Missing
Mona

Praise for **RATS**

"Joe Klingler's debut is an intelligent, non-stop page turner. The characters are well written and believable, the technology detailed always engrossing, the story moves along almost effortlessly." — **Manhattan Book Review (5 of 5 stars)**

"This is a good, well written page-turner, written with staccato prose and sharp scene-setting." — **Rubery Book Awards**

"Klingler's debut offers a deep logistical jungle sure to entertain buffs and newcomers to the techno-thriller genre. Throughout, he displays fierce writing chops." — **Kirkus Reviews** *(Featured Selection of the Month. Kirkus Recommended List)*

"Fans of international thrillers and espionage books will enjoy this novel." — **Foreword Clarion Reviews (4 of 5 stars)**

"RATS...is a fun romp-and-motorcycle-ride through intrigue, explosions, action, betrayal, politics, and victory." — **San Francisco Book Review (4 of 5 stars)**

Praise for *Mash Up*

2015 Winner National Indie Excellence Award - Thriller

"Klingler's new thriller is a ride into the dark side of computers and comedy. Klingler's plot definitely has a Quentin Tarantino-feel to it." — **San Francisco Book Review (5 of 5 stars)**

"Klingler makes supreme use of his tech knowledge in a grisly mystery that strives to address the ethics of content ownership. His effortlessly clever prose makes the subject thoroughly entertaining...a thoughtful, well-constructed tale." — **Kirkus Reviews**

"Klingler is skilled at writing action scenes. He puts the reader directly in the line of fire, and he doesn't let up." — **Foreword Clarion Reviews (4 of 5 stars)**

"[Klingler] has fantastic talent for imbuing wit into situations that normally wouldn't be witty...almost every character offers some sort of unique perspective and really great moments where I laughed aloud. If you can make me laugh while simultaneously making me wonder what the hell is going on, then I'll read any book you have to write. The author's writing style actually reminds me a little of Dean Koontz, if you take out Koontz's supernatural leanings."--**Literature Typeface**

"Cleverly designed, *Mash Up*, makes the perfect detective read, as well as a classic addition to the noir genre." — **San Francisco Book Review**

Also by JOE KLINGLER

Mash Up
RATS

Please don't let impersonal corporate-driven social
networks come between us...

Join *Joe's Readers* directly at:

www.joeklingler.com

to occasionally receive news on book releases, previews,
discount promotions and more.

Missing Mona

A *Tommy Cuda* **MYSTERY**

Joe Klingler

CARTOSI LLC

Published by

CARTOSI LLC

Dedicated to

Joseph William Klingler

...and the mechanic's magic in his hands.

One

"I really like a lot of other kinds of music, but the blues just
does something to my insides."
— *Johnny Winter (1944-2014)*

THE MORNING AFTER MY twenty-ninth birthday I began
to realize privacy in the 21st century was the melting wax of
Icarus. This thought intruded as molecules of tequila
conducting chemical experiments in my head painted the walls
around me a Matisse of browns—the walls of my parents' house
left to us by my grandmother on my mother's side in the tiny
burg of Gates Mills, Ohio. I lay curled around a pillow with one
eye studying orange light penetrating a drawn shade. Like many
of my generation I had spent beautiful years testing the efficacy
of medical marijuana while downloading the latest app for my
mobile gadget; majoring in Math, English Lit, Sociology, and
Philosophy (none for long); finally managing to matriculate a
Poli-Sci degree before boomeranging back to a no-upward-
mobility job as car mechanic at the two-year old Walmart just
across the county line.

I didn't yet understand my circumstances as my open eye
roved the room amid recollections of Betty going on last night in
the back seat of my car about age and clocks and waiting.

Girls liked to go slow—until they were in a hurry.

Shifting shadows on that orange shade told me wind was
lifting the branches of the big elm in the backyard. But I didn't
quite know then.

Not yet.

Of all the people and objects inhabiting my life, the situation was finally fully illuminated by my gadget: a golden iPhone with a gazillion bytes of storage. Enough, the genius at the bar told me, to hold every movie, song, game, and message I would see or hear in my lifetime. It shuddered against the hard oak of a nightstand I had been looking at each morning for over twenty years.

A voice some marketing department had named Siri, which made me think of women's clothing, serenaded my contemplative state with information the moment it arrived from the big computing cloud in the sky:

Message from Betty. Where are you? Take me to breakfast. You know back-seat boogaloo makes me hungry.

Message from Willy. Race day, Thomas. You're getting old and slow. I'm coming for you today.

Willy was on a futile quest to shave tenths off his Pontiac GTO's quarter-mile time and keep my Chrysler in sight at the finish.

Then:

Message from Betty. I know where you are. You left auto check-in on in Foursquare. Call or I'm coming over.

That moment I knew.

Knew for sure.

Knew like I knew I had been named after a missing disciple in the Bible.

My friends knew where I was; expected an instant response to inane messages; texted within moments to ask if I had seen the latest selfie posted to the Land of Instatwits—billions of pixels that I just had to see *right this very second.*

I knew...

I didn't have those seconds anymore.

My life was filled communicating vapor to and fro. Hours consumed building mountains of digital clouds that dissipated instantly in the scorching sun of continuous updates.

As I entered my thirtieth year on the planet, this was…like…um…having a fast car but no gas.

I heard the atomic clock in bad sci-fi flicks:

Tick.

Tock.

Time waits for no man.

My life should be…evolving.

Something should be *happening*.

My open eye settled on the shiny gold phone.

The problem crystalized like supercooled water becoming ice in the split of a second—technology isn't invented to help me live a long and happy life. It's purpose is to make the geek kids in Silicon Valley wealthy. Such is the nature of capitalism: growth, IPO, valuation, capital gain. I was an afterthought. Maybe even collateral damage.

I sat up.

My privacy. Freedom from observation. Freedom from *disturbance*. That was the price of admission.

I immediately fell back to the pillow at the insistence of the naked screaming midgets dancing in my head.

Siri said, "Message from Betty."

I shouted at the midgets.

"I'm sorry, I don't understand. Would you like me to search the Internet for 'Goat Thockaway?'"

I struggled to recall how had I ended up here; I wouldn't drive my Barracuda blind-eyed on blue agave. My eye saw the keys on the nightstand beside my gold gadget. I never put keys on the nightstand; I left them in my pocket right where I would want them.

Someone had driven me home.

I rolled over. Where could I find a life as exciting as a detective novel? Or at least a pop song?

I stretched my back, which brought sensation to my feet.

"New message from Willy," Siri said.

"Tell him you will never beat me."

"Tell Willy 'You will never beat me.' Send message?"

"Yes, Siri."

"Message sent to Willy."

I groaned

Mistake. Now Willy knew I was awake; he would be in my driveway in half an hour.

I had made impulsive decisions in my life: buying a mahogany guitar, changing my major, approaching that curly-haired brunette in the S-aisle of the library and asking if she was looking for books on Sewing or Sex. Those had worked out okay.

So I made another one.

The midgets applauded.

"Siri, turn off location services."

"Maps will no longer be available."

"OK."

"Location services off."

"Message to all contacts: I, Tommy, am going off the grid. So long, and thanks for all the fish." One of my friends would figure out *The Hitchhiker's Guide to the Galaxy* reference. They could Tweedledee the dolphin story to everyone else.

"Sending message to two hundred and fourteen contacts."

Staring at the ceiling I had painted Taffy Egg Shell Surprise after finishing college, I said: "Post message to all social networks."

"Posting."

"Thank you, Siri."

"I am here to help."

"Siri, turn off power."

"All services will be unavailable. Are you sure?"

"I am totally sure."

"I'm sorry. Would you like me to search the Internet for 'I.M.T. leisure?'"

"Siri, shut down now."

"Goodbye, Thomas."

My iPhone became an inert block of black glass and aluminum.

I breathed easier. That could be Apple's new mantra: not *Think Different,* but *Breathe Easy.*

I rolled my head in circles; my neck crackled along like a drunk drummer. When my friends received that message they would immediately attempt contact to find out why I had gone mad. When I didn't respond Willy, Betty, or someone would coordinate a siege on my house. Eventually Mom would let them in because she's polite that way. Which meant...

I sat up fast. My head did barrel rolls, but landed upright.

I blinked to clear my eyes.

What did I need?

The '59 gold-top guitar (reissue) I used in college bands. Vinyl record collection—the way it was when Eddie Cochran sang about blues in the summertime. Six shelves of mystery novels; I would have to be selective.

And superman-in-a-phone-booth quick.

I tossed back the blanket and saw that I still had pants on. I stripped, jumped in the shower, stepped out, and ran a towel through the hair my mother insisted made me look as handsome as the blond guy on reruns of Route 66 that she had the hots for as a teenager growing up in Kansas. I tossed on blue jeans, a black T-shirt with *Mopar* emblazoned across the chest touting Chrysler's original equipment motor parts (the only kind I ever used), and gray tennis shoes.

Raiding my Hemi-under-glass funny car piggy bank yielded $437. The rest of my personal wealth sat earning too little interest in a bank whose logo made me think I was the stagecoach and the bank was Jesse James.

I stuffed the records, books, turntable, speakers and a scratched black suitcase made of recycled cardboard filled with one sport coat and handfuls of clothes under the curved rear window of my Chrysler. On the way back to my room to search for more stashed cash I passed mom coming down the stairway wearing a Saturday tennis outfit she'd probably call Perfect Peach. She was relaxed and smiling and not in any kind of hurry because she allowed for travel time as reliably as a Buddhist monk meditated.

"Uh, Mom, could I borrow a couple hundred?"

She stopped three steps from the bottom and redid the elastic ring holding her blonde hair behind her head. Buying time.

"Not if you're going to spend it on Betty. You throw too much of your money at her already."

"I'm taking a solo vacation. See the USA in my Chrysler. Try to figure out how to break out of the Walmart rut."

Her hands stopped moving. "Really?"

"Yeah. But, I have to leave fast before the tribe shows up and talks me out of it."

She crossed her arms. "Well, Thomas Benjamin, it's about time. When you graduated I told you to travel, clear your head. Don't fall back into the same rut with the same crowd or you'll never find your element."

I tried to remember what she meant by *element*, but all I could think of was the periodic table on the wall in General Chemistry, and a girl named Georgette whose skirts seemed to shrink during class.

"You were right, Mom."

She smiled and hugged me with both arms. Then pushed me away.

"A few hundred isn't enough. Let me loan you a thousand."

"Thanks, Mom. You're the best."

"Where are you going first?" she said as she turned to go back to the second floor of our four-bedroom on two acres that had been built before I came along. Halfway up I glanced out at grass I had cut countless times — not something I would miss. I spoke to the bobbing blonde tail on the back of her head. "I was thinking Detroit, the soul of Motown. But then I thought maybe

6

Memphis to find out what's happening in rockabilly these days. I want to see the building where the famous Sun Records were made."

"They haven't done that music right since the Stray Cats broke up. You know that's when I met your father."

This story I had definitely heard before. "I'm in a hurry, Mom."

"You wait years and now your pants are on fire." She sighed. "At least you're getting out of the house."

She strolled toward the master bedroom. I blasted to my room, looked under the bed at dustballs, wished I could take my too-tall Fender amp, and said goodbye to the dresser where I had hid all the things boys need to hide (including my first picture of a topless girl) by taping them to the underside of its drawers. The iPhone lying on the nightstand beckoned me.

To take or not to take?

My skin felt electrified. Maybe I would need a phone. And music files. But not more text messages. Or Twitter temptation. I weakened, shoved it into the front pocket of my jeans and took mental inventory. Jacket, three shirts, underwear. Shaver. Blue brothel creepers. Sunglasses. Where were my sunglasses?

I pulled open drawers. Flipped through shirts, socks. Scanned the room. Found them hanging by one temple over the back of the lampshade. I grabbed the Ray-Ban Aviators (timeless style since 1936), slipped them over my shirt collar, and turned to leave.

Mom was standing in the doorway with cash in her hand.

I stepped forward, hugged her hard until she whispered, "Oh, Tommy," stepped back, smiled, and slipped the money gently from her palm.

"Bye, Mom...yes, I promise I will call."

She wasn't smiling any more; she had already started the worry-mobile. "If you don't, I'm sending a private eye to find you."

"Please don't worry, Mom. I just...um, I can't really explain it."

She held my shoulder with her right hand. "You just celebrated your last twenty-something birthday. You see the big three-oh coming at you down the long highway of life, so you want to run away to find something before old age pins you to the mat." She smiled and let go. "And makes you cry uncle."

Mom was okay. I didn't think so back in high school, but she seemed smarter now.

"Mom." I could see she might cry like the day I left for college. "I'll be back, but please, I gotta go..."

She stepped backward into the hallway and shooed me with one hand. "You drive safe, Tommy. No beer and car keys."

The keys!

I pressed my hand against my front pocket where the keys should be; turned toward the nightstand, found them right where I hadn't put them, and squeezed a key older than me in my left hand.

I should take the spare. Where was it?

I dropped to one knee in front of the nightstand while Mom watched. At the very bottom I found the wooden box I got as a kid at a Mackinac Bridge souvenir shop. Man, the view from that bridge was vast: water for miles in both directions; I wanted to build one so much I started off majoring in Math in college.

I flicked it open.

The key was at the bottom under a high-school class ring and assorted ancient coins I had traded for slingshots and knives. I slipped it into my pocket and made a mental note to hide it someplace I could access in an emergency.

Mom was still there as I raced for the door, but she stepped back. As I reached her she said: "Goodbye, Tommy. I love you."

I hugged her again, "I love you too, Mom. Thanks for the loan."

Then I was down the stairs and outside.

Sunny. Saturday. High noon.

I stopped to admire the chocolate-brown metallic Plymouth Barracuda with a 426 Hemi V8 my Granddad had generously left to me in his will. Only a few Barracudas with the 426 were ever manufactured; all specifically for Super Stock drag racing. He had arranged for one to become street-legal; though he never explained why it had a 1965 title.

Restored it myself after college with parts from scrap yards.

I hopped in, fired that big motor into a gentle rumble, and waved to Mom, who stood motionless in the window of the living room where a teenage Betty had offered me my first glimpse of a real girl.

Two

TEN MINUTES OF WINDING through side streets so I wouldn't be spotted by Betty or Willy carried me to the monster: Interstate-80, a ribbon of concrete that could take me all the way to the Pacific Ocean without a single red light. What amazing technology made a road: pulverized stone and water poured into flat, smooth rock wherever you wanted it.

Engineering was an unseen art.

I listened to the Hemi barely idling as we cruised along at the speed limit. I patted the pack of money in the breast pocket of my black leather jacket made by the same company that had sewn them for Steve McQueen: the *master of cool* according to the former owner of my car. With each passing mile the gas gauge leaned further left, the throbbing in my head faded, and my grasp of what the hell I was doing and why slipped a notch.

As I rolled past a bright orange semi, the bearded driver gave me a thumbs up. I waved. That happened a lot. Guys love cars, especially cars for the drag strip. Rocketing in a straight line. Hundreds of horsepower fighting to thrust tons of steel forward across 1,320 feet of asphalt. Reaction time, torque, traction. Big $F=ma$ forces Newton would love. I could almost smell burning rubber.

I eased the accelerator toward the floor, cranked down the window, and rested my elbow on the sill. Wind roared in my ear. The exhaust sounded beautiful, angry, sweet, steady.

I daydreamed.

Music, work, cars, girls, computers, life, liberty. Computers. Computers created their own brand of problems. I could reach out and almost-but-not-quite touch anyone anywhere on the planet. Like eating a famous Big Boy burger without the patties, computers created an unsatisfying virtual life funneled through snippets of text and selfies. That character in Woody Allen's Paris movie, who wished he could return to an earlier era when things were more vivid and exciting, came to mind.

I felt a magnetic pull on my brain.

Like the past where my Granddad drag raced on country roads using telephone poles for the start and finish lines.

And rockabilly music.

I flicked on the AM radio and pressed the leftmost button. I kept that one set to AM 800, CKLW The Big 8 out of Windsor, in honor of Granddad who had lived through the glory days when their Big 30 songs mattered to almost the entire country. Lots of people thought it originated in Detroit. The station wanted you to think it came from Motown. But it didn't.

The broadcast towers were in Canada.

It was now a pale shadow of its former 50,000 watt rock-and-roll self; an automated shadow programmed by a media conglomerate that had moved to talk/news format years ago; calling itself *The Information Station*. I listened to a woman describe the clear weather I was driving through as 'sprightly,' then pushed the second button on my old radio to flip to AM 580, CKWW: the frequency where the old CKLW format had been moved after a buyout. 580 was now essentially just an oldies format so thousands of people could go about their day listening to *(I Can't Get No) Satisfaction* by The Rolling Stones. I thought of music passing invisibly through the air to all those people—more unseen engineering. We were brothers and sisters. A community listening together.

I grinned and flicked on my cell phone. It would be nice to hear Eddie C sing *Twenty Flight Rock*. The phone beeped and blipped.

Siri said: "You have three urgent messages from Betty."

I drove with my left hand at nine o'clock, holding the phone in my right. A thought crystallized: I didn't need a magic car to go back into the past; I just needed to make clear-cut decisions about what I wanted in my life — and what I didn't. That yoga instructor, what was her name? She sat next to me in Theology. Name sounded like a fruity drink. Brendina. She advised me to choose my own path.

Do not enslave yourself to the wishes of others.

Especially not college-dropout entrepreneurs in California who tried to make everyone feel like they were behind in life if they didn't use the last thing invented. As if *new* was somehow better than *proven*.

I tossed the cell phone out the window.

And immediately wondered how I'd call Mom.

Then shrugged. I didn't need a digital tether. Mankind had lived for millions of years without a chunk of silicon in his pocket bugging him.

I just needed something to do.

Like eat.

A road sign promised a Frisch's Big Boy up ahead, a restaurant chain that began in Ohio back in 1905. I eased into the right lane and took the exit. That date was stuck in my head because Willy and I had stopped for lunch at a Cleveland Frisch's on a trip to the Rock and Roll Hall of Fame. We argued about who was the best guitar player of all time; reached no conclusions. Hovering over our booth hung a framed vintage black and white poster of a shapely girl sipping Coca-Cola through a striped straw. She wore a long skirt and a sweater emblazoned with 1905.

Some things don't change — not even in a hundred years.

I idled into the Frisch's lot wondering how many burgers they had served in a century, and parked under a corrugated roof suspended on angled steel poles painted white. A concrete sidewalk separated two rows of cars facing each other, like boxers about to start a match.

I couldn't stop a grin. Curb service.

I ordered from a waitress with long curls and a short skirt and imagined my grandfather sitting here ordering a burger when the Barracuda was new and not carrying a historic license plate.

Maybe not so different.

"Gramps would like her curls," I said to the dash that was playing The Chantays version of *Pipeline* from a single speaker embedded inside: a speaker I found on eBay because the owner was parting out his car after a bad crash.

I missed Gramps; he had style. And I admired his work ethic: making a living fixing cars after serving in Vietnam; then having my Dad when everyone else was tuning in, tuning out, or rolling in the mud in a farmer's field listening to Hendrix play *The Star-Spangled Banner*.

All we did was add new words to the dictionary like *selfie* and *clickbait* and *social network*.

The curly-haired girl came and took away my tray. I considered trying to find a pay phone inside and calling Mom, but I'd only been gone an hour and a half.

I started the Barracuda and rolled through the parking lot slowly.

A woman was standing beside the driveway leading to the frontage road.

Holding her thumb out.

I pushed in the clutch and coasted toward the exit. Red, wavy hair, black jean jacket, black and white leopard print pants. Black boots to her knees suggested motorcycle more than horse. A black backpack with silver sections that probably reflected light sat at her feet.

I touched the brake pedal with my toe.

Curved, rectangular sunglass lenses fully covered her eyes. Laser-cut black aluminum temples disappeared into red hair.

Under thirty. Out of high school.

I reached over and cranked down the window on the passenger side. It moved smooth as the day Chrysler built it.

Gramps never let me forget: if you're going to have it, take care of it.

She stepped close. A shiny silver belt holding up the leopard print pants caught my eye. She leaned in. Red bangs played against the top of her sunglass frames. One hand came up and lowered the glasses, revealing silver makeup surrounding green eyes that were fixed on my face.

"Hi," she said.

I tipped my head toward the diner. "Just get off work?"

Her face moved toward the restaurant and back. "Wouldn't work there." She pushed the dark glasses back up. "Where you going?"

The first words into my head were *wherever you are*. I almost said Detroit, but intuition pushed me toward vague.

"West." I had to go west before I could turn north for The Motor City.

She moved her jaw, lips pressed together.

"How far?"

Good question. The ink wasn't dry on my getaway plan. I improvised.

"Maybe Chicago."

She pulled the glasses down again. Studied me. A green pickup pulled around from behind and into the street. The driver glanced my way. Surprising me, he gave a thumbs up with his free hand. I couldn't tell if he liked the car, or was encouraging me in my quest.

She stepped back and moved her head right and left, scanning the side of the car. Finally she said: "Looks like a turd."

Some people didn't initially appreciate the rich beauty of Turbine Bronze, first used on a production Barracuda in '67. They had to be educated.

"Think of it as a giant sixty-five percent fair-trade chocolate bar. Good enough to lick."

She stared at me. A smile crawled into her cheeks. She bent, disappearing from view, popped up with the pack on her arm, opened the door, slid a slender rear end across black vinyl, and held the pack on her lap.

"Let's go," she said.

I couldn't remember asking if she wanted a ride as I eased the clutch out, maneuvered back to the Interstate, and made a show of going through the four-speed Hurst shifter to about 90 up the entrance ramp. She didn't seem to notice, so I slowed.

Her face was tilted out the passenger window, red hair streaming toward the back seat, eyes hidden behind dark glass. Wind roared inside the cabin, but Gramps had finangled A/C—available all the way back in 1965—so we had an option.

"Air conditioning?" I asked.

"Mona, what's yours?" she shouted.

I concluded she enjoyed open windows, and I'd have to speak louder.

"Tommy. Tommy—" I stopped. I should be careful with information. I was trying to leave a world where everyone knew where I was and what I was doing; where privacy was only something you asked for when you were going to kiss a girl. Then I realized I wanted to impress her, and Thomas Benjamin Kelsey lacked charisma.

"What?" she called out over the rush of the wind.

My eyes caught the silver letters on the dash above the glovebox.

I leaned toward her. "Cuda. Tommy Cuda."

Three

MONA SMILED, POINTED AT the front of her jacket, and said, "Meyers." Her right hand reached across the gap between the bucket seats. I lifted mine from the steel grip of the Hurst to shake hers, and instantly didn't want to let go of its soft warmth. She took her hand away and leaned her head back into the wind.

I drove with my elbow on the doorsill and left fingers on the wheel. My right hand fiddled with the radio, touched the shifter now and then (though I didn't need to do anything), and laid limp on the seat the rest of the time. She wasn't talking, so I had time to fabricate a reason I was going to Chicago, and what I planned to do when I got there.

Fortunately, I had been there a couple of times on road trips. And had read about it in one of the two history classes I passed. The Windy City: named not for the weather but for the bluster of its politicians in the nineteenth century. Some of my favorite crime novels had taken place there: *Big City, Bad Blood; Deader by the Lake; The Litigators.*

Oh. And it sat smack on Lake Michigan. Maybe I could get a place by the water.

And do what?

Be unreachable for starters.

"Mona, where you headed?"

"Wherever you're going."

I tossed a sideways glance her way. She was facing the roof liner letting the wind take her. She appeared to be serious.

"I'm thinking a hotel near the beach in Chicago. Relax, listen to the waves. Find some of that famous Chicago blues music."

"I was going to South Bend to meet a friend at Notre Dame."

Past tense.

"It's on the way. I can drop you off if you like," I said, and held my breath. Chicago would be way more fun with a curvy redhead. Even one who didn't say much.

She leaned toward the window, the wind creating fluttering flames behind her.

"South Bend is boring," she said.

I accelerated to indicate that I would be happy to roll past this boring town where she had a friend who might be male who could put an end to our minutes-old adventure.

"We could liven it up," I offered, trying to be open-minded. Maybe her friend was a slender brunette who liked old cars.

She rolled her head across the back of the seat until dark lenses pointed at me.

"Sounds like more work than driving to Chicago." She smiled.

I shrugged. "OK. We drive to Chicago. What about your friend?"

Her left hand came up and dragged the glasses down her nose. Green rings glistened at me.

"What friend?" she said.

I fought a grin, not knowing what game she was playing, or what my score was.

We stopped for gas. She carried her backpack into the minimart. I pumped. She came back with three kinds of potato chips, a can of cheese and two bottles of water. We were back on the road in minutes.

As we approached Gary, Indiana, a sort of industrial back alley entrance to Chicago, I spun the radio dial and landed on the tail end of a news story about a cop being shot somewhere in Michigan. Then the DJ spun *Get a Job* by the Silhouettes. I tried to think how many years it had come out before my car rolled out of Detroit.

Mona took off her sunglasses even though the setting sun was glaring through the windshield.

"What do you do, Mr. Tommy Cuda?"

I drove for a few seconds (corn field, elevated irrigation pipe, a distant silo) processing my new name, savoring the sound of it on her lips, and wondering what a good answer would be before coming up with a one-word response.

"Do?"

She rolled her head my way again. "You know. Work. Money. Get a job. It's an easy four-mile question."

"Four-mile?"

"On the Detroit City scale of one through eight." She apparently read my confusion. "Road names." She made little karate chops with her left hand. "The roads are a mile apart. Eight Mile is special. It divides the gritty city from the silly suburbs."

I had seen a movie named *8 Mile* about a white rapper working in a factory. I turned and noticed two things: she had barely perceptible freckles on her nose, and the mystery novels I had been reading since the fifth grade were stacked on the back seat. I made a quick decision and tried to sound as confident as the guys in those books.

"I'm a private investigator."

Her eyebrows shifted up...then down, as if they had answered a question. She laughed, slipped her glasses back on, and turned her face to the sun.

"What do you privately investigate?"

"Whatever the client wants; I'm not picky. Though I like to work regular hours when I can."

"Why's that?"

"More restaurants are open."

Get a Job faded and a weather lady told us it was going to be sunny in Chicago for the remainder of the weekend. I had been there to see museums and concerts, but it never struck me as sunny.

We curved through Gary on a raised slab of concrete watching smoke rise from blackened chimneys and spiral into Rorschach forms. I saw two faces, and maybe a basketball. Wind whooshed as I passed a Walmart semi towing a double trailer and realized I hadn't given notice to my boss.

"How much?" she asked.

Tire noise from the truck crushed her words.

"Sorry. How much what?"

"For private eyeing? What would you charge me?"

I mentally adjusted amounts I had read in novels for inflation.

"Five hundred dollar retainer up front, and two hundred a day plus expenses." She didn't react, so I added, "But it depends on the length of the job. I give discounts for long projects because it saves on paperwork."

She was quiet.

The weather lady was replaced by The Beatles singing *I'm Looking Through You.*

Maybe I had overpriced my nonexistent skills. I watched the sun hovering close to the horizon and hoped we weren't too late to score a decent hotel on a Saturday night. Then I wondered where she was really headed. And when. And why.

She rolled up her window.

I did the same, quieting the car.

She unzipped the backpack on the floor between her legs.

I tuned the radio to get static out of the AM station.

She placed a hundred dollar bill on the console between us. Then another. When she had placed five she started another stack until she had six bills on it.

"I want three days," she said. "Do you need expenses up front too?"

I thought about the fourteen hundred and thirty-seven dollars I had started the day with. And the eleven hundred lying behind the Hurst shifter. And the fact that I had just told a complete stranger I was a private eye, and she was calling my bluff.

"Depends on what you need done. Will there be travel involved?"

Her forehead furrowed above the metal frame of her sunglasses. She shrugged and laid down three more hundreds. "Not sure. How's a hundred a day?"

I had no idea what I needed to do, or possibly how to do it. So I said: "Perfect. Would you like a receipt, Miss Meyer?"

She shook her head, didn't correct the Miss, and seemed unfazed by the amount of money she had just spent.

It was getting warm in the car.

I scooped the hundreds together into a stack, and with some twisting pushed them into the left pocket of my pants. The thought that a pretty girl with so much cash on her shouldn't be hitchhiking drifted through my brain, but didn't park.

"How can I help you?"

She rolled her window halfway down while looking my way.

"I want you to find someone."

The only missing thing I had ever found was our terrier Smudge when he got lost chasing a particularly exuberant squirrel in the woods. And I essentially just wandered around with a flashlight most of the night until he came running to me near a creek.

"That can be tricky. Depends on what we know about this person. Who are you trying to find?"

A long windy silence. Then: "I'll tell you in the morning. Can we get some food on your expense account?"

"How about a place with live music?"

She studied the right side of my face. "Why do you listen to this old crap?"

I eased the accelerator toward the floor to pass a truck lumbering up a long curved piece of expressway.

"Crap because it wasn't written by someone your age? Crap because it's old? Or crap because you don't understand it?" It was my car and my gas. I could be indignant if I wanted to — even if she was my client.

"Touchy."

I grinned. "Testing your sense of humor. I started listening to music outside the stuff chosen by marketing departments to optimize advertising revenue my second year of college. Got the radio DJ job on the night shift and began experimenting with the humongous library of vinyl the school had collected, mostly through donations from alumni. We called it the *College of Musical Knowledge*. My grandfather would dial in requests, and I'd dig records out of our archives."

"That's how you got old, huh?"

"No," I said. The Chrysler rumbled along just above the speed limit.

Finally she dipped her sunglasses and said, "No?"

"That's how I got educated. That's when I learned people of all eras and ages pour out their feelings in song not to communicate their world, but to survive it. In some cases, to discover it. That's when I learned people from the past had a lot to say about the present and how to live. That's when — "

She waved both arms. "OK, OK. I get it. College boy wakes up one day, takes his hand off his dick, and realizes that other people have feelings too." She laughed.

It was a nice laugh. The kind that didn't have any edges.

"Yeah, something like that. But the people around me weren't really hearing music. They were using it as an ear vibrator for stimulation between text messages."

She pushed her glasses up. I wondered if it was a habit just to keep her hands busy—like stroking a worry stone.

"They were doing something else too," she said.

I did a quick review of my philosophy and sociology experience. Came up empty. I watched the highway for signs to a blues bar that might have food. I waited as long as I could, hoping she would elaborate without making me ask. She didn't.

"What's that?"

"Pumping cultural myths into their brains that will pop up for years without the poor creatures knowing where the hell they came from."

This I remembered. "You mean repetitive media consumption creating a person's value system through subconscious imitation?"

She nodded. "That's how a college boy would say it."

I wasn't loving the word boy. "Hmm. How would a pretty hitchhiker say it?"

I watched her with one eye, the stripes zipping by on the road with the other. Her lips twitched.

"Brainwashing."

"Like everyone being in love with the music they listened to during puberty?"

She shook her head; her hair bounced like a shampoo commercial. "No, that's hormones and timing." She turned my way. "Better be careful what you put on the radio tonight." She laughed again.

I exited Highway 41, known locally as Lake Shore Drive, at Fullerton. We drove a switchback pattern until Mona saw a sign that read B.L.U.E.S. on Halsted only blocks from the exit. A window poster informed us a band named BLU44 wouldn't start for hours, so we cruised in expanding circles with her pointing at restaurants as we talked about the foods we were craving.

She wanted tuna.

I wanted a burger.

She wanted rare steak.

I thought fish and chips sounded great.

Most places were jammed with patrons, traffic was just shy of gridlock, and pedestrians strolled everywhere in the dusty golden richness of dusk. At a stoplight, a guy my dad's age wearing a Tommy Bahama shirt with sailboats on it pointed at the Barracuda while trying to direct the attention of the woman with him toward the car. I couldn't make out his words, but was confident he was telling his own Barracuda story. Minutes later, I made a left turn after sitting through three light changes burning prodigious amounts of fuel in the 426 cubic inches of fun under my hood.

We had come full circle and were back on Fullerton.

Mona gestured toward a brick Victorian house hiding behind a black iron fence.

I read the sign. "The Bourgeois Pig?"

"Sounds perfect for you."

I smiled. We had become so close she felt comfortable insulting me.

I parked on the street and we entered a converted house that had a library with shelves on two walls and a fireplace without a fire. Surrounded by books I felt sure were as old as my car I found a tasty sounding sandwich on the menu called the Muffaletta. Mona covered the last six letters with her thumb, licked her lips, and broke into her edgeless laugh.

The sandwiches arrived faster than I could heat up a can of soup.

"Why are you traveling?" Mona asked, her face suddenly serious.

I shrugged. "I was bored. I own a car. *See the USA in Your Chevrolet* seemed like an obvious choice for an all-American boy." There was that word again.

She chewed and studied me.

I said: "Yes, I know it's a Chrysler."

She didn't laugh. "Taking off alone? Bored doesn't seem like quite enough..." She chewed her lower lip. "Incentive."

"Ever see that movie *Groundhog Day* with Bill Murray? My mom loves it, bought the DVD. I woke up today feeling trapped like that weatherman. Life going in circles. Tick-tock, time passing me by. Stuck in a rut." I grinned. "Pick your cliché of the day."

She nodded, face calm, skin smooth as freshly whipped cream. "That I understand."

"I also got really pissed off at my smart phone."

Then she laughed.

Later, inside B.L.U.E.S., a singer named Demetria Taylor hit the *Wang Dang Doodle* with a voice that demanded attention. Behind the stage a sign read: *Over 150,000 songs played.* Being surrounded by dozens of music fans and pulsing music while sitting close to Mona made me think about space. I realized we were close to the lake.

I wanted to see it.

To my left posters three layers deep clung to the wall. Below them a wooden rack held a dozen brochures: Lincoln Park Zoo, Field Museum of Natural History, and a hotel with a big W overlooking blue water. It was on Lake Shore Drive and sounded expensive, but I had a client to impress, and an expense account.

I reached over and unfolded the brochure on our table. The band's volume made talking an auditory challenge, but Mona nodded as my finger pointed back and forth between us and the W.

The drive was brief. Mona stared out the car window through glass twice her age, backpack between her knees. I self-parked in a concrete structure and she dragged me toward the beach where I got sand in both shoes while carrying my suitcase in one hand and my gold guitar in the other. We stomped the sand off in front of a glittering W on a blue background and entered the lobby.

I stopped on a hardwood floor, recently shined.

"I have a question for my client."

"Shoot."

"Since the client is paying expenses." I caught her eye. "One room or two?"

She didn't blink. "One. In your name."

On the twelfth floor a few minutes later, I pushed the door to our room open for her with my shoulder.

"You're sure you're okay with one room?" I asked.

She stopped in the doorway, turned to face me. "So long as you keep your hands to yourself college boy." Then she laughed and went in. She seemed to laugh a lot, then grow quiet as the nighttime after rain.

Two queen beds filled most of the room. I took the one by the window, spreading my suitcase on the floor. She dropped the backpack she hadn't let out of her sight all night into a chair, slipped off her boots, surprised me with a hug and kiss goodnight, and crawled into bed wearing her leopard pants and jean jacket.

I fell asleep with my cash inside my pillowcase wondering if I was being careless sharing a room with a hitchhiker. I figured her as being okay, maybe even a little cautious herself. I also wanted her in that way my body can crave a woman after knowing her for three or four seconds. But what filled most of my head was that I had my first case as a private investigator — and no idea how to go about it.

Four

I WOKE LYING ON MY BACK with darkness on the other side of my eyelids and wind rushing into my right ear. I opened my eyes; a hotel ceiling, colorless in the dimness, slowly replaced my inner fog.

A heavy weight pressed my right arm into the mattress.

Fingernails scraped down the left side of my chest.

No, not wind. Breath.

"Mona?" I whispered.

Her head nodded against my shoulder. The breath came in short bursts. She slid her body up on top of me, pressing bare breasts against my chest.

The bursts continued in my ear.

Her fingernails reversed direction, moving slowly up my left side and across my neck until fingers slipped behind my neck and wrapped themselves into my hair.

The wind ceased.

A whispered, "Kiss me, Tommy," preceded soft lips against mine, rotating, opening. Her hand pulled me to her.

I moved my now free arm up and around her slender waist, along the smooth curve of her spine, her back expanding and contracting quickly against my palm. The hot pressure of her kiss held me suspended. Darkness and desire blended into a sense of moving fast through outer space in our own private starship.

I mumbled, "Should we slow down?" through the kiss. I doubt she understood the words, but her head shook no. I relaxed my shoulders and focused on the softness of her breasts, the intense pressure on my mouth, the grasp of her hand.

She inhaled sharply; froze; pulled my hair toward her. Her body shuddered. My body shuddered in response.

She slipped back to her original position along my right side, the dampness of our skin lubricating the motion. The soft breath in my right ear returned.

"Thank you for the ride, Tommy," she whispered.

Then she was gone into the darkness.

I heard her scuffle into the sheets of the other bed as the words of a Catholic college girl who was saving herself for marriage came to me: *There's a lot you can do without having sex.* Then I skydived into deep sleep.

The whoosh of traffic woke me.

The other side of my eyelids was now orange.

I laid on my stomach wondering if what I thought had happened aligned with the reality of the cosmos. I rolled toward Mona's bed.

It was empty.

No backpack.

I sat up. Listened. Nothing but traffic.

I dropped back against the pillow. The first day of my thirtieth year had been a doozy. I reached to grab my cell phone from the nightstand to check the weather before remembering it was on an Ohio highway in a hundred pieces. I twisted back to count the money inside my pillowcase. My $1437 was down to $1050 and change. I hadn't touched the cash Mona had given me — all $1100 plus $300 was accounted for. I flipped off the covers and gazed at the sheets, wondering if Mona's visit had been a dream, then shuffled to the window and pushed the curtains open.

Morning light pierced both eyes.

Far below, the glittering blue of Lake Michigan invited me to dive in.

I took a shower. Still no Mona.

I dressed in my jeans from the day before, put on a charcoal sport coat over a black and white polo shirt, and packed my leather jacket into my black suitcase.

No Mona.

I looked for a note, used towel, lipstick smudge on a pillow. Nothing. I hefted my suitcase, said, "Goodbye, Mona" to the empty room, and headed for checkout. When I reached the street in front of the W, a dozen people dressed more for dancing than church were waiting for valets to bring their cars around.

I turned right for the garage.

Inside the gray shadows of the parking structure I passed status logos: BMW, Lexus, Mercedes. A low car I thought might be a Ferrari from a distance turned out to be an Aston-Martin fifty steps later.

I found my Barracuda and peeked through the window; my records and books were where I had left them. I loaded my suitcase and guitar. Slipped behind the wheel. Now what? The expense money would cover the hotel, but I still had eleven hundred dollars.

And no client.

I studied the car key, marveled at the crudeness of a thing etched from steel, pushed it into the ignition, and turned.

Silence filled the space where a Hemi should have been.

I tried to recall when I had replaced the battery. Last summer. Plenty new. Besides, it should have been charging all day yesterday while Mona and I were rolling down the highway.

Charging system failure? No idiot light had warned me.

I got out, slipped my fingers through the grill, raised the hood. Someone had disconnected the negative terminal of the battery. The wrench they had done it with was lying on the battery case: Sears Craftsman—like I used. Maybe they had been interrupted while stealing the battery.

I reconnected the battery and leaned over to check the V-belts as I had seen my grandfather do a hundred times. *Always check the belts: they crack, loosen. A weak link in an otherwise strong machine.* But I couldn't see them because a backpack had been stuffed between the radiator and the fan.

A black backpack.

With silver accents.

I worked the pack free, careful not to rip the material on the fan blades. The front and back were streaked with the black grease engines attract, but it was otherwise unharmed.

"Mona, you're one crazy cat."

I started to unzip the main compartment before remembering she had pulled hundred dollar bills from inside. I surveyed the parking garage. A white sedan was backing out to my left. A family with two little girls dressed in matching yellow shorts walked toward me from the far end. I slammed the hood down, moved to the driver's door, tossed the pack over the seat, dropped the wrench on the floor, and got in.

The Barracuda roared to life.

I needed privacy to find out what was in that pack — and what she wanted me to do with it. Had to be important, or she wouldn't have hidden it.

Assuming Mona hid it.

I drove downtown streets gray-dirt-bland in shadows cast by Sunday morning light. Traffic inched along, as if Chicago were yawning after a tough night on the town. Not knowing many restaurants, I stashed the car at the top of a parking garage near the Pig where it wasn't visible from the street, and took the backpack with me. I found the Pig open for breakfast, ordered an egg panini, and headed to the restroom. It only had one stall, but that stall had a door.

And a lock.

I sat down and put the pack on my lap. In the main section I found packets wrapped in brown paper. One was torn open. A peek inside revealed hundred dollar bills.

My mouth was suddenly dry.

A quick count indicated a hundred bills per pack: ten thousand dollars wrapped up no bigger than a good hot dog. I rummaged around: ten, twenty, maybe fifty packs. I did the math. Blood swished in my ears in rhythmic pulses.

A half-million dollars.

I forced myself not to whistle.

The outer door to the restroom opened. I counted to ten, then reached behind me and flushed.

I checked the small pockets of the backpack. Found a phone. It asked for a security code; I put it away. Another held a wallet-sized photo of Mona that could have been taken in an amusement park photo booth. I flipped it over.

Find me, Tommy – M.

I stared at the picture. Red hair flowed to her shoulders. Recent. Bright painted lips reminded me of a chewing gum commercial. Or maybe all-natural mango hair conditioner.

I'll tell you in the morning.

I jumped when the outside door slammed. I flushed again, and on my way out passed a guy in his dark blue Sunday best looking uncomfortable.

The panini was on my table when I reached it, the coffee still steaming. I sat down and put the pack between my feet the way Mona had done in my car. Now I knew why private eyes in novels were always smoking a cigarette: it was nerve-wracking having no idea what was going on.

Five

I BIT INTO THE PANINI and watched a young couple near the window hold hands under the table while I dug out Mona's cell phone. I tried to sort the items bouncing around in my head into some semblance of order: the phone, the money, where Mona had gone, why I claimed to be a private eye when I hadn't investigated anything since trying to score a phone number by texting a coed's friends. The guy behind me bumped my chair hard as he stood up to clear his gut past the edge of his table. I turned. He didn't even look my way, let alone apologize. I let it go and focused on practical issues: where was I going to sleep tonight? How long did I want to stay in Chicago now that I had missed Detroit? And since it was my only real source of funds, what about Walmart? I hadn't told them anything. And…was I going to try to find Mona?

Of course. I had to. I had taken her deposit. That seemed like a sort of contract.

Or bond.

Her thin smartphone wanted a four-digit number to let me inside. She couldn't be silly enough to use her name, but Mona *was* four-letters. The phone showed a row of circled numbers, not an old-school dialing pad. I couldn't remember which letters corresponded to which numbers. I scanned the room.

A waitress with short brown hair noticed me rubbernecking and came over. Bright red crinkled cloth clung tight to her torso from just above her belly button to slightly above her breasts. A clear plastic strap over each lean, toned shoulder helped hold it up.

"Is there a pay phone around?" I asked.

She glanced at the cell phone lying on the table and back at me.

"I need to see the letters on a keypad."

She pulled a phone from her pocket, tapped it, and showed me a keypad. "Like that?"

I nodded, looked for the letters. MNO were all on the 6 button. So Mona was 6662.

"Thanks." As she turned away I noticed her hair was short in back, maybe shorter than mine.

The 666 niggled at my mind even though I didn't buy any of that superstitious mark of the beast mumbo. It had to be a coincidence; but then, I didn't really believe in coincidence either.

I tapped the numbers. The phone unlocked. Long odds.

Six messages. I took another bite of egg and cheese. The first text had come in yesterday at 5:02 am. Early for a Saturday morning.

Did you get out?

Mona hadn't answered. I scrolled down and up. She hadn't answered any of them.

Hey, are you out? Let me know.

An hour later:

We're on the road.

Just heard, pigs got everything.

Then:

Contact me asap.

The last had arrived at noon Saturday, less than 24-hours ago.

FIND ME!

Sort of a theme developing around Mona.

The sender was identified as *Z-Rox*. Didn't help much, and made me think of dinosaurs.

I checked for email, wondering how many federal regulations I was violating.

Nothing. The phone hadn't even been set up with an email account. I checked to see if the browser had a history that might show where she accessed an account in the cloud.

The history was empty.

Contacts only contained the number of the phone itself, assigned to *redhoof.* How many twenty-something girls had only one entry in their cell phone?

I put the phone away and thought about a hitchhiker hiding a huge chunk of cash in my car. Go to the police? I had driven across two state lines, never asked her age or where she was from, accepted a cash deposit and prepayment. And why would they believe a guy from Ohio who told them: "She left the half-million under my hood, I have no idea why."

Solving this myself sounded like a better idea.

A newspaper abandoned on a neighboring table caught my eye; I reached over and collected it. The waitress with the clear straps watched. I waved her over.

"Do you have chocolate cake?"

"For breakfast?"

I smiled. "Anytime is right for chocolate and coffee."

"I have a brownie leftover from yesterday. Half-price."

"Yes, please." I hesitated. "Could I ask you a question?"

Her eyes held onto me as a BS deflector went up over her slender face: small nose, no makeup, like an athlete ready to run. She nodded.

"I need a place to stay in Chicago for a few weeks. Something simple, like a spare room in a house."

The shield dropped slightly. "Find someone who needs a roommate."

I recalled Billy Denster at Oberlin who thought bathing was for sissies. I definitely did not want a roommate.

"Maybe a little more private, but still cheap."

She tilted her nose toward the ceiling, scrunched her lips, tapped a finger against her cheek just the way actresses did in sitcoms.

"Victoria's. That's a bed and breakfast." She pointed with a capped ballpoint pen. "That way."

"Close?"

Her head bobbed. "Oh yeah. You can walk it easy."

"Thanks, I'll check it out. Do you have a backup suggestion?"

The smile tilted. "You could rent our spare room, but my boyfriend wouldn't like it."

"Narrow-minded, huh?"

She laughed and said, "One day-old brownie coming up," before spinning away.

By the time I finished the brownie (fresh by my standards) and washed it down with brew, the white-faced clock on the wall told me it was nine o'clock and (with my old phone shattered to bits on I-80) I needed a watch.

I found a tourist's walking map on a shelf near the cash register at the Pig, hefted the backpack intensely aware of its contents, and started wandering the city. As I walked along dodging pedestrians texting or pressing a cell phone to their ear, I thought about the vinyl records in the car. And my guitar. More reasons to find a safe place. As I turned onto Clark Street the three gold balls of the Medici family crest hovered ahead of me.

Pawnshop. Second score of the day, counting the free brownie.

I stopped out front and gazed through a window that had last been washed long ago by drunken frat guys. I didn't much like wrist watches (too much like a hand grabbing my arm), but amid a sea of leather and metal straps a dozen pocket watches glistened. Unbelievably, one had a Chrysler winged logo on the face, and a slender silver chain. With my cash in my left pocket, the retainer from Mona in my right, and a backpack that made me feel like a thief, I walked through the door to the jingle of bells. A short rotund gentleman appeared from a back room covered in monochrome: white shirt tucked into gray pants held by both a black belt and suspenders, overlaid by a wide slate tie. A study in shades of gray except for the suspenders — they were red with a narrow gray stripe. I thought of the Ohio State Buckeyes, but didn't ask, since this was Illinois.

His eyes followed me.

My jaw tensed as the thought that he had guessed what was in the backpack fleeted through my brain. I cleared my throat.

"I need a watch. You have anything with an automotive logo on it? Maybe a Chevy?"

"Ford wristwatches." He motioned toward a cabinet to my left.

I walked over and studied them. Ford was popular, as was Chevy and Toyota.

"Pocket watch?"

He considered me. My sport coat, backpack. "Not many young guys carrying those."

"Trying to get ahead of the hipsters," I said. "Jeans all come with this little pocket." I poked my index finger in the small pocket on the right side of my pants. "But no one ever uses it."

"Most kids don't know why it's there," he said, as he shuffled through the shop, apparently searching for my request. As he passed by the window display he said, "How do you feel about Chrysler?"

"Does it have a Hemi?" I asked, mimicking the TV commercials.

He answered with a low grunt of a laugh. "People don't know what to think about Chrysler. Government bailout. Mercedes buys them. Then Fiat. What a circus. That's worth two hundred easy. I'll let you have it for ninety-seven."

He handed me the watch. It showed 9:21. I held it to my ear: ticking. I wondered when he had last set it.

"Fifty if you guarantee it keeps time."

He shook his head. "It'll keep time like a Swiss Army captain. Seventy-eight, plus tax."

This guy liked unusual numbers.

"Do I have to wind this every day?"

"Not if you carry it. Check the back. Self-winding. The motion of your hip keeps the spring tight."

A bonus feature.

"No tax," I said.

He nodded. I debated if this was a legitimate expense for Mona. Decided it wasn't and pulled a hundred out of my left pocket.

My new friend held the bill up to the sunlight coming in from the window, turned it sideways, exposed it to bluish light from a small silver tube, and finally tilted it back and forth a half-dozen times. Satisfied, he gave me a twenty and two singles, and studied me as I slipped the watch in my pocket, attaching the chain to a belt loop.

I left the shop with an idea scraping the inside of my skull, the backpack feeling heavier than when I walked in, and Mom's voice hounding me to never pick up hitchhikers because they always had secrets.

Six

A DON'T WALK LIGHT interrupted my progress as I hoofed along Fullerton wondering how to keep my meager belongings safe. I goggled at the architecture to help me resist the urge to cross against the light. On my right a plain brick building sported white block letters: Chicago Public Library, Lincoln Park Branch.

A library should have suggested books, but I thought *public Internet access.*

I went in and was directed to the Web terminals by a young woman in a bright yellow top who gestured without speaking, maybe an occupational hazard of working in a whisper-quiet library every day. I set the browser to *Private* and went to DuckDuckGo.com: the search engine that promised not to track me. I surely didn't want anyone to record me typing "counterfeit hundreds" into a search window.

It instantly found holograms, A100 coding, pictures of presidents embedded in special paper, and the number 100 in the right corner changing from green to black depending on the viewing angle.

Maybe because part of me wasn't ready to find out, I killed time by checking my new watch. Ten o'clock. I compared it to the digital time on the computer. Exactly correct. I smiled. My friend with the red suspenders probably set all the watches in the window just before he opened every day.

I dug into my right pocket for one of Mona's bills, held it to the light, found the hologram: A100. Tilted it. The 100 changed to green from dark black. I pushed it back into my pocket and moved on to the next article from my search.

Counterfeit currency in Michiana.

Michigan and Indiana. I had picked up Mona in Ohio, not far from the Michigan state line.

The link led to YouTube. I wasn't doing a good job of escaping technology, though my new watch was a start — at least it didn't have a battery.

Two other people, both men, were using terminals on this quiet Sunday morning, but seemed to be ignoring me. I watched the video with the sound low. A guy in a suit described how to test the bills and showed a map of where they had been identified. The dots looked like an amateur had thrown darts at the Midwest: Chicago, Toledo, Detroit. Fake bills had been showing up for months, which inspired this newscast that had made its way onto YouTube.

I unzipped the top of the backpack just enough to get my hand in, pretending to dig for a candy bar. I found a packet in the middle of the bunch, worked the end open with my fingers and carefully extracted a bill from the center. I rolled it into my palm, brought out my hand and zipped the pack closed. I placed the bill on the desk and stood so I could move my head around to vary the viewing angle. The 100 stayed black. I checked the holograms; they didn't do anything unusual. I rubbed the bill; it felt like the ones in my left pocket.

I shook my head and whispered: "Mona, Mona, Mona."

Had she really slipped me half a million in worthless paper? One more question I wanted to ask when I found her — something I wasn't going to be able to do sitting in the library. I stared down at the pack between my feet. I needed a place to hide things, so I asked the Duck.

It found a storage unit over on Halsted, the same street as the Pig.

An hour and a half later my guitar, records, novels and Mona's backpack sat in secure climate-controlled self-storage; the Barracuda was tucked away in a parking garage, and I lay stretched out on a queen bed in a top floor room of Victoria's

Victorian B&B with rent paid in advance for a week, my suitcase under the table, and a lot on my mind.

While stowing the goods in a rarely cleaned eighty-square-foot storage space I had locked the door from the inside, trapping myself in a giant safety-deposit box, before opening the backpack. Only after counting forty-nine packs did I think of my fingerprints. I wiped the waxy paper down with a Handi-Wipe from my Dopp kit and put on a worn pair of leather driving gloves before opening a seal. To my eye, the seals seemed pressed by a machine, as if someone had an assembly line and could wrap dozens of these packages in minutes. Then I carefully counted the hundred-dollar bills inside, some new, some wrinkled and worn. A hundred total. Ten grand to each pack.

However.

Of those hundred, only the first and last five passed my crude, and likely inaccurate, test for authenticity. Ten per pack, a thousand real dollars, close to fifty-thousand in the entire backpack. That would cover my expenses for a long time. But forty-nine was an unusual number if you weren't a fan of San Francisco's NFL team. There had probably been fifty, and Mona took one.

Why leave the rest with a complete stranger?

An image of her chair-dancing at B.L.U.E.S. in her leopard print pants came to mind: lithe, sensual, free.

Followed by the obvious answer to my question.

She left the cash because she had to get rid of it fast.

I took a shower to clear the dust from my hair and mind and changed into my second pair of jeans. It was growing dark, so I switched to my leather biker jacket. On the way out of Victoria's I noticed a pay phone in the lobby and stopped. All the classic detective novels had a pay phone. Now everyone owned a cell.

Times change.

That reminded me of Mona's phone hidden in her backpack in locked storage. It likely had GPS. And those signals would shoot right through this old building if I brought it here. But I had turned it off. For a brief moment the uneasy feeling of doubt drifted through me. Yes it was off. I was almost sure.

I mentally reviewed my day, picked up the black handset, and read the directions to reverse the charges. Mom accepted them right away.

"Chicago. I stayed near the lake last night. It was beautiful."

"Are you relaxing?" she asked.

I hadn't thought about relaxing since picking up Mona. "I've been walking the city. I stopped at the library."

"Library? Oh Tommy, are you running a fever?"

"Funny, Mom. I, uh, broke my phone, and dropped in to learn a bit about the city."

"Be sure you eat," she said.

I smiled. Moms and food. "I found a café that serves all day."

"Good. Remember, you are what you eat."

We said goodbye and I hung up staring at the MNO on the number 6 key. No, I wasn't relaxing, but I was having fun. I turned for the front door.

A gray-haired woman standing in the next room near the little registration desk motioned me over with two fingers. She hadn't been there earlier when I registered; a young girl with flowing hair the color of a fawn had checked me in.

The woman stepped behind the desk and her hands disappeared below it. Scenes from a dozen stories where establishments kept sawed-off shotguns under the counter flashed to mind. Her hands came up holding a flat plastic card.

"Twenty-five dollars," she said.

"I, uh..."

She tapped the plastic card on the counter. "Tommy, you just called your mother." She held out her hand. "I'm Victoria."

I shook her hand gently; it was warmer than mine. I returned her smile.

"Now, the next time you call, use the prepaid card." She paused until our eyes locked together. "Do not call your mother collect."

I reached for the cash in my left pocket, my mother's cash, and nodded.

"Yes, Victoria, that's a very good idea."

She smiled, which made her face wrinkle in a happy way. "I hope you enjoy your stay with us." She considered me top to bottom. "We do have a monthly rate."

"Thank you. My plans are a bit, uh, fluid at the moment. But I could use a washing machine."

"A one suitcase man," Victoria said. "Washer and dryer in the basement. Ask for the key here at the front desk. And since you didn't read our brochure, breakfast is at seven." She held my eyes again. "In the morning."

I grinned.

"And Tommy, if we have to answer the pay phone for you, it's a dollar per message."

Seven

I WALKED AWAY FROM VICTORIA'S intending to stop at my storage room to retrieve Mona's cell phone. The thought of having it in my possession made me nervous, cell phones did things I didn't understand, but it was my best option.

No, I just wasn't thinking like the private eyes in books. In those stories they *always* went to the last place the missing person had been seen. So I swung by the W and stood near the main entrance trying to recall details of Saturday night while watching valets hop into expensive cars. Mona had been with me past midnight, but gone in the morning. Someone must have seen her. I fingered the small picture she had left, and watched a tall African-American in a red vest leaning against the building reading a paperback. He had the confident air of someone waiting for his Bentley to be retrieved.

I walked over. "Hi."

He slipped the book into his back pocket, nodded. "Got a ticket?"

I shook my head. "A quick question." He stiffened. "I stayed here with my wife last night."

He relaxed back against the wall. Maybe something he heard all the time.

"Was the hotel to your liking?" he asked.

"It's superb. Only problem. She left during the night and hasn't come back."

"Women," he offered, flashing a big white smile.

"Any chance you were here last night?"

"Sure was. I'm here every night I can get. A man has to fight his way through a recession."

I placed Mona's picture on the top of his stand and held it with one finger.

"I know this is a long shot, but did you happen to see her?"

He stepped forward, glanced up to make sure there were no cars waiting, then leaned in to study the picture.

"Black boots, red hair." He moved a hand up and down. "Striped jacket made me think referee."

The jacket was news to me. "Yeah, probably her."

"Haven't seen her."

It was my turn to stiffen. His face was flat. Then the smile began.

"Just jivin' you, man. She flew out of here, oh, maybe one, two in the morning."

"Somebody pick her up?"

"Nope." He pointed. "Taxi stand right there. The lead cab was dark green. I remember because the guy behind him was pissed he missed the hot-babe fare." He nudged the picture toward me. "Not much action that late, even on a Saturday. This place draws a mellow crowd."

"Think I could find him?"

"The cabbie? Sure. He'll be back. But he won't tell you anything. Paul don't remember much. You want, I'll ask him."

I introduced myself. His name was Marvin.

"I'd appreciate that." I slipped him twenty for his troubles. Figured it as a legitimate Mona expense. A thought came from nowhere. "Marvin, are you a musician?"

"You picked up on that, eh? Bottom man." He shifted one hand in a polish-the-car motion. "I lay a smooth groove."

"Where might a guy go for a guitar besides a pawn shop?" I had my gold top locked in storage, but no way was I going to let that lie in a hotel room while I was out looking for Mona. We were too close.

"How much green you want to mow?"

I blew out, considering my budget. "Less than five hundred."

"Old Town School of Folk Music. Proceeds go back into the community. They teach too, if you feel the need."

"Thanks. Not a place I would have tried."

"But I can get you something real fine for three. Gibson or Fender?"

"I lean Gibson."

"Right. We all have preferences. Makes us unique, like a song. Color?"

"Not gold." I met his eye. "And not hot."

He held up both hands. "No man, Marvin's clean. I know a lot of brothers. Someone'll have something. You stop back later tonight. I'll have your axe, and maybe news about your lady." He hesitated. "Might be bad news."

I nodded. "Whatever you find." We shook. His long fingers enveloped my whole hand. "Thanks, Marvin."

I drifted into the hotel thinking about referees. Mona hadn't been wearing a striped jacket, and I had been with her every second (a little voice said: *except when you were sleeping*). I figured the W for a gift shop and wasn't disappointed. Like everything else at the hotel, it was large and extravagant. I found rain coats for the blustery Chicago weather, but nothing that could pass for a ref.

A young woman came out of a back room and walked to the cash register. She sat on a stool, picked up a *Vogue* magazine, and ignored me. I stepped up to the counter and tapped softly on the glass top. She looked up.

"Do you sell jackets here?"

She tilted her head toward the aisle I had just left.

"I was thinking something more elegant. Leather. Maybe stripes."

She lowered the magazine and stared at me with very dark irises.

"Stripes?" She dragged the word out like she was hearing it for the first time. Then shook her head slowly. "No stripes."

"Anything else?"

"I have one," she said. "In back. It's black, basic. Would you like to see it?"

I shrugged, "Sure."

She disappeared and returned in less than a minute wearing the black jean jacket that Mona had been wearing.

"That's very nice. Is it yours?"

She nodded. "A woman came in yesterday, traded me." She hesitated. "Mine was like this but," she moved her hand up and down, "it had contrasting stripes pressed into the material. Do you like it? I'll make you a good price."

I smiled. "You should keep it. Looks great on you."

She glanced down at the jacket and back up at me, pulled it closer around her and gave me a model-on-the-runway smile.

So Mona had found herself a new jacket. Why?

"How late is your shop open?"

"Depends on the night. Weekdays until ten. Friday and Saturday until two. Some people like to spend money when they're drunk." She smiled again. High-wattage. Almost made me want to spend money.

As I walked out the main entrance Marvin was slipping behind the wheel of a green Jaguar. He waved. I waved back.

Dark clouds covered the city. If those had been in Ohio they would mean rain in a couple of hours. I wasn't sure what they meant this close to Lake Michigan. I pulled on the chain. My new pocket watch read almost seven o'clock. I headed for the Bourgeois Pig, wondering if the clear-strapped girl might still be working.

Eight

I STROLLED THROUGH THE Chicago dusk trying to imagine a half a million bucks as a stack of one-dollar bills instead of hundreds. I could buy a parking lot full of cars with that kind of money—so long as they weren't Lamborghinis. I struggled to put it into perspective, like a quarter million miles to the moon. But the more pertinent question was…

Why did Mona have a backpack full of fake dough?

The voice in my head I figured all private eyes argued with said: *Find her and she'll tell you.* I wasn't sure Mona would tell me anything, or if the little she had told me was true. But I had been paid for three days of gumshoe work, and didn't exactly have pressing commitments on my calendar. Except Walmart. They were expecting me for second shift today. Maybe if I didn't show, they would never take me back.

As I walked into the *Bourgeois Pig* I scanned for the bare shoulders of a slender girl a bit over five feet with wispy short hair. A waitress behind the counter matched the hair but not the shoulders. I made my way to a two-top in the far corner that people seemed to be avoiding, perhaps because one chair faced the wall, wondering why, if she had worked all day, she was wearing a black shirt now.

I scanned the menu of stupendous sandwiches with outrageous names. The Beggar's Opera (TM trademark included) with homemade basil pesto and grilled chicken jumped out. I was considering if I might be up late and should get coffee when the black shirt appeared.

"Hey," I said.

She studied my face. "You're back."

"And you're still here." I nodded to the shirt. "But you dressed for dinner."

She shook her head. "Not still here. Back like you."

"Two shifts? You must be rich."

She laughed, a gentle sound I liked a lot.

"I go to college. Spent today in the library trying to catch up. What would you like?"

I ordered the Beggar's and coffee and didn't find out what she studied before she disappeared. According to the menu the Pig didn't close till ten, and was going strong now. When she returned with the coffee I checked for a name tag, came up empty.

"I'm Tommy."

"Penny. My last name is not Lane, and yes, my parents like the Beatles." She held out her hand and shook once, the trained businesswoman.

I released her hand and pointed at her. "Kate Hudson."

She tilted her head back and gazed down her tiny nose at me. "*Almost Famous*, right? Penny Lane was quite the character in that movie." She smiled, then disappeared.

I thought boyfriend, and, traveling through.

Halfway into the sandwich Penny came back to check on my dinner. I assured her all was fine. Then added: "Thanks for the pointer."

She tilted her head again. Maybe she did it all the time. Soft eyelashes fluttered. Still no makeup.

"I got a room from Victoria."

"Nice. You're welcome." She swiveled her head to check on the other tables. No one seemed to be trying to flag her down.

"What do you study when you're not overseeing your restaurant empire?" I asked.

"Crime and criminals."

I held out my wrists. "You going to slap the cuffs on me?"

She put a finger to her lips. "We'll see." And she was off again.

I finished the sandwich and a second cup of coffee while thinking about how to find a missing person. Maybe Marvin would provide a lead. All I had so far was a girl in a striped coat that bailed out of my hotel room in the middle of the night, leaving a warm memory behind.

And I had a half-million dollars.

Sort of.

Why would anyone leave dangerous money with a person they had just met, and might never see again? I got only one answer: wherever she had gone, she couldn't take it with her.

Penny came back and removed my plate. There were empty tables now, so no pressure to vacate mine. I ordered a fresh baked cookie with M&Ms in it. Then said: "Professor. If you wanted to find a missing person, where would you start?"

"Milk cartons," she said as she turned away.

When she came back with the cookie, she brought a tiny carton of milk like I drank back in elementary school with the mid-morning snack. It had a tiny picture of a missing girl on the side: Carla, age 8, a curly-headed African-American kid with a beautiful smile.

"Not her," I said.

She watched me for a moment, giving me a chance to study the way she swooped her hair across her forehead.

"You need to get the word out," she said. "Crowdsource." She left me with a cookie the size of a DVD, and the milk carton.

I broke it in half and contemplated about how to get someone in Chicago who had seen Mona to tell me where. *Assuming she was in Chicago.* She could have thumbed her way into a long-haul rig (Walmart came to mind) and be most of the way to California by now. That was a disheartening thought. I reviewed and chewed.

Mona traded her black jacket for a striped one. Walked out of the hotel. Left the money under my hood.

And a note. Don't forget the note.

Penny came back, broke off a piece of my cookie and stood there eating it.

"Would you like a bite of my cookie?" I asked.

She pushed a tuft of short hair behind her ear with her free hand. "Do you have a picture?"

I reached inside my jacket, placed it on the table.

She munched our cookie. "Kind of glamorous. Doesn't seem like your type."

"My client hired me to find her."

Her eyes grew wide. She glanced around the café, then sat down at the table, facing the wall behind me.

She whispered, "Client?"

I nodded.

"So you're a private investigator licensed in the state of Illinois?"

"Ah, not exactly. I'm just starting out."

"You're helping a friend?"

"Acquaintance."

She stole more cookie, which was fine by me; the thing was huge.

"I get it. You have no idea what you're doing, but you want to help someone out."

"Do criminologists study private eyes too?" I asked.

She nodded. "Mostly to understand how you civilians complicate things for us." Her eyes moved to my chest and back up. I got an inkling of what a woman must feel when a guy drops his eyes to her breasts while talking to her.

She leaned across the table and lowered her voice. "Are you carrying?"

I shook my head. "Not even a cell phone."

Her jaw stopped moving.

"I'm in a technology reallocation phase," I said. "It had become intrusive, people wanting immediate responses to nonsense, phones tracking my location, all that next-big-thing stuff. I've returned to simpler times."

She nodded, possibly thinking I was an idiot.

Then she grinned. "How are you going to call me?"

"Victoria's has a pay phone."

She laughed.

"What time do you get off work?" I asked.

"We close at ten."

"Since you're an expert on crime, would you care to consult with me on how I might crowdsource this problem?"

She stood. "You buying?"

"For sure," I answered, not at all sure what I was buying.

"Get here early and I'll score you a free cookie." Then she was off to another table to check her customers.

I watched her small bottom move a bit longer than was absolutely necessary before leaving cash for the check and kicking myself for not getting her phone number in case things went wrong.

Nine

I UNPACKED MY SUITCASE into a four-drawer dresser that had probably seen the civil war. Then reorganized it. Twice. Unable to concentrate on anything except failing to generate ideas on how to find Mona. I was back at the Pig with five minutes to spare, but Penny came flying out before I reached the door. She was still wearing her black shirt, but had slipped on a blue jacket with a slender animal skin collar. As we met on the sidewalk she pushed a bag into my hand.

"For later, when we're hungry."

I felt a curved shape inside and slipped the bag into the pocket of my jacket then raced to catch up with her because she hadn't stopped walking.

"In a hurry to escape repression from the Pig overlord?"

She shook her head. "No, I just like to keep moving. You know, Newton and all that."

What had Newton done? Calculus. And laws. Which law was she talking about? She must have read my expression.

"A body in motion remains in motion unless acted upon by an external force."

"I didn't know Newton was a criminal."

She punched my arm. "Don't they have high-school physics on your planet?"

"Let me think back. Yes, I'm remembering something about getting high." She moved fast. I lengthened my stride to stay with her. "Are we in a rush to be someplace?"

"We have work to do."

She stopped.

I walked two steps beyond her before realizing she wasn't beside me. I backed up.

She was staring at a poster taped to a metal lamp pole advertising a performance by a band called Splinter Group. I wondered what they had splintered from.

"Where was she last seen?" she asked.

"The W hotel."

Her brown eyes rolled my way. "Fancy client. Let's go to Kinko's"

Penny dragged me to an all-night place that said FedEx over the door where we made our own page-size poster on orange paper. A quarter of it was Mona's picture and the remainder a $200 reward for information about her whereabouts under a heading in bold italics that read: *Missing Mona.* I listed Victoria's pay phone number, figuring a dollar per message wouldn't cost much. We left the harshly lit center with a hundred flyers under my arm, a roll of packing tape, and a box of colored thumbtacks.

"So?" she said.

"You have a plan?"

"Do you have wheels?"

We walked the few blocks to the garage. When I pointed out the Cuda she ran a finger along the rear fender.

"Looks like a giant chocolate bar," she said.

I laughed and unlocked the door for her.

"I think we fan out from the W," she said. "In ever increasing circles until we run out of flyers."

"You think she's close?"

She shook her head. "I think if someone saw her, it was while she was making her getaway."

We became a well-oiled machine. She put tape along the top and bottom of flyers while I drove. When she pointed at a telephone pole or kiosk, I pulled to the curb, she pushed herself out the open window and stuck the flyer up, adding thumbtacks if the surface was soft enough.

Traffic was light on Sunday night, so in an hour we ran out of flyers. But I had at least done something to earn my per diem from Mona.

"Where to now?" I pulled out my watch. "It's eleven-thirty."

She stared. "Is that made by Luddite?" She laughed. "I've got to get some sleep. Two shifts and school tomorrow. Back to the Pig."

In a few minutes I stopped at the curb. The Pig was dimly lit inside; a tilted sign in the window read CLOSED in bright red against midnight blue.

"I've got a pay phone," I said.

She smiled, scribbled on a piece of tape, tore it off and stuck it to my forehead.

"Call only at seven in the morning. I leave for work at seven-thirty." She kissed two fingers and touched them to my cheek. "Keep me posted about Mona. Maybe I can use her for my Master's thesis." She hopped out and leaned back through the window. "Bye, Tommy."

I drove halfway to Victoria's before remembering that Marvin had told me to come back, so I swung north on Lake Shore Drive. The deep water of Lake Michigan to my right, black under the stars, reached to empty beaches bordering the highway. I couldn't find the moon. I saw the W, but there was no exit so I continued north, passing high-rise after high-rise, wondering how many people lived in Chicago.

And if Mona was out there somewhere.

I backtracked to the W's entrance. Marvin took long strides toward the car. When he got close and recognized me behind the wheel, he whistled like he'd seen a sexy girl in a tiny bikini.

"My man has a *sweet-ass* ride."

"My grandfather left it to me. Restored it myself. So don't go raising the price of the guitar."

Marvin's face busted into a huge grin. "Wait till you see what I got for you." He stepped back and waved his hand. "Right over there, sir, beside the black Mercedes."

I parked and waited behind the wheel. Marvin had disappeared. I revved the Hemi a couple of times just to listen to it sing before shutting it down.

Marvin slipped in beside me holding a tan guitar-shaped flannel sheet. "Guy Billy knows was just about to pawn this. I told him you'd make him a better deal." He leaned forward to check the passenger's side rearview mirror for customers.

I pushed my door open, careful not to scratch the shiny black paint on the Mercedes, and slid the instrument across my lap. It was powder blue metallic, but most of the paint on the back had been worn off. The fretboard was worn. I moved through a few chords and a couple of scales listening to the natural tone of the wood.

"Feels good," I said.

"Guy played a lot. Swears by it. Hurt his hand, needs the cash."

I examined the grain of the wood. Made in Korea. A lower cost line, but good quality.

"How's it sound through an amp?"

"Everything works."

I laughed. "Doesn't matter, I don't have an amp." This was plenty good for noodling at the B&B. And it wouldn't take a part of my soul if it were stolen—no memories had advantages.

"What's he want for it? It's worn bad."

"Well-played," Marvin said. "Pawnbroker offered two-fifty."

I'd have to do better, and Marvin would need a finder's fee. It was set up nicely, guy must have been using it as his primary instrument. Made me sad to buy it and take it away from him.

"Will he take three hundred, and another fifty for the Marvin retail outlet?"

Marvin nodded. "We can make that work."

I hit an E9 chord and let it ring. "Tell him if he ever wants it back, he can have it for the three fifty."

Marvin nodded, his face somber. He knew what selling your instrument meant.

"Thanks, Marvin. You're okay for a middle man." I smiled, paid him, rewrapped the guitar and placed it on the floor behind the bucket seats. He hopped out and came around to the driver's side. He eased my door closed like he had just returned the car to me, then leaned over.

"I talked to our cabbie. He remembers her real plain. Pretty. Red hair. In a hurry. Leaving at night like that; he figured her for a local whore."

I nodded, listening for details that might help find Mona; trying not to think about her breath in my ear, and her body pressing down on my chest.

"She made him drive around town. Kept changing her mind where she wanted to go. Ran up nearly a hundred bucks on the meter."

I bet she did. "Paid him with a hundred?"

Marvin nodded.

"Where did she get out?"

He smiled. "Cabbie remembered exactly. Or, claimed he did. You can never tell with Paul, he makes stuff up faster than a paperback writer."

"Your opinion?"

"Too creative for Paul, probably really happened. She wanted out at Dunkin' Donuts. The one down on Ashland. You gotta be careful, there's a million of 'em around here. Says she made him keep the meter running while she ran in and got him a donut and coffee. I quote, 'That cute little ass got me a cinnamon donut.'"

I nodded. "Worth checking out."

"It's right across from Fearon's Pub, in case you need a drink by the time you get there." His eyes flashed to the guitar on the seat behind me, then back to my face. "You coming to open mic at BLUES tonight?"

"I'm sort of out of practice, that's why I wanted this." I motioned with my head.

"You don't practice the blues, my son, you channel it. That's why I got it for you so fast, so you can back me up tonight." He glanced at his wrist. "I'm taking off at twelve-thirty and heading right over." He backed away from the window. "See you there."

I waved and started the car. Marvin grinned at the sound of the engine.

I had half an hour and a cookie in my pocket. I started on the cookie and drove to the storage facility. They had promised 24-hour access and rewarded me with a night clerk who buzzed me in and checked my key. I resisted the urge to grab a few more hundreds and found the phone in the outside pocket of the backpack. I logged in, but there were no new messages. I locked up and grunted at the clerk on my way out. He grunted back.

Before I reached the car the phone went crazy with blips and bloops. I pulled it out. A stream of messages was arriving from Z-Rox. I counted eleven: asking, requesting, demanding a response. The last one ended: *or else.*

Z didn't seem so friendly to poor little Redhoof.

I considered responding. But Z-Rox might figure out someone besides Mona had her phone. I wasn't ready for that.

A phone meant GPS, cell towers, location updates to faraway computers. I had heard some kept tracking all the time, which was one intrusion too many. I leaned against the rear fender, right about where Penny had blessed it with her fingers, and thought about how to disable a cell phone so it couldn't tell anyone anything, without breaking it.

I turned it off, then flipped the case over and fumbled until I got the SIM chip out. I didn't think any phone could communicate without a chip, though I wasn't certain. I tucked the phone up near a taillight, and slipped the chip under the floor lining near the driver's seat.

I stared out the windshield. What did *or else* mean?

I drove back to the parking garage. My spot on the third floor was open, and seemed safe, so I grabbed it.

I finished the cookie, tucked the guitar and its makeshift case under my left arm, and started walking toward B.L.U.E.S.

Ten

I ENTERED A HALF-EMPTY CLUB where Marvin was pushing an amplifier into position on a low stage. I ordered two beers from a jean-clad waitress with a black bra showing under her green silky top.

"How's this work?" I asked Marvin.

He pointed at me, then to himself. "We open as a duo, heat things up a little. Then Kahlil—" He stretched to scan the room, shrugged. "He'll join us on drums when he gets in the mood."

"You have tunes in mind?"

He nodded. "A couple classics, then one of mine." He saw my face. "Not to worry, my friend, I can carry them if I have to. Just give me some rhythm backup. And when I point at you, do something."

Something. I guessed I could do something.

"It's open mic. We only do three tunes," he said.

"How come we get to go first?"

"Because I'm Marvin," he said, flashing his grin.

I found a little Fender guitar amp at the back of the stage glowing on standby, plugged in, flicked it on, and checked the electronics in my new acquisition. The guitar's tone was bright and full. I kept the volume low and played fast in an effort to warm the nervous frigidness out of my hands, remembering my last performance had been at a frat party: a time when I still hoped to prevent myself from getting a real job. Then came Walmart mechanic to provide the necessities of modern life: gas, food, alcohol, cell-phone contract, and required-by-law health insurance. The back of my neck felt prickly. I turned around.

A girl appeared to be watching me from the shadows along the wall.

At first I saw Mona, then mentally slapped myself for seeing what I wanted to see, rather than what was there. This girl had straight black hair and wide rectangular sunglasses. The blush in her cheeks reminded me of the paintings of long-legged girls on the noses of World War II bombers.

Her black skirt reached to mid-calf and her short-sleeved blue sweater to ward off the chilled air rolling off the deep waters of Lake Michigan was furry enough to be alive. The hug of the skirt and heels made her appear tall and slender. And shapely, like that secretary in *Mad Men* on TV.

I winked.

She sipped a blue martini the shade of seawater in the Caribbean.

Maybe she wasn't watching me; I couldn't see her eyes through the glasses. I wondered if all of the open-mic clientele were going to be classy.

I played through a bit of *Seventh Son* and smiled at Willie Dixon's reference to "flesh quivering on lovely bones" as the martini girl's shape held inside my head. I switched to *Hoochie Coochie Man*. Something told me Marvin would be singing that one for sure. I checked over my shoulder.

She was staring at the stage. Sipped. Turned around and walked the length of the bar.

The room swayed slightly.

I held a note to see how long the guitar would sustain and realized I had been on the road for only a single day, met new people, even landed a job. I was digitally-officially out of touch, yet life felt almost…fuel injected.

"You ready?" Marvin said. "Let's open with Hoochie Coochie Man."

I laughed, nodded and waited for him to count it off.

Marvin had a naturally smooth voice that made girls look our way. I stood to the side and kept it simple. Halfway through the song, Kahlil appeared behind the drum kit wearing a black beret with a green emblem above his forehead, and started playing so loud I could barely breathe. Marvin turned up, so I did too.

People started dancing. I took my first solo. No one grabbed me with a hook.

We did another classic and a Marvin original, then a multicolored gaggle of girls swarmed him and I felt more energy inside me than I had since my last drag race on an Ohio back road.

The blue martini returned and leaned against the wall in the same shadow. I wrapped the sheet around my guitar and tried to watch her without being obvious. She had a fresh drink in her left hand; reflections from her glasses hid her eyes. She lifted the garnish, and removed a small orb from the toothpick with very red lips.

I went over to thank Marvin, who introduced me to his fans. They were generous with compliments and one girl in a tight red dress jumped onstage and gave me a hug.

I leaned toward Marvin and spoke over the jukebox playing a version of *Badge* I hadn't heard.

"I'm going to get a cinnamon donut."

He shot me his big grin.

As I dropped off the stage my heart sank a little; Martini girl was gone. I scanned the room: left, right, front, back. No blue sweater. An empty martini glass at the near end of the bar had a toothpick in it, and lipstick on the rim so bright I could see it from the stage.

A girl in a hurry.

I considered waiting to see if she'd come back, but the donut shop beckoned, so I walked back to the Cuda. I slipped my new purchase in back and realized it had already taken me places I hadn't expected. A glance at the phone hiding near the taillight motivated me to send a reply to get things rolling. A little voice countered that starting a conversation with a stranger who wrote *or else* remained a bad idea.

I drove the speed limit, admiring yellow-warm streetlight reflecting from asphalt as I traveled south towards Ashland, feeling the vibration of the music still inside me, and the strange beauty of Marvin's chorus: *Why wait for fate, when you're holding me in your arms?* It seemed every traffic light installed since Chicago's founding in 1833 by real estate speculators (as described by the free magazine at Victoria's) decided to turn red as I arrived

A brightly lit Dunkin' Donuts sign claimed *America runs on Dunkin'.* An overweight man on a stool faced the largest paper cup of coffee I had ever seen, and a plate with three donuts stacked into a tower. He was chewing, so the three must have had a friend. I pulled up to the other end of the counter.

"What can I get you, honey?" a voice said from somewhere.

"Orange juice and a donut."

A slender black woman in a pink dress floated from a side door to the opposite side of the counter. "What kind of donut would you like?"

"A fresh one."

She stopped and put one hand on her hip like I had insulted her child.

"Sorry. I meant, whichever you made most recently."

"That would be the white frosting," she said, pointing.

I nodded.

"Just one? You look a little thin."

"Been working too hard."

"Ain't we all, baby. Coming right up."

I took the picture Mona had left and placed it on the counter, facing her way. When she brought the juice and donut her eyes touched it. She hesitated.

"You've seen her?" I asked.

"All depends on who wants to know."

"My name's Tommy."

"Theresa."

I motioned for her to turn the picture over.

She flipped it, read the note.

I said, "Her name's Mona."

She studied the writing, flipped the picture back. "Yeah, that's what she said."

"She was in last night, wasn't she?"

Theresa nodded.

"Paul the cabbie told me he dropped her off out front."

She smiled. "Sure did. Girl ran in here and bought the man coffee and a donut. Not many fares would do that for a driver."

"She's thoughtful that way."

Theresa glanced at her other customer. One donut remained on his plate, and half of one in his hand. He was chewing in time to a watered-down instrumental version of *Roxanne* by The Police.

"Anything you can tell me that might help me find her?"

"She didn't seem lost," Theresa said. "Anyone can write on the back of a picture."

I nodded. Smart lady.

"Your name really Tommy?"

I found my wallet and held up Thomas Kelsey's driver's license. She studied it.

"Not Cuda?"

Mona had definitely been here. No one else knew me by that name.

"Nickname." I pointed through the window.

She whistled through fabulous white teeth. "Pretty color." Then she walked away and disappeared through saloon-style swinging doors into the back.

The donut was indeed fresh, and welcome; gigs made me hungry. I downed half the orange juice and saw Theresa coming through a glass partition. She placed an envelope on the counter. It had *Tommy Cuda* written on it.

I flipped the picture over. I was no expert, but I'd guess the handwriting was the same. Maybe even the same blue pen.

"Should I open it?" I asked Theresa.

She shrugged. I zipped the end off. There was a note and a stack of bills I'd count later. I worked the note out with two fingers. Theresa watched me unfold it.

Tommy. Keep looking. — M (No, you weren't dreaming)

The girl knew how to provide motivation.

I finished the donut and juice, slipped Theresa a twenty-dollar tip, and headed back to the hotel. I was tired and more than a little confused from my first day on the job.

Stretched out on the bed wearing only shorts I decided I needed to start a journal. But all I got down on a piece of hotel stationary before my eyelids drooped were the names of people I had met today: *Penny, Marvin, Kahlil, Theresa, pawnbroker who might be an Ohio State fan, Victoria, huggie girl in red dress.*

And ones I hadn't: *Paul the cabbie, Penny's boyfriend, Martini girl in the fluffy sweater…*

I checked my pocket watch, after two AM, put it on the nightstand, crawled under the covers, wrapped one arm around my new guitar, and drifted off fast.

Eleven

A TWANG STARTLED ME AWAKE. Strings beside me were vibrating. I blinked my eyes clear. The room was dark save for a night-light glow seeping in through lace curtains.

I got up, shuffled to the bathroom, went to the window, pushed a curtain aside with one finger. Streetlight circles on the sidewalk seemed more like 3D effects in a modern animated movie than nighttime in Chicago. The human mind was tricky: retrieving things from memory without regard to where they came from, mixing up the virtual world and reality as if they weren't different.

Two cars sat on the far side of the street: an asphalt-gray sedan whose dark windows reflected a corner of Victoria's yellow building, and a small aqua SUV parked in front of it that had likely never seen a dirt road. The remainder was empty, still. For a moment not a leaf moved in Victoria's yard, dead or alive. I hadn't expected any part of Chicago to be so much like Gates Mills. But at four in the morning, most sane people everywhere were apparently sleeping, giving the night over to owls and pussycats.

A dark-haired woman with a blue martini intruded. Not because she meant anything, she was just nice to think about. Then Mona took over. The envelope Theresa had given me contained another eight hundred dollars: three or four more days of paid work if I kept expenses low.

I had almost a week to find her.

A page of a newspaper blew out from between the two cars, danced on the centerline of the road, then drifted toward me. It stopped at the curb, unable to make the leap. Standing in my underwear, watching the night do nothing, it hit me why Mona was gone, yet leaving a trail.

She was running.

But not from me. From someone or something that came before me. And if that someone found her, it would be bad to have the money in her possession. It might even help if she didn't know where it was — which she didn't. Of course it was about the money.

It was always about the money.

That helped me relax. It didn't answer anything, or help locate her, but I felt better having one little puzzle piece inside my head that made sense. I crossed to the bed, strummed the guitar and crawled back in. I put one arm around the rosewood fretboard and thought about the dark-haired girl whose name I didn't know walking away from the stage.

$ $ $

The room was bright and my throat dry. The sharp edge of the guitar body pressed into my cheek. I reached for the watch: seven-fifteen. I jumped up, splashed water on my face and got dressed, switching to my leather jacket to give the sport coat a day off. This was an incredibly early time to roll out of bed, let alone to eat, but I couldn't miss a free breakfast.

I walked down steps carpeted in flowing patterns that I associated with the roaring twenties, and turned toward the dining area. Two tables of four were occupied and a table for two was empty. I grabbed it.

Victoria was on me before I had even repositioned my chair.

"Would you like a wake-up call tomorrow, Thomas?"

I smiled. "Wouldn't want to trouble you."

She smiled too, so I guessed I wasn't late. She didn't take my order, just started bringing out food: orange juice, coffee, cream, a plate of fruit, a baguette. Since food was arriving, I started eating. Halfway through the fruit, the young girl with fawn-colored hair who had checked me in brought out an omelette with green peppers and mushrooms in it.

"Is she angry with me?" I asked, nodding towards Victoria.

She studied me. "How so?"

"She told me last night that breakfast was at seven."

The girl's face tightened. "She's having tease-the-slacker fun with you."

"She thinks I'm a slacker?"

"Anyone she sees who isn't working at that very moment is a slacker. But it's worse if you're under thirty. Worse still if you sleep past dawn."

I nodded. "Tell her I'm here working on a case for a client in Ohio."

"Are you?"

"Well, last night I was jamming in a blues club. But yes, I'm working."

"Sounds fun." She leaned close and whispered, "Breakfast is served from seven until nine. You can come down anytime."

"Thanks. I won't reveal my source."

She refilled my coffee and vanished.

My eyes drifted to a bay window. The sedan across the street was gone, but not the aqua SUV. I worked my way through the omelette and thought about what I would do if that pay phone didn't ring. I also remembered I should have called Penny at seven, so a stop at the Pig was on the agenda.

More cars flowed past as the morning matured: Chicago waking up on a Monday. A moving van obliterated my view for a moment. My first time in the city all on my own. A woman holding hands with a little girl in an orange coat disappeared behind the SUV, then came out the other side.

I didn't miss school.

I finished the omelette and was draining the last of my coffee when a car pulled in behind the SUV. A gray car. I lowered the cup, looked closely. Possibly the same gray car I had seen last night.

"More coffee?" the fawn-haired girl asked.

She poured, I studied the car. The driver didn't move to get out, just stared straight ahead. I glanced up at the girl, no name tag.

"Thank you. My name's Tommy."

She laughed. "I know, I registered you yesterday. I'm Kim, but my friends call me Slim. It's a long story."

"OK Slim Kim. Nice to meet you." I glanced back at the car.

She saw my eyes move and followed them. We both watched a man exit the right rear door and step onto the sidewalk: maybe five-foot-eight on a good day. He looked up and down the street, taking his time. He straightened his jacket by lifting the lapels. That made me wonder if he wore a shoulder holster under there and was shifting it to a more comfortable position. Maybe my mom was right, I did read too many detective stories.

"Friend of yours?" Slim asked.

"Never saw him before."

I cooled my full cup of hot coffee with cream and waited. He had a short mustache, the fair complexion I associated with Russians, and hair combed straight back almost to his collar. He walked between the two vehicles, which reminded me of the windblown newspaper in the middle of the night, and turned toward Victoria's. I watched him enter through the front door, a businessman in a business suit on business, and go straight to the registration desk. In a moment Slim lead him around the corner. They stopped at my table.

"Tommy, Mr. Hosco here to see you."

"Thanks, Slim," I said, bringing a smile to her face as she turned away.

I stood and shook his hand. It felt damp, but Bruce Lee powerful.

He gestured to the chair across from me. "May I?"

"Please. Would you care for breakfast?"

"Coffee. I won't be staying long."

European accent I couldn't place accurately. Slim was watching from around the corner, so I pointed to my cup, then to my guest. He sat down; I followed.

"What brings you to Victoria's, Mr. Hosco?" I asked, sounding like hurriedly written pulp fiction. Nerves. And my subconscious remembering half a million dollars I was trying hard not to think about.

"Business."

He reached inside his jacket. My spine stiffened. It was daylight and there were eight other people in the room, not counting Slim, who would soon be back with coffee for Hosco.

I tried to relax by tensing and releasing my jaw.

He unfolded one of my flyers and spread it flat on the table.

Slim arrived, filled his cup, slipped silently away. I glanced down at the flyer, then back to him. Something in his sandy hair made it shiny. I smelled the too-much-cologne aroma of a high-school locker room. I put him older than me, maybe thirty-five, and stronger: the muscles of his neck suggesting a poster hawking a Vegas boxing tournament.

"Is this yours?" he asked.

I nodded.

"You're looking for Mona?"

"I'm trying to locate the girl in that picture. I've been told her name is Mona Meyers."

He grew taut at the use of her full name, as if I had uttered a top secret code.

"Why?" he said, then tore the tops off two packets of sugar in a single motion and dumped them into his coffee with one hand.

"I don't know."

He stared at me. His high forehead was smooth, as if carved from stone.

"You have reasons," he said.

"Mr. Hosco, I'm a private investigator from Ohio. A client gave me that picture and asked that I spend a few days trying to locate her."

The pay phone in the hallway jangled. Slim raced around the corner.

"And have you?" Hosco said.

I smiled in a meager attempt to diffuse the invisible, building tension. "Would I still be in Chicago having breakfast?" I gestured toward the picture. "Those went up yesterday. You're the first to respond."

Hosco studied my face, sipped coffee, studied my face some more.

I said: "Do you know Mona?"

He drank for a long time, then placed the cup on the table without looking down. "Not your business." He stood. "Tell your client Mona is being cared for." He stared down at me. His eyes projected darkness, though the irises were halfway between blue and glacial gray. His Hollywood jaw shifted. His clothes were a little loose, but I got the sense that beneath roamed an athletic build that used a panther as a role model. "You should go back to Ohio, Tommy. Stay away from Mona. Chicago isn't your kind of town." He turned and exited through the front door without looking back.

My chest had tightened so much I wasn't breathing. I forced an air stream out slowly through my nose.

This sure wasn't Walmart.

Slim zipped around the corner and slid into Hosco's chair. She passed me a folded slip of paper.

"Who was that?" she asked, breathless.

"I have no idea." I pointed to the flyer he had left on the table. "He knows Mona."

Slim picked up the flyer and read.

I opened the note.

Pink Monkey. Tonight. Seven sharp.

She said, "You owe me a dollar for taking that message."

Twelve

I FOLDED SLIM KIM'S NOTE and pushed it into my jeans, wondering what a Pink Monkey was and how far I'd have to drive to reach it. The table of four closest to me rose to leave. The guy with his back to me dropped a newspaper on the seat of his chair and slipped on a red windbreaker. I waited for the group to turn the corner before reaching for it. He must have been a paperboy in his youth, because it was still in its original form; not many people could read a paper without making chaos of the sections.

The headline was about BP paying millions to recall gasoline that had been misformulated and was damaging car engines. How the heck could BP suddenly forget the formula for gasoline after so many decades? I scanned the article: *polymeric residue at higher than normal levels.* Below that: *16 Wounded in Separate Shootings Since Saturday.* A 13-year-old boy was mentioned in the second paragraph. Men walk up, fire shots. Cars drive up, fire shots. One guy was shot by someone on a bicycle. I stalled on that. A bicycle?

I flipped the paper over.

Counterfeiters Shoot Cop

I read faster. The headline needed a question mark. A cop had been shot in a raid near Detroit. Reams of paper were confiscated along with chemicals and a printing press, but no counterfeit bills. The operation, hidden in underground tunnels, had been located by specially-trained bloodhounds. A single gunshot was heard above ground by fellow officers. There was hope that the policeman, now in critical condition, would be able to identify his assailant.

I glanced around Victoria's little restaurant. The remaining table of four were eating, ignoring me. I kept reading.

A truck driver came forward and said he picked up a female hitchhiker in the area before dawn Saturday morning. She hadn't been identified and was wanted for questioning.

A one-inch square artist's drawing, what the paper called a *facial composite*, of the hitchhiker accompanied the article. She had bangs and her ears showed, as if her hair were short or pulled back in a ponytail that wasn't visible. I slid the flyer Hosco had left next to the paper. The crude sketch wasn't convincing.

Mona had been hitchhiking west. But then, lots of people hitchhiked west. In fact, almost all hitchhikers traveled west: toward the land of sun and gold, Hollywood fame, and liberal marijuana laws.

I carefully tore the article out and put it in my jacket with the flyer. Eight-thirty. I left a tip for Slim, slipped out the front door, and jogged most of the way to the Pig.

Penny saw me as I raced through the door. Her snug black shirt had been traded for a snug blue one. She frowned and held her thumb and pinky like a telephone to the side of her head. I gave the universal gesture for sleep. She laughed. I sat at the out-of-the-way table for two I'd had the night before.

"Lazybones," she said, looking well-rested, and what my mother would call chipper.

"Sorry. Time change got me. Ohio's on Eastern."

She shook her head. "If you're going to lie, at least figure it right. The clock turns back an hour as you go west; you should have been up early. Not so sharp for a *private eye*. Coffee?"

I nodded. "And a leftover cookie if you have one. I had breakfast at Victoria's."

"I see. Penny gets to wait. Victoria gets the attention."

"Victoria was buying." I grinned.

"Hmm," she said, and left.

I pulled out the pictures and placed them side by side on the table; studied the sketch; wished they had printed it in color. But the finger was pointing at Mona—she had the cash.

Penny placed a mug of coffee on the table and a big sugar cookie beside it. Then stood behind me and leaned over my shoulder.

"What do think?" I asked.

"I think you flunked art class."

"It was in the *Tribune* this morning."

She looked closer. "I vote a big fat maybe. Why?"

"Story about counterfeiting in Detroit. A cop was shot."

"Why would Chicago care about Detroit?"

"Hundred dollar bills are floating around the Midwest. They're just following the story, to warn people."

"They think this girl came here?"

"They don't know. A trucker picked her up at dawn. He helped make the sketch."

Penny left to wait on customers. The contents of the backpack insisted Mona was connected somehow. Unclear if the trucker picked her up, or some random girl running from her parents.

Penny came back and refilled my cup.

"What does your education tell you the cops would do with these two pictures?"

"Question you," she said. "Find out what you know about her, and her whereabouts. Especially on the day this went down."

"Friday night," I said.

"So, where were you Friday night, Mr. Tommy?"

"At my birthday party in Gates Mills, Ohio."

"Well, happy birthday. We'll have to celebrate."

"When you're not studying." I smiled. "Wouldn't want to interfere with grad school."

She tilted her chin up. "You're just jealous of intellectuals. How did our flyers work?"

"Two leads. A guy stopped by the hotel and asked me what I knew. He suggested I close my file."

"He came by?" Penny put one hand on her hip and held the coffee pot with the other. Her eyes rolled up and left toward the antique tin ceiling.

"Got it. There's a website that lists the location of public pay phones in the U.S. I used it once when my car battery went dead the same time as my cell phone."

"Bad luck. You think he got the address from that site?"

"It'd be easy. How do you think he found you?"

"Didn't think to ask him. He had his own driver. Slate-gray sedan."

"Not many of those in Chicago." She laughed and left.

I pulled out Slim's message from the pay phone; it didn't give me new ideas. A dozen people around me chattered, their caffeine-fueled speech spattered with *value-process, client-centric, push-pull strategy* and my favorite business-BS word of all time, used daily by the store manager at Walmart: *synergy.*

Penny came back with another cookie and I slipped her the note. She left right away, but read it as she crossed the room. I figured I'd go to the meeting. Worst case, I paid two hundred dollars and the caller's information led nowhere.

Not much of a risk.

Chicago isn't your kind of town echoed in my ears.

My brain conjured up the threats Hosco hinted at in a city where sixteen people had been shot between Saturday and Monday. I had a big stack of unhappy thoughts and an empty feeling by the time Penny came back.

She slipped the note into my hand, then tapped her forehead to let me know she was thinking about it. I worried about the connection to Detroit. Was I now involved? What had I been thinking about, loading up my car and heading west?

Certainly not a girl's picture in the *Tribune* and half a million dollars of funny money.

Two uniformed police officers came through the front door, both African-American, both female. They waved to Penny and took a table on the opposite side of the restaurant. I made an executive decision to keep my mouth shut; let the grand plan of the Universe unfold. I was looking for a girl who was paying me to look for her.

Simple enough.

Penny came back. "Exotic dance club on the South side. Should be quiet so early."

"I'll let you know what I find out."

"I'm back here at five. Don't keep me hanging." She slipped me another piece of paper. "Phone number for the Pig. Ask for Penny." She laughed.

I finished the second cookie before realizing I had eaten too much for one morning, said goodbye to Penny on my way out, and decided to walk along Fullerton toward the lake. Morning sunshine sneaked down alleyways, splashing on humans hustling to work in un-neat rows. Drivers practiced using their horns. The buildings held noise and exhaust fumes around me like a torture chamber.

No street in Gates Mills was like this.

I reconsidered turning everything over to the police. Driving west. But unanswered questions haunting me seemed a poor way to start a new phase of my life.

I reached Lake Shore Drive and watched the blue surface of Lake Michigan roll with white caps the color of fresh snow. I passed the W hotel wondering where I should go once I found Mona — or failed. That was my job: find her, nothing else. It was day two of the three she had prepaid for. Not counting the money she had left at the donut shop.

I headed for the library, arrived early and had to wait fifteen minutes for a woman no more than five feet tall to unlock the door from the inside. She had a shiny stud through one side of her nose, and eyes surrounded by so much dark makeup I thought they were in a well. She loudly tripped a lock, then walked away. I shrugged and went in. The first counter I reached she was standing behind: jet black hair and a loose shirt such a bright green it probably used batteries. I knew my way to the computer room from my earlier visit so I waved to her and turned right. She didn't smile, but did lift a finger in response.

I was alone with a couple dozen computers, all of which were dark. I chose one in the back facing the door so I could see the green shirt. She glanced my way but didn't acknowledge my existence.

I read the directions on how to start the computer. While waiting for it to boot itself into usefulness I watched her movement behind the counter: down, up, down again. I had never worked in a library, but keeping track of books was probably like arranging the parts when dismantling an engine.

I logged in as a guest and went to Amazon.com. A quick search revealed half a dozen books on private investigation: *The Complete Idiot's Guide to PI, Secrets of the Investigation Trade, Advanced PI Guide, Getting Your Way Legally*. I certainly wasn't advanced; Penny would likely vote idiot after that time zone mistake.

I saw green reflect from the monitor in front of me moments before I sensed a body near my right arm. I turned. She was pixie-cute up close, except for the deep-dark-well eyes, although I'd bet she hated the word pixie. She had on black pants with stitching like jeans but that fit like paint, and shoes with what must have been a two-inch foam platform covered with green fur that made me think of a neon cheetah running through the jungle.

"Hi," she said.

"Hi. Am I in the wrong place?" I asked, figuring I was on a computer that wasn't public.

"Not if you want to be in the library."

I smiled.

"You want coffee? I was just going to drip some."

"Fantastic. Yes, thank you." I dug in my pocket. "How much?"

She shook her head. "It's for employees, but I hate to drink alone."

I glanced around the room and out through the door.

"This is a big place for one person."

"There'll be more, but it's so slow in the morning I work this floor by myself. You need anything?"

"I'm good. Just doing some searching."

"Why don't you do it on your cell phone?"

"I don't have a cell phone."

The wells stared down at me. "Get one. You could do research, then download the books you want, and read them wherever you are."

"But I'm here," I said.

She crossed her arms. "But you wouldn't have had to come here. You could do everything from wherever you were."

I nodded. "I agree. But two things would happen. A dozen people would be bothering me right now with a stream of text messages interrupting my work, then whining if I didn't reply fast enough to assure them that their blathering is the most important thing in my entire life. And," I paused. "I wouldn't be about to have coffee with the librarian I just met."

She studied me, then pulled out her cell phone and took my picture.

"Making a record of the last dinosaur before I go extinct?"

"Sort of," she said. "No one will believe I met an attractive guy that doesn't own a cell." She held up her gadget. "My proof."

Then she was off, apparently to brew coffee for the Luddite dinosaur.

I returned to the computer and opened the sample pages from the book for idiots. The table of contents convinced me there was a lot about this business I didn't understand: licensing, when to carry a weapon and when not to, how to use white pages, public records, the court system, secrets of interrogation, and something called The Outhouse Routine. Reading it gave me the same feeling as the first time I dropped the oil pan off a V8 engine and stared up at the crankshaft, rods and pistons; and realized I was somehow going to take that all apart, and magically put it back together again.

It had taken me a long time.

Now I had less than ten hours before meeting a lead at the Pink Monkey who might tell me something worth $200.

Curiosity led me to the Outhouse, which turned out to be a clever trick to entice a guy faking a workmen's compensation claim to leave his house. Not what I needed. Then I read about skip tracing and was instructed to accumulate as much information about the skip as possible.

I searched the web for Mona Meyers. There were a whole bunch of hits including a dozen websites that wanted to sell me an address. I set the age range from twenty to thirty-five. There were still ten. Two in Michigan.

Her phone. I had her cell number. Or someone's number. But did I want to put the chip in and let it connect and maybe identify itself to someone just to find out it belonged to an address in Plymouth, Michigan? I wasn't sure how that would help me.

The green cheetah arrived with a paper cup and placed it next to my keyboard. She dropped three paper packets next to it, two sugars and something masquerading as cream, and stood beside me sipping coffee from a big mug.

"Thank you." I dumped the cream in and stirred with a little wooden stick. "What do you do when there aren't customers?"

"Stand around and wait. I'm not allowed to leave the counter in case someone walks in."

I blew across the top of my coffee and tasted it, my hand already shaking slightly from morning caffeine at both

Victoria's and the Pig. "This is really good for someone who didn't leave that counter way over there."

She made a little gun with her fingers and shot me in the head. "Thanks. We have a special machine." She splayed her fingers out like fireworks. "Sprays water over the grounds for a more even taste."

"You could do a TV commercial."

Her smile said she was tolerating me with some effort. "It's cold in Chicago most of the year. The kind that rips through clothing and paints itself on your skin. Good coffee is a requirement for survival."

My turn to smile. "Hey, I found a book here on Amazon but can't wait for it. Is there a good bookstore around?"

Her face stopped like someone had pressed the pause button on the giant DVD of life.

My right eyebrow tensed.

"Duh," she said, waving her head in a circle.

I choked into laughter. The last library I walked into was at Oberlin College to meet a thin blonde girl who brushed pictures on her body with edible paint and asked me to lick them off. Hadn't occurred to me that libraries actually held *books*.

"Do you think you might have this one?" I pointed at the *Idiot* entry.

She leaned forward, careful to hold her coffee to one side.

"We have loads of stuff for idiots," she said. "Give me the ISBN; I'll check for you."

I scrolled to find the number she wanted and sipped coffee while she wrote it down.

"Right back." The green animal skins sauntered away.

I scanned the table of contents of the other books from my search, realizing how useful a TOC could be. I couldn't remember ever having read one before.

My new friend came back carrying a thick paperback book and placed it on the table.

"That's great, thanks again."

"So you're a private investigator?" she asked.

I shook my head. "I'm a wannabe looking for pointers for a project I'm working on." I remembered primary school. "Is there a way I can get a library card and take this with me?"

"Do you have a picture ID showing your residence in Chicago?"

"No. I'm staying at a B&B."

"How long?"

"Just got here Saturday. Only staying till I wrap up this project."

"No can do...unless." She paused.

I waited. She didn't go on. "Unless...?"

"Unless I can trust you. I'll put it on my card if you promise to bring it back on time."

"I don't want to trouble you. I can stay here and read." I couldn't get over how much black surrounded her eyes. Made me wonder what she really looked like. "What happens if I don't bring it back?"

"Besides that you're a lying P-O-S?"

"Uh, yeah, besides that."

"I have to pay to replace the book." She sipped from her cup, her eyes never leaving mine.

I dug in my pocket for a twenty and placed it next to the book. "How about, since we just met, if I promise to bring it back, *and* put up the twenty as insurance?"

She grabbed the money. "You're on. Happy reading."

I paged through the book carefully, trying to locate skip-tracing techniques that were at least gray-area legal without a license.

Posting flyers was never mentioned.

Thirteen

EVEN WITH COFFEE FROM the dark-eyed cheetah, by
noon my eyes were drooping from too much reading. *The Guide*
had tremendous breadth, and approaches I had never heard of
for searching online databases, many of which charged a fee.
But it struck me as anthropology. I didn't think Mona had a
house, car or utility bills I could trace. She seemed free of such
encumbrances. I needed something forward facing; something
that would point me down the road to where she was *going:*
mind reader, psychic, maybe a shiny crystal ball.

I closed the book and stood to stretch my back. On my way
out I passed the front desk. The girl with the cheetah shoes was
working beside a skinny white guy wearing a black button down
over a white T-shirt. I stopped at the counter.

"May I help you?" she asked, with a sly little smile. The
skinny guy watched, and listened.

"I was wondering if you get a break for lunch."

"Maybe."

I held up the book. "I owe you. May I buy you lunch?"

"Are you trying to seduce me?"

I cleared my throat, then met her dark eyes. "Don't know
yet, I just met you."

She laughed and turned toward the clock. "I can get off in
ten minutes."

I smiled, didn't comment. Watched her face reveal
realization. Then said: "Great, I'll wait outside. Okay to take
this?"

She nodded. "You've been stamped and spindled."

I walked through the glass doors realizing we hadn't exchanged names. I realized another thing too: I was having way more fun than I ever did texting. There was something about not having dozens of interruptions every hour that felt free and natural, like I was out on the Serengeti grassland hunting wildebeest with a spear.

I stopped at a low brick wall and put one foot on it, not feeling like sitting any longer. Traffic flowed steadily in both directions under a sunny sky. I was still waiting for the bluster of a storm in the Windy City. My eyes followed a gray sedan and landed a block away on a sign for DePaul University. It occurred to me that cheetah girl might be a student. I had counted eighteen gray sedans when she came through the door with a black scarf wrapped around her neck and flowing over her green shirt like a movie star stepping out of wardrobe.

"My name's Tommy, nice to meet you."

She held out her hand and shook mine half a dozen times like she was trying to get water from a well.

"Lizz with two Zs. What are you hungry for?"

"Love. Money. Meaning to my life. How about you?"

She studied me. "That was payback for the seduce-me comment wasn't it?"

I glanced down toward DePaul. "Are you a student?"

"Only of life," she said. "So, where shall we dine?"

"Anything that isn't snake or chimp brains works for me."

She took my hand and dragged me toward the corner.

"You really don't like chimp brains?"

"Too close to cannibalism."

She nodded gravely, her black hair glistening. "Yes, I see the resemblance: no cell phone, knuckles close to the sidewalk."

I tried to stop myself, but I laughed aloud.

We passed a parking lot for U-Haul trucks and climate-controlled self-storage that reminded me of a certain backpack. She stopped under an orange awning.

"Thai," she announced.

"No brains?"

"No brains," she said, and pulled me through the door of a place called the Duck Walk.

An entire wall was washed by a watercolor study in shades of orange that could have been an abstract sunset except for a seated Buddha and green splotches suggesting trees. The furniture had been assembled with narrow leather strips, probably handmade in a distant village that didn't have steel saws so the natives filed everything smooth with a rock. I instantly felt warm and comfortable. It only had six tables, but one at the end near the kitchen was empty.

"This place feels good," I said.

"Feels? The dinosaur feels?" She smiled and led the way to the table.

An Asian girl about the size of Lizz took her order for Chili Pepper Dish. I ordered Madness Noodles because I was curious what they were. We both had Thai iced tea.

"Why do you work in a library?" I asked.

"Balances the rest of my life."

"Is the library the calm part, or the exciting part?"

She closed one eye and wagged a finger at me. "I like fashion and music, culture. Own a little clothing shop where we do custom stuff."

"Stuff?"

She lifted her platform shoe. "This was originally black and white. We dyed the green in for me. Special dye. Colorfast, but when I get tired of it, we hit it with UV light to break it down, wash it out, and then it becomes whatever color I want next."

"Doesn't the library job interfere?"

She shook her head. "Shop doesn't open till six in the evening. Most of our customers prowl at night. We modify clothing too."

"You modify stuff?"

Her finger came up again. "A girl will come in wearing a pair of blue jeans and yellow T-shirt. Maybe sneakers. We'll custom dye the jeans, razor the shirt, maybe take it in a little here or there, hand paint the shoes, all interactively. She feeds us her preferences, and we guide her while she watches it happen in the mirror. Walks out an hour later way more hip. Might even get her laid."

"Ah, the ultimate goal of fine fashion."

"The goal of everything. Not to be cynical, but that's all evolution cares about."

"You're a biology major?"

"Theology." She held a straight face for few seconds. "OK, I lied. Comparative Art. That led me to the library." She laughed.

"Was there a plan?"

"Sure was. Get the hell out of my parents' house. College was a path they would pay for."

"Stop me if this is too personal," I said.

"It's not about chimps?"

"No, your eyes. Why so much black?"

"Makes people think I'm evil. Keeps them away from me." She paused, sipped her tea. "Doesn't seem to work on dinosaurs."

"How was art school?"

"Lots of pretty pictures and boys who wanted a muse that would put out and cook dinner."

"Sounds fun."

"Which part?" she said.

Our food arrived. It smelled worth eating.

"Being a muse."

She shook her head. "No matter what happens, it's always your fault. I switched to criticism." She started eating.

"You critiqued their work?"

"Yeah, sometimes before they finished. It was way more fun, and they improved, because I'm good."

"That your goal then, become a famous art critic? Artists everywhere fearing the stroke of your pen?"

She studied me as I tried to eat my noodles without getting a bad review.

"Not so into fear." She paused. "Except for my eyes. I like to design things."

"Things?"

"Like this spoon. It's too narrow. Or that wall. I like the color wash, but the images don't hang together thematically."

"Is that what you do with clothes? Hang them together thematically?"

"I try. Some people—" She shook her head. "There's no helping them because they won't listen to reason."

"Reason and art. Polar opposites."

"Art is eminently reasonable. You just have to understand the vocabulary."

"Angles, perspective, that vanishing point stuff? I'm not so good at math unless an internal combustion engine is involved."

"Most dinosaurs aren't. One of the reasons they're extinct."

Old car. No smart phone. Maybe I was going dino. I changed the subject.

"What's the name of your shop?"

The sound of the front door opening drew my attention. Two guys about my size walked in, both Caucasian. I thought of Hosco, felt vulnerable, remembered the *Idiot's* book warning about the downside of carrying weapons. I glanced toward the kitchen, inside my head Howlin' Wolf sang Back Door Man.

The guys sat up front; I relaxed a notch.

"It's called Get Over It, on Halsted. Really small though, don't blink or you'll walk past it."

"I bet rent's high in this town."

"Millions of people all wanting to be in the same place. Shrinking supply."

I stopped chewing, spoke through my noodles. "Shrinking?"

Her head bobbed. "Big money likes high rises, millions of square feet on ground the size of a postage stamp. Doesn't leave room for the little person." She squinted at me. "No short people jokes."

I held up a hand. "Got no reason." I smiled.

"You and Randy Newman can go sodomize each other."

"It was satire, a big, er, short metaphor. Really, I called and asked him."

She smiled broadly. I realized she had perfect teeth, like Donny and Marie meet Beyoncé.

"Fortunately, I never wanted to be a supermodel. No one cares how tall a designer is. How about you?"

"I never wanted to be a supermodel either."

Her face did something between a scowl and an *I'll get you for that.*

"Oberlin. Ended up in political science after tryouts in math, sociology, and philosophy."

"Politician or lawyer?" She finished her last pepper.

"Neither. It was the one degree that would accept all of my credits."

"Politician for sure." She laughed.

We walked back to the library, her dragging me by her soft, warm hand again. She stopped on the library steps.

"Are you going to seduce me now?" she asked.

"No time. You have to get back to work."

Her eyes studied mine from their dark wells. She pointed at the book with her free hand.

"I don't know what you're up to, Tommy. But be careful. Chicago snacks on humans. We didn't invent crime, but we're working to perfect it."

On an unbidden impulse, I lifted her hand and kissed the back.

Fourteen

WHEN MY LIPS TOUCHED LIZZ'S hand I felt guilty about Penny. Crazy. She had a boyfriend, and was simply helping out a new friend—maybe only because she found crime intriguing. I should have been thinking of Betty after years of on and off, spinning in circles as if we were lost moons. Intense and driven, she would predict futures that'd flatten my enthusiasm like a spatula pressing a burger on a hot barbie.

Then there was Mona of the midnight visit.

I stopped walking; leaned against a lamppost we hadn't put a flyer on. And the furry sweater at the blues club. Who was *she?* I explained to myself that it didn't matter. The job was to find Mona, earn my paycheck, and get back on the road.

I pulled out my new watch: a little after one. Six more hours.

I wanted to be relaxed and clearheaded when I arrived at the Pink Monkey, so I made my way toward Victoria's. When I reached my room on the second floor a folded Post-it note sticking to the door greeted me.

Detective Braden would like to speak with you. Please call 555-1379 and ask for him.

Not relaxing.

I debated whether it would be harder to sleep not knowing what he wanted, or having talked to him. I knew one thing: he was going to ask why I wanted to find Mona Meyers. I couldn't tell him the missing Mona had hired me; he'd think I was loco. I didn't have a license to be a real PI, and I sure couldn't talk about the backpack.

So what *could* I talk about?

I went downstairs to the pay phone and didn't see Victoria. Slim Kim stood in the little office behind the desk talking on a telephone with a wire. I pushed coins in, dialed and waited. A computer answered and told me to state the name of the party I wanted. I obeyed. The phone clicked and left a gap of silence that felt like the Grand Canyon.

"Braden."

"Detective Braden, you left a message at Victoria's for me to call."

"Your name?"

"Tommy Cuda." I turned away from the receiver to clear my throat. "With a C."

"Thank you for calling, Mr. Cuda. According to flyers posted all over town, you're looking for a woman named Mona."

"Yes, sir."

"Why?"

The *Idiot's Guide* said *never lie to the cops,* it always led to bad things happening to the PI. I wanted to say, "Because she's missing," but he didn't sound like a fun guy.

"I met her on the road. She was heading to see a friend."

"When?"

"This past Saturday. She said it was okay if I looked her up in Chicago, but we, uh, parted ways before she gave me a way to reach her."

"So you're hot for this girl and posted flyers to try to find her."

It wasn't a question, but I answered anyway. "We talked a bit." I skipped the dreamy kiss, and the electricity of her hands. "I was hoping she would show me around town. I've never been to Chicago." Not precisely true, but explaining field trips and concerts struck me as overkill.

"Seems like a lot of trouble."

"She's a lot of girl." I was sticking close to the truth, hoping it made me sound sincere. "Is something wrong, Detective?"

"No, Mr. Cuda. There's just..." He paused. I held my breath. "A coincidence we're trying to sort out. I appreciate your calling me quickly, and please, if you find this girl let me know immediately. We would like to talk to her."

"Is she in trouble?"

I counted to four before he answered.

"She's only wanted for questioning at this time." Another pause. "Where are you from Mr. Cuda?"

"Ohio, near Cleveland. I'm on my way out west. Vacation."

"We would appreciate your staying around town. Is that convenient?"

"I'll be here through the end of the week for sure."

"Good. Please call before you depart. And remember to remove your posters, Chicago takes littering seriously."

He hung up. What had I said? I promised to contact him. I promised to hang around. No promises I couldn't keep.

I went upstairs, definitely feeling better than having that call hanging over my head. I grabbed my guitar and strummed through Marvin's song *Roll With No Rock,* about why waiting for marriage was a bad move in the 21st century. The girls in his gaggle hadn't acted like they were even going to wait for him to turn off his amp.

Almost two o'clock. I eyed my *Idiot* book on the nightstand, but wasn't up to more studying. That's when I realized I hadn't checked the obvious technological wonder: social networks. And immediately remembered Weinergate forcing Anthony Weiner to resign from Congress for tweeting a picture of his boxer shorts. The ensuing news articles made it clear that anything posted to a social media site became corporate, trade secret, property. Even something as innocuous as a search could be subpoenaed into a court of law.

Not breadcrumbs I wanted followed.

I laid back into Victoria's down pillow, hoping I wouldn't dream about privacy in the new millennium.

Fifteen

I WOKE TO SUNSHINE AFTER dreamless sleep feeling like I had been through a sci-fi time warp because it wasn't morning. I tried to formulate a plan, but too many unknowns made it a guessing game. I took a shower, decided to shave, then sat around naked gazing out the window at the afternoon light turning orange. I paged through the *Idiot's Guide.* Learned how to bug a telephone. Learned a little about subpoenas.

Then realized I didn't know how to find the Pink Monkey.

I dressed: sport coat, black pants instead of jeans. Boots. I put five hundred of my money in my left pocket and five hundred of Mona's in my right, after checking each bill to be sure Uncle Sam had printed it. Last thing I needed was to be picked up for passing a bad hundred in a strip joint. And with that backpack in my locker.

Hard to explain.

I stopped at the pay phone to call the Monkey for directions, had another idea, and poked my head around the corner. Slim was in the office with a black wire dangling from a fat handset in her left hand. Her back was to the front desk and I could hear bits of conversation. It didn't sound friendly.

I walked over. Waited.

She slammed the receiver down, and I recognized the sagging shoulders of a woman who wasn't happy. Maybe even crying.

I debated leaving. Before I could reach a decision she turned around, saw me, wiped her eyes on a sleeve and came out.

"Hi, Tommy. Can I help you with something?"

"How about we turn it around?" I pointed at the phone.

"Men." She tried to smile, but it came out like a limp rag.

"Tough customer?"

She shook her head. "Boyfriend. Hates it when I work late. Wants me to quit."

"And do what?"

"Be home when he is so I can cook for him like his mother did."

My lips scrunched up to think. "We all need love."

"Can't eat love," she said, and rubbed her thumb and index finger together. "I'm saving to go to school. If I don't work, we can't save a penny. Chicago is super expensive."

"So it's a temporary problem?"

"That's what I keep telling Frank. But he can't spell patience."

"Tough spot." She seemed so young. She should be having fun following her dreams in college, not worrying about some guy's dinner. "How can I help?"

"Tell me it's okay for a girl to want an education."

"Kim, it's been okay for a girl to want an education since Eve studied botany. Colleges are full of girls. And lots of them are super smart." I smiled. "I can attest to that personally."

This time her smile was real as she blinked away tears.

"Thanks, Tommy. You going out?"

She knew where I was going; she had taken the message.

"Sightseeing. Would you happen to have a computer back there with a printer?"

She ducked below the counter. "You mean something that could access maps on the Internet and print directions for an out-of-towner looking to see the local sights?"

"You could be a fortune teller."

She pushed two sheets of paper toward me. One was a map, the other turn-by-turn directions to the Pink Monkey.

"That car you parked out front when you registered looks like something from the Stone Age. I figured they didn't have built-in navigation back then."

"Iron," I said. "It was the Iron Age. Big iron." I picked up the pages. "Thanks, Slim. You're one step ahead of me."

"Only one?" She reached under the counter. "Gin or vodka?"

"Vodka, if I get to choose."

She placed a silver hip flask on the countertop. "Since you didn't do your homework and get directions, I suspect you also don't know that the Monkey is bring your own."

"Complicated liquor laws in Chicago, huh?"

She pointed a finger at my chest. "Full report tomorrow. I'm seeking a high return on my investment."

I reached in my left pocket. "May I contribute to your college fund?"

She shook her head. "You don't have to do that."

I placed a hundred flat on the counter and covered it with my palm. "I want to. I got to go to college. Maybe didn't use the time as wisely as possible, but stumbled upon some good advice. Tell Frank that Tommy the college boy said he'll be a lot happier if you're a lot happier."

She looked in my eyes, then at my hand. I thought for a second she was going to cry again. She nodded. I gave a little wave and turned around fast before she could refuse to accept it.

On the sidewalk in front of Victoria's I considered taking a cab, thought about needing a quick getaway, stuffed Kim's papers in my jacket, and headed for the Barracuda. I slipped behind the wheel. Both shoulders relaxed in the familiar surroundings. I patted the dash. Granddad's voice in my head said very clearly: *If they can't catch you, they can't hurt you.*

A couple of turns and five miles later I reached a square, two-story brick building on a corner lot. It could have been a warehouse except for pink lights over the upper-floor windows, and a dark gray awning leading to a double glass door. No one was out walking the street. A pair of streetlamps in the building's shadow flickered on. I pulled up to the curb in front of the awning and checked my watch. Two minutes after seven, if it was keeping time correctly.

The traffic light cycled.

I pulled forward and drove around the block, stopping for another red light. Shortly, I was back in front of the door. Slim's papers showed that the Monkey opened at seven. It was eight after.

I revved the hemispherical-head V8 just to hear it rumble.

The glass doors to the club swung open and a man in a white shirt and black slacks came jogging out. He ran around the front bumper and pulled my door open.

"Welcome to the Pink Monkey, sir."

He was breathing like he had run up a flight of stairs.

"Hi, are you open yet?"

He nodded and tore a ticket off a fat stack he had pulled from his pocket. He handed it to me. His skin was a golden darkness that made me think of Central America.

"Are you in a hurry?" I asked.

He seemed shocked that I had bothered to talk with him, but shook his head. "Not really. You're only my third car tonight. Monday is slow, early is slow. You put them together." He shrugged.

"Do you park a lot of cars on a good night?"

"A couple hundred easy."

"Thanks. I'll be less than an hour."

"This is a tough place to leave," he said.

I circled around the rear of the car and kept one eye on it as he pulled away nice and easy. I wondered if that changed once he got to the parking garage. I looked up at a building that had flat castle towers on each end, like the rooks in a chess game.

The tall windows between them were opaque, like the ones at the Oberlin chapel.

I passed through double doors and was struck by two things: pink light is really hard on the eyes, a sort of packaged glare; and a large oval bar with a chicane like a race track covered in shiny copper. Illuminated raw glass ten inches deep and two inches thick ran around the outside of the copper creating the impression of Arctic ice during a nuclear weapons test.

The greenish glow pulled me.

There was more: a pink wall, a stage, an elevator, booths with tall dividers, four-top tables surrounded by leather chairs, and two girls wandering around in lingerie as if they were getting dressed for a date.

The Arctic bar was empty, so I took a place facing the pole on the small stage behind the bartender. The stool was soft-cushioned leather, with a back. Built for long hours of comfort.

A bartender in a black shirt with Pink Monkey embroidered over the pocket arrived with a black napkin with the same pink and gray logo.

"Welcome to the Pink Monkey."

"You wouldn't have fresh-squeezed orange juice would you?"

"We would. I just started squeezing for the night. Rocks or up?"

"Rocks." I pulled out Kim's silver flask loan and placed it on the bar. A lowball glass arrived with room for a shot. I poured short, took the flyer out of my pocket, folded it so Mona's picture faced up and pressed it onto the copper bar.

Two middle-aged guys at a table off to my right were talking more than drinking. I imagined myself at forty sitting with them and suddenly eleven years didn't seem very long. Beyond them sat another stage, also empty. Silent television monitors showed sports, but I noticed there were no mirrors. I wondered if someone had done a study that demonstrated men didn't like seeing themselves when they were lusting after nubile females.

A body arrived at the chair to my left. I didn't turn. An aroma Shakespeare could have written a sonnet about floated past me.

A hand reached over and touched the paper, rotated it away from me. I turned slowly.

A tall African-American woman whose face could have been on the red carpet at the Oscars gazed down. Curls cascaded to the middle of her back. The paint on her long fingernails suggested an abstract by Pollock.

She didn't smile, didn't blink, simply studied my face.

"Another white boy in love with Mona?"

I pointed at myself.

"Yes, you."

I shook my head. "Just doing what she asked me to do."

She unfolded the flyer, read it top to bottom. I had imagined I'd be meeting a rumpled guy who would salivate over the two hundred bucks the flyer promised. This lady likely did better than two hundred an hour. I reached into my jacket for the original photo. Placed it next to the flyer.

Her eyes moved to it. She picked it up. I reached my hand out and turned it over with her hand following along. She read the inscription.

"Hmm," she said.

"Would you like a drink?"

She glanced at the flask standing on the bar.

"All I have is vodka," I said.

She waved to the bartender and a giant martini glass with pink liquid arrived. It might have had an LED in the stem, because the liquid was glowing.

I poured for her until she gave a sign.

"Thank you," she said. "You're Tommy?"

I nodded.

"Where did you meet Mona?"

"Hitchhiking west."

She nodded. "Mona can be adventurous. I was going to ask if she knew you were looking for her." She waved the pocket photo. "But this sort of says it."

She took a long sip of the pink liquid.

"Is that good?" I asked.

"Custom made for me. The bartenders know what I like to feed my body. It works well with vodka."

"Can you help me find her?"

Her nod reminded me of a queen allowing her subjects to rise.

"Will you?"

She smiled for the first time. "Yes, Tommy. I'll help you."

I pulled two hundred from my left pocket and slipped them onto the counter.

She waved her hand. "Just pay for the drink, the boss will be happy. Save that for Mona."

"Your call, um..."

"Sorana. It's nice to meet you."

We shook hands. "My pleasure." Her fingers were longer than mine, even without the nails. I wanted to ask about Mona, but directness felt rude. Some private eye; I couldn't even ask a question.

She sipped her pink drink. I appreciated the orange freshness the bartender had delivered.

I said, "I have a friend who would like you."

"What's your friend do?"

"Sings, writes songs, plays bass."

"So he's broke."

"Only in his pockets."

She pointed. "There's a room upstairs. They let bands jam. Stage is all set up."

"Never heard of that. Can anyone play?"

"Anyone who knows me...and passes a little audition with the boss. If customers complain though—" She dragged a finger across her throat. Then she spun her bar stool and leaned a slender bare back against the Arctic glass. "Better turn around, Tommy."

I held my drink in my right hand and slipped the two hundred off the bar, happy to spend it on Mona as instructed.

Lights popped on around the stage across the room as the music grew louder.

A girl pranced onto the stage wearing white fishnet stockings with openings the size of a quarter, and translucent-white everything else above heels as tall as my vodka flask. Pink lights gave her skin the otherworldly glow of a virtual reality simulation of an alien Amazonian culture from the Alpha Centauri binary-star system arriving on earth to dominate all men.

"Mona's a dancer?" I said far too loudly.

"She is."

"Thanks for taking the time to call me."

"Someone would have. I wanted it to be a friend."

"Have you known her long?"

Sorana spun back to the bar, so I did likewise.

"About a year. She's not always here. Travels, works other jobs." Then she was standing. "Would love to talk, Tommy, but I'm in the batter's box." As she left, the green Arctic-ice light faded from her Greek-sculpture body. I wondered if she spent time in the gym, or if a beautiful figure was an occupational hazard of dancing.

The bartender came back, but I still had half a tank. *About a year.* So Mona was a regular in Chicago. What was that story about South Bend? Maybe she did have a friend. Maybe she had friends in lots of places.

My glass was empty by the time Mona walked down the steps from the stage in her five-inch heels. She was stunning in a way I hadn't appreciated in leopard pants and a backpack. I waved to the bartender for a refill.

"My first time here," I said. "How do I talk to Mona?"

"You catch her eye. Buy her a drink. Go to a private table. Talk all you want."

He looked a bit like the guy parking cars; I wondered if he had gotten his cousin a job. I suppressed a grin as Jimmy Buffet sang *Everybody's Got a Cousin in Miami* in my head. Maybe people in Chicago had cousins too.

"Thanks. If you know what she likes, would you set one up?"

"You got it."

I spun around and waited. She was halfway across the room.

Sixteen

MONA HELD HER HEAD ballerina high as she strolled, surveyed the room, gave me a slight nod...and kept walking. Maybe it was the pink light, but I saw no sign that she recognized me. I watched her take two more steps, her body breathing beauty, then stood up from the bar stool. The motion caused her to glance back my way.

I waved her over.

She turned mid-stride and stopped close, smelling like warm rain. We were eye-to-eye, which made her six-feet tall in the outrageous heels she had been dancing in.

"Hi," she said. Her eyes flicked to the bar. "Is that for me?"

"Ordered special."

She stepped past me and flowed onto the bar stool, crossed her legs. The shoe on the dangling foot had a clear platform thicker than a stack of pancakes.

"Thanks. Did you like my dancing?"

She leaned forward to sip from a giant swizzle stick. In the club lighting, the custom drink matched the hair draping forward across her pale cheeks.

"You move like you enjoy it," I said.

"There are far worse ways to earn a living."

I laughed. I had said those exact words to myself at Walmart a hundred times.

"Well," I said. "I found you."

She pushed the drink back on the bar.

"Yes you did. Now what?"

I blinked, and took a moment to find my spiked orange juice.

"Now we do whatever you wanted me to do after I found you."

She stood, placing me at eye level with a bra commercial.

"Let's dance."

"The check?"

"It'll follow us." She walked away.

I grabbed my flask and drink and trailed her to the elevator. We were alone as we took a brief ride up one floor. I watched her reflection in the shiny door and thought about a drive across Indiana. And a foreshortened night that her donut-shop note claimed wasn't a dream.

We stepped into a room half the size of the downstairs with a bar in front of windows that had been blocked by shades, and a bandstand at the far end holding amps and a drum set. She walked to a booth made for a DJ. A slow jazz piece by someone who knew how to work the saxophone began playing. Then she walked to the middle of the room and faced me.

"No private room?" I said, placing my drink on a table.

"Not that kind of dance." She motioned me toward her with two fingers.

I stepped forward. She put her left hand on my shoulder like we were going to waltz, then pulled me closer. I held her bare back lightly with my right hand and took her hand in my left. We started swaying.

"This is my first time here. Is this some sort of special dance?"

I couldn't see her lips to know if she smiled.

"Don't worry, there's no charge. This is a Mona feels like being held by a gentleman dance." She put her head not quite on my shoulder. "So Mr. Gentleman, do you have a name?"

I confirmed red hair and crazy long bangs. I noticed a small tattoo over her left breast I hadn't seen before, and couldn't decipher in the dim light.

"We've met," I said, disappointed she didn't recall my name.

We danced in a slow circle.

She said softly, "You said this was your first time here."

"It is." The stage came into view. "Do you have live music?"

"That's for famous people, so they can jam between girls. We get loads of musicians after their downtown shows. But sometimes locals get to play." She paused. I felt her hands squeeze me a little tighter. "Do you play?"

"Guitar. Blues mostly."

"Oh, that would be fun. Come here and play. Dedicate a song to Mona."

"Could I dedicate one to Mona and Tommy?"

"Bad boy. My boyfriend would get mad if he heard that."

We swayed. My hand on her back felt hot, like energy was flowing into it.

"Cuda," I said.

"What?"

"My last name."

"Tommy Cuda. Kind of cute."

"Does it remind you of anything?"

"Hmm…Buddha?" The edges of her lips curled.

"Do you remember a turbo-bronze Barracuda? What you said?"

"A what…oh, wait, that's a fish, isn't it? A big ugly one."

I laughed. "It's a car. From the sixties. Remember what you said when you saw it?"

"An old brown car?"

Her nearness generated those good vibrations the Beach Boys sang about. But her expression said she was thinking, and coming up empty. I leaned away and she met my gaze with a soft smile and eyes made darker by pink light. If she was high, she hid it well. I pulled her back close.

She let me.

Maybe this was a test. She wanted proof she was important to me, and not just a passing hitchhiker.

"What did you have for dinner Saturday night?" I asked, recalling taking her to the Bourgeois Pig.

"Hmm, a two-mile question. Today's Monday right?" Her head shifted on my shoulder. "I was working...let's see...chicken breast. From our kitchen here. I peel off the skin."

The sax stopped playing. *Two-mile* echoed in my ears. I held on as long as a respectable gentleman could, released her and squeezed a bare shoulder in each hand. Her green eyes met mine with a dreamy kind of focus.

"You were here Saturday night? This past Saturday. Two days ago."

"Yes, your honor," she said, laughing. "There were witnesses."

"I'm sorry, I have you confused with someone else."

"An old girlfriend I bet. We get that a lot here. Everyone on Earth has a double, you know. My astrologist says it's a rule of math."

I shook my head. "Someone I just met Saturday."

"You met a girl who looks like me?"

I nodded. "Yes. A gorgeous redhead. Just like you."

She stepped away. "What's her name?"

"Mona."

The space between her eyebrows furrowed.

"Where?"

"A restaurant in Ohio."

"I better go." She spun on a toe and sprinted to the elevator. I grabbed my drink and followed with long strides. She let me into the car but stood to the back. When the doors closed she reached over and hugged me while whispering in my ear, "Forget you met me. And get out of here. *Please.*" Then she stepped to the back of the elevator, stared straight ahead, and hugged herself. When the doors separated she flew toward the stage to the right in that shuffling way girls run in high heels, her translucent white robes floating behind her.

I crossed the club toward the beacon glow of the Arctic bar in a daze. The bartender didn't blink at the hundred I used to pay for the hefty price of the girls' drinks. I maneuvered through a maze of unoccupied tables toward the front door, stopped near the glass, and gazed at reflections from inside the club.

No Mona.

I took a deep breath, pushed the door open to the outside, and handed my ticket to the young guy who had driven my car away.

"Chocolate Barracuda, right?"

"Good memory," I said, and fished for a bill in my pocket. Waiting in the late dusk watching traffic and subconsciously counting gray sedans, I realized why private eyes drank so much in those noir novels I loved. I always thought it was just a literary device to keep characters busy and provide a gritty edge. But the turmoil in my head — facts colliding and refusing to bond into a narrative that didn't violate the laws of physics — made me feel like chugging Slim's flask.

Then I remembered Penny.

Had to see her first.

My car rounded the corner and I smiled at the unmistakable rumble. The valet stopped directly in front of the main entrance, hopped out and stood holding the door open. First class service. I walked around the rear bumper and held my hand out with the folded bill in it.

"Thank you, sir," he said. Then his eyes lifted over my shoulder and his smile dropped away.

I felt a hand on my left arm. It pulled hard and spun me.

"Wha — ?"

The blow hit just below my sternum, doubling me over against the car and driving the air out of me. I managed to stay on my feet and gasp, but nothing would come in.

A voice near my left ear said, "I told you...stay away from Mona."

I fought for breath, saw Hosco poised for more action, his left hand clenched. Flashed to images of a gray sedan.

"This is your second warning." His boots stomped away.

I exhaled and began to breathe enough to uncurl my body. The valet was still in the street with one hand on the open driver's door of my Barracuda and the other holding the tip I had given him. I struggled to slide behind the wheel.

"Thanks," I managed. "Nice club."

His face was serious. "What did you do to piss off Mr. Hosco?"

I dragged in a slow breath. "Who is he?"

"He manages the girls." The young guy leaned closer. "Rumor is he's connected. Cop trouble went away after he showed up."

I managed to nod, still barely breathing, wondering why a well-connected guy needed a killer left hook.

I said: "I waltzed with Mona."

Seventeen

I FOCUSED MY EYES ON the road like it led to Oz, waiting to see how my insides were going to react to high-speed compression. I hadn't been hit that hard since football tryouts in high school when Pete Blake's gold helmet rammed my belly, convincing me running track would be a better choice. The Cuda and I wound our way back to Lake Shore and drove north until I found an exit that let me park near the beach. I turned the car off, rolled the window down, and listened to waves dying on the sand.

Mona hadn't recognized me. Mona had been at the Pink Monkey on Saturday.

Option 1: She was lying.

She warned me to stay away from the club. Just like Hosco had done.

No, Hosco had warned me to stay away from Mona. Not the same thing.

I leaned back and let the fresh lake breeze dance on my face.

She told me to forget I met her. Did *she* want me to, or had someone (Hosco?) told her: *if a guy comes around asking questions, chase him away.*

Option 2: She was scared.

No one asked about the backpack. Was it possible they didn't know I had it? Mona knew. I rewound. I assumed Mona had left the backpack, but anyone can pull a battery cable and write a note. She didn't recognize the name Tommy, or the car. Her eyes had eluded contact, pointing at me but focused on the moon at the same time.

Option 3: Drugs.

She had talked, then gone quiet, then talked, then gone quiet. She matched the hitchhiker down to the barely-there freckles. And money and drugs were common bedfellows.

Option 4: Whacky mental disorder: split-personality, amnesia, stuff I had never heard of.

Maybe she really couldn't remember me. What was that called when people can't remember things that just happened? I needed a smartphone to access Wikipedia. It started with an 'A'...anterograde?

Option 5: The odds seemed small, but maybe I found the wrong girl. That meant there was another gorgeous redhead somewhere. Her astrologer thought so.

I pulled out the small picture of Mona and studied it in the moonlight. Flipped it over.

Find me, Tommy. – M.

I put the photo away, and took a sip of vodka from Slim's flask. I got out of the car, opened the trunk, and found the phone where I had hidden it. Debated. When it connected to towers, would anyone know but me?

I hoped not.

I put the chip in and turned it on. The last message said *or else*, but it was days old. I sipped from the flask, my stomach aching from the punch. New messages scrolled down the screen. Z-Rox wanted a reply. Z-Rox wanted to know Redhoof's whereabouts. Z-Rox was becoming less polite.

The most recent message was two hours old. I shut the phone off and pulled the chip out, returning both to their hiding places. Z-Rox must usually get fast replies; the silence was driving him crazy.

I started the car and listened to the motor idle. Cranked the window up. I drove to the Pig and found street parking. Walking along I wanted to kick myself for not mentioning the name Z-Rox around Mona to see her reaction.

Penny was busy delivering food. I sat down to wait. When she came by, I ordered roast beef I hoped I could keep down. Then

I thought about the details of what had happened, and how to explain them to her. When my food arrived, I ate in tiny bites, chewing thoroughly. My stomach made minor complaints, and continued to ache. Halfway through the sandwich, she sat down across from me.

"How did we do?"

"Found a girl named Mona. Looks like the hitchhiker I picked up in Ohio."

"That's great. And those flyers were cheap."

"You're a genius, Penny."

She frowned. "Something's wrong."

"Sure is, but I can't diagnose it, can only give you the symptoms. Mona doesn't remember me. Claims she was at the Monkey on Saturday. When I mentioned I had met someone who looked like her, she went into hyperdrive, told me to forget about her, and get out of the club. Like I was toxic."

"That's weird even for Chicago. I mean, maybe not know you. But chase you away? Be right back." She jumped up and grabbed an order from the counter. Passed me on the way to delivering it.

I was missing something. I shook my head. A kid from Ohio that took nearly six years to get through college? Yeah, I was missing a lot. I wished I could just turn the page and read about what happens next, figure out where that Maltese Falcon is hiding.

Penny slipped a bag onto my table without stopping. I opened it to find a huge cookie with all red M&M's embedded in it. Her boyfriend was a lucky guy, probably didn't appreciate her. Monday night. Odds were he was watching baseball with his buddies in a sports bar.

Cowhide balls got me thinking. Maybe Mona was playing a complicated game I was supposed to figure out. There was a big payoff in a certain backpack, maybe I needed to go on offense.

Penny sat down. "Weird."

I pointed to the cookie. "Thanks."

She shrugged, but smiled. "What's the next step?"

"I'm thinking offense, but haven't picked a play."

She nodded her head vigorously. "Let's take the flyers down. Broadcast that we found her."

"If we found her."

"We can always put them back up next week."

"She could be long gone by next week." I examined the cookie for the perfect place to take the first bite. "Let's pull them, though. The cops warned me about littering."

She laughed. "In this city? The whole place is a trash can." She broke off a piece of cookie and stuffed it in her mouth. "So Mr. PI, I'm off at ten. Let's plan our next move. But I have to be home before midnight."

"Glass slipper?"

"Test tomorrow. Need an hour to review."

I pulled out my Luddite watch. Just after nine.

"Okay if I just sit here and contemplate?"

"Sure. I'll bring you a decaf."

I found the page of hotel stationary I was using for a journal and passed the time trying to write down everything Mona had said, word for word. Then the events that led up to the punch I hadn't told Penny about. I hadn't heard footsteps, nor seen anyone on the sidewalk while waiting for my car. Hosco must have come out of the club fast. I added what I recalled of the text messages, including a rant that ended: *Dumb lady gets smacked,* which sounded like a rap lyric.

Penny came by and dropped a black pocket notebook on the table. It had a Bourgeois Pig logo on the front and lined pages. The logo consisted of a wild boar embossed on a black and red shield under a crown. Classy for a bistro. She had good timing, both sides of my sheet were full. I folded my notes into the back of the book, and continued on the first page.

Penny managed to sneak out at nine forty-five. We started pulling flyers right away, retracing our path from the day before.

"You ever hear the name Z-Rox?"

She frowned in thought, then crumbled a flyer into a ball and tossed it into the garbage bag on the back seat. "Nope. Sounds like a Chinese copy machine." She pulled out her cell phone. "Google says Z dash R O X is an online game written by Evil-Dog. A visual puzzle." She faced me. "I love puzzles, they're like solving crimes."

I stopped the car. She stuck her arm out the window and pulled down another flyer.

"Why are you asking?"

"He punched me outside the Monkey."

"That's assault and battery. Be careful, gamers like to keep score. You okay?"

"So far. Just once to the midsection. Knocked the wind out of me good."

"What did you do, insult his girlfriend?"

"No, danced with her." I pointed to the picture on the flyer she was holding.

"You danced with Mona?" She grew quiet, and folded the paper slowly instead of crumbling it. "You said she didn't remember you."

"She didn't. Says she had skinless chicken at the club Saturday for dinner. That means she wasn't at the Pig with me. She also didn't react to my car."

"Can't help there, I didn't work Saturday night. And girls don't like cars, so we don't remember them."

"Guys are wasting their time?"

"Oh no. It's like male birds preening their colorful feathers," she said.

"Girls like feathers?"

"Of course not. They like a male specimen who is healthy and strong enough to have good ones. It's the implication."

"So guys aren't wasting their time?"

"Not at all."

"She called it a turd," I said.

"Mona?"

"The hitchhiker. Took one look at the color and said, 'It looks like a giant turd.'"

Penny laughed. Kept laughing. Doubled up, smacked her forehead against the dash.

"Instant karma," I said.

"Sorry, that's so funny. She didn't say 'polished' did she?" She started laughing again, but put a hand out to fend off the dash.

"If you had said that about this fine piece of machinery, would you react to the word Barracuda by talking about ugly fish?"

"Hmm," she said. "Do you think she was high?"

I pulled to the curb and stopped. There was no poster. I turned to Penny.

"Do you mean mood-altering prescription medication, or street drugs?"

"I was thinking street. Hallucinogens affect the brain. Addicts don't remember much."

I gazed past her at the sidewalk and on to a building front. White letters read: VINTAGE FASHION. I thought back, nodded. "Yeah, she could have been stoned. But her speech was okay."

"Practice," Penny said.

"There's something else." I smiled at the way her short brown hair framed her face. "You have lovely hair."

"Careful, I have a stun gun."

"And a boyfriend. Sorry, it's the moonlight."

"That's the traffic light on caution."

She was right, because it turned red, tinting her hair closer to Mona's. "You look good as a redhead too, but that's not the something. I have her cell phone."

"Tommy! You pick-pocketed the girl's cell phone while you were dancing?"

"No no. She left it."

"No girl forgets her cell phone. She'd sooner forget her panties."

"That's what I figured, but it was in my car Sunday morning. I turned it off and took the SIM chip out. I figured she might track me with GPS."

"You're supposed to find her but she's tracking you? Is this one of those alternate universe scenarios like that movie uh, uh, Run something Run?"

"Seems wrong, doesn't it?"

"Yeah. And paranoid. So what did you find on the phone?"

"A black hole. No addresses. No photos. No saved message streams."

"Prepay I bet."

"And incoming messages from...are you ready?"

She held up a hand. Rubbed her lips together. "Z-Rox."

"Bingo."

"The perp is usually someone known to the victim," she said, with the knowing expression of a graduate student who can quote relevant statistics.

"Why?"

"Why leave her phone? To help you find her. This way you know about someone named Z-Rox. And sure enough—" She pointed at me and winked. "You found her."

"An excellent hypothesis, Watson. Only one little deductive wrinkle. Mona doesn't seem to know it."

Eighteen

PENNY AND I TRACKED down the rest of our flyers and recycled them in a mammoth steel container half a block from her apartment. I stopped the car at her door just before eleven. She stared at me and chewed on the nail of her index finger, her brown eyes never wavering.

"Good luck on your test," I said.

She stared. Chewed.

"Sorry if I kept you too late."

No reaction.

"Do you work at the Pig tomorrow?"

Slight nod.

"You're not going to tell your boyfriend about the moonlight and get me punched are you?"

A smile around the finger and a shake of the head.

"Thank you for helping me."

"You're welcome," she said.

"I'm stumped. Let me know if you have any advice. You're the grad student." I paused. "What made you pick criminology?"

"Longish story. Revolves around prejudice and hate. Me hating the way the world is mostly."

"This isn't a good time to talk, is it?"

She shook her head. Stared. The finger came down. She twisted, knelt on the bucket seat and leaned forward. "Kiss me." Her lips pressed mine before I could get my hands off the wheel. Something soft grazed my forearm. Her lips pressed harder. Then disappeared.

"Goodnight, Tommy."

She popped the door open and skipped up the brick walk to her apartment. I watched until she opened the door, and turned around to wave at me.

"Goodnight, Penny," I said softly, my lips buzzing.

I slipped the Cuda into first and rolled away, glancing back once to see a window light up. I had been to college, and raced vintage muscle cars. Learned a bit of Eastern philosophy in karate class. Played guitar. Experienced the pyramidal tribute to the gods of sex, drugs and rock and roll at the Hall of Fame in Cleveland. Of all the things I thought I knew, why did I seem to know nothing about women?

I shifted to second.

I did know what to do with a spinning brew of confusion — find some blues music.

I drove to the parking lot at Children's Memorial Hospital on the corner of Lincoln and Fullerton (where parking turned out to be free on Mondays), retrieved the cell phone from the trunk, and walked the short distance to B.L.U.E.S. Rodney Brown and Hot Rod were on the bill. I liked their name, ducked into the club, ordered a draft, found a table in back; then tried to clear my mind by not thinking about Mona, hoping my subconscious would get creative.

Rodney played a nasty raspy tenor and his band carved a groove a mile wide, massaging the nerve endings in my body right down to Penny's kiss.

I turned the phone on without putting the chip in. It complained it couldn't connect to the cellular network and only had half a battery. I poked around for saved text, email, an address book. Recent calls. All blank. I found a notepad app. There was an entry so far down at the bottom I thought the page was blank and almost missed it.

Friday midnight. Kinkos. No Theology.

Note to self? Text message without the sender? I checked the camera roll again, hoping there was a picture hiding deep inside. Then I found an app called FotoOp with a recover option that came up with one picture. It matched the one in my pocket with the note on the back. I spread my fingers to zoom. A pillar showed in the background. A pillar I had seen before. I shifted the picture with my finger and found the rear fender of my Barracuda behind her left shoulder. She was wearing the backpack, something I couldn't see in the cropped version on paper.

I stared at the phone and sipped beer. Hot Rod switched to a slow shuffle blues half-a-century old.

History.

I switched to the browser...poked around...located a list of four recently visited pages. I opened the first.

Yahoo news story from Saturday: *Officer Shot in Catacombs.* I read the first paragraph. It was a hastily written article about a canine patrolman being shot while investigating a potential crime site. It didn't mention the dog. I went to the next page.

Bloodhounds on the Trail told the story of dogs used by the police for drug investigation, tracking and guarding. Special attention was given to Lilly, a four-year-old bloodhound who uncovered a counterfeiting site outside of Detroit.

Why hadn't Mona cleared this history? Did she forget? Not know how? Been in a hurry?

I moved on to the third article. It was a blog from early Saturday morning spreading an unverified rumor that a dozen people in a huge underground cult encampment had been raided by the police without a warrant.

The fourth page was a shopping site for women's hair supplies: bottles of potions in rainbow colors, hair extensions, brushes.

I tapped my beer glass to watch bubbles rise. The backpack tied Mona to Michigan. Maybe. Probably. I had suspected she was involved. But seeing these searches on her phone, from before I picked her up...

I thought about a poor cop with a hole in him and the dog he probably spent more time with than his wife.

"Damn," I said.

"Is that any way to greet a lady?"

I turned and saw a pink sweater. I tilted my head up to a girl with long dark hair standing close, wearing glasses with gray-tinted lenses—like those automatic sunglasses that don't turn clear fast enough when you walk inside.

"I'm sorry," I stood. "Just had a bad thought." I recalled a similar sweater; it had been blue.

"Bad thoughts in a blues bar? How original." She laughed. Her voice was hoarse, like she had been screaming at a loud rock concert. She brought a cigarette to her lips, but it wasn't lit.

"Would you care to join me?" I asked.

She tipped her head. "I don't know. You're awfully busy with that cell phone."

"Doing homework."

"What are you studying?"

I grinned. "The phone."

She slipped into the chair opposite me. "Are you taking advanced cell phones for dummies?"

I sat back down. "Not yet. I was looking for something in this particular phone."

"Did you lose it?" She smiled, the cigarette back in her hand.

"In a way." Rodney started a slow smoky tune on his sax I didn't recognize. "What's your name?"

"Tracy. Tracy Kane." She reached her hand across the table.

"Tommy Cuda. Is that like Cain and Abel?"

She wagged her head. "No, like sugar with a K."

"Aren't sweaters too warm this time of year?"

"Air conditioning gives me chills." She shivered to demonstrate. "And the lake air is from the arctic."

I looked for a server. "What brings you to BLUES?"

"You."

"Isn't that supposed to be my line?" I waved at a girl carrying a round tray.

"You came to see me? How nice." Her lips were very red, made larger by gloss. The waitress arrived.

Tracy said, "Blue martini, please."

"Have you tried our Memphis Blues? Blueberry Schnapps, Curacao, and vodka. Tastier than a blues song." She smiled.

I'd bet that line had sold more than a few drinks.

"Sounds fun, I'll have that," Tracy said.

The waitress looked at me, I was half full. "Later." I watched Tracy roll her cigarette like a magician about to make it levitate. "Why did you come to see me?"

"Heard you play last night. Thought you might be back."

I pointed at her. "Blue sweater?"

She nodded.

"Did you like Marvin's song?"

"The one about not waiting for a rock before you roll?" She grew quiet for a second. Then said: "He seems to enjoy singing it."

"Marvin has passion. Sorry, we're not playing tonight. Sundays are open mic, we were just jamming a little."

"When can I hear you again?"

Her question triggered an idea. "Maybe tomorrow."

A martini arrived that was indeed quite blue. She nibbled at the orange garnish. She sipped. Her eyes found mine. It was probably the lighting, but I'd swear her irises were violet behind the dark lenses.

"I'm working on a gig at a place called the Pink Monkey." I didn't mention I had only been working on it for fifteen seconds. "Not a blues club though." I considered elaborating, decided to wait; new ideas often turned out to be less than brilliant. "If it happens, it'll be early, around seven."

Her lips rolled together and back. Lipstick still perfect.

"Dinner party?"

"Upstairs room. We have to, um, audition. Have to check with Marvin, though. It's coming together at the last minute."

"Lot of things are like that these days." She took a slow sip of the martini, her eyes drifting to the bandstand where Rodney was blowing strong. "Why do men like to look at women?"

"I read a study that claimed the chemical reactions in the male brain while looking at naked women are similar to the effects of cocaine and heroin."

She smiled. Played with her unlit cigarette.

"Could I ask you something?" I said.

"Something? Sure."

I cleared my throat. "My grandfather has a book of nose art."

Her cheeks puffed in a grin. "You're into noses?"

"Pinup girls. Painted on bombers. World War Two mostly."

She nodded, and didn't turn away.

"Those girls had a certain style," I said.

"And you're going to ask me why I also have that style?"

"You're psychic." I reached for my beer.

"I love the past: forties, fifties, maybe a bit into the sixties. When women had shape."

I felt hot. Maybe blushed.

"But what you really want to know is: how? There are two critical factors. They used makeup a certain way, didn't try to hide that they were wearing it. Lots of rouge, bright lipstick, you can tell this is not a natural look I was born with."

I nodded.

"It's not supposed to be. It's supposed to excite men."

I swallowed. Licked my lips, searching for something suave to say.

"Don't bother to deny," she said. "I knew you liked it the first time you saw me."

I stared into my beer.

"But there's another secret." She watched my face, sipped her martini. "Maybe I'll tell you when I know you better."

I grinned, wondering if being a tease was the second secret.

She pointed down. "You were studying that phone?"

"Just seeing what it remembers." It might have been a reflection of stage lights, but her eyes seemed to flicker.

"Not to be nosy, but why?"

"For a client. I'm trying to —" What was I trying to do now that I had found Mona? "Satisfy my curiosity."

"Is someone paying you?"

I nodded.

"So you have a consulting business?"

I liked the sound of that. Not a private eye without a license who might get busted by the cops, but a *consulting business*.

"Part-time. It's not like I have a whole floor downtown and a hundred employees."

She moved a shoulder. "Employees are the ultimate headache anyway. People have too many private agendas."

I lifted my beer. "To agendas."

The soft ping of her glass sounded like an invitation.

Nineteen

I WHISPERED HIGHLIGHTS of my evening to Slim while ordering breakfast to provide return on her vodka investment. Then I sat at my table at Victoria's mulling over my failure to convince Tracy to give me a way to contact her. Slim returned and eyed me as she filled my coffee, likely wanting more skinny on the Monkey.

She finished pouring and slipped the morning *Tribune* onto the table.

It was folded to an article that included the same artist's sketch, though smaller this time. The officer in Detroit remained in critical condition. Blunt trauma to his head led to speculation he had collided with a stone wall as he fell. He was mumbling random words the hospital had recorded and the police were trying to decipher. The article mentioned "bricks" and "fire." It went on to cover the way dogs were trained, how to spot counterfeits, and a request for anyone with information to please contact the police. This time it referred to a "substantial amount" of cash found in what they were calling catacombs, probably because a word referring to an underground cemetery helped sell newspapers.

I absently tapped a rhythm on the white porcelain handle of my coffee cup while admiring the blue and yellow tablecloths Victoria was using today. Who might know how much cash had been stored there? The people who had printed it. Perhaps the people who were to receive it.

And who knew how much cash had been recovered?

Only the police. I shook my head slightly to correct myself. Or anyone with a mole at the police station who might leak an unimportant detail like that.

Did any one person know both things? I knew, and Mona knew, that at least five hundred thousand dollars was missing. Surely someone would care.

Or would they?

I broke off a corner of a maple muffin and thought about cops. They didn't care how much they recovered; they cared how much went into circulation. How about the guys who printed it? Why would they care if half a million had gone missing instead of being confiscated? They were out the fake dough either way.

However, if a third party benefitted...both sides would care.

I drank the fresh coffee from Slim. If unknown persons (I refused to say Mona in my mind) burgled it, not only had they stolen big money from the kind of people you should never steal from; they might also have led cops to the catacombs.

The guy, gal, gang who had set up those catacombs would be mighty irritated about that.

Slim came back. "Coffee, sir?"

"Yes, please." I tapped the paper. "Good article."

"Not much news. I wish that poor cop would recover enough to tell what happened."

I nodded. "What do you want to know most?"

She screwed up her lips for a second. "Why did the guy punch you?"

"He came here yesterday, told me to stay away from Mona. I sat at the Monkey's bar — beautiful ice simulation by the way; you should check it out." She wrinkled her nose. "Mona and I made small talk, then went upstairs and slow danced." Her eyes opened wide. "Her suggestion. I was hoping to get more information."

"Did you? Like her cup size?"

"Indirectly. She panicked when I told her about the hitchhiker."

Slim held the pot handle with two hands. "But she's the hitchhiker."

"Correct. However, at that moment she learned I *remembered* the hitchhiker, which is apparently a bad thing. She told me to forget about her, then chased me out of the place. That was just before I got punched."

"Are you okay?"

"Not spitting up blood, but my sternum is super sore."

Slim sat down, whispered, "What's next?"

It was after nine. I checked the room. The last two diners, two women I had overheard talking about Chicago's seven-story shopping mall, were standing to leave.

"Not sure. My client told me to forget about her. That sounds like I was fired. Or at least finished what I was supposed to do, even though I don't really know what it was. Being a pawn is a tough job."

She laughed and flipped her long hair backward over her shoulder; it immediately fell forward and dangled by her narrow chin.

"What are you going to do?"

"Since I don't have instructions from my client, I was thinking of enjoying my vacation in Chicago."

"You're lucky to have this sunny weather." She leaned close. "You going to keep poking around?"

I moved even closer. Her haired smelled of the summer rain we weren't having. I whispered in her left ear, "Yes."

She nodded, confirming that in her estimation I had made the right decision. She stood.

"And you're going to keep your secretary, who faithfully answers the pay phone for you, duly informed of the latest developments, right?"

I grinned. "On a need-to-know basis."

She punched my shoulder with a soft fist and followed her coffee pot out of the dining room.

I could understand why Mona had left the backpack: she wanted me to keep it safe. I sipped hot coffee and woke up a bit more. That meant wherever she was right now *wasn't* safe, at least for that backpack. And the photograph was so I could show it around. That had worked quickly.

Why the cell phone?

I imagined Mona standing in the parking structure of the W late Saturday night, deciding to slip the phone in the pack, hide the pack under the hood.

It had been powered on too, so it could receive messages, and maybe drop electronic breadcrumbs.

The messages. Had she wanted me to learn about Z-Rox?

I left Tuesday's *Tribune* on the table and walked out the front door and down freshly swept brick steps. As I strolled away a voice suggested that I really should be practicing, given that I was hoping for a job at the Monkey.

But it was too early for the blues. And sunny.

I strolled toward the lake. Wind swirled a yellow candy wrapper along the curb in my direction. I tried to catch it with a toe; jogged for a bit in my black converse sneakers and jeans; stopped before raising a sweat. Lake water extending to the horizon suggested an ocean promising far-off lands. Made me wonder what Chris Columbus and his sailing buddies did when they got the blues.

I walked up the curved driveway to the W hotel. A slender white kid with acne stood behind the valet desk. I asked if he knew how to reach Marvin, told him I might have a music gig. He promised to call Marvin at noon when he might be out of bed. I thanked and tipped him, went back to walking.

It was going on eleven when I reached the library. My favorite librarian was standing behind the counter chewing gum and paging through an oversized magazine printed in black and white. She wore a black jacket over a black shirt. The counter blocked the lower part of her body. Her eyes were again floating in jet-black wells that reminded me of the Kiwi shoe polish I used to shine my leather boots while listening to Mom's Stray Cats collection.

She looked up. "Are you back to seduce me?"

"Hadn't thought about it yet, too early." I stopped opposite her. The stud in her nose was blue today. "Vintage magazine, before the invention of color printing?"

She squinted with one eye. "Perhaps you're lost?" She tilted her head. "The Docks of Boon are further west."

"Was wondering if you have any real newspapers."

"What year?"

I laughed. "Good one. I like your blue." I touched my nose.

"Thanks, it's my birthstone."

"Today's *Detroit News*."

She closed her magazine. "How could we fulfill our civic duty to the grand City of Chicago, that has just passed the one thousand shootings mark, if we didn't have the Murder City News available for comparison?" She glanced around, pointed with her head, and walked to my right.

I followed.

As she stepped out from behind the counter shiny sapphire slacks that matched the gem in her nose slapped me awake. They stretched tight over her thighs down to knee-high black boots with thick flat soles suitable for marching. I tried not to stare, and partially succeeded.

Lizz's pants led down a flight of concrete steps. At the bottom we passed through a half-glass door painted light green, along a cool hallway whose damp paper smell brought catacombs to mind, and into a room lined with racks of newspapers hanging from long wooden sticks.

She stopped and faced me.

"You could get a Kindle and read anything you want."

"But then—"

She held up her hand. "I know, you wouldn't have the thrill of not trying to seduce me." She smiled, white teeth and gray makeup transforming her face into an Ansel Adams portrait. "I understand."

"I'm curious how a certain story is being covered."

She stretched out her arm. "A dozen major newspapers for at least the past week at your fingertips. Dead trees dangling from more dead trees for your edification. And that's not counting the dead dinosaurs used to ship them here."

"Lot of dead things around here."

"It's Chicago. This way." She went straight to the *Detroit News* and pulled the main section off the rack. The pages floated lazily from a yard-long stick as she carried them to a tilted table wide enough to lay out a full newsprint page.

"Thanks, Lizz. You must be the best librarian in all of Chicago."

"At least."

"I know I'm late. But is there a chance of sharing a cup of your fine coffee?"

"'Wait on me hand and foot' is not a recommended seduction strategy. That's supposed to come later." She glanced at the front page. "See, Murder City. I'll see if I can make coffee appear out of a top hat." She headed back for the stairs. I watched her go in case she gave me a last-minute backward glance.

She didn't.

The headline shouted *Two Found in Shallow Grave.* I read the article, though it wasn't what I had hoped to find. Two males had been found under a foot of dirt near the St. Claire River by a boy and a German Shepherd he called Pause. Each had been shot twice. A ballistics investigation was underway. The grave had been covered with an alcohol-based fluid the police said may have been intended to slow the decomposition of the bodies.

I turned the pages carefully, scanning for the word counterfeit. On page nineteen I stumbled into a pharaoh's tomb of wonder. The top half of the page was a labeled architectural diagram with color-coded sections. The bottom half was a numbered index with explanations of each label.

I felt Lizz by my side placing a cup on the table. I grabbed her hand before she could retrieve it and kissed the back gently.

"Thank you, Mistress of All Knowledge, for your generous gift of the dark nectar of life."

Her face was still, but her torso jiggled with contained laughter under her jacket. She let me hold her hand as she gazed down into my eyes from her towering five feet plus heels.

I held my best poker face.

"Is that all?" she finally said, and her lips spread into a smile.

"It's still early for me. Just getting warmed up."

"Find something interesting?"

"Maybe. The *News* has a detailed story on that counterfeiting operation. Was just about to read it."

She pulled her hand away. "Well, don't let the Mistress of Knowledge slow your pace. It's eleven. Mistress dines between noon and one." She went away again. I marveled at her blue pants. Then read carefully.

The underground location had been used during Prohibition by the Purple Gang of Detroit to store bootlegged liquor after bringing it across the river: boats in summer, walking the ice in winter. Someone unknown had carefully expanded it, and cleared nine access tunnels. That made sense. Once they shot the cop, they knew how to sneak out without being seen.

I looked up from the paper and stared at a sketch of the basement hanging on the concrete block wall. *They?* Why plural? How did I know if more than one person had been caught off guard by that cop and his dog?

Another reason to douse that grave: slow down the dogs. I'd bet that fluid could dissolve ink. The Detroit cops probably knew, but weren't telling the press.

The underground facility turned out to be a series of storage rooms interconnected with narrow tunnels tall enough to move whiskey through on handcarts. The room where cash had been found was indicated. It had wine-cellar equipment for controlling temperature and humidity powered by interchangeable battery packs. But the trump card was the print room. It was only a sketch, but appeared to be a modern press that used metal offset plates. Through serendipity (the article never used the word *luck*) the police had entered the tunnels while someone was at the press.

I leaned back with Lizz's brew and tried to imagine the shock the cop experienced when he turned a corner and saw one, two, maybe more, people silently working over a printing press. Someone pulled a gun and fired at least once, then cleared out before the cop's backup arrived. That scenario made sense if the police thought they were exploring just another abandoned hole left over from Prohibition. I wondered if the cop had time to fire back.

A section labeled FOOTPRINTS estimated there had been at least three different people in the print room based on analysis of the dirt floor. It gave shoe sizes, including one for a woman: size seven. I closed my eyes and visualized Mona's feet in her platform high heels.

Maybe.

Experts were working to reconstruct the event, but looked forward to Officer Tyler's eyewitness account. I took the time to commit the layout to memory. What struck me most was the compactness: each section was smaller than my room at Victoria's. I imagined firing a handgun from my bed, then running through a narrow tunnel hundreds of yards long. I would reach the tunnel's exit—and come out where?

While contemplating possible scenarios my eye landed on a white round-faced clock on the wall with a thin red hand that jumped from second to second like it was scared.

Just after twelve.

I folded the paper over the rod and returned it to the rack, then ran up the stairs two at a time. Lizz was waiting by the front door tapping her boot, but she smiled as I came jogging around the corner.

"Mistress has been waiting."

"I hope her hunger hasn't abated."

"Ravenous," she said, and took a bite out of my bicep with her fingertips. "I know just the place."

"No Duck Walk today?"

She shook her head. Her black hair, that normally hung straight down like it was in Jupiter's gravity, swayed.

I filled her in on what I had learned as we walked. She nodded thoughtfully, and didn't say much until I inadvertently mentioned my second warning from Hosco.

"He punched you? That's battery."

"You think I should register a complaint?"

She stopped in the middle of the sidewalk. "You mean like cops?"

"Uh, yeah."

She stared up at me. I didn't know what to make of the look in her eyes.

"Didn't you say you were a private eye?"

"Well...this is my first gig."

"You have to stay away from cops. Your clients must be confident that hiring you isn't going to get them an interview with the local constable."

"Constable?" I laughed. "You're serious?"

"Of course. Didn't you hear Marlowe in those Chandler novels? Protect your client." She grinned. "While not getting yourself arrested."

"Comparative Art major, huh?"

"A few of us can read." She started walking again, and stopped three blocks later in front of a Dutch door. The top half was open and the bottom had a crude faded painting of a giant hamburger. She walked up to the door and waited.

A voice from inside a narrow room called out, "How many you wish?"

"Two, with," she answered. "Coke. Coke."

The voice came back, "No Coke. Pepsi, Pepsi," followed by deep rolling laughter.

"You learned standup in art school?" I asked.

"José is a John Belushi fan. Grew up around that time."

"Now he's a chef?"

"You jest. Wait till you taste his burgers."

Since there was no restaurant and no chairs, we carried our food to the bus stop and shared fries with waiting riders. As usual, Lizz was correct. I don't know what José hid inside, but the meat was charred for a barbecue competition, and cheddar cheese drooled over the sides onto giant potato slices so crispy they crunched; a perfect pairing for a huge plastic Pepsi.

"Hey Lizz, can I ask you something?"

"Is this where you start to seduce me?"

"Maybe," I said, half meaning it. She was awfully darn smart, which was awfully attractive. "The guy that punched me."

"Need a good lawyer?"

"He told me not to come back. Said it was my second warning."

"When was the first?" She stole a fry even though she still had half a plate.

"He came by Victoria's with a flyer. We chatted over breakfast yesterday."

"Hmm."

"Yeah. Number three could be bad. Three strikes and all that."

"Don't go back."

"But Mona works there."

"Mona, huh? Is this part of the stealth seduction you're laying on me?"

"She's my client."

"And your job was to find her?"

"Correct."

"For which she paid you?"

"Correct again."

"So now the problem is..." She pushed the last of her burger into her mouth.

"Now the problem is...I don't know what the problem is. Mona didn't recognize me, and told me to stay away from her."

She sipped her Pepsi until it slurped. "Consider your client's needs. Punching man says stay away. Mona says stay away. Even Lizz says stay away. Why don't you just..." She turned in my direction.

"Stay away?"

She tipped her head and made her deep-well eyes big.

She was stating the rationally obvious. I had found Mona (well, maybe I had found her). But I was in possession of a great deal of money someone had hidden in my car. He or she knew I had it. He or she would want it. I couldn't just toss it in a trash can and drive west; a move like that would catch up with me.

"But I don't know what's going on."

"Not good for a private eye," she said. "On the other hand, is someone paying you? Are there damsels available to seduce?"

I shook my head. "No, no damsels."

She punched me, maybe a little harder than necessary, then got up and tossed the food carton into a gray can.

"Did you ask me your question?"

I shook my head. "Was wondering. That business you have."

"You need a new dress for the ball?"

"You mentioned 'makeover' yesterday. Could you make me unrecognizable without taking off body parts?"

She faced me, held my chin in a hand that was soft and warm and had midnight blue polish on the nails. Turned my face one way then the other. Released me. Pulled at my clothes with two fingers. Spun me around. Poked at my butt.

"How long does it have to last?" she asked.

"Couple of hours. I'm going to be on stage playing guitar, and observing."

"How good are your eyes?"

I had no idea what she meant. "I don't wear glasses."

"I meant, can you see in a club through dark glasses? The eyes help people recognize faces. One of the reasons famous people wear sunglasses."

"The other reason?"

"It's harder to tell if they've been using drugs. Look at Keith Richards with and without sunglasses sometime." She was still studying me. "You want to look like a blues musician?"

I nodded.

"How successful?"

"Scraping to get by."

She pursed her lips and I realized they had black makeup outlines around the dim red lipstick.

She put her hands on either side of her head like she had a headache. Her eyes danced over me.

"How much money do I have to work with?"

"How much would you like?"

"Well, we can't use designer base products; no musician could afford them. A couple hundred maybe."

"You got it."

"Walk me back?"

We walked in silence for a couple of blocks.

Out of nowhere she asked, "Do you have a favorite color?"

"Turbo Bronze."

She laughed. "Sounds like something that would shoot out of an exhaust pipe."

131

"It's the color of my car. Brown with gold metallic flakes."

"Hmm," she said. "We'll see."

We stopped in front of the library with about two minutes to spare.

"Come by Get Over It around six. Don't shave."

I bowed and kissed the back of her hand again. "Thank you."

"Better," she said, before gliding through the glass doors.

Twenty

I WALKED TOWARD VICTORIA'S in seventy-degree sunshine wondering why Chicago had such a bad reputation for weather. Maybe Kim was right, I had hit a rare good spot. I passed the self-storage building, thought about that backpack, and the key to the storage locker taped to the underside of the nightstand at Victoria's. Not particularly clever if someone were motivated to find it.

I stopped by the pawn shop to see my friend with the Ohio State suspenders. I told him the watch was working fine, which seemed to please him, and bought a brown nylon guitar case with shoulder straps. He probably overcharged me, but I liked his casual style and it was less than fifty bucks. Just before leaving I remembered something from the plot of a noir novel whose title I couldn't remember.

"Do you have a safe?" I asked.

His narrowed eyes studied me.

"I have something that needs to be secure. Was wondering if you could hold it for me?"

He nodded. "That I could, if it's not large." He glanced at my case and shook his head. "No guitars."

"Small," I said. "A memento."

"Bring it by. My fees are quite reasonable."

A long walk took me back to Victoria's. I stopped to see Kim at the front desk. She handed me a message from Marvin: he was up for the gig and had dictated a list of song titles. She asked about my stomach; I told her it was improving. She warned me to stay away from the club, those places weren't good for my health.

I said she sounded like my mother.

She made a funny face and reminded me of their dollar per message policy.

I practiced for an hour, dredging my memory for *Politician, Girlfriend Blues, Seventh Son,* wishing I had access to my records. The titles I didn't recognize I figured for Marvin originals; I'd just have to hide behind his playing. Then I took a nap with a T-shirt tossed over my eyes.

I woke but didn't get up, trying to decide what to wear in case Lizz decided to razor my clothing. Then I decided it didn't matter because the few clothes I had were too Tommy, she was going to have to start with something else. So I put on jeans and a green button-down shirt and tossed my sport coat over it. Then I peeled duct tape off the bottom of the nightstand and removed the locker key.

I slipped my blue guitar into its new bag, carried it to the parking garage, and locked it in the car. I had no idea how long Lizz was going to keep me, so I wanted to be ready to head right to the Monkey. The weather was still clear so I walked to the self-storage, rented a second, smaller locker, and moved the backpack to it. Knowing it was soon going to be harder to access, I opened a brick and pulled off the ten good bills. This was Mona's money, so I took out my Pig-logo notebook and made an entry in the back. According to my scribbles, I was still holding the five hundred retainer, but the per diem money lasted only through tonight. I also had the donut fund. But if I stayed on the case, I might need this thousand too. On the way out I waved to an attendant watching online video of girls washing a little red Corvette.

He grunted.

I stopped at Walgreens, whose painted window told me their first drugstore opened in 1901, and bought a white carousel music box with a rainbow on top. For a moment I wondered if Tracy liked music boxes. Then I worked the bottom off and tucked the key to the cash up inside. I wound it and listened to

Somewhere Over the Rainbow, feeling like one of those little horses going round and round and round.

I bought a second box with a Degas ballerina in a ceramic tile on the top. It played *Swan Lake.* Then I went to see my friend the Buckeye fan.

I showed him the rainbow box. Still wearing his red suspenders, he looked it over, petted a horse, and touched the lever to start the music. His face seemed to soften.

"It was my mother's," I said.

He nodded, wrote a ticket, and said he'd keep it for sixty days. I asked him to please lock it in the safe, but to feel free to listen to it anytime he wanted. Then I walked to the Cuda and drove toward the Pig feeling energized.

Almost five o'clock.

Penny ran out the front door as I approached. She grabbed my arm and dragged me along the sidewalk away from the entrance.

"We have to talk," she said.

"Sure, Penny. You okay?"

"I...I..."

She looked okay: her soft hair fluffed, either no makeup or some natural style that looked like no makeup, and black jeans with cute strapped sandals that I pretended not to notice. I waited.

"Last night."

"Hey, thanks for helping me take down those flyers; I know you wanted to study. How did your test go?"

She shook her head. "Forget the test."

"Is something wrong?"

She sucked on her lower lip. I realized with an emptiness that Hosco might have seen us together.

"Did someone threaten you?"

"No."

"Is your boyfriend mad?"

"That's the thing—" She stopped and licked her lip where she had been chewing it.

"It was only one kiss." I smiled. "Nice though."

She lifted a hand and started on the knuckle of her bent index finger.

"Did you tell your boyfriend?"

"I hate lying," she said.

"Then tell him."

"No, that's not it."

I waited.

"I hate lying," she said.

"So come clean. What's bothering you?"

She lowered her hand. "I don't have a boyfriend."

The surprise reached my face.

"I'm sorry. I just say that to guys so they stay away from me."

It didn't seem to me that she had been staying away exactly.

"You want me to stay away, but you offer to help me. So we're friends?"

"I hope so," she said.

I nodded. "Sure we are." But then I had no idea why she had kissed me. Fortunately, my mother had explained to never try to understand a woman, not even her.

"But..." she said.

I watched her eyes. She met mine, then twisted away like a car she loved was coming down the street, though the road was empty.

"Is this about that kiss last night?"

"Sort of."

"I'm sorry if I didn't hold up my end, you surprised me." I grinned.

She punched my arm. "You're fun to hang around."

"Then hang. We can be cool."

"No," she almost shouted. "I mean, I'm not saying that."

I took her hand. "Penny. You helped me a lot. You're a fabulous girl. You're smart. I'm glad I met you. Could we please go have dinner? I have a meeting at six and have to play tonight. Whatever's bothering you we can work out later. I promise not to hate you, and I promise to come back tomorrow."

She squeezed my hand, found my eyes. "Promise?"

"Yes, I promise. Now take a deep breath." I waited. "Let it out real slow." I led her up the sidewalk toward the Pig. She was smiling by the time we got to the door.

I wanted something light so I ordered mushroom quiche, a salad, and a smuggled cookie. Penny came by the table a couple of times but didn't say much. I let her know I was working on another gig with Marvin. She asked how long I would be staying in Chicago: a question I couldn't answer.

It was ten minutes before six when I walked out the door. The soon-to-be setting sun had been joined by a cool breeze from the Northeast, directly across the lake. I flipped the collar of my sport coat up, though it didn't help much, and walked toward Lizz's shop.

The sign above a narrow green door read: *GET OVER IT – Transform Yourself from the Outside In.* That sounded like the fake-it-till-you-make-it mantra from a self-help seminar: imitating confidence yields minor success leads to real confidence in a positive feedback loop like a microphone squealing on stage. I wondered if it really worked.

I opened the door and a metal bell above my head tinkled. A flash went off in my eyes. Twice.

The spots cleared to reveal a room a couple of car lengths long, clothing along both walls like a Hollywood star's walk-in closet, and a single barber chair at the far end looking lonely. Lizz stood in the center of the room holding a camera the size of a brick spewing out paper photographs like the original Polaroid. Behind her a man with very short hair and blue-rimmed glasses studied me. He was about forty-years old and a handful of pounds overweight.

"What do you think, Mikel?" Lizz said.

"Midwestern chic. Reminds me of my dentist."

"Tommy, this is Mikel. He'll be doing your hair."

I shook hands, was led to the barber chair, and leaned back for a shampoo.

"I'm glad you didn't shave," Lizz said. "We're going to do a little jazz thing."

I was glad I forgot, because I just remembered she had told me not to. "Blues," I said through the sound of running water.

"You smell of college," she said. "We want a slightly offbeat beatnik pseudo-intellectual look. Think you can handle that?"

"I feel typecast."

Lizz laughed.

Mikel tilted me up and electric clippers started running in my ear.

"Hair is a key identifier in a portrait," she said. "So most of it is going away, the rest will be dyed darker. And we'll shape your five o'clock shadow."

Minutes later Mikel finished and Lizz held up a hand mirror. The sides of my head were short bristles, but the top was dark and swirly.

"Put these on."

She handed me gold wire-frame sunglasses with small circular lenses. I was beginning to look like someone I didn't know. Mikel dropped me back and worked on my face with his buzzing machine. When he flipped me up I had the start of the stereotypical goatee of jazz artists of the fifties. I realized that I could pass for forty, and wondered if this is how I would look in eleven years.

"I'm thinking lid," Lizz said, and tried on a hat I associated with sports cars, a brown beret, and something that a railroad engineer might wear. She stared at me. "I think beret."

"I feel like a painter." I turned the sports-car hat with the top snapped to the brim around like the great bluesman Buddy Guy often wore. "How about this?"

"Good. Let's keep working." She peeled off my jacket and shirt and folded them into a double-handled black bag with the words Get Over It on the side. She handed me a midnight blue short-sleeved shirt with silver down the right front like the broad stripe on a Ford Cobra. She worked her way down my body until I was wearing a punched-leather belt with a Fender belt buckle (she didn't have Gibson) and shiny metallic pants that came fairly close to Turbo Bronze, only darker. They were tight and stretchy and had modest bell bottoms.

"Awfully conspicuous," I said.

"That's the best way to not get noticed. They'll give you one glance, write you off as a wannabe rock star, and be on their way." She pointed and said: "Shoes."

I was given a choice between cowboy boots and black dress shoes. I had no idea which would work better with metallic pants, so I put one on each foot and turned back and forth while Lizz and Mikel studied me.

"Boots," Mikel said. "More Texas guitar slinger."

Lizz nodded. "Can you play in a jacket? It'll do a better job of hiding your body. And it's cool enough outside for one."

"Sure, if it's not too tight in the shoulders."

She found a black leather sport coat on the rack and slipped it on me. The supple material moved when I did.

"I'm feeling a bit metallic."

She nodded. "Good. Not like anything you've ever worn, right?"

"Pretty much. These pants are...shiny."

"They'll be perfect on stage. Just don't wear them in daylight." She laughed. "Well, Mikel?"

"What color is your guitar?"

"Powder blue," I said.

139

"Ouch, that'll pop."

"It'll be fine," Lizz said. "Especially under pink lights with one arm of the jacket over it." She walked around me, tilting her head up and down, left and right. "Walk."

I walked the length of the narrow store thinking about how runway models must feel surrounded by crowds and cameras.

"Relax," Lizz said. "You're a blues player. Your steps are too purposeful. Walk like you're not sure where your foot is going to land."

I strolled, relaxed my eyes, shifted my gaze.

"Better. What about the face?"

"Sunken cheeks, deep-set tired eyes. It won't take me long," Mikel said.

They put me back in the chair and Mikel started applying makeup.

"I don't usually wear makeup," I said.

Lizz gave me her *duh* look. "Guys don't, though many should. It'll help change the shape of your face, reduce the recognition triggers in people who have seen you before."

"You sound like a spy," I said.

"It's called shape from shading. Artists were doing it centuries before Pixar brought it to the big screen. Can you play wearing a ring?"

"On my right hand."

I felt cool metal slip onto my fourth finger.

"We need a statement on a chain. What means something to you?"

"Guitar pick."

"Too obvious. Down home blues artist. What would he wear?"

"Talisman," Mikel said.

"Oh yes," Lizz agreed. "I've got just the thing."

Mikel worked on my face. In a few moments I felt a chain being fastened behind my neck and a cool lump against my chest.

"I need to trim these eyebrows, they're killing me," Mikel said. No one commented but I felt the edge of steel scissors over my eyes.

"Let's review." Lizz lifted me by the arm and stood me in front of a full length mirror, then spun me around. The heels on the boots made me an inch taller, the makeup made me ten pounds thinner. The jacket and pants combined to hide most of who I was in a blatant sort of way. A silver skull with brilliant blue jewels for eyes hung inches below my chin.

"The hat?" I asked, feeling odd under the little circle of the reversed sports-car lid.

"Perfect," Lizz decreed. "Suggests a beret without being one. You'll stick out and be remembered. Not like that other guy." She popped her fingers. "What's his name?"

"Tommy," I said.

"Yeah, him. Speaking of which, what're you going to call yourself? You have to be careful, if someone shouts at you, you had better answer. And *not* to Tommy."

I hadn't thought about it. I just didn't want Hosco to recognize me when I walked in.

"Any suggestions?" I asked.

"Something with a T," Mikel said. "It'll be easier to cover a mistake. Pretend you misheard."

"Don't blues players always have a bunch of names?" Lizz asked.

"You mean like Pee Wee Crayton or Blind Willie Johnson?" I said.

She nodded, thoughtful. "Long. Hmm. Fowler. Scottish artist, painted mythological landscapes. Got it. Long Toe Fowler. We'll call you Toe for short."

I looked down at my boots, trying to remember how long my second toe was.

Lizz added, "You're smart enough not to valet your car, right?" She handed me a pack of Lucky Strikes with a slender gold lighter clipped to it. "Cover if you need it."

I slipped the smokes inside my new jacket.

She stared at me, then held out her hand, palm up.

It took me a second to realize she wanted her two hundred.

Twenty-One

SEVEN-FIFTEEN. I PARKED SIX blocks north of the club and practiced my blues walk, carrying the guitar in its new brown bag. An occasional glance in passing windows revealed a stoop-shouldered musician inching his way toward a gig accompanying me. I grew to like the reversed cap, and wondered where Tommy Cuda had gone while repeating *Long Toe Fowler* to myself over and over. I stopped two blocks from the Pink Monkey and stood on the corner like that guy in the Winslow Arizona song. I replayed each meeting with Mona. What was said. What had been left unsaid.

I leaned the guitar up against a building that may have once been a bank, and put one boot up against the stone. I lit one of Lizz's cigarettes and dragged slowly to test the feeling. The sky had gone cloudy and the moon could be seen rising as a hazy glow, even though the sun hadn't yet set. I kept my head down and one eye on the entrance to the Monkey while running lyrics through my head that all seemed to be about men whose women didn't understand them.

My mind had drifted to Lizz's deep-well eyes when a green and white cab stopped in front of the Monkey. A black man hopped out, pulling a bag behind him that I'd bet had a bass guitar in it. He was wearing a black trench coat that made me think of a hidden shotgun.

I put the cigarette out with my boot, couldn't find a place to toss it, slipped it into my shiny pants, and started walking.

The cab was gone and the man stood staring at the entrance when I stepped up beside his left elbow.

"Hey."

He turned and gave me the once-over, evaluating a stranger. His eyes lingered on the pants.

"Long Toe Fowler," I said.

He considered me.

"Cuda sent me. You located a guitar for him."

His mouth slowly worked its way into that smile. "Long Toe?"

I stuck out a boot. "Call me Toe."

"OK, Toe. Let's wake this place up." He started for the door.

"Uh, Marvin, let's talk." I pulled him away from the entrance. "They have a stage on the second floor for jams: drums, amps, sound system."

"Good, that's good. They're all ready for us."

"Well, that's the thing. They don't know we're coming yet."

His squinted left eye suggested I had better talk fast.

"But there's a girl here who wants to meet you, and I'm confident you can talk us onto that stage."

"Does she know we're coming?"

"Eventually."

"So Marvin better be sharp?"

"Marvin's always sharp," I said. "Her name's Sorana. She's met Tommy. Let's stop at the coat check and ask for her. Maybe you can save us the cover; it's steep for a blues player."

He picked up his instrument then stopped me with a hand on my forearm. "Hey, word is they only serve fruity drinks in this place."

"Yeah," I showed him the flask. "We're covered."

He nodded and we advanced through the glass doors shoulder to shoulder.

I asked a not quite skinny girl with blonde hair pulled tight back over her head and bright blue eyeshadow if it would be possible to chat with Sorana. Told her I had been in earlier in the week and made an appointment for an audition. Her eyes said she didn't believe me, but a ten spot convinced her of my sincerity, and to abandon her station for the sixty-seconds it'd take to deliver the message.

She came back and asked us to wait. We stepped aside to make room for real customers. Marvin studied the club while rocking back and forth on the balls of his feet like a boxer before a match.

"When Sorana gets here, I'll go to talk to the coat check girl," I said.

"Good idea, Toe. Don't want to distract her."

We had waited less than five minutes when the mound of curls flowing from Sorana's head made its way across the bar. I left Marvin and stepped over to introduce myself to the girl with tight hair whose name turned out to be Anna. Her eyes matched the blue eyeshadow. I told her blue was Toe's favorite color, which she didn't believe until I showed her the eyes in my magic skull pendant, and unzipped the guitar case. I was running down a list of songs with blue eyes in the title for her: *Behind Blue Eyes* by the Who, *Blue Eyes Blue* by Diane Warren, *Blue Eyes* by Elton John, and *Suite: Anna Blue Eyes* by CS&N, which she knew I had changed from Judy when Marvin stepped up beside me with Sorana on his arm.

"Lady says we should take the elevator," he said.

I looked at Anna who looked at Sorana who communicated something with subtle body language; then Anna tore off a couple of tickets and handed them to me.

"You going to play a song for me?" Anna asked.

While I was trying to think of one so I could say yes, Marvin interjected, "We'll write one for you. Maybe call it *Double Blue Love*."

Anna smiled and squeezed my hand that was holding the tickets. I reached into my pocket for another tip, but she shook her head no.

We were behind the closed doors of the elevator before anyone spoke.

"Marvin promised to dance with me," Sorana said.

My palm tingled, remembering my dance with Mona.

"Toe here's going to do a ballad for us, ain't you Toe?"

Sorana tried to see eyes behind my glasses.

I nodded. "Two if you want, you can hold her longer."

Two smiles reflected in the gold elevator doors as they opened.

I plugged into a new model of an old Fender amp, tuned my blue guitar, then did a simple instrumental version of *Don't It Make My Brown Eyes Blue*, wondering if Anna could hear me downstairs. I owed her for fetching Sorana, or we'd still be standing on the sidewalk. I soloed for three choruses, keeping things mellow. Marvin and Sorana danced close, the only two people on the floor. A dozen male customers drank, two petite dancers I hadn't met gyrated gracefully near their tables, and a bartender wiped off an empty bar. When I stopped, Sorana kissed Marvin quickly on the cheek and headed for the elevator.

Marvin watched her walk away. I watched Marvin watch. He finally turned and stepped onto the low stage.

"Toe, my man, what have you gotten us into here?"

"Complexity," I said. "The depths of which have yet to be sounded."

He shook his head, but he was smiling.

I checked the bar clock. Seven thirty-eight. We launched into a Marvin tune called *Lonely Man*. Just as I was about to start my solo the elevator doors opened. I strummed a chord and pointed at Marvin. He played a slow moaning melody high on his bass: a whale longing for its mate.

I watched a long black skirt emerge from the darkness. Dark hair touched a blue sleeveless top shinier than my guitar. I played the next chord, Marvin worked the solo. She came closer. Tiny silver sequins flickering on the shirt formed the outline of a barely visible dollar sign.

She stared at the stage, didn't smile.

I had seen her before, sipping a blue drink. Tracy. Like sugar with a K.

I turned away and almost missed the chord change. I forced my eyes to the neck of the guitar and finished the song behind Marvin singing:

Lonely is time standing still / Hues of you I cannot kill.

Tracy gave us a little applause, which drew the attention of a bartender in a white vest that appeared pink under the lights. She caught his eye and turned toward the bar. We launched into a shuffle blues to rev the place up, though we were still subdued as a duo with no one pounding the silver metal-flake drum kit behind us. I played a solo. When I looked up Mona and Hosco were on the dance floor twisting and sliding. I swallowed hard and tried to make my jaw relax.

We let the last note fade out. Marvin turned my way, eyes smiling. Hosco approached the stage with Mona on his arm. She had forgotten to put her flowing translucent angel robe over her dark lingerie. Her skin was magazine-cover perfect in the dim lighting, her body the idealized curves of a sculpture. But up close, it was her svelte dancer's strength that held me in suspended animation.

I blinked and avoided eye contact.

"You guys are okay, where you from?" Hosco asked.

"Mississippi," Marvin said without hesitation. I had never been there, but it seemed like a fine answer for a couple of blues guys.

"Got a name?"

Mona was looking my way. I couldn't tell if she recognized me, liked guitar players, or was just resting her face in my direction because Hosco was ignoring her.

"Toe the Line," Marvin said.

I nodded, but kept my eyes behind the glasses and pointed mostly toward Tracy, who had scored a tall drink with a light in it, and was sitting at a table far to my right.

"Words to live by," Hosco said. He flicked a thumb toward the idle turntable. "I'm spinning later. Hang around, I'll buy you guys a round."

Marvin gave him his signature smile. "Not much of that music down our way."

"Try it, you'll like it. Tell Sorana Mr. Hosco said you guys are okay to play here. I like that you keep the volume under control." He put an arm around Mona and pulled her close. "How about something for the deck of a cruise ship in tropical moonlight?" He turned and guided her to the center of the dance floor as if she were on a string.

Marvin lifted an eyebrow my way, then started a ballad in G. As we played I kept my face pointed at the neck of the guitar and flicked my eyes behind the dark lenses from Hosco's undertaker-gray suit slow dancing against Mona's bare skin, across to Tracy's glowing drink, and back to Hosco. Near as I could tell, no one had seen Tommy Cuda.

We finished and leaned our instruments against the amps. Hosco dragged Mona toward the elevator faster than she could gracefully walk in high-rise heels. Tracy gazed into the room, ignoring us. I crossed to Marvin.

"You're good with girls, Marv," I said softly. "Would you tell the curvy brunette that Long Toe is sitting in tonight for your regular guitar player?"

His eyes danced over to her and back to me.

"She's from BLUES isn't she?"

"Good memory. She's met Tommy."

"Trying to avoid her?" He looked me over. "Clever disguise. Be careful talking, girls remember voices."

"I want to shadow Mona, will you keep her occupied?"

"Next time, give me a hard problem." Marvin headed for Tracy's table. I loosened my walk the way Lizz had instructed, found the elevator, dropped a floor, went to the main bar, and avoided the bartender from my first visit. I ordered cranberry

148

juice, spiked it, and watched a chrome reflection of Mona finishing a dance for a table of three forty-something guys whose paunches stuck out far enough to rub against the edge of the table.

I drank and waited. Sorana crossed behind me and disappeared into a back room. The elevator doors opened. Tracy stood in the car alone. She stepped out and scanned the crowd. I dropped off the stool into a crouch below the bar, and heel-toed until I was in dark shadows behind a wall that formed the back of the bar's stage.

"Hi."

Still in a crouch, I spun. Mona was standing inches from my face. I reminded myself Toe had never met her.

"I like your playing," she said, eyes bright, smile wide.

"Thanks," I said in a low baritone, striving to sound like anyone but Tommy Cuda.

"Really. Most musicians are drunk up there and want to show off, jump around and stuff." She looked down. "I really like your pants."

I hesitated, lowered my face a bit. "I really like your legs."

She blushed, surprising me. Dancers seemed so extroverted and experienced with exposure, I didn't think they ever blushed. She squatted and ran the tip of her index finger along the stretchy bronze material above my knee while looking straight into my glasses. "Do you want to touch me back?"

"You were dancing with a guy." I motioned with my head, glad it was almost pitch-black behind the partition.

She sighed, said nothing.

"Are you and he?"

"He's been ignoring me, showing off his silly car, going out of town, playing the great DJ Z-Rox." Her head danced as she spoke. She sighed again, longer and deeper. "He makes me work too much." Her eyes drifted along my body but didn't stop anywhere. "Girls have needs too…hugs for example."

The phonemes *zee-r-o-k-s* stuck in my ear and clanged around.

I managed to croak: "They call me Long Toe."

She thought about that. "I'm Mona." She reached her hand out and shook. It was smooth and hot, like her back the night we danced. Then she guided my hand and waited until I ran one finger along her kneecap.

Low and slow I said, "I'd like to be the masseur the day you visit the spa."

She tilted her head, stared at me with an expression I couldn't read. "You're a funny guy, Toe." She stood and pranced away.

I peeked around the corner. Sorana was sitting at the bar between two tall black men facing a half-dozen drinks lit by neon ice. On the far side of the room beside the second stage Hosco stood with his back to me, talking to someone I couldn't see. I slow-walked to my bar stool. When I got there, I leaned against the ice and feigned watching two Asian girls dancing on the far stage in a choreographed love scene while keeping my eyes on Hosco's back. Mona returned to the table with the three chubby guys.

Hosco spun his head around, then turned left toward where the girls came and went for the stage. The person he had been talking to moved with him. A blue flash almost convinced me it was Tracy.

I sat down.

Why would he talk to Tracy? Easy. He was trying to hire her. As much as I'd have liked to see her dance, part of me hoped she didn't do it. My experience with Hosco suggested he'd be an overbearing tyrant as a boss.

A big hand landing on my left shoulder made me spill my drink.

"How about another set?" Marvin said. He glanced down the bar where Sorana was talking to the two guys. "This place sure has great scenery. It should be a National Park." He swung back to me. "Then I should get to the W."

"Hey, Marvin. Why do you work as a valet?"

"Because I dropped out of premed." He read my surprise. "Yeah, Marvin has a past. You want to hear a short version of a long story?" He didn't wait for an answer. "Organic chemistry. Did you take that? Carbon atoms everywhere. You know what the symbol for Carbon is? C. Like the key of C." He put a hand on my shoulder. "Good old C-major white keys on the pianoforte. So there I was, taking the final exam my second semester of organic. That stuff is complicated, with all the different bonds going on, but I'm doing okay. Halfway through the test, the answer to a question is the semi-structural formula for butane."

My eyes must have glazed over a bit.

"You know that one? I'll never forget it: CH_3 CH_2 CH_2 CH_3. " He released my shoulder and gestured with both hands. "Suddenly, the H jumps out and I see B natural, the way Germans do. I hear that half-step motion between C and B, like the *Jaws* sound track, but funky. C, three Bs, another C, two Bs—bar of seven, then swapped. I start writing a melody. Lyrics about Charlie, another C, jump into my head. Could be about a guy, you know, like a tribute to Charlie Parker, or slang for cocaine. But turns out to be a woman, puts a little twist on the meaning of the whole song. " His long fingers found my shoulder again. "I've got three verses, a chorus, and am working on the bridge when the professor calls for the exams."

"You did this?"

"The Universe did it to me. That test sent me a message."

"Did you pass?"

He shook his head. "No way was I handing that test in. I walked out humming with it in my pocket. The whole class thought I was nuts." He shook my shoulder. "Made a decision to give music a chance. This is year two of five."

"Five years. That's your time frame?"

He nodded. "That's how long Dean Koontz's wife agreed to support him so he could become a writer. I heard that on a podcast. Figured the Universe was giving me a model for artistic creation."

"You read Koontz?"

"Only the Odd stuff. I like that brother." He released my shoulder.

"So butane made you a valet?"

"Great perks. Third shift, so on my time off, I'm primed to work late in the clubs. Not many cars to park at night. I stand at my desk and write songs, scribble lyrics, listen to music. No one cares so long as I'm there when a customer needs a car."

"So they're paying you to write music."

"Pretty much. Tips are lousy; I don't park many after two. But I could be sitting in my bedroom scribbling crappy songs instead of doing it for minimum wage plus tips."

"Your songs aren't crappy."

He gave me a grin. "Thanks, Toe. Let's heat this place up. Window shopping is making me nervous."

His long strides led us to the elevator. We visited my flask on the way up, turned up the volume, and poured blues into a roomful of guys being worked by a half-dozen beautiful women.

I didn't see Mona.

Or Tracy.

And couldn't stop thinking about Hosco.

Twenty-Two

MARVIN ENDED OUR LAST tune with a sighing vibrato. Two guys applauded. Tracy stepped off the elevator carrying a full glowing drink in two hands; I looked back at my amp so she wouldn't see recognition in my eyes and say something like, "Is that you, Tommy?" I wasn't hiding from her, but I was hiding.

I turned to Marvin. "You staying for the DJ?"

"Got to get to work."

"You guys finished?" Tracy asked as she reached the edge of the stage.

"Marvin has a day job," I grumbled.

"Someone's got to pay for your pretty pants," he said, pulling a cell phone from his pocket.

"You need a ride?" I asked, still trying to pitch my voice low.

He shook his head and pointed at the phone. "Got to go see Brenda before clocking in, take a little ride in her Mustang. Later, Toe." He shook my hand, kissed his fingertips, touched Tracy's cheek and drifted across the floor: a confident blues king passing among his subjects.

"I could use a ride," Tracy said.

I tried to assess risk. "When?"

"Right now if you can."

I slipped my guitar into its new case and thought about my goals.

"Was hoping to stay for the DJ."

"I think he's leaving."

I stepped off the stage with my guitar. "Not my business, but did Hosco try to hire you?"

"Who?"

"Guy up here earlier with a redhead. Saw you two talking." I watched her drink. "Is it the lights, or have you been to the beach?"

She lifted her hands and turned in a circle. "Do you like it?"

"Very natural. Makes you look...Italian." I tried to smile casual, like the way Lizz wanted me to walk.

"Passionate lovers I hear." She paused. "He thought I would make a good dancer."

We started for the elevator. "You have the curves." I imagined her in lingerie dancing with a pole; stopped myself.

"I have help," she said, moving through the shiny doors as they opened.

Yoga, ballet, the gym came to mind as we descended. "Doesn't seem like you need help."

She finished the drink. "You'd be surprised."

The elevator stopped in sunglass-assisted darkness.

"I like surprises."

She laughed and led me toward the front door. I waved to Anna.

"Where's my song?" she called after me.

I pointed to my temple. "Marvin's head."

Anna wagged a finger, but she was smiling.

I stopped on the sidewalk under the club's gray awning. "I'm a few blocks away. Nice night for a walk." I glanced down at mules with high heels. "Or wait here, I'll pick you up."

"I'll walk if we go slow."

I extended an elbow, waited for her to loop her hand in, and turned right. We strolled away from the pink lights on the building into a dark hole before reaching a streetlight, then back into darkness, retracing the steps of the slouched bluesman I had seen on the way over.

"Do you like Chicago?" she asked.

"Haven't been here long. Only my second gig."

"Do you have a day job too?"

Would Long Toe Fowler work a real job?

"Try to avoid that. Cuts into my energy level."

We were a block away when I saw the Cuda looking lonely beside a streetlamp.

"You from Chicago?" I asked.

"No, came here for a job."

"Anything you like to talk about?"

"Boring banking stuff."

I stopped, sniffed the air. "Definitely smell money. Thought it was your perfume."

She laughed, her painted lips forming a full curve that a cheap novel would call voluptuous. As we approached the Barracuda she slowed. Her eyes roamed over it from back to front so I stopped beside it. She twisted to get a better look at the car, then back at me. Something crossed her face that I read as curiosity.

"You like old cars?" I asked.

"That one's special. Love the curvy glass."

I stepped over, popped the lid with a key, and slid the guitar in.

Her eyes grew. "This yours?"

"Loaner. Cars are beyond my budget." I closed the trunk. "Let's go for a ride."

I cruised back the way we had come until the pink glow and gray awning of the Monkey came into sight. The bright taillights of a silver sports car parked directly in front of the entrance spilled red on the dry asphalt. Its passenger door stood open. I slowed before the intersection to intentionally catch the stoplight.

As Tracy and I sat at the light in Hemi-rumble silence, Mona and Hosco came out of the club together. She was wearing a beige trench coat. Her shoes implied she was still wearing her dancing outfit underneath. Hosco hadn't changed his undertaker suit. As he walked, it moved loosely around him. The *Idiot's Guide* advice on how to hide weapons came to mind.

Both car doors slammed and the interior lights went out. The low car moved forward. My light turned green, bathing Tracy's tan and sequins in the color of money. I pulled away slow to keep the exhaust quiet, and maintain as much distance between the two cars as I could.

"That Mr. Hosco has a very nice car."

Without looking my way Tracy said, "If you like that sort of thing."

"Are you going to work for him?"

"I prefer banker's hours."

Hosco stopped at a red light. I didn't have choices so I pulled up behind him and hoped he didn't associate the grillwork of a vintage Barracuda in his rearview mirror with a guy he had punched recently.

"Where to?" I asked.

"Sixth Street," Tracy said. "Straight for a couple more lights, then left."

A man in a dark brown suit and hat stepped off the curb and into the crosswalk in front of Hosco's car. He was wearing large sunglasses, as if channeling Elwood Blues. Seemed like I was part of a trend. Through the slanted rear glass I saw Hosco nuzzle Mona's ear, and her lean away.

"You seem to like blues," I said.

She turned in her seat to face me. "Depends on who's playing it. I find it releases tension."

The pedestrian reached Hosco's low hood.

"You get tense counting all that money?"

The man stopped.

Hosco's brake lights glared in my face even through the sunglasses. He was kissing Mona.

"We have machines for that," Tracy said with a laugh.

The man's arm pumped into and out of his jacket.

My eyes locked onto a fat gray tube. Silencer. That meant semiautomatic. And a magazine with rows of bullets.

Mystery novels had real-life applications.

The tube pointed at Hosco's windshield.

"Oh shit," leapt out of my mouth.

Tracy turned forward.

A giant bottle of champagne opened.

A spider web appeared in the windshield of the Ferrari.

Tracy's hands raced each other to her face. She breathed, "Rosco!"

The champagne opened again. Mona screamed so loud in the silver car I thought she was in my lap. Another champagne popped. The brake lights of Hosco's car went out.

I let out the clutch.

Easy.

The Barracuda crept forward and tapped the silver car near the rearing-stallion logo of the Ferrari Corporation. I could hear Mona screaming over the sound of my engine. The gunman's sunglasses turned toward her. Tracy yelled something into her hands I couldn't understand.

I stomped on the gas.

Both rear tires screeched as they spun into smoke and heat, the old Chrysler Sure-Grip differential doing its job.

The gunman's face snapped up.

The silver car accelerated toward him.

The low front bumper hit his knees and tripped him onto the shiny hood. I kept my foot pinned to the floor and accelerated both cars through the red light. He slid off the driver's side and landed in the street, scrambling to roll away as my Barracuda swept past.

With no one holding the wheel the silver car drifted right. I swerved left to pass and checked my mirror. A pewter sedan made a right turn from the cross street. The gunman was on his feet, yanking open its back door. The Ferrari coasted up the curb and over a fire hydrant that snapped off and geysered water into the chassis as the airbags deployed.

I couldn't see Mona.

I turned right at the next intersection, left at the next, right at the next and stopped at a pay phone stuck to the side of a brick building advertising bagels. I shut off the car, ran to the phone, punched 911, put Toe's leather jacket over the mouthpiece because I had seen it done in old movies and yelled, "Accident on South Clinton Street. A car hit a fire hydrant." I hung up, sprinted back to my car and blasted away, breathing hard, sweating, and trying to make my brain focus. I had driven a mile before realizing my hand was shaking on the Hurst shifter...and Tracy was sitting beside me stone still.

"You okay?"

She didn't respond. I glanced sideways. Her tanned face had lost its color. Even her lips were pale.

"Tracy!"

She turned toward me.

"Directions to your place."

She shook her head.

I yelled louder than I wanted, "Where do you want to go?"

Her eyes came alive. "Stop the car."

I swung to the curb in front of Green Day Dry Cleaning — 20% off through Friday.

She opened the door, stumbled out, leaned in, her face blank, tears streaking her cheeks.

I flashed to Mona with her elbows on the windowsill in the Big Boy lot.

"Go away," she said. And ran.

Twenty-Three

I PUSHED THE HURST INTO first gear and wondered if pushing a Ferrari off of the road counted as a hit-and-run. Then I drove without attracting attention until I pulled into the main entrance of the W where Marvin was standing behind the valet stand whistling. I didn't get out. As he walked around the car his eyes dropped to the front bumper. He stopped at my window.

"How bad is it?" I asked.

He shrugged. "A little paint on your shiny chrome. Maybe a crack or two." He poked his nose inside the car. "No girl?"

"She got out after a very weird moment with a handgun, a redhead, and a silver Ferrari."

"You're into some kinky shit, Long Toe." He laughed. "You bluesmen are something."

"Say a guy wanted his car to be invisible. Maybe have a chance to touch it up a little..."

"You got tools?" Marvin asked.

"Can get them," I said, thinking about my storage locker.

"Then you just need a place." He scribbled on the back of a parking ticket and handed it to me. "Brenda has a long garage in a row of identical apartments. Tell her you're there to detail your car and will detail her Mustang too. Give her fifty for storage. She'll probably leave to go shopping."

"At midnight on a Tuesday?"

"The girl can window shop anytime; turns her on. Plus, she likes that all-night fitness place." He studied my face behind the circles of dark glass. "You okay?"

"Stunned. It happened fast."

"We'll talk later. Marvin'll be here."

He patted the roof and I pulled away. First stop was to get my tools out of the storage locker, second stop was a gas station to buy cleaning rags and paste wax. I even found a plastic bottle of paint remover. Third stop was a two-story townhouse a mile across town. A blue Mustang was parked on the street with a note under the windshield, handwritten in sparkly pink ink: *T. Moved my car for you. Garage is unlocked. Gone shopping. — Brenda*

I checked the address on the ticket and pulled up to the correct door. The headlights revealed a brass Master lock hanging on a flap hinge. I got out, yanked on the lock and it opened. I swung the door up to reveal a concrete floor and a narrow garage that ran the entire length of the townhouse, leaving room for two and a half cars so long as they were parked bumper to bumper. A box spring and a mattress stood against the right wall beside a stack of brown boxes.

I pulled my car to the back, being careful not to touch the box spring, leaving six feet in front of the bumper so I could work. I killed the engine and sat in silence, my heart rate still not back to normal.

I faced the empty seat where Tracy had been and heard her gasp, "Rosco!" Of all the possible reactions to a gunshot...seemed strange, but I wasn't enough of a shrink to know what it might mean.

I got out and went to close the door. On the inside wall was another note tacked beside a hook that held a ring with keys and a tiny teddy bear. The bear was wearing a yellow shirt with Marvin on the chest in red capital letters.

For my Blue Beauty. — B

Brenda was on top of the situation. I pulled the Mustang in and closed the door. There was a mated latch on the inside, so I slipped the shackle of the brass lock through the hasp.

Then got to work.

The Ferrari paint was barely more than a silver scuff on my chrome, and came off with the remover. It hadn't been much of a push once Hosco's foot dropped off the brake pedal.

I polished the bumper, the rubber push bars, the front lights — everything that might have touched the Ferrari. First with my power drill's attachment, then by hand, using the better part of two hours working under a single naked bulb.

Brenda must be having a heck of a workout.

I wiped down my entire car with detailing spray then set to work on hers. It had been recently washed, so I polished the wheels and sprayed every inch of the sea of blue. I did the best I could on the carpet with the mini-vac in my toolkit; then focused on her dash, instruments and windows, finishing at a quarter to three with my adrenaline running low.

I rolled a fifty-dollar-bill inside her key ring, and hung it on the inside of the door.

I stored my tools in the trunk, took my guitar, and thought about Mona's phone. Decided to take it with me, then locked the Cuda. I debated, but took the keys with me too, including the spare; no one had reason to start my car.

I replaced the padlock outside in its semi-locked state so Brenda could get back in, and started the long walk to Victoria's. After two blocks I pulled the sports-car hat off my head, stuffed it into a trash container, and put the sunglasses into a pocket of my jacket.

The night air cooled my head around my ears. I missed my hair.

A taxi slowed as it passed, but a cabbie might remember me, so I kept walking even though I felt exposed to a thousand windows hiding men with long-barreled rifles pointed in my direction. Would there be witnesses? Would a stranger provide a description of Long Toe Fowler as his face hit the pavement?

The *Idiot's* advice *don't lie to the cops* should have a footnote: *don't fantasize about bogeymen.*

So fast. And a silencer. Who bothered with a silencer?

More cars went by, including a sleek silver Jaguar that made me do a double take. None slowed, or even seemed to notice a musician walking home after a gig. I switched the guitar to my other hand; hummed to the tattoo of Toe's borrowed boots on Chicago concrete; wondered why Hosco had sent messages to the phone in my pocket.

When I reached the door to my room there were three notes sticking to it.

Tommy, Stop in soon.—Penny.

Hey Idiot, Did you see the late-breaking correction on the Murder City News website today? – The librarian you probably don't remember.

Tommy, What did you find out? Kimmy (P.S. You owe me $2.00)

Kimmy? I thought she liked Slim.

I locked the door and put the chain in place. Didn't bother to turn on a light, pushed the guitar underneath the bed, and fell onto it in Long Toe's shiny pants.

I woke an hour later, sweating from a bad dream I couldn't remember. I turned the TV on with the sound muted, tossed the black leather sport coat Lizz had provided across the bed, and started flicking through channels. The third one had news. In ten minutes it showed a silver Ferrari. Both doors stood open. Water poured out over the rocker panels like a fountain in front of the Capitol building. The ticker along the bottom mentioned gunshots, car crash, anonymous caller.

There was no one in the car.

I waited.

One person pronounced dead at the scene; no details being released. A passenger had been taken to the University of Chicago. Stable condition. No mention of a second car. Or witnesses. A picture of three bullet holes in a windshield replaced the fountain.

I got a glass of water that was hard to swallow. Kept watching.

A round-faced white guy with colorful government flags on either side of him pounded on a podium with a clenched fist. The text said he was Alexander Clyde, campaigning for city council on the slogan: Rein in Chicago Crime.

"Plenty to go around, Alex," I whispered.

I watched for twenty minutes, but the info didn't change. Alex pounded the podium again. The ticker said he was for safer streets and neighborhoods.

I switched it off. Thought of Tracy running away, flopped onto the bed, and pulled the quilt over my shoulder.

$ $ $

When I woke again my watch was digging into my leg, the room glowed gold, and I had a headache. I rolled over. Ten o'clock Wednesday morning. I had missed breakfast, so I took a shower to wash away the face-thinning makeup, shaved off the goatee, and dressed as Tommy Cuda. My hair was darker than it had ever been. I thought about having Lizz dye it back while staring at the leather coat, bronze pants and pointed boots. What were the odds I would want to become Long Toe Fowler again? It had been a ruse to hide from Hosco. That game was over. And Toe had been at the scene of a crime. I folded the clothes, found a plastic bag for sending laundry down, and packed everything inside.

Then headed for the Bourgeois Pig with Toe's clothes under my arm.

The Pig had a flat-screen TV turned on for the breakfast crowd. I was almost finished with a pair of eggs and another chapter of the *Idiot's Guide* when the Ferrari came on, followed by faces. Rosco Hosco, 34, financier, shot to death. The only witness an elderly man sitting at a bus stop who said the Ferrari had raced forward and swerved. Beside Hosco was a picture of Mona Meyers, an employee of the Pink Monkey who had been in the car. She was in stable condition after being injured by the opening of a side airbag. The next story showed the sketch of a woman wanted for questioning in the Detroit case.

I choked — but maybe only because I had seen Mona at Frisch's. A phone number to call displayed along the bottom of the screen. I was staring at the sketch when Penny arrived.

"How was your evening?"

"Not as much fun as the night before."

She blushed, her face pure like a young girl's before she starts reading *Vogue* articles about the cosmetics required to be attractive.

"Stop that. Did you find anything out? And what happened to your hair?"

"I was in disguise. I talked to that girl before the accident. She complained her boyfriend doesn't fulfill her needs."

"That's not news." She laughed.

"You see the guy who was shot?"

She nodded. "They've been running that story every hour. Must be a slow news day."

"That's the guy who punched me."

"You didn't have to shoot him." She held a straight face.

"Funny."

"You're close to something ugly." Her eyes danced around the café. It was in morning slowdown between the early rush-to-work crowd, and the slacker brunch-for-lunch group.

"It gets worse. He worked as DJ at the Pink Monkey. Seemed to be in charge of the music, and maybe hiring girls."

She watched me. "What aren't you telling me?"

"He called himself Z-Rox."

She blew out. "Wow."

Facts fell into place like a winning Tetris move. The sketch was Mona. Mona really was Hosco's girl. Mona had been in Detroit. Mona was lying.

"Penny, you're a smart criminologist." She crossed her arms. "If a person wanted to pass information to the police to protect a client, how could he do that and remain anonymous?"

"Call the hotline number they show on TV."

"Yeah, but that's monitored and recorded. I bet they can subpoena the recordings under the right circumstances, maybe identify the caller."

"They can subpoena anything, for a hundred reasons. Some of them even legal." She held up the coffee pot.

I nodded. Caffeine seemed like a good move; science had shown it could improve performance on cognitive tasks. "So how then? They can trace paper, inks, the impact of a typewriter. Even something called touch DNA that requires just a few skin cells from a doorknob or pair of panties. Anonymity seems impossible."

"Panties? My my, aren't we the super spy?" She grinned.

"Bedtime reading. As you've probably guessed, I don't know much."

"You kiss okay," she said.

I watched her eyes. Brown. Warm. Liquid chocolates wanting to be tasted.

"Haven't you forgotten about that yet?"

She shook her head. "Silly boy. Who's your target?"

I frowned.

"Who do you want to send info to?"

"The lieutenant who called me."

"Call his assistant from a pay phone. Use a voice changer to sound like a woman. There's a bunch you can buy as home safety devices."

"No wonder you're in grad school."

"Or use the synthetic voice in your cell phone to speak the info you want to send."

"But the cameras on traffic and street lights can record video of who was there at the time of the pay phone call."

"True. So you better be smart. Or..."

I drank coffee and waited.

"Just go in, talk to him, tell him what you know. Develop a relationship."

"Risky."

"You drive a car a half-century old, no crumple zones, no airbags, no ABS brakes, and you worry about risk?" She laughed and waved goodbye as she headed off to another table.

I grabbed my package and headed for the library. On the way I turned on Mona's phone to see if I could make the voice say what I wanted. It hooked up to a Wi-Fi network named *Emanon.* A new message popped in.

Your number is prevalent in the late Mr. Hosco's cell phone. Perhaps you could help me.

It had come from someone named Theo.

Twenty-Four

I TURNED THE PHONE OFF without doing the voice test and kept walking. Lizz was alone behind the counter when I entered at eleven-thirty.

"Well?" she said.

"Your work performed beautifully." I put the bag on the counter. "Okay to give you these things here?"

Her mouth shifted side to side like she was tasting something good. "Sure you're not going to be Toe again?"

"Not for a while. Things happened."

"Like every other day," she said, glancing in the bag. "You like the hat?"

"Sorry, I had to get rid of it fast. And I still have your sunglasses."

She slipped the bag off the counter and bent to place it on the floor. When she came back up I noticed her black hair had a broad red streak in it.

"New hair?"

"Yeah, I have it replaced every time I change the oil in my car. Runs better that way."

"New look for you."

"Lots of redhead talk these days. Thought I'd see if it helped me." She pushed a two-inch square of newsprint at me. Her fingernails were painted black, except for the ring finger. It was orange-red, a close match to the stripe.

I read the article. It was a correction to the story of the Detroit catacombs. They had found plates for twenty-dollar bills, but no other denomination.

"You know anything about printing money?" I asked.

Lizz leaned her elbows on the counter. She wore black frame glasses with little red dots near the temple. Her light gray eyes floated under gray eyeshadow, spotlights compared to her usual wells.

"Sure do. I print mine right after changing the oil."

"Your money runs better that way?"

"Faster."

I laughed, held up the article, she nodded, so I slipped it into my jacket next to the circular sunglasses.

"Took an art of money course in college," she said. "Mucho thought goes into designing that paper."

"Do you know how big plates are? You know, the plates that article said are missing."

"They'd fit in your pocket if you were old-school printing one bill. If you're printing a whole sheet like the big boys do, your pants would fall down." Her eyes narrowed. "Thinking of starting a new business?"

"Can't, I'm busy seducing my local librarian."

"How's that going?"

"Slow. She's too smart for me."

"College girls. Maybe you should go for a stripper."

I shrugged. "Too tall. Thanks for the article." I wandered back to the room full of computers and sat at one where I could watch Lizz work the front desk. The room was empty, making me wonder when anyone used it. Then I remembered a question, so I walked back to see Lizz.

Her eyes widened when I arrived.

"You're an artist. What kind of people have purple irises?"

"Well...people who like flowers, aliens from the far side of Uranus, and thems that wears tinted contacts to mix with their normal eye color to produce purple."

"Thems that wears?" I asked.

"Stripper talk," she said.

"Elizabeth the First. Woman of many faces." She held a straight face. "What about, um...structural undergarments?"

"Sounds like something for building bridges."

"You know, not revealing lingerie, but the other things girls wear."

"The Victorians were big on corsets to enhance the female form. All manner of torture devices were devised in the early twentieth century, mostly by men trying to get rich. Most of that went out with the arrival of hippies; though it's found new life in the all-things-retro movement." Her eyes danced and her mouth parted. She stepped away from the counter and ran both hands down her body. Today her jacket was green and the tight pants were black. "You trying to tell me something?"

"You of the golden-ratio body of a Greek goddess? Of course not. I'm trying to understand why women wear such things."

She stepped forward and leaned her elbows on the counter again: something she was short enough to do without bending at the waist.

"Multitudinous reasons. She desires a smaller waist, or the appearance of a bigger bottom. Enhancement for small breasts: up and together. Or a smoother look under clothing so no little bulges of blubber stick out."

"All ways to look different than she really is," I said.

"Ever notice a girl wearing high heels? Now why would anyone do that? To be taller, well, I might do that, but who wants to be tall? No, they want the walk: short steps, swaying hips. Do they like walking that way? No, it's slow and troublesome." She held her finger and thumb together. "But it triggers a tiny primal switch inside what men use for brains that causes them to chase the wiggle."

"You're saying clothes are shape-changers that create triggers?"

"Distracts you from parts she doesn't want you to notice."

"A kind of warfare, like multiplayer computer games?" I said.

"And here you thought Sun Tzu was writing about bows and arrows when he said, 'All warfare is based on deception.'"

"I should have gone to art school."

We laughed and I returned to my corner computer thinking about women's undergarments. When I got there I checked Yahoo for news.

I learned Rosco Hosco had lived in Detroit, worked as a bodyguard, trained in Tae Kwon Do (that explained the power of that punch), and frequented Tigers baseball games. There was nothing to explain a silver Ferrari that cost more than most people earned in years.

His suit hung on my mind. Some guys had physiques that were hard to fit. Or maybe he liked them loose. Still…a former bodyguard might carry weapons.

The girl in the car had been moved; she was now being treated over at Mercy Hospital on South Michigan Street, three miles from the Monkey. I'd bet the media had staked out her room.

And I knew someone calling herself Mona had hitchhiked to Chicago. I wanted to tell the cops, even though I was working for her.

I went back to the counter where Lizz was staring at a thick book that contained beautiful color reproductions of paintings from something like the Middle Ages. Golden halos made the three people on the left saints; I wasn't sure what that meant for the guy on the right.

"How would you get information to the police?"

"Hey officer, could I talk to you for minute?" she said, without looking up.

"Anonymously."

"I wouldn't."

"Meaning?" I asked.

"If I wanted to remain anonymous, I'd keep my mouth shut. Any connection and it's bound to be revealed. Recordings.

Digital footprints. You've heard of Eric Snowden, the NSA, leaked celebrity nudes on the Web. Therefore, no connection."

"Spoken like a concerned citizen."

"In a highly litigious, network-based, surveillance society," she said, still reading.

I leaned on the counter and thought about the risk. I hadn't done anything; I was just storing a backpack for a friend. I didn't know what was in it. I laughed at myself.

Lizz lifted her eyes. "So?"

I blinked.

"Are you taking your librarian to lunch?"

"Sorry, I slept late and just had breakfast. I'm way behind."

"Ah." She waited.

"My schedule is in chaos. I would love to ask her to dinner, but if I miss she'll be mad."

"You're psychic. Maybe you could stop by her place of business around six-thirty if you're free, and ask her then?"

I grinned. "That's a great suggestion." I patted my jacket. "Thanks for the article."

"Don't mention it. We librarians live to serve."

Twenty-Five

I PUSHED THE DOUBLE glass doors of the library open wide and stepped into a lack of sunshine delivered by floating mood suppressors the color of steel wool. I visited my friend the Buckeye fan and got the rainbow music box. That reminded me the second box was still in my room. I also bought a pocketknife with a two-inch blade and white pearl handle for five bucks.

A different guy at the counter buzzed me into the climate-controlled storage area. The backpack was exactly as I had left it. I strapped it on and left, not even taking time to visit my gold guitar. I tried to connect the dots of everything I knew, and ended up with a cool fear in my chest as I counted bodies: two in Detroit, a guy in a Ferrari at a traffic light, cop with a dog. Not to mention a missing redhead with amnesia.

Lizz was correct: *remain anonymous by keeping mouth shut.*

Outside of the climate-controlled storage building with Mona's pack on my back, I realized no one had ever shown me an ID. The thought that maybe there *was* no Mona Meyers stayed with me all the way to Victoria's.

I waved to Victoria at the front desk as I passed. She held a hand to her ear reminding me to call my mother. No notes on my door. I pulled the curtains, locked myself in, dragged a chair over, stuck it under the doorknob for added security, and sat on the floor. I took the packs of money out two at a time and lined them along the bottom drawer of my dresser. Then I stared at the backpack standing upright on the floor.

I squeezed the top and the sides. Blocks of foam inside the nylon made it hold its shape even when empty. I lifted it with one hand: a few pounds, certainly less than ten. I felt along the inside, looking for a seam that was stitched poorly. I pounded around with my knuckles.

And got nowhere.

I hated to destroy the pack, but there was only one way to be certain.

I flicked open the pocket knife, preparing to cut the seams to reach the foam blocks, when I realized I hadn't checked the outside pockets where the phone had been. I unzipped them and found at the bottom of the upper pockets a stiff flap hiding a slender nylon zipper. Opening it provided access to a block along each side of the pack. I worked the one on the right out; it was two pieces of stiff foam wrapped with tan packing tape.

I cut the tape carefully on three sides and separated the two blocks like a clam shell. The reversed impression of a hundred dollar bill etched in shiny metal gaped at me. I don't know how long I had been staring at it when a knock at the door stopped my breathing. I folded the blocks together, put them in the drawer with the money, and stuffed the backpack into the drawer on top of the cash.

I pulled the chair away from the door.

"Yes?"

"Sorry if I woke you, Tommy," Victoria said. "There's a Lieutenant Braden here to see you. What should I tell him?"

I wanted to say: *Tell him to check Hosco's gun.*

"I'll be right down. Just, uh, give me a minute to dress."

"Don't rush. I'll serve him coffee."

Victoria's footsteps moved away.

What was that saying about anything that can go wrong?

I scanned the floor for a stray bill or scrap of paper, then opened the two drawers and tossed my clothes on top of the backpack. I splashed water on my face, toweled it off, and combed what hair Mikel had left me. I took a deep breath, looked in the mirror, whispered, "Don't lie to cops." I heard Lizz's voice telling me to protect my client if I wanted others to hire me. Right at that moment, however, someone else hiring me seemed like a worse idea than going back to Walmart and changing oil for people who couldn't spell it.

The music box I had picked up as a gift sat on top of the dresser beside the key-hiding carousel. I slipped it into the inside pocket of my leather biker jacket and headed downstairs, the little dancer etched into the ceramic cover giving me comfort.

Braden sat at a table for four on an enclosed porch that I had thought was part of the dining room, but was now partitioned off by a wide pair of French doors. Victoria was giving us privacy, or protecting her other guests. He was facing the window, his blue suit reflecting a sunbeam that had managed to cut through the cloud cover. His tie was tight enough that his neck hung slightly over the collar of a clean white shirt. He was maybe fifty, and didn't get enough exercise. When I walked up, he pushed a copy of my flyer across the table, and invited me to sit down with a hand gesture.

"You were looking for someone," he said. "Did you find her?"

I sat facing him. "Found someone. Not sure it was her."

He rubbed the bridge of his nose with his thumb, as if he sometimes wore glasses and had the habit of pushing them into place.

"You're not sure?"

"No." I kept my answer short so I wouldn't say too much. It was the absolute truth; I wasn't sure at all.

He tapped the picture. "Tell me, Mr. Cuda, why do you want to find this girl?"

"Because she asked me to."

He leaned back in his chair and lifted his coffee cup, but didn't drink.

"How long have you known her?"

"Today is Wednesday. I met her Saturday afternoon."

His eyes stayed glued to me. I hoped my body language translated to: *this guy is telling the truth.*

"Would you mind elaborating?" he said, then drank from his cup, casual, relaxed, encouraging me to talk too much.

"I picked up a hitchhiker in a Big Boy parking lot back in Ohio." I pointed to the flyer. "Red hair, bangs, green eyes. Attractive."

"Why were you there?"

I almost said 'because I was hungry' but caught myself. "Vacation. I'm on my way to California. Want to see the ocean, maybe try surfing. Was thinking of following old Route 66, if I can find it."

He nodded, put his coffee down. Calm, slow motions. Nothing to excite me. I forced my mind away from the dresser in my room.

"She first wanted to be dropped off in South Bend to see a friend, but changed her mind when I mentioned Chicago." I paused to give him a chance to ask questions. He didn't. "She rode to Chicago with me. We had dinner, stayed at the W...one room, two beds."

His mouth flicked toward a smile then relaxed. "Sounds like a nice vacation."

"Sometime during the night, she quietly left. Because she wasn't there in the morning."

"No forwarding address? Phone number? Email?"

I shook my head. "She left this." I took out the picture I had put on the flyer and handed it to him. "There's a note on the back."

He studied the picture, flipped it over. His lips moved like he was about to speak, but he didn't.

"I figured it for a game: a test to see if I would make the effort." I left out the part about Mona hiring me to find someone, and that someone turning out to be her.

He nodded. "And did you find her?"

"A woman named Sorana called after seeing my flyer. She works at the Pink Monkey."

His jaw shifted. "Go on."

"She insisted I visit the club, then quizzed me. Why was I trying to find Mona? Where had we met? That kind of thing. I must have passed, because she had me wait at the bar until Mona took the stage."

"I see."

"Then I talked to a girl named Mona Meyers, which was the name the hitchhiker gave me. Mona the dancer, also a green-eyed redhead, to my eye was the hitchhiker with fewer clothes."

He handed the picture back to me and said: "But."

"But Mona the dancer didn't know Tommy Cuda, or claimed she didn't. She also hadn't been in Ohio on Saturday, she had been working at the Monkey. Had chicken for dinner. Took the skin off."

"So you found the wrong girl?" He glanced at his coffee, but didn't touch it.

"There are a fair number of green-eyed redheads in the world. Odd that two would be named Mona Meyers. For the record, no one showed me ID, so many things are possible."

His eyes shifted to the window. I could feel his cop brain working, generating options. Eventually he said: "A girl playing games with you, wondering if you would chase her. You did and that's all she wanted. Lost interest. Or, two girls. The hitchhiker gives you the name of a stripper. Coincidence. Or she knows the stripper. Or maybe just lifted the name off a website."

I nodded. "I didn't get any other calls, so I took the flyers down and recycled them." Hosco hadn't called; he stopped by. Still not lying.

He smiled. "Most residents aren't so considerate of our city."

I recalled my own list of options. "Maybe it's not a game," I said. "Something is really wrong. This Mona could have a psychological problem. Or —"

"The obvious," he said. "She was doing drugs like millions of other people, and doesn't remember anything about you. Hard on the ego, but happens all the time. What do you do now, Mr. Cuda?"

"The W was too steep for my budget, so I have a room here for a week. Thought I'd see the sights, and find Route 66."

"Do you have a number where you can be reached?"

"Just here. I think you already have it."

"No cell phone?"

I shook my head. "Don't own one."

His eyes studied me from below low lids. I imagined he was thinking that everyone has a cell phone, so I must be lying. Maybe had been lying all along.

"I'm vacationing old school: no cell phone, paper maps, cash. The way it was in the sixties when my Grandfather fought in Vietnam. I'm fed up with electronic gadgets beckoning me like a stable boy."

"Unusual approach, vacationing in the past." He paused. "I stopped by because I was in the neighborhood. This girl," he tapped the picture on the flyer, "was in an automobile accident last night."

I shifted in the chair and hid my secrets behind a forced frown. "Oh no. Is she okay?"

"Better off than the driver. I was hoping you could tell me something about her."

"I don't know much. We had very little conversation after I found her."

"How about before?"

"We talked about the music scene in Detroit while driving. Small talk about bands, songs. She asked me why I listened to 'old crap.'"

Braden grunted. "Did she have anything with her?"

I envisioned Mona standing at the Big Boy exit.

"A backpack like hikers carry. No suitcase. No purse."

He nodded. "A not uncommon way to travel." He clasped his hands and leaned forward onto both elbows until his stomach touched the table. Speaking more softly, he said: "Mr. Cuda, you're new to Chicago. No one knows your face." He paused, studying me. "You may have occasion to see things, overhear conversations." He leaned back, paid close attention to his coffee while he drank, placed the cup back on the table. "These might be things I would want to know about."

I studied the closed French doors; made sure no one was within earshot.

"Are you asking me to be an informant?"

Twenty-Six

MY FINGERS FOUND THE coffee cup Kim had left on the table for me as I watched Lieutenant Braden make his way to a dark blue Ford sedan. I waved as he drove away, but he didn't look. The coffee was lukewarm. He turned left at the corner and my heart rate finally began to slow. How did killers stay so cool while talking to the cops? I had felt naked just chatting with a detective about a hitchhiker.

I drank the coffee fast and stopped at the front counter. Slim was counting money.

"Hi, Kimmy," I said, using the name she had signed on the note. "Is there a chance you have wrapping paper?"

She stopped counting; stared into me for a long moment. "Foreign guy visits you here at Victoria's, punches you at a club, then his face shows up on the TV news. Now a cop stops by asking questions. And you want wrapping paper?"

"You know about curiosity and cats?" I said.

"Ha ha." Her gaze didn't shift.

"Detective Braden asked about Mona; I told him what I told you. He didn't mention anyone else."

She waited.

"Neither did I," I said.

Her slender jaw shifted side to side, touching her long hair.

She blinked. Nodded. Put her money away. Then said: "Sending mom a souvenir?"

"A friend in the hospital. Trying to cheer her up."

"Not attempting to seduce some poor girl?"

I placed the box on the counter. The ceramic image of the ballet dancer faced me. She was a redhead.

"Well, there is the librarian."

"You don't seem the librarian type."

"Neither does she."

Kim laid out white tissue paper. "I have plain-Jane green or festive balloons?"

"Green, please."

"You know, you shouldn't think of it as seduction," Kim said. "More of a journey where you both succumb to the power of love, a mysterious thing."

"Curious."

"Huh?"

"A *curious* thing. It's from an old song."

"Oh. It's one of those meme thingies bouncing around in my head. I don't know where it came from."

"Isn't that dangerous?" I said, putting my finger on white ribbon as she tied a bow.

"Love?"

"Ideas bouncing around in your head that you don't know where they came from."

She shrugged.

I said, "Huey Lewis."

"Huey?"

"Your meme. It's a line from a song by *Huey Lewis and the News*. California band. *The Power of Love* was used in a movie."

"Maybe that's where I heard it. What movie?"

"*Back to the Future*."

"Back to where?"

"Maybe you didn't see it." I smiled.

"Do you want a card with this?"

"Sure." She pushed a miniature folded card across the counter. I wrote a simple get-well-soon message, and taped it to the top of the package. "You seem happy today."

"I'm always happy."

I stared at her. Might have been the color of her hair, but she sort of resembled the proverbial deer in headlights.

"Oh, that. He backed off a little."

"Figured out that getting you to college is a good plan?"

She shook her head. "No. He has to work double shifts twice a week for the next month. I laughed when he told me."

"You didn't? How heartless."

She grinned. "Couldn't help myself. I told him very seriously, 'You can't. I'm off those nights, who will cook my dinner?'"

We laughed together at her boldness, but part of me worried for her future.

On the sidewalk in front of Victoria's I considered the distance to Mercy Hospital. Being on time for Lizz. And the secrets hiding in my dresser.

I arrived before two o'clock, which was good because visiting hours ended at three. A woman in a tan skirt and sharply pressed white blouse standing behind a gray counter told me room 438, then glanced at a computer screen, and said I couldn't go up unless I was immediate family. I held the wrapped package in my hand and tried to show concern.

"I'm not officially family...yet. Could you ask Mona if she'd like LT to come up? I have something special for her. No flowers, she's allergic to flowers." I shook my head. "Best if she's not around flowers. But if she's too tired, I'll come back later."

Her brown eyes softened and she reached for a desk phone off to her right. I drifted around a modest lobby: thin brown carpeting, rows of much thumbed magazines on a glass table, empty chairs waiting for visitors, and pictures of a group of men with a spade beside a huge artist's drawing of the building I was standing in. Somehow, artists made stone and glass look really impressive on paper. I heard the receiver clunk into the cradle.

"Take the elevator to your left. Don't excite her, she's had a head injury."

"Thank you, ma'am. Have yourself a pleasant day."

She beamed. I dashed for the elevator. The door to 438 stood open six inches. I couldn't see Mona so I pushed gently. The bed was tilted up. Her eyes were closed. One was bruised and her nose was swollen, though she remained quite beautiful. I stepped inside. Her eyes opened. Her lips twitched.

"Come in. I want to see the guy I'm going to marry."

I let the door go easy back to its propped state and walked over to the bed, holding the package.

"Sorry about talking my way in."

"That's okay, I haven't had visitors. The doctor says I have to rest and it's boring stuck in this little room." She squinted. "I've seen you before."

"Last night. The great blues guitarist Long Toe Fowler, at your service."

"Shiny pants. Yeah. I liked your hat."

"We were auditioning. I was sort of incognito."

"A good thing to be in the Monkey." She shifted in the bed, stretched. "What are you doing here, uh...what's your name?"

"My friends call me Toe. I brought you a present." I held out the green package.

"Stand close," she said. "I want to be sure it's not a bomb."

"Bombs are bigger."

She laughed again, a gentle soft sound.

I moved so close to the bed I could feel heat from her body. She untied the ribbon carefully and handed it to me. I let it float into a white wastebasket. Her red hair was pulled tight behind her head and her bangs clung to her forehead. I noticed a bit of tattoo behind her white and blue hospital gown, just below her collarbone. She undid the tape carefully, unfolded the paper and handed it to me.

She stared at the box. Then, holding it on her palm, lifted the lid with her other hand. Tinkling sounds of Tchaikovsky filled the room. She let it play for a long time before lowering the lid so slowly I heard the pin engage to stop the music wheel. Her green eyes were damp. She reached out with her left hand, grabbed the sleeve of my jacket and pulled until she could kiss me on the cheek.

"How did you know?"

"I didn't. I only saw you on stage one time."

She pulled her gown lower. The tattoo was a pair of ballet slippers whose ribbons rose up to form a heart.

"I wanted to be a real dancer." She paused, stroking the tile figure on the top of the box. "Life didn't work out that way."

"You are a real dancer. I saw you on stage. You put your heart into it."

"No one goes to the Monkey for the dancing."

"Your life is a work in progress; you'll find a way. Open a school. Become a choreographer. Hey, you could go to Hollywood and be the body double who does the complicated dancing for movie stars — like they did in that old *Flashdance* flick."

That made her smile.

Footsteps in the hallway coming hard and fast interrupted my motivational speech.

"Close your eyes," I said, and flipped up the lid on the music box so it would tinkle, then dropped to my knees, bowed my head and mumbled, "Our Father, who art in heaven, hallowed be thy..." The footsteps stopped. I wanted to turn around, see who was checking on Mona, but I kept at my mumbling. Mona did a good job of resting her eyes. The box's music slowed.

Footsteps started up again, and faded away.

"Are you a priest?" Mona whispered.

"Altar boy. I never got promoted."

She laughed softly, but her eyes had a dreamy complexity. Shock maybe, or the head injury.

"You haven't told me why you're here," she said.

"I danced with you."

"That did it, huh? Smitten. Kneeling at my feet." She closed the lid on the music box. Turned it over. Wound it with a sound that reminded me of a socket wrench.

"It happens," I said.

"Uh-uh. Not this time. I can see it in those bright boyish eyes. You want something."

"I have questions that only a beautiful green-eyed redhead can answer."

"Do me a favor first." She motioned with one finger. I leaned in close. She whispered, "You're a musician, right? I need drugs."

I got a white plastic chair from the corner and brought it close to the bed so our heads would be at the same level. I held her left hand in case I didn't hear them coming the next time they checked on us.

"You became an addict instead of a dancer?" I asked, trying to begin at the beginning.

She spoke quietly, like she was inside a confessional in a cathedral. "Real dancing jobs are hard to find. I made piles of money dancing upside down with a stupid pole. Then my shoulder wouldn't stop hurting." She stared at the wall beyond her toes, looking frail and small in the whiteness of a chemical-clean hospital room. "A doctor at the emergency room prescribed Oxycontin. Told me to rest my shoulder. That stuff worked great." She paused. "But I knew a guy." A longer pause. "He promised to make me famous. I didn't get much rest."

"Opiate pharmaceuticals catch out a lot of people. Was that part of your plan, work in a club until you found a real job?"

She turned to me. "I had a little girl's dream, not a plan."

I thought of a gold guitar. And Walmart. Then pushed my attention to Mona's bruised face — dreaming would have to wait.

"Drugs are dangerous with a head injury. Painkillers can mask important stuff. That's what I've read." I didn't mention my knowledge derived from stories about a Dr. Watson.

She breathed in. "I've got to have *something*."

"Have you told the doctors?"

She shook her head in slow motion.

"Will you? Ask them to move you to rehab?"

"Stay longer? You're crazy...even for a priest."

"Stay. Get help." I squeezed her hand. "Be protected from whatever happened last night."

She met my eyes. "Rosco traveled. Wouldn't take me along like he used to. He liked having me around. But sometimes..."

"Something went wrong?"

"We were doing so well. He even had a Ferrari."

"Too well?"

She frowned and the bruised skin near her right eye became a deeper purple, but she didn't say anything.

"Musicians travel too. I was driving across Ohio, dreaming of seeing the Pacific Ocean. A pretty girl with a backpack and tight jeans held out her thumb as I was leaving a Big Boy parking lot."

"The original double-decker," she said, her eyes somewhere else.

"She had green eyes just like you. A fabulous smile, like you. She rode with me all the way to Chicago with her long red hair flying in the wind, then disappeared in the middle of the night. But she left a note."

Her face didn't change.

"The note said 'Find me.' And was signed, M. She even gave me money for expenses while I searched."

"She disappeared?"

"While I was sleeping. Told me her name was Mona Meyers."

"But that's my—" Her eyes widened. I was no expert, but her expression started as surprise, shifted to fear, and landed as anger. "That bastard."

I waited, hoping emotion would fuel her tongue.

"Business trips my dancer butt." Her jaw set. "Stupid Hugh Hefner." She punched the mattress with her fist hard enough to make the bed shiver. Then whispered: "Good riddance."

I wasn't following.

She released my hand, face taut, spat out: "Mala."

Which sounded like a war cry in an ancient African language.

Twenty-Seven

MONA FLATLY REFUSED to talk more about Hosco. Instead, she tried to make me promise to sneak drugs to her room. I beat the rehab drum, suggesting she use the accident as an opportunity to get the monkey off her back. After I had dodged promising once too often, she clammed up entirely and pressed the call button. In short order I was standing on the sidewalk in front of Mercy Hospital under a truckload of confusion.

A white police car with a long blue stripe down the side pulled to the curb next to me, facing up the street in the wrong direction. The driver's window powered down.

"Mr. Cuda?" asked an African-American woman with beautiful teeth and arms that could win a wrestling match.

I nodded.

"Lieutenant Braden would like you to come in and chat with him."

"I talked with him a few hours ago."

She held her eyes on me. "That was before you visited Ms. Meyers."

I remembered those footsteps in the hallway. Of course they were watching Mona, see who would show up.

"Sure. Would tomorrow morning be convenient?"

The door swung open and she stepped out. She had to be six feet, no heels.

"He was hoping now would be good for you."

I checked my pocket watch: two-thirty.

"If he insists."

She opened the rear door and I slid onto a dark blue vinyl bench seat wondering how many people had taken this ride in handcuffs. The view through the steel-mesh divider made me think of a shark-diving cage. A round-shouldered Hispanic cop in the shotgun seat didn't turn around or speak. We cruised past a solid wall of buildings (brick, stone, glass), then a flash of green leaves close to the car, stopping at red lights like everyone else. Pedestrians stole glances at me and moved away as if the car were carrying an infectious disease. I mulled over my conversation with Mona, and what parts of it I was going to tell Braden.

The car pulled to the curb in front of a plain two-story building with block letters on the side identifying it as the police department. A cathedral with a green roof stood across the street. The officer riding shotgun got out and opened the right side door for me. I slid across the full length of the seat and stepped to the curb, glad to be out of that cage.

The driver spoke through the open door. "Second floor, room two fifty-four. Lieutenant Braden is expecting you, Mr. Cuda." She paused. "I don't have to waste more time with a personal escort do I?"

"No, officer. I'm on my way."

Her partner slammed my door, slid in and slammed his. He pressed a cell phone to his ear as the car departed with a brief squeal of rubber. It clearly didn't have a Hemi. I figured his call was to Braden.

I crossed the sidewalk, thoughts of the dresser in my room making me less and less comfortable. Braden would ask why I had gone to see Mona. He would want to know what she told me.

I pushed through a pair of glass doors into the hallway of an office building and found two elevators on my left. On the second floor a brown sign indicated the 250 section. Voices muffled by closed doors accompanied the tap of my feet on tile. Number 254 stood open. I knocked gently on the frosted glass.

Braden waved his hand. I stepped into the small office and took a wooden chair with a green wicker back near a bookcase filled with brown folders that matched the one he was reading. He spoke without looking up.

"Did she tell you anything of interest, Mr. Cuda?"

Calmly I said, "Of interest to whom?"

He turned a loose page, letting it float into place on the right side stack.

"To you, for starters."

"She asked me to help her."

His lips moved with the words he was reading, but no sound came out. I waited. He put a finger on the page.

"Help her how?"

"She's not feeling well."

His finger tapped the page, like he was trying to remember something important.

"She is in a hospital."

"I don't mean from the accident." I paused, thinking of how best to say it. "She misses her life, hates being stuck in that boring hospital bed with nothing but saltwater running into her arm."

He studied my face, but didn't speak.

"She should be in rehab. Maybe you could help make that happen before they release her. Once she goes home..." I shrugged. The little green chair squeaked.

"Why so interested?"

"She asked me to get drugs for her. Rehab wasn't what she had in mind, but it'd be a good choice."

This time he smiled. Small, but a smile. "I see." He closed the folder. "When did you first meet Mona Meyers?"

"Saturday afternoon I picked up a hitchhiker who told me her name was Mona Meyers. But the Mona in the hospital says the hitchhiker wasn't her."

"At least your story hasn't changed. And what do you think now?"

"She looks like the girl I picked up: bangs, those green eyes, that smile. But she doesn't remember our ride. It's all kind of weird."

"Yes, Mr. Cuda, weird is a good word for it." He moved the folder to a stack of them on his far right. "Where is your car now?"

"I loaned it to a friend, since I've just been hanging around the city."

"Would you mind if we examined it?"

I recalled rubbing the front bumper beneath a single naked bulb. Maybe I could go over it again in daylight.

"Uh, sure. I'll arrange to get it back. Any special reason?"

"One." He pulled a folder from the stack and opened it, studied a sheet of paper. "Was the Mona currently in the hospital ever in your car?" He paused. "To the best of your knowledge?"

"The ride from Ohio to Chicago."

He held up the page. It was too far away to read.

"A preliminary DNA report for human hair," he said.

"You want to check my car for hair?"

"Have you cleaned it since Saturday?"

I felt my shoulders relax. This wasn't about my bumper kissing the Ferrari.

"The outside. I like to keep things shiny."

Braden returned the paper to the folder. "Ms. Meyers was present during a homicide." He paused, maybe considering how much to share with a civilian. "She remembers very little." He rubbed his chin the way people do when they're stressed. "The chief wants this homicide closed fast; he's concerned about pretty statistics. We spent all night going over the crime scene with fine-tooth combs. Ran fingerprints and a couple of hair samples against every database we have, including CODIS. That's the FBI's system."

"A homicide?" I tried to act surprised without sounding like a soap opera.

He nodded. "Yesterday evening. At an intersection near her place of business."

"A car as a weapon?"

"No. The weapon was a nine-millimeter pistol." He stood and lifted the stack of folders from the desk. "A hair matched an open investigation in Detroit." He looked right at me. "It also matched an elimination sample we took from Hoskova's passenger. We collect those for everyone present to help us make sense of the crime scene."

"I saw in the *Tribune* an officer was shot in Detroit."

He stopped, and remained motionless for a long while. I felt my heart thumping in my chest.

"An odd case of stumbling into the wrong place at the wrong time." He sighed, seemed to squeeze the stack of folders harder. "Could you bring your car in tomorrow?"

"Sure. How long will you need it?"

"Depends on what we find," he said, and motioned for me to exit the little office first.

Braden walked me to the elevator talking about how Chicago could double their police force and still lose the war on crime. As we shook, he looked me in the eye, then turned back toward his office.

I stood on the sidewalk staring across the street at the gold inlay high up on the cathedral. What an incredible piece of work, and made to stand up to that destroyer of everything: the weather. I turned the corner and headed for Victoria's on foot. Odds were good they would find Mona's hair in my car. They might even figure out the front bumper.

Entangled in unintended consequences. I should stay away from hitchhikers.

No messages on my door. I stepped inside and locked it behind me. The bed had been made. The towels on the floor were gone. I checked the drawers, pulled my clothing away, and gazed upon stacks and stacks of printed paper.

"Why, Mona?" I asked the money. The answer came back fast:

Because I can't be caught with it.

Then I better not be caught with it either.

First Z-Rox on her phone making threats. Then Theo's text message with the "perhaps you could help me" approach.

I opened the soft case, stood my blue guitar in the corner, and stacked packets of money from the bottom of the case up along the slim neck portion until I was staring at a guitar-shaped half-million-dollars. I zipped it closed, removed the two foam packets containing the plates from the backpack, and put them in another Victoria's laundry bag. With the case on my back and the plates in hand I headed out to visit my vinyl records.

When I reached the storage company, I bought a cardboard box from the wordless clerk, and rented a small locker. My walk-in room smelled like the basement of a church, but my Les Paul, books and records seemed to be happy. I moved the cash from the guitar case to the new box, sealed it with packing tape and pushed it into the hallway. I locked up the room and carried the cash to my new locker. The future was blurry; whoever came to pick up the cash didn't need to know about my belongings.

I stared into the blackness of the inside of the new locker at the box of cash, debating what to do with the plates.

I locked up 1214, put the plates into the empty guitar case, and strapped it to my back. On my way out I waved to the clerk whose face reflected game show contestants competing for the best scream.

Just after four o'clock.

The first two savings banks I visited consisted of cubicles and an ATM machine. The third was a Citibank branch with a row of small offices. A clerk wearing a white shirt and blue tie shook his head: no safety-deposit boxes available large enough to hold a guitar. I explained my desire to store important documents while on the road. He gave me box T36, and two gold keys as shiny as jewelry, then asked me to please hurry because they would be closing soon.

I put the two foam blocks, each containing a plate, into a long metal box and forced the foam down so I could lock the sliding top. I put one key in my pocket, and the other in the guitar case, trying to think of where I could hide them now that both my room and car weren't safe.

It was after six by the time I reached Victoria's. No sticky notes today. I unlocked my room. The backpack was on the bed. I tried hard to remember where I had left it.

I eased the door closed behind me and flicked the wall switch for the table lamp. The drawers of the dresser were standing open, and what little clothing I had was on the carpet.

I took a deep breath, feeling like I had just used up my luck for the entire year.

I checked the rack behind the door. My jacket and pants were hanging in a row, with the pockets pulled inside out. I considered calling Braden. And tell him what? Someone had searched my room. Found an empty backpack.

I tossed the empty guitar case on the mattress. Looked for my guitar in the corner. Not there. Found it on the far side of the bed on the floor. Picked it up, still in tune. Slipped it into the case, and under the bed. Not a simple burglary, they wouldn't leave an easy-to-pawn guitar.

Who then? A third warning from the late Mr. Hosco? Mona coming for her backpack?

I checked the window.

The curtains were closed. I parted them with one finger. The window was down, but the latch hadn't been rotated to lock it. There was no screen.

Had there been a screen? Had that lock ever been rotated closed?

I gazed down at the green grass of summer and a row of shrubbery up against the house one story below. A tree waved to me from thirty feet away. Nothing a ladder couldn't solve. I turned and studied the varnished inside of the door. Locks could be picked. There were even videos on YouTube showing how to do it.

I showered to clear my head. While rubbing my hair with a white towel I stared at four keys next to the carousel music box. Two storage units, two keys for the bank's box. Thankfully, they had all been with me.

I put on black jeans, a pullover knit shirt and leather jacket, glanced at my creepers, grabbed the boots. I stuffed the backpack into a drawer now that there wasn't anything important in it, then thought briefly about getting rid of it because it connected me to Mona. I sighed. I was already irreversibly connected to Mona. I tossed my remaining clothes into an empty drawer.

Now the keys.

I taped the locker key for the cash inside the carousel and put one deposit box key in each boot. I dropped the storage key for my record collection with Kim at the front desk, who was still happy. She promised to put it in the hotel safe for two dollars a day. Gold keys pressed into the arch of each foot as I walked toward Lizz's shop, feeling more prepared for the next uninvited guest to visit my room.

Six-ten.

I picked up the pace and reached the pawn shop in minutes. I asked how he thought Ohio State was going to do in football this season. He grinned and pointed out his scarlet and gray suspenders, told me his son had studied architecture at OSU, and was now working for the City of Chicago renovating hotels. He promised to take good care of my little horses.

I slipped the pawn ticket into my pocket, turned left, and fifty yards later was stopped at the corner by a television visible through the window of The Goal Sports Club. The big screen was showing a closeup of a silver Ferrari parked on the sidewalk. Water flowed over the curb like a Chinese fountain in monsoon season. I tried to read the closed captioning, but it was too far away.

I lifted my chain: six twenty-three.

I went through a door with a soccer net painted around it into the bluster of a happy-hour crowd trying to drink, talk and watch TV all at the same time. I turned sideways to elbow through bodies to get closer to the Ferrari. The sound was low, but a voiceover said Chicago had triple the murder rate of New York and was ahead of Mexico City and Moscow, as if they were competing to qualify for the Olympics. Violent crime was up double-digit percentages from the previous year. Murderers were bolder, openly shooting victims in Chicago streets. Most offenders were male. But when women killed, they chose a spouse half the time, which seemed like a sort of gender equality gone mad.

The Ferrari disappeared and the screen went black for a few seconds before a pudgy head in a blue suit popped on. He ranted about budget cuts reducing the effectiveness of the great Chicago police force, and he slipped in what an excellent job he was doing fighting crime with fewer and fewer resources. Then he quoted per capita statistics on the reduction of homicides over the past five years that made me wonder how a homicide was defined, and by whom.

"You like our mayor better than football?" a woman's voice asked.

I turned to see a waitress with a yellow scarf wrapped around her neck holding a tray of empty glasses.

"There was a Ferrari up there a second ago."

"They show that a lot. Not everyday you get to see a wrecked Ferrari, even in Chicago. Can I get you something?"

I was going to be late.

"Can I buy a bottle of wine and take it with me?"

"We don't have great stuff, but sure. What would you like?"

"Red, but not heavy."

The camera backed off to reveal four men sitting on a dais behind the mayor's podium. The mayor had moved on to taxes and how lack of investment was crippling Chicago, which was contributing to the increased crime rate. People pressed up to the dais on three sides. Behind it, a dark-haired woman was speaking to two men in tailored business suits.

I moved closer to the screen. Glasses. Long skirt. She turned to look up at the mayor, who was asking the public to report any information regarding the shooting.

Tracy?

I hadn't figured her for a girl who would hang with city officials.

An electric shiver accompanied the thought that Tracy had gone to the police and disclosed everything she saw the night Hosco was shot. Maybe that was the real reason Braden wanted my car.

The waitress returned with a bottle and two plastic wine glasses on her tray.

"Sorry I don't have a bag," she said.

"You're an angel for bringing glasses."

I paid and tipped her in cash, then made my way back to the street with a glass in each pocket, the wine bottle inside my half-zipped jacket, and Tracy Kane on my mind.

It was six thirty-seven.

Twenty-Eight

LIGHT FLOWING THROUGH the glass door of Get Over It made a rectangular block on the sidewalk. I zipped up my jacket with the image of Tracy and a politician still behind my eyes and walked in.

"You're late."

Lizz's voice from somewhere in the rear of the store.

"But I bear gifts," I responded to the empty room.

She stepped out from behind a maroon room divider wearing a variation on her librarian outfit: brown leather heeled boots; skin tight emerald green pants; brown jacket.

"Those pants are amazing."

"For an amazing girl," she said. "What did you bring me?"

I pulled the bottle out of my jacket and placed it on a shelf displaying pairs of leather gloves in the bright colors of Ferraris. "And..." I removed one glass from each pocket and placed them next to the bottle.

Her lips drew together. "Hmm...so alcohol seduction is your next move?"

"A toast to the prettiest librarian in Chicago."

"You've seen them all?" she asked, grabbed the bottle and disappeared into the back room.

I shook my head not knowing quite what to make of Ms. Lizz, but enjoying the movement of emerald sheen. She returned with an opened bottle and poured for both of us.

"To idiots everywhere," she said.

I laughed, touched glasses, drank. She chugged hers, placed the plastic glass beside the bottle and took mine out of my hand.

"Are you free for dinner?" I asked.

"So long as you take me to a place I can wear these pants."
She turned toward the back of the store, motioned for me to
follow, and pointed at the barber chair where I had been
remodeled by Mikel. "Have a seat." I slipped onto the cracked
leather cushion. The overhead spotlights that lit the clothing
went out. Then the neon OPEN sign in the front window
flickered off.

"Closing?" I asked.

"Have to, the proprietress is busy."

Light leaked in from the street, but the room was so dark her
pants had turned silver. She moved behind me, her boots
tapping a floor covered with wide white marble tiles. The front
door clicked, locking electronically. She took my left hand,
eased it down and tied a pink scarf across my wrist and around
the arm of the chair.

"A gentle reminder," she said. Then she did the same to my
right wrist, with a blue scarf.

"A reminder of what?"

"To not touch." She stood directly in front of me sipping
from my wine glass, then held it to my lips so I could drink too.
We went back and forth until the glass was empty. "Would you
like another?"

"I can wait for dinner."

She smiled and placed the glass to the side. Tiny colored
lights popped alive in the ceiling.

"We use these to see how our outfits will look in nightclubs.
Hold tight."

I gripped the arms of the chair, not knowing how else to hold
tight.

She placed a boot onto the built-in metal footrest and
launched herself up, straddling me. Her gray eyes, encircled by
black eyeliner and metallic shadow, floated above the
phosphorescent glow of her lips. Orange light glinted from the

diamond in her nose. She gazed into me, then took my face in both hands and leaned close.

She didn't kiss me.

She moved very near. Images popped into my head: summer rainstorm, snow-capped mountain, open meadow of wildflowers in sunlight.

"Love your perfume," I managed.

"I like subtle," she whispered, so close I felt warm puffs of air against my lips. "I hate people who act as room fresheners."

Her hands were velvety warm. She turned my face gently left and right; her pupils, dilated in the darkness, following as my head moved. Our upper lips touched and she froze in position. Hers moved microscopic distances across mine. Then our lower lips touched, and she repeated the motion. She backed away, moved forward and made contact, did the microscopic swirl, backed away. She slipped her coat off to reveal a deep purple shirt with glistening sequins, tight and curved over full breasts she had kept hidden until now.

The chair moved. I smiled, thinking I was imagining it, until the low hum of an electric motor convinced me we were truly rotating beneath the colored lights.

She pressed forward so slowly I could feel the flesh of her lips spread against mine as they compressed. Her right hand left my face. I started to lift my arms to embrace her, but the scarves said no. Her breath came faster, she pressed harder, the chair spun, her tongue touched my lips, teeth, tongue. She moaned soft and low and long, the way a tugboat in the distance blasts its way through fog. Her eyes closed, her body rocked against me in rhythm with her breathing until she arched and flexed and pressed her open mouth full and hard against mine for what felt like hours.

The spinning chair slowed. Her breathing softened. She pulled away. Her lipstick was askew.

She smiled. "What would you like for dinner?"

"The second course of that."

"Boys. Not satisfied with first base?"

"Appetizers make me hungry."

She slid off my lap. "An excellent start." She untied the scarves and disappeared behind the room divider.

I stood with some difficulty, and walked on weak knees to the restroom in back where I removed lipstick that was glowing in the dark on me too, making it easy to find. If her plan was to ensure I would remember our first kiss, she had succeeded like Neil putting the first bootprint on the moon during the Apollo 11 mission. I locked eyes with my mirror image. Had I just taken a small step, or a giant leap?

The colored overhead lights blinked off and she came out from behind the screen wearing her jacket and a long purple scarf around her neck, black hair flowing down over it on all sides, face luminescent.

"You look like you just won the state lottery," I said.

"The manufacturer named this rouge Afterglow. Do you like it?"

I coughed. "You, uh..."

She took my hand and we walked to a restaurant in Lincoln Park called North Pond that had begun its life as a warming hut for ice skaters. Surrounded by lush greenery, overlooking placid water, and imagining an open fire's warmth as snowflakes fluttered, the hustle of Chicago disappeared like a Vegas magic trick. Salads, sizzling steaks and the eyes of the shortest librarian I knew filled the next hour. While sipping a 10 Year Tawny port Lizz picked from the menu, the key in my right boot nudged a toe.

"If you wanted to hide a key, where would you put it?"

"Hide from whom?" she said.

"Everyone."

"Good guys *and* bad guys?"

A Ferrari windshield shattered behind my eyes. I nodded.

She watched me over her glass. "This is difficult. If you hide it, say bury it in your garden, someone may see you hide it. Or they can torture you until you tell them where it is."

"Avoiding torture is a plus."

"But if you give it to me, they force you to tell them who has it, then they torture me until I tell them where it is."

"Looking good so far," I said. "Glad I asked."

"Plots of entire movies revolve around how things are hidden. So why have a key at all?"

"I have something in my possession that needs to be secure."

She put her glass down and lifted both elbows to the table. Her purple top had shiny narrow straps that I thought were called spaghetti but resembled ribbons on a birthday present. My eyes found her shoulders.

"You like skin, don't you?" she asked.

"I like *your* skin."

"Ah, the kisses are beginning to work. So you put this object of great desire in a safety-deposit box and now you have a key you want to hide."

"Have you been following me?"

"Easy guess." She held out her hand, palm up.

"And you think I have this key with me?"

"Of course. In fact, you probably have two because leaving them in your hotel room would be risky and stupid." She curled her fingers twice.

I slipped a boot off and dumped the key onto the floor under our table; bent over, picked it up, polished it with my napkin and dropped it onto her open palm.

"Good quality," she said. She closed her hand around it and let it fall between her breasts, the way actresses did in Hollywood glamour flicks. "I'll take care of this one."

I shook my head. "No way. I can't put you at risk."

"Sitting here having dinner with you puts me at risk. Some old guy with a bad haircut is probably taking our picture right now and texting it to his boss over a secret NSA-proof network." She finished her port. "Besides. I'm only going to have it for one day." She stood and walked away, her jacket hanging on the chair, the purple shirt clinging to her slender waist.

Her joke about the photographer rang in my ears. If I could observe Mona, her friends could observe me. I focused on the street across the pond. Cars passed, several were gray sedans. Doorways and windows capable of hiding a person were everywhere along the street. I thought about the gunman's eyes focused on Hosco. What would he remember? Long Toe's goatee? A bronze Barracuda? He had leapt into the back seat of a sedan. His driver had eyes. Were there other witnesses in that car?

Lizz's return with a sheet of paper and an envelope put the brakes on my paranoia train.

"Who can you mail the key to that will for sure mail it back?"

"They'll think I'm crazy."

"Tell them you're doing a study of shipping performance."

"My economics professor at Oberlin would be into that."

"Good," she said. "That will add institutional delay."

She slid the envelope across the table. "Do you know his address?"

I wrote his name and the address of the college. I figured they could find the Economics department.

"No return on the outside, put that here." She shoved a sheet of paper at me. "Write a note asking him to mail it to your hotel."

I scribbled a letter and retrieved the second key from my left boot. Lizz gave me the four-inch piece of Scotch tape stuck to the back of her hand. We taped the key to the bottom of the page, folded the letter and put it in the envelope. I sealed it and noticed a Forever stamp in the corner.

"You carry stamps?"

"Do I look like a prepared-for-anything Boy Scout?" She smiled. "Our waiter found one in the office for me."

We strolled back to Get Over It, the night growing cooler and the conversation revolving around why Chicago felt like no other city. I argued it was the proximity of a deep freshwater lake and its unique boating community. Lizz said it was the historical location of Chicago as the commercial gateway to the west where the flow of money attracted the special kinds of people who follow money: inventors, captains of industry, liars, thieves, politicians. I was countering that it was really the evolution of the Chicago electric blues sound led by Big Bill Broonzy, Magic Slim, Willie Dixon and a host of other African-Americans that made the city unique when we arrived at her car: a red Fiat coupe half the size of my Barracuda. Her green pants shimmered in the halogen brightness from the streetlight, and reflected in the glossy red paint.

"You two would make a good Christmas present."

She smiled. "If you pay attention, you won't have to wait that long."

"Do I get a good night kiss?"

She shook her head. "They get me all excited, then I can't sleep. But you can have a hug." She opened her jacket so I could slip my arms inside. I squeezed her tight and let her perfume conjure mountainsides and waterfalls again as my hands felt her small frame through the thin purple cloth.

"Thanks for a unique evening," I said, preparing for her smart comeback.

"You're welcome, Tommy," She slipped behind the wheel and started the car. The window rolled down in jerks as she turned the crank. "Long Toe was a good choice." The car angled out of the parking spot and stopped.

I walked up beside the window, leaned over, lifted my eyes to hers.

"You're on first. No action until we meet again."

The car moved six feet and rocked to a stop. I walked up to the window a second time.

"Including onanistic rituals." She blew me a kiss. "Talk soon."

The car purred into the street.

Twenty-Nine

I STOOD ON THE PAVEMENT thinking about the location of a shiny gold key for half a minute before the meeting with Braden swirled into my head like an Ohio funnel cloud. A DNA test could put Mona in the catacombs, and in my car. But she didn't remember. I had visited blues clubs years ago, enjoyed shots of tequila, didn't remember much. If alcohol could do that to me, what was Mona's habit doing to her?

I headed for the lake, brewing ideas, hoping Marvin would be at his station. I stopped to watch huge swells undulate like a giant sleeping animal. So incredibly peaceful, yet able to erupt into the wild hallucinations that inspired sailors' sea chanties. Deep hidden power.

Like an idling Hemi.

I laughed and turned south toward the W. My feet felt better without keys pressing into them.

Maybe Mona was lying because the items were hot. So, admitting knowing me was dangerous.

Which made *being* me dangerous.

I took a long breath and thought about my twenty-ninth birthday party and Betty and the gang back in Ohio. I resolved not to go back to Walmart just because it sounded safe and comfortable right now.

Marvin was sliding behind the wheel of a long black BMW when I walked up the driveway. He stopped halfway out.

"We gotta talk," he said. "Be right back." And the car accelerated away.

I sat on the hard edge of a huge flower pot holding a skinny tree that had just been watered and daydreamed about my ride in Lizz's rotating chair. Marvin came jogging up the walk wearing all black under his red valet vest, startling me back to Chicago reality.

"There's a problem," he said.

"Someone stole your last song and now it's number one but you're not getting royalties?"

"Hey hey, not that big a problem. It's your car."

"I know. The forensic cops want to go over it."

"That's a different problem." He rubbed his chin with long bass-player fingers. "It's been stolen."

"My car?"

"Yeah man. Last night."

Long Toe had been followed. "Is Brenda okay?"

He nodded. "Perfect. Saw the whole thing, about three a.m. Fried the lock, backed her car into the street. She keeps the keys hanging in the garage because she always loses them. Drove yours away."

"They knew it was there."

"Had to. No way to see into that garage. Hey, Brenda loved the detail job, thanks."

I nodded. "What'd she see?"

"Bunch of stuff." He dug into his pocket. "Shot this from her window with that little pink camera I bought her for her birthday." He handed me a SIM chip. "All here in HD, baby."

"Did you look at it?"

He shook his head. "Will if you want. But at this point I figure Marvin's ignorance might come in handy later."

"Probably better if I don't mention Brenda either. Cops milling around and stuff."

"She's cool if you need her. But if you don't." He shrugged.

I held the chip up. It had *16 GB* printed on it.

"How do I explain this?"

"Explain what?" Marvin asked, followed by his signature smile.

"Good plan. I'll let you know what I find. You write that song for Anna yet?"

"In progress, but Brenda thought maybe it was getting a little personal. I'll stay on it tonight. When we going back?"

"Not sure, had a little mishap." I outlined the story of the gunman, Ferrari and fire hydrant for him.

"Mona in a Ferrari? You're getting close to some heavy shit, brother. Watch your back."

"Someone saw the Barracuda."

"Yeah, and followed you. They'd have to be fast if you tucked it away like you said."

"Why not stop me, take it away?"

He shook he head. "Don't know who they're dealing with. Boosting a car is easy. Safe."

"You know, they saw Long Toe. Maybe he should lay low."

"Good idea. Your identity has been compromised, Agent Toe. Go see that little lady you told me about."

I laughed, though he was right. "I'll go see her tomorrow."

"First thing, dude." He pointed a finger at me. "First thing."

I walked south toward Victoria's, glancing over my shoulder every few seconds. If someone was tailing me, I couldn't ID them. When I reached the B&B I walked around the block twice; no cars made turns to stay with me.

It was almost eleven when I unlocked the door to my room and hesitated with my hand on the knob, remembering the backpack on the bed. I shook off the little spike of fear, feeling stupid, and pushed it open. Antiseptic air carried me back to Mona's hospital room.

I stood in the doorway, my shadow cast in front of me by the low light in the hallway.

A woman's voice said, "Hello, Tommy," so softly I could barely hear it.

I stepped inside, closed the door and pressed my back against it, one hand still on the knob. A sliver of synthetic moonlight from a streetlamp sneaking between the curtains painted a white stripe across a pair of shapely legs. Behind the stripe, a silhouette sat motionless: taller than Lizz and wearing a hat like Long Toe's; only rounder, as if it had been inflated with a tire pump.

I said: "You're trespassing."

"I thought you would like me in your bedroom."

"You're supposed to be in the hospital for observation."

A long hesitation. Then: "Too much like prison."

"Do you need a place to stay?"

"No. I wanted to touch base."

I reached to the wall and flicked the switch up. Nothing happened.

"I unplugged the lamp. This way, no one can tell we're here."

She was right, given everything that had happened, a certain amount of paranoia was called for. I took a step and sat on the end of the bed.

"Touch away."

The fingers of her left hand stroked her neck below her ear. Her hair must have been tucked up under the puffy hat. "There are complications."

I waited for more; it didn't come. "A silver Ferrari?"

She was quiet. Then reached out and pushed the curtains together. The sliver disappeared; her silhouette was now barely visible.

"That's one," she said. "I wanted to pay you."

"What for? I don't know why you left the W, or wanted me to find you, but here we are."

She crossed her legs. She might have folded her hands on her lap. Now I could see the edge of a tall boot. "My luggage is empty."

She had poked around.

"This room didn't seem secure." I grinned even though she probably couldn't see my face. "Guess I was right."

"Hotels aren't safe..." her voice drifted off. Which side of unsafe she had been on, I wasn't going to guess. "Is my secret in a good place?"

"Yes. And I'm holding expenses down."

"Men and money." The silhouette remained still, except for the left hand near her neck. "Here in Chicago?"

I debated how much to tell her. Then remembered it was her stuff, and she was my client.

"Yes."

The big hat nodded in the darkness. She shifted in the chair, her body barely a shadow in front of the window. "How long will you be in Chicago?"

Braden's question. "Now that I'm unemployed, I'd like to head west in a few days." I thought of Lizz's marathon kiss, figured I should get out right away, or I might not get out at all. Then remembered my car had been stolen.

"I'd like to hire you for another job," she said, more softly than before, almost fearful.

I shook my head; the bed squeaked. "Can't. Found out I need a license to do private-eye work in Illinois."

She laughed. "Store my luggage. Would that cost much?"

Chicago had its good points, but I hadn't counted on nine-millimeter fireworks.

"Maybe you could take possession of your property. I'm more involved than a traveling-through guy should be."

"Me too." A car hissed by outside. She didn't speak until its sound disappeared. "We know things."

We did. And we were learning more. And I didn't care for any of it.

"So you want me to hide your stuff?"

"Out of sight is out of mind. *Level 42* sang about that."

"There are songs about everything; minstrels carried the history of mankind in their heads for thousands of years. Since you would be my client—"

"We would be all confidential."

Probably not true for a hack with no license. "Is there an option?"

"We could turn everything over to the police."

My threat meter jolted red, but it wasn't her voice. It was subterranean. Something I knew I didn't understand.

She added, "You could grab everything and blow town."

"That's no way to treat a client."

She giggled. I hadn't ever heard her giggle.

"So, we have a deal?" she asked.

I had come this far. "Standard rate. Two hundred a day plus expenses. Call the donut money a storage fee."

I heard shuffling in the darkness. Hands reached over the table like a blackjack dealer. She stood, made taller by the inflated hat; crossed the room, leaned close. I felt a hand on the back of my neck, and another on my leg. She kissed me quickly on the mouth; then a whisper near my ear. "Thank you, Tommy."

She glided silently away.

I saw a lovely silhouette as the door opened, then swung closed.

Thirty

ON THURSDAY MORNING a tiny sunbeam snuck past the curtains to illuminate a row of bills fanned across the corner table. I had left the light off the night before on the chance that Mona's paranoid intuition had been right. Now, curiosity pushed me to the table to count with my eyes: two thousand dollars. I picked up the first one and did the checks, including the color changing ink. I examined the next, and the next.

All real.

Mona didn't want me passing fakes around Chicago.

She had searched my room, had she found...

I went behind the door and dug into my jacket. Her cell phone was there; she hadn't even asked about it. Of course she had another phone; this was a throwaway. Maybe she had been planning to track the package with it.

But now I had the package.

The law cared about possession. I should have given her a receipt like my Buckeye buddy had given me. If she claimed the luggage wasn't hers, nothing said it was; therefore, it had to be mine, because only I could find it. Mona even denied knowing me. She knew I wouldn't go to the cops: too much explaining to do.

Seven-ten and one time zone behind. I went downstairs and called Mom using the card Victoria had sold me. I told her about the gigs with Marvin and she asked for a recording. I asked about Dad and she said he was still working weekends, busy with that silly stock market. I paused too long and she asked if I had really gone to a library.

"I found a little restaurant near a pond. Used to be a warming shack."

"Was that in the card catalog?"

"No, Mom. The librarian knew about it." She didn't say anything, but I knew her head was forming mom questions. "She's cute. Dark hair, gray eyes. Wears crazy makeup. Art degree from here in Chicago."

"Since you've been gone less than a week, I won't ask if it's serious."

Which told me she wanted to know. "We just had dinner, Mom. And she helped me with some research."

"Thomas Benjamin doing research? Do you even know where the library is in Gates Mills?" She laughed.

I hung up feeling better. While I was standing there inhaling to determine what was being served for breakfast in the dining room, the pay phone rang. I stared at it. Kim came bounding around the corner and stopped short.

"Should I answer it?" I asked.

She held up a finger and grabbed the handset.

"Victoria's Victorian, how may I help you?" She watched me as she listened. "One moment please."

She covered the mouthpiece with her palm and whispered, "It's lieutenant Braden asking for Tommy Cuda. Are you in?" I took the handset and waited as she ran around the corner, fawn-colored hair flying.

"Hello Lieutenant, I was about to call you, but I thought it was too early."

"Mr. Cuda. We have a shit-brown Barracuda registered in Ohio to a Thomas B. Kelsey. Would you know anything about it?"

"That's mine. Turbo Bronze sixty-five built around a four-twenty-six Hemi. My friend told me it was stolen last night."

The line was quiet for seconds.

"That could be. It was blocking a residential driveway in South Chicago. The owner called to have it removed. It's at the station now." Another long pause. "I'm afraid it hasn't been handled gently."

I closed my eyes and saw Granddad's car with no wheels, no hood, no doors...and because it was so rare, probably no engine. I had let him down big time.

"I'm sorry, I should have brought it in right away."

Braden inhaled. I couldn't tell if he was angry his investigation had been interfered with, or if the car was in such bad shape he felt sorry for me.

"With your permission we'll do the search now."

If I didn't give permission, he'd get a warrant. But that would take time, irritate him, and make him wonder what I was hiding.

"Sure. Do I need to come in and sign something?"

"That won't be necessary. Did you have anything of value in the car?"

I visualized my car in Brenda's garage. "Just tools. Those old locks are easy to pop so I don't keep much inside." I hung up and wondered if *not gently* meant the thieves had helped disguise the fact that it had pushed a Ferrari.

Maybe a silver lining to a bleak cloud.

After breakfast I started toward Mercy Hospital, hoping they would tell me something about Mona. I walked fast in sneakers, stroking the smooth back of her cell phone in my pocket like a worry stone, realizing half-way there that it might have useful fingerprints. I zippered it into my breast pocket, vowing not to touch it. If Mona's prints were on it, that would be something I could lean on.

Mona's phone made me think of Hosco's. Surely it had been with him in that Ferrari. The gunman didn't stick around, so the police should have it. Yet Theo had texted that Mona's number was *prevalent;* wanted to know if I could help.

213

I fed quarters to a metal newsstand and stuck a paper under my arm. At a corner Starbucks I thought about more coffee. The line reached the front door, so I plopped down at an empty table and turned pages. The catacombs article arrived halfway through the second section. My eyes latched onto a computer rendering of a man's face. The officer had regained consciousness and told how he stepped into a room to surprise at least two men at a machine. He pulled his automatic and was calling for backup when a shot hit him. He didn't understand who could have fired it, but the doctors made it clear trauma does strange things to memory.

To my eye, the picture was Hosco, though the mustache was missing, and he looked thinner in the drawing. I read carefully, twice, but it was unclear when the officer had regained consciousness. The article was silent on why the cops had gone to the catacombs on that particular day. I thought about guys in a shallow grave and how it all added up to a plan gone awry.

Or a double-cross.

I tore the article out and stuffed it in my pocket, leaving the paper for the next caffeine junkie. A few minutes later I was talking to the woman at the hospital who had let me in to see Mona.

"Released yesterday," she said. "Checked herself out. Not much we can do when someone wants to leave." Her eyes moved to the computer screen, then back to me. "She loved the music box."

I smiled. "Thanks. I tried to talk her into rehab."

Her eyes widened.

"Does it say anything about where she went?"

She blinked. "You're a brave young man." She typed. "She entered our outpatient option." She bent and pulled a trifold flyer from under the counter. "This describes the program in detail. She has to report every day."

"That's great. She likes structure."

The woman studied me, finally smiled. "Good luck."

I wandered out of the hospital studying the little map on the back of the pamphlet. If I had my bearings correct, Mona might be two buildings south.

And she was, sitting alone in a sunroom with screened windows that let the breeze flow through and remove the smoke from the cigarette in her hand. The music box tinkled Tchaikovsky from beside a glass ashtray. She glanced up as I walked in, managed half a smile, moved the cigarette to her lips with a shaking hand, and crossed jean-covered legs that ended in black suede boots.

"Congratulations," I said.

"You call this getting me drugs? The stuff they give me could be sold in a candy store. It even comes on a little strip of paper."

"It's the first day." I held up the flyer. "This claims it will get easier the longer you stick with it." I pointed. "Never saw you smoke before."

"I hate these, but I don't have any choice." She waved the cigarette. "They haven't banned nicotine."

I sat beside her and spoke softly. "You're not seeking a new supplier, are you?"

She blew smoke just past my forehead and closed the lid on the box. "If I had that we wouldn't be chatting. But a supplier is only step one." She rubbed her thumb and index finger together.

"You're working."

"The Monkey? Barely keeps me in groceries. I need a new place to stay. And clothes. And the heating bill when this city turns to an icicle." She paused. "I'll miss the penthouse."

"Hosco's?"

She inhaled, came closer to my face with this exhale. "He took care of things. But..." her voice drifted off as she turned to the window.

215

I waited, gazed out the window too, enjoyed the bright sunshine, and a little brown bird sitting on the edge of an empty birdbath. Eventually she filled the silence.

"Things were different lately."

"How lately?"

Her lips pursed. She flicked ashes into the sail of what I now saw was an ashtray shaped like a yacht.

"Couple months maybe."

"When did he get the Ferrari?"

She faced me, the cigarette dangling from lips glistening with pale pink lipstick.

"Month ago. Says it was the most powerful one ever built."

"New then. Must have been doing well."

"Yeah, he had something big going. Was really excited about it. Said we were *set*." Her jaw shifted left and right like it was lost. "You know, for life, in that smug way he had whenever he had money in his pocket."

"Were you?"

"Us?" Her eyes found the little bird, still waiting for his bath. "No. He was distracted. Jumpy. Said he was focused on the money, our future. But a girl can tell when things aren't right. I think success was going to his little head."

I waited. She didn't elaborate.

"The police found a hair in Detroit."

"Huh?"

"In an underground facility used for counterfeiting money. They found a red hair."

"Lot of redheads in the world." Her smile wasn't much more than a twitch. "Some of us are even natural."

"This strand matches yours."

She dragged on the cigarette. "How do they know that?"

"I think they borrowed a bit while you were in the hospital."

She flicked the ashes off. "Can they do that?"

"You were in the Ferrari. They needed an elimination sample for everyone present. Ran a match against Detroit for some reason."

"I don't go underground; caves scare me. And I stay away from Detroit. Except for concerts. Went to see KISS because of that movie *Detroit Rock City*." She faced me. "Remember the song about losing your mind?" Her head danced as she sang, her voice rough from the cigarette.

I took the article out of my jacket and pressed it flat so she could see the drawing. She leaned forward to study it.

"They think Rosco was in that cave?"

"Eyewitness says so." I waited. "The hair could have come from his jacket."

Her jaw moved in small circles. "We hugged a lot."

"What was he doing in Detroit?"

She exhaled and shrugged. "He wouldn't talk about business. Liked to play that whole Godfather bit. You know, women don't get to know anything. He's from Eastern Europe; they have their own ways. He just got me the drugs I wanted, and gave me little things to do."

"Like working at the Monkey?"

She nodded. "To entertain his associates so he could look important. Show he had a beautiful woman. All that macho shit. But other things too."

I waited, hoping she would think of the other things, and want to talk about them.

"Like tonight," she said. "I'm supposed to attend a fancy dinner as a favor to someone. I don't know who, and I don't know why." The coals glowed brightly as she inhaled. "I pay cash at the door. I'm afraid to not go." She grew quiet, stared at the end of her cigarette, licked her lips; brightened suddenly. "Hey, would you escort me? It's a flashy political thing so we get to dress up." She smiled, her perfect white teeth complementing her red bangs. "We can slow dance again."

"You don't seem the political type." I moved to a plastic chair to face her. "Who do you usually go with?"

"An older guy thrilled to have me hold his arm as we walk in."

I wanted to ask, but kept my mouth shut.

"Escort stuff. Maybe a private strip show." She shrugged. "Depended on how important he was I guess."

I watched her eyes, still managed to keep my mouth shut.

She shook her head. "Never. Rosco was very jealous."

Maybe that's why he had punched me. "You have lovely green eyes."

"It's the sunlight." She smiled. "So?"

"I'd be honored to go with you. But I don't have a thing to wear."

She laughed. "Pewter gray suit. Tux is even better if you can rent one. Wait till you see my gown."

She lit another cigarette off the end of the first one, both hands shaking.

"You going to be okay today?" I asked.

Her eyes told me the jury was out. "I get more this afternoon. But don't let me sneak anything tonight; I have to be back here tomorrow. If they throw me out I won't even get their crappy drugs."

I watched her smoke half of the slender cigarette, filling the room with cheap menthol.

"You mentioned something yesterday," I said.

"My head hurt. I was pissed about my face. How can I dance like this?"

Her face was red and purple, although she had done a remarkable job of hiding it with makeup.

"What about Hosco?"

"Risky to ask questions. Maybe someone smarter than me will figure it out." She shifted her body to move closer. Her green eyes opened wide. "You want to find out for me?"

"Do you think I could?"

"People don't know you." She paused. "I'd pay you." A hesitation. "Eventually."

"What is it you want to know?"

She turned away to flick ashes at the sailboat. "He must have done something really stupid, I want to know what it was."

"And you want any money he left lying around."

She smiled around the cigarette. "I'm the closest thing he had to a wife."

Thirty-One

TWO DOZEN VEHICLES that had all parked too close to *Your Car Will Be Towed* signs lined the perimeter of a cracked asphalt lot surrounded by chain link fence and razor wire. I stood beside Lieutenant Braden, struggling to digest the state of a brown Barracuda. The outside wasn't even scratched, though the bumpers had been removed and stuffed in the trunk. Only reason I could think they were in the back was so they wouldn't attract attention lying along the road somewhere.

But the interior.

Foam had been sliced, pieces of the dash removed, seat frames bent, even the steering wheel had been unbolted and was lying on the floor of the passenger's side.

"Sorry about your car," Braden said.

"When my friend told me it had been stolen, I figured someone wanted a classic and was going to repaint and sell it. This is carpet-bombing."

"Either a gang doesn't like you and is sending a message, or they were looking for something they think you have."

"I don't own much, a few books and records in storage. I was afraid they might tempt someone to break a window."

"Windows are all good," he said. "No idea what they wanted?"

"Could they have thought it was a drug runner?"

He shook his head. "No one would use a car like this for drugs. Too easy to identify. Figure silver Toyotas for that kind of work."

I walked closer and forced myself to peer inside.

"You can touch it," Braden said. "The forensic guys were here late finishing up."

I put a hand on the roof and poked my head through the open driver's window. The rubber floor had been lifted, exposing the naked steel of the chassis. I flashed back to the day I started to restore it and realized with horror I'd have to take most of the car apart to put it back together again. At least this time I wouldn't need to overhaul the Hemi.

I went to the front and popped the hood. The battery and air cleaner were missing, but otherwise the engine appeared untouched.

"Did they find anything?" I asked.

"Load of fingerprints we'd like your help sorting out. Our flashy new lab computer thinks some are from a woman."

"Betty, my friend back in Ohio, was in the car late Friday night. And the hitchhiker I picked up Saturday afternoon." I reached into my pocket and rubbed the SIM chip Marvin had given me, wishing I had taken the time to review it before seeing Braden. "Oh, and Penny, a waitress at the Bourgeois Pig. She helped me post the flyers. She's been in it this week."

"The flyers about the girl you were trying to find?" He motioned me away from the car and led us back toward his office.

"Yeah, the hitchhiker."

He nodded. "Quite a coincidence."

I wondered what coincidence he was referring to, but let it go. "Thanks for getting her into rehab."

Braden shrugged. "She requested it. I just filled out the paperwork."

"She's outpatient. Do you think that's safe?"

He stopped walking. "Do you mean will she stay clean?"

"I was reading about her accident in the paper. Something weird went on."

He started walking again. "She happened to be in the passenger's seat. There's no law against that. I think she's told us everything she remembers, though it isn't much."

"Did she see the guy?"

"Yes and no. She saw a man with a gun, sunglasses, and a brimmed hat. So far she's done a lousy job with a description. Computer models, photos, nothing seems to help. I think it happened too fast; her short term memory got flushed."

We rode the elevator up a floor.

"Do you think she's safe?"

He entered his office and sat behind the desk. This time the top was entirely clear except for a telephone with a wire draping over the side and a jar of mostly red pens. I leaned against the wall.

"Anyone sitting in a car while the driver is gunned down is not living a safe life. And since we don't know the why of it, I have no opinion."

"If she saw the guy again, do you think she would recognize him?"

He interlaced his fingers and stared past me through the open door. "Sometimes people aren't so good when presented with too many options. A real face might trigger her memory."

"Were her prints in my car?"

He shook his head. "No, but the absence of data proves nothing."

I chewed the inside of my left cheek. "She was in the car for hours. Does that seem odd to you?"

"Wearing gloves? Holding a Coke? There are many things to do with one's hands."

Like guard a backpack containing half a million dollars.

"Could I borrow copies of the fingerprints?"

Braden studied me, but didn't respond.

"I'm confused. I know she was in my car, yet no prints?" I paused. "And suddenly I don't have a car."

"We found hair," Braden said. "It's at the lab." He picked up the phone, asked for forensics, gave a case number and hung up. "Copies are on the way. They were on your property, and who knows, maybe you'll stumble into something useful…if you keep your eyes open like we discussed." He motioned for me to sit. "Do you have identification, Mr. Kelsey?"

I handed across my Ohio driver's license, the same one Theresa at the donut shop had inspected. His eyes passed over it, snapped up to my face, back down. He held it out to me.

"Who is Tommy Cuda?"

"That's me too. Just a sobriquet though, nothing official about it."

"What exactly is your interest in this case?"

"I started out on vacation. Picked up a hitchhiker. One thing led to another."

"And now?"

"Now I'm trying to help a young woman struggling through rehab."

He opened a middle drawer and brought out a small notepad. As he reached for a pen from the cup he causally asked, "Are you in love with her?"

Lizz's long kiss popped into my head, I blinked the warm feeling away. "Mona? I hardly know her. Although we slow danced once." I smiled.

"When did you two first meet?"

"Saturday. In Ohio. Then again Monday at the Pink Monkey."

"Are you sleeping with her?"

I laughed before realizing I was being interrogated.

"No."

"So you're not her fiancée?"

I shook my head. "Fabricated story to sneak past hospital protocol."

He leaned far back. His was the first office chair I had ever come across that didn't squeak.

"I'm more curious than anything," I said. "I started out on vacation, met a dynamite redhead who turns out to be a dancer in an exotic nightclub." I shrugged. "Not my average day."

He stood without warning. "Call me if you find out anything. Especially if your new friend Ms. Meyers starts to remember what happened Tuesday night."

I went to an office on the first floor and a clerk made me sign for a manila envelope and the keys to my car. The Chrysler logo was still on the leather fob. I managed to stuff foam into the driver's seat and test the seat belt, but the back was bent away so it felt like sitting on a bar stool. I retrieved the steering wheel, found the nuts needed to attach it lying underneath, and my tools tucked in the back corner of the trunk where I always kept them. While I was working a guy in blue coveralls walked up to the driver's window and handed me an invoice.

"Pay the lady at that window," he said pointing, and walked away.

The invoice was for a new battery and installation. A note along the bottom showed Braden had ordered it.

I crossed my fingers and turned the key. The Hemi started on the first try. I left it running, found the window and paid in cash. I could have done it cheaper myself, but not faster.

I drove to the Pig and parked around the corner. I wrestled with the bumpers and managed to push them forward so I could close the rear lid. What I saw through the curved glass looked like it had been in a fight with a chainsaw. I took a deep breath and took to heart the words Granddad uttered at the start of any project: *let's see how we're going to fix this.*

Penny was in. She saw me and pointed with an elbow to my table in back. She zipped by with coffee, said, "We need to talk," then disappeared while I studied the menu. Before I had even ordered she showed up with a BLT.

"Someone ordered a Hobbit and didn't want it. Thought you might like it. On the house."

"Thanks Penny." I smiled. "Just what I was going to order."

I put the menu aside and carefully lifted Mona's cell phone from my front pocket and placed it on the table. I was a couple of bites into the sandwich when Penny came back.

"You want to talk?" I said.

She shook her head. "Not here, it's too complicated."

I almost laughed wondering how my life was going to get even more complicated, but said, "Did you study fingerprinting?"

"A whole lab section on different techniques. Still have my kit."

"Think you can lift prints off a phone?"

Half grin. "If you bring it to my house."

"And then we talk?"

"You're quick, Tommy Cuda, like that car of yours."

A boulder pressed down on my shoulders at the mention of the car. "When?"

"I'm off in twenty minutes. Got an hour before class." She ran off.

I put the phone away and concentrated on the thick sandwich, Mona's hair in the catacombs, a shattering windshield, one more gunshot in a city of gunfire. Now hair in my car. Maybe Betty's, but it might be Mona's. I was staring into an empty coffee cup when Penny danced out wearing a lavender leather jacket.

"Nice," I said.

"Thanks. I bought it from a biker girlfriend who sold her scooter."

"Did she give up riding?"

She shook her head; her short hair didn't shift a millimeter. "Nope. She bought a faster bike and switched to a black jacket with broad green stripes like a neon tigress."

I said, "You have fun friends," while thinking of a late-night jacket swap.

She hooked my arm and we walked.

When she saw the car she circled it and said, "Looks like a crime scene."

"Stolen. This is how the police found it." I opened the passenger door. "Sorry about the seat, we'll have to improvise."

She ended up lying back on what was left of the seat with her hands interlaced behind her head and the belt tight across her lap.

"You really should have a sun roof. I could watch the clouds go by."

"If I can't repair the interior, I'll put one in for you." I made a left turn, feeling the pull in my lower back from lack of support. "Since you can't admire the lovely grayness of Chicago, how about we talk fingerprints?"

She was quiet for a moment, but I couldn't see her face to know why.

"Humans leave oily residue on smooth surfaces; geeks figured out chemical ways to make them visible. We take pictures and a smart computer in the clouds knows how to match them to help identify people. Although trained humans are still better."

"It can't be that easy."

"It would be if crooks left nice fat impressions on a flat surface. When we did our class project there were a dozen overlapping prints and smears so it was more *Where's Waldo* on a topology map of Mount Everest. Why are you after a fingerprint?"

"I want to know who used this phone." I took it out by the edges and handed it to her. She held it up near the torn roof of the car.

"Loads of smooth surfaces. Have you touched it?"

"A little," I admitted. "There are text messages on it."

She rolled her head toward me. "You mean someone is trying to reach this person?"

"Yeah. I don't know who they are. Or for that matter, exactly who they're trying to reach."

"Someone misses Mona." She laughed.

I lucked into street parking half a block from the two-story building where Penny lived. She led me directly to a bedroom on the first floor.

"This is the darkest room we have. Highlighters will work better." She pulled down beige shades and disappeared into a walk-in closet. I sat on the edge of the soft double bed to wait, taking in the smell of shampoo, perfume, and leather shoes.

She returned with a case she placed on a light-colored vanity in front of its mirror. In minutes she had fingerprints glowing all over the front, back and sides of the phone. I opened the metal clasp on the manila folder the clerk had given me, and removed a dozen sheets of fine paper with four prints to a sheet.

"The bed," she said.

I laid out pages in three rows while she took pictures of the phone from a dozen angles and sent them to a printer in her kitchen.

"Be right back," she said, and trotted out of the room.

I studied the pages, trying to see differences in the swirls. Penny was right, a computer would be good at this. Maybe Braden would help.

Penny returned and added two more rows of four pages each. We stared. She moved closer. Our arms touched. We studied the images. The patterns blended in my head, although the third Braden page and the fifth Penny page became similar if I squinted.

"Do you like me, Tommy?"

The suddenness of the question startled me. I coughed. Tried to think of where it had come from. Then replied, "You're great. Thanks for helping me with this. I know you have class soon and are squeezing me in."

"You're welcome. But do you like me?"

My brain retrieved her quick goodbye kiss from a few days ago. "You're incredibly cute. The way your hair frames your face is hard to forget." I coughed again. But I could see in the mirror she was smiling.

She pointed. "That whorl, and that one."

She was right. I studied the tips of my fingers and held up the index finger of my right hand.

"This one?"

She took my hand. "Wait." She found a magnifying glass in her kit and studied my finger. "Yep, that's you. If we scan these into the computer, it will give us probabilities of a match."

She picked up two more pages and held them next to each other, then over each other, then at arm's-length. "These peaks are similar."

I agreed. Braden said they hadn't found Mona's prints in my car. Now I had a print on a phone matching a print from my car.

"Tommy?"

I turned. Penny was two inches away.

"The boyfriend was a smokescreen, right?"

"That's what I want to talk about. I don't have a boyfriend." She lowered her eyes. "I have a girlfriend."

Chicago. Big town. Pretty college girl.

"Hey, that's cool. Whatever is best for you."

Her face came up. "But I like you."

"Just not like that. I get it."

She shook her head. This time it disturbed her hair so the left side pointed out.

"I like guys sometimes." She paused. "I just don't like guys, you know, as long term partners." A longer pause. "I'm considering adding you to my bucket list."

I grinned. "A grad student already has a bucket list?"

"Life is short; you had better start yours soon. I know a psychologist who says I could be emotionally gay, but physically bi."

"And I am officially confused." I laughed to relieve the tension I was feeling, but not too much, because Penny was clearly serious.

"Think of it like guys do, a little no-strings attached roll in the hay. None of that big R relationship stuff."

No strings? I thought of Lizz driving away in her little red car.

"You're awfully attractive, Penny. And smart. Working with you is a blast."

She stepped away, her face frozen.

I said: "I'm not sure Tommy can handle the no strings part."

A smile crept onto her face. She hugged me, then kissed me lightly on the cheek.

"You're right. Guys think they can be detached, then get possessive and jealous and do crazy shit that requires a restraining order. However..."

Close up her hair contained a dozen shades of brown. I smelled cherry wine over ice shampoo.

"However?"

"I'm still considering you for my list," she said.

"Uh-oh."

She smacked my butt and stepped back. "You can say that again." She collected the papers from the bed. "I have to go to class. Let's meet back here at noon." She waved the pages. "I'll scan these and ask our lab computer for help." Then she ducked into the bathroom, still carrying the pages.

"Uh-oh," I repeated under my breath.

The shower hissed. I checked the time; worried how fast Lizz could find a tux. I stepped to the bathroom door and knocked with two knuckles.

Penny called out, "It's not locked."

I inched the door open. The bathroom was already filled with steam. Her shape was barely visible behind fogged glass.

"Did you come to see what you're missing?" Joyful laughter carried over the sound of the shower.

Her exuberance was inspiring. "Didn't want to leave without saying goodbye."

"Goodbye, Tommy," she called out, then the shower door cracked open. "Hey, when do we get to see the messages on that cell phone?"

Thirty-Two

I DROVE STRAIGHT TO the library. Luck gave me a parking spot fifty feet from the entrance. Half past four on a Thursday afternoon, on time for Lizz, but worried Chicago commuters would make us late for wherever Mona was taking me. I leaned against the bent seat, closed my eyes, and tried to do a Zen-style letting go of all thought—hoping a new one would pop up to explain why Mona was afraid to skip that dinner.

I was running barefoot between vivid green bushes eight feet high on either side. Round and round a curved maze in hazy sunlight shouting Mona's name. Staccato machine gun fire erupted behind me, I spun and spun and…was shocked to see the inside of my Barracuda.

Lizz was standing on the sidewalk tapping the windshield with the spiked heel of a leopard-skin mule. I reached over and unlocked the passenger door.

"Who's Mona?"

"Someone I only dream about because I'm saving myself for you."

She smirked. "You just made that up." Her eyes scanned the interior and landed back on me twice their normal size. "Who did you piss off?"

"Car was stolen. Cops found it. This is the leftovers."

She slipped in and struggled to sit upright. "I hope you have insurance."

"It's old. They'll want to total it."

She turned and stared at me. The shadow over her eyes almost matched my car. Then I saw the color of her pants.

Metallic and shiny, they cast her as a bronze sculpture at a gallery opening. She continued to stare.

I finally got it.

"A dancer at the Pink Monkey. Wants to take me to a fancy fundraiser. I need a tux."

Her expression didn't change and her eyes didn't move.

"I mean, Lizz, would it be possible for you to find a tux for me on short notice, preferably gray, and make me over into a guy that looks like he belongs at a fundraiser? Naturally, I will pay for everything; and moreover, be forever grateful for your assistance."

Her eyes blinked but remained on my face. "Forever?"

"At least through the end of the week."

She faced the windshield. "More accurate, but not nearly as romantic." She leaned back further and further until she was lying flat on the bent seat back. "How much time do I have to work this fashion miracle?"

"Lots," I said. "I don't have to be to the club until seven." I started the car.

She pulled out her cell phone, dialed, visually scanned my body, then rattled off sizes. She moved the phone to her chest. "You want to pick it up or have it delivered?"

"Whichever you recommend."

She put the phone back to her ear. "Delivery please." She hung up. "Get Over It," she said, and stared up at the steel roof of the car.

I drove toward her shop in silence. At the third red light she said, "So I have to eat alone tonight."

It wasn't a question, but I said, "I bet you have loads of friends; have a nice evening out. Or stay in and watch a movie." Then I realized that as an artist, she might hate movies.

"You're not getting my drift."

"I'm working."

No laugh. "At a fundraiser where they'll have lobster. I love lobster. With a stripper. And I'm not a stripper."

"You're an artist." I flicked my signal on and made a left turn. "And you may be the world's best kisser. Further research is required."

She didn't say anything, but I could see in the rearview mirror she was fighting a grin.

"I like your pants," I said. "There's something beautiful about liquid metal over curves."

"Thank you."

"They almost match my car."

"I got as close as I could."

"I didn't know you liked Turbo Bronze."

"I don't particularly," she said to the roof.

"You look great in it." I turned to face her, which I knew I shouldn't do while driving so I lifted my foot off the gas. "Really great." Then, knowing a girl might not appreciate this, I said anyway, "Even better than my car."

"That's what matters."

"That I think you look great?"

"Essentially. The male needs to be properly stimulated." She reached into the purse at her side, came back with a gold tube and applied lipgloss without looking.

We didn't talk the rest of the way to Get Over It. I parked close. We walked into her shop just after five. She closed the door behind us, and locked it.

"You're not opening tonight?"

"Later. I have a special order. One of those customers who calls on short notice with ridiculous demands and expects us to work miracles."

I kept my mouth shut and followed her to the back of the store.

"Your throne," she said, gesturing to the barber chair. She kept walking so I took off my jacket and sat down, figuring she'd have me try on sizes, or mousse my hair or something. But the next thing that happened was the lights went out except for the LED spots in the ceiling. This time they were all the color of a candle flame.

I felt something soft touch the back of my neck, then my right cheek, and a lime-green scarf floated to my lap. Lizz did the same on the left with a second scarf. A black one. A third she held over my eyes like she was going to blindfold me, then she let it too float to my lap.

"Will these match my tux?"

She stepped around to face me and shook her head, her face locked in a half smile. I noticed her eye shadow again, bronze, like the pants.

"I like bronze," I said.

She removed her jacket and tossed it on the floor, revealing a tight white shirt that let her bra show through. Her breasts held my gaze while my lips began remembering her feathery kisses.

"Your eyes are saying the right things," she said. She peeled her shirt up over her head in one motion. A bronze chain around her neck came together and disappeared into a shiny bronze bra.

"I really love Turbo Bronze," I said.

She stepped closer until her thighs pressed against my kneecaps, then reached behind her with both hands and hesitated. With her hands behind her she stepped onto the chair's footrest and then up into my lap like she had the night before, straddling me on her knees. Her bra touched the tip of my nose.

It loosened.

"Watch carefully," she whispered. The bra fell away in slow motion, allowing her breasts to flow outward. A bronze pocket watch hung between what had to be the eighth and ninth wonders of Chicago.

"You got a new watch," I said quietly.

"Open it."

I reached up carefully with my right hand and squeezed the watch until the cover flicked open. The knuckles of two fingers grazed her breast.

"It's ten after five," I said.

"We have until-five thirty." She reached down between us and came back with the black scarf. "Tie my wrists."

I opened my mouth to protest, closed it, and reached my arms around her body, feeling her breasts pressing through my shirt.

"Now my arms." She saw my confusion. "Above the elbows."

I located the lime scarf under her leg, looped it around both of her biceps and made a half hitch.

"Tighter."

I pulled a little more.

"Lean back," she said. "Tighten it and watch my chest. Stop when you like it best."

I pulled the scarf tighter bringing her arms together and shoulders back, and lifting her wonders. I pulled more. That seemed perfect to me so I knotted the scarf there.

"You do unusual things in a barber chair," I said.

She looked directly at me, her glossy lips reflecting orange light. "Love is an art form. Most people never evolve beyond finger paint."

"Ahem. Speaking of fingers."

A smile curved her lips. "You're wasting time with all this talking."

I lifted my arms and stopped, remembering our first slow-motion kiss. I lowered my hands to the chair and held on, then moved my mouth within a millimeter of her left nipple and let my breath warm it. I touched it with the tip of my tongue. Lizz's breath escaped in a sigh. I focused my attention until it was standing and she was moaning, repeating on the other side.

Then I stopped, gazed up into gray eyes under sparkling shadow, and touched her tied hands with my fingertips; micro-inching up her taut arms and over her shoulders and down her sides, touching her everywhere.

Except her breasts.

She began begging to be untied, her breasts quivering, her breath moving in short bursts.

I unhurriedly removed the knots in the two scarves.

She slipped one hand between us, used her arms to push her breasts together into my cheeks, managed to reach a hand behind my head, and began moving on my lap. I held her bare back firmly in both hands, supporting her go-horsey riding motion. She arched forward; bit my shoulder through my shirt; screamed, and collapsed against my chest.

I wrapped both arms around her, relishing the soft dampness of her white skin and the warm feeling of her heated body pressing on me. She brought her hand to my lips.

I kissed her fingers.

She hugged me hard for half a minute, whispered something that might have been Latin I couldn't translate, then jumped off the chair and disappeared behind the dressing screen. I picked up scarves, jacket, bra, shirt, and hung them over the screen.

She called out. "You better get a shower. The tux arrives at six and we have to do your hair first."

"You haven't told me about your new watch."

She came out from behind the screen wearing a tight black T-shirt with nothing under it. The watch hung on the outside over dripping red letters that said: *l'art pour l'art*. She stepped close, turned the watch over and unscrewed the back using a dime as a screwdriver. I looked in at tiny gears and springs and bracing holding everything together.

"Nice watch," I said.

"Jewel movement. Any watchmaker would recognize it as a fine piece of craftsmanship." She held it up. "Matches my earring."

Until then I hadn't even noticed one long earring made of small fragments of bronze hanging from her right ear. I got a queer feeling inside my chest. "Was it a gift?"

She grinned. "In a way." She reached up from her five foot height to my six foot with one hand and pulled my head down. "Look close."

"I see a watchtower guarding tall mountains in the dark of night."

She smacked the back of my head. "Silly. Remember the key you gave me? Kenny scanned it with his laser. Then he melted it and built watch parts with a 3D printer. You should see it put down layers of metal like a *Super Mario* midget welder. In an hour he can melt the parts and print you a new key from the CAD files." She lifted my head up. "We had an industrial 3D printer in sculpture class. I scanned half of a fresh tomato and built one in steel."

I studied the gears trying to find something that resembled the key; barely found metal the right color. I held out my hand.

"What?" she said.

"Aren't you going to give it to me? I'll trade you for mine if you need a watch."

"No way."

"You're stealing my key?"

"Storing," she said.

That word conjured *cash and plates.*

"Too dangerous."

She smiled. "Owning a watch? Or knowing me?"

Knowing a redhead. I brought my hand to my chin in the thinker pose. "It's close."

She punched my arm, shaking loose Mona's word.

"What does the word 'mala' mean to you?"

She dropped the watch down her shirt and wiggled until it settled.

"Hindu prayer beads."

Thirty-Three

I WAS VISITING RED LIGHTS on the road to the Monkey by 6:45. The gray tuxedo with a charcoal stripe felt tailor made, but my back ached from sitting upright in the bent driver's seat—or maybe I had strained it in Lizz's chair. The skeletal internals of the passenger door stared at me, the seats had been sliced, the rubber floor was missing in the back seat. I added dollars in my head, sighed, and wondered how I would ever find a complete interior for a car a half-century old.

I parked on the same street Long Toe Fowler had used and walked to the club. Anna looked me up and down, apparently approving of both the tuxedo and the way Lizz had made the hair Mikel left on top of my head flow in waves like volcanic sand sculpted by the wind. I leaned on the counter and she leaned in to get closer, her pink name tag visible on a gray sweater.

"I hear a guy is writing a song about a beautiful girl named Anna who works here."

She blushed so hard her cheeks matched the tag. "He said he would," she said softly.

"You must have done something to inspire him. He worked on it all night."

"And you are?"

I held out my hand. "Tommy Cuda, Marvin's manager."

Her hand was tiny, but the nails were long. I tried not to get scratched.

"You look familiar."

"Must be the tux," I said.

"Awfully formal for this place."

"No monkey in the Monkey jokes, please." That drew a smile. "I'm here to meet Mona."

She pressed close and whispered: "Did you see her boyfriend on the news?"

"She has a boyfriend?"

"Had. He's dead. Shot." She pointed over my shoulder. "Right down the street. A couple days ago."

I leaned an elbow on the counter to get closer to her height.

"Is there something about Mona I should know?"

"Look around. She works in a strip club. Oh sorry, I'm not supposed to call it that." She waved a hand as if it would erase the words. "She's beyond beautiful. Dances like an angel Satan would have in his entourage. And..." She shifted her eyes left and right. "Don't repeat this, but she likes candy." She sniffled. "You be careful, Mr. Manager."

"Thanks. I see why Marvin is writing that song."

Her face glowed a little. "I'll get Mona for you."

The black beads of a wide curtain swayed with Anna's passing. I counted only three empty tables. Sorana danced on the far stage. She could be in that entourage too. There was a stocky black guy built like he had been born in a gym wandering around in a dark three-piece suit. His face was stone calm but his eyes were everywhere—maybe filling in for Hosco's sudden absence, watching out for the girls.

Three soccer-player lean white guys in pants that didn't reach their sneakers came in bragging about how they were going to entertain the dancers.

"What's with the outfit, you getting married?"

The guy in the middle was grinning.

"Got a date," I said.

"Who would go out with a monkey like you?"

They laughed. I stifled my smart-aleck comeback; they might not have a sense of humor about their clothes.

"Hang around, you can meet her."

"Here?" the short guy on the end said. His head swiveled toward the club and back. "What kind of girl is she?"

"A dancer," I said.

More laughter. "Yeah, some dancing." The short guy put his hands on the back of his head and tried to rotate his hips in a circle.

"A real dancer," I said. "You know, footwork, choreography. You must watch music videos."

"Yeah," he said. "But they don't make them here."

"Tell you what." I pulled out my pocket watch, which got them chuckling. "If in the next five minutes all three of you guys don't wish you were me, I'll pay your cover charge."

"You're on," they said in unison, then formed a huddle and I had to listen to them snort and guffaw, planning some stupid strategy.

Anna arrived behind the counter. "On her way."

"Thanks, Anna. I'll put in a good word with Marvin." I dropped money in her jar.

"May I help you gentlemen?" Anna called out.

One came out of the huddle. "In a couple of minutes." He pointed. "That guy is going to pay our cover."

Anna turned to me, eyes wide in surprise.

"Maybe," I said. "We have a bet going."

The curtain parted as Mona walked through with her red hair scooped up onto her head in a swirl of architecture. Her gown was the blue of sapphires but it sparkled purple points of light. Sleeveless, tight and (as she waved to Anna I saw) backless. I'd never seen anything like it except during the Academy Awards on TV.

"Hi, Tommy," she said, and grazed my cheek with a kiss. "Will you hold the tickets?"

She handed me two envelopes a half-inch thick. I slipped them into my jacket. The main door swung outward and a muscular Asian man in a black suit wearing a chauffeur's cap held it open. A freshly waxed black limo sat at the curb reflecting the Chicago night. I held out my elbow. She laced her hand under my arm and an etched gold bracelet I surely couldn't afford dangled against my sleeve. We turned.

The three guys were gaping.

"Well, guys?" I asked.

Mona's gaze moved to the short pants, then to me, then back to the guys. She smiled, parting full red lips meant for kissing. "Hi boys, are you friends of Tommy's?"

They were remarkably still and sober staring at her. Each managed a quiet hello.

"We good?" I asked.

All three nodded.

"Have a great evening, gentlemen."

"Bye, guys," Mona added, waving a clutch purse coated with hundreds of glittering stones the size of the BBs I shot out of my air rifle as a kid.

Outside the chauffeur opened the door of the limo for Mona. She glided in despite the fact that the gown barely let her ankles separate. Shortly we were rolling.

"Were they friends of yours?"

"Just met. We had a little bet."

"You bet strangers? You don't seem like a risk taker."

"It was a sure thing. I bet them they would want to be me the moment you showed up."

Her eyes considered me, then she laughed and shook her head.

"How do boys come up with things like that?"

"To avoid fighting over women, which is our default behavior from millions of years of evolution."

"That's silly. There are plenty of girls to go around." She opened her purse, pushed things around with a finger like it was a tiny bulldozer, then snapped it shut.

"Mona, in case you haven't looked in a mirror today, there are precious few women who are even remotely as beautiful as you."

She studied my face. "You're serious aren't you?"

"Why would I not be serious?"

"Because guys only say stuff like that when they're trying to get laid. At the hospital it felt like you were really trying to help me."

"I am trying to help you. And you are beautiful. Plus, you hired me for, uh," I glanced toward the driver, "that project you mentioned."

"So you're not thinking about getting laid?"

I took a slow breath. "Mona, if I could look at you in that gown and not think about sex, I'd have to be dead."

She burst out laughing, then grew suddenly quiet. She turned to me.

"Men always lie to me, Tommy. No one has said anything nice and really meant it for..."

"I won't lie to you, Mona. Okay?"

She leaned closer so I could put my arm around her.

"Okay," she said so softly I barely heard it.

"You look fantastic, and seem...less nervous than earlier."

"I told them I had to go to this dinner. The doctor gave me more little dissolving strips to put under my tongue. They really help."

I gave a little fist pump and said, "Go Rehab!" happy she had sought help. Happy they had found a way to chase her monkey.

She tipped her head down and smiled with her lips pressed together; maybe embarrassed, maybe thinking I was silly for cheering her on.

The driver stopped under a pink neon sign: The Drake. The old majestic building had layers of floors in the shape of an H, and hundreds of rooms. But what was it with Chicago and pink?

242

"We're slumming?" I asked.

Mona poked me in the arm. "You behave, Mr. Cuda, this isn't the Pink Monkey."

"So we don't get to dance?"

Her eyes ran down my tux. She squeezed my thigh. "Maybe."

The driver opened the door and Mona led the way to the Grand Ballroom: two-story gilded ceiling, balcony all around like an opera house, bandstand, polished wood dance floor, and dozens of huge round tables covered in white with leather chairs holding hundreds of women in clothing that shimmered when they moved. We were stopped at the entrance by two guys on either side of a greeting girl in a black skirt and ruffled blouse.

"Welcome to The Drake, invitation please?" she said.

Mona looked at me.

I pulled two envelopes out of my jacket.

"I'm on the list," Mona said. "Mona Meyers. This is my friend, Mr. Cuda."

The girl reached under the table and came up with a leather-bound registry, flipped pages and made an entry.

"That's with a C," Mona said, as the girl wrote my name. "Like barracuda." Mona smiled at me. "The big ugly fish."

"Two plates," the girl said, then hesitated. "I'm sorry, there's no indication of prepayment."

Mona motioned with her head. I handed the envelopes to the girl, who seemed surprised by them. She slit one open and took a short breath. "Thank you, Ms. Meyers, have a wonderful evening." She didn't bother to open the other envelope.

As we strolled into the ballroom I glanced back over my shoulder. One guy held the envelopes, the other was talking on a radio.

"Would it be rude to ask how much this fundraiser costs?"

"It would," Mona said. "But since you're working for me I can share; it might be important to our project." She leaned close to my ear. "Ten thousand a plate."

"Must be good steak."

"And wine," she said, lifting a glass from a tray passing by on the hand of a waiter whose tux fit even better than mine. He stopped and waited for me to take a glass, smiled at Mona, stared at her pile of red hair, then dashed off.

"Do you have that effect on all men?" I asked.

"I wouldn't know." She sipped red wine from a huge round glass. "I haven't met them all."

I laughed and gazed up at the chandeliers. Fabulous sparkles, but I knew they weighed tons and worried an old bolt might decide to retire.

"What kind of people pay so much for dinner?"

"The boring kind," she said, "who want favors from the guy we have to listen to drone on and on after dinner."

"No sneaking out, huh?"

She shook her head. "They always have a great band with trumpets and trombones like the old days." She twirled. "Can't you just feel the elegance of the past oozing from this place?"

A woman in a silver gown sitting ten feet away looked at Mona and frowned. If her face ever launched a ship, it would sink.

"You mean like Prohibition and two World Wars?"

"No, silly. I mean music and dancing and fashion and laughter." She came closer and touched my glass with hers. "That's what little girls are made of."

"And envelopes full of hundred dollar bills."

She tilted her head down and her eyes up. "Did you peek?"

"Wild guess. You surprised the hostess."

"Rosco always gave me cash. I don't know why, but I bet it's for something important."

The overhead lights flashed and a bald guy in a navy-blue suit appeared at the front. He thanked everyone for coming and asked that we please be seated for dinner. I followed Mona to the second table from the front and pulled out the chair she indicated.

I sat to her left.

Partway through steak with a pink warm center, colorful vegetables I couldn't name, and a small lobster (Lizz had guessed right), I leaned toward Mona and whispered: "What charity is this for?"

She coughed slightly into her hand.

"Mr. Cuda, I'm not that kind of girl." Then she laughed. Four people at the table turned our way: two women twice our age, both wearing lacy gowns; and their husbands, who managed to appear twitchy and bored—simultaneously.

"You did that on purpose. Trying to cause trouble."

"Trouble finds me, I don't have to cause it." She waited while the waiter poured a golden dessert wine, then waved her glass at the room, but spoke softly. "This is politics. I bet the big guy tracks every dime. When the time comes for a favor, he checks a secret app on his cell phone and knows to the penny how important we are." She moved to drink, but lowered the glass. "In the old days you had to be seen, be elegant, make conversation. Now you're a number in an app. I bet he doesn't even have my picture in there."

"What office?"

"Representative of something. But he wants to be governor. Rosco complained..." She stared into her wine, then rotated the glass to make the liquid move. "He would say stuff like, 'LaRuche has it all figured.' And sometimes when he was drunk on vodka, he would even pay a compliment: 'That guy can see around corners.' You know, like the all-seeing eye of those Pinkerton detectives."

I tried to hide my shock. "You know about the *We Never Sleep* company? I just read about it in a, uh, library book. And Hammett, *The Maltese Falcon* guy, he worked for Pinkerton before he started writing."

"They're from Chicago, you know, really famous around here. There was an article in the paper all about their history."

"Please don't be insulted. You read about private eyes?"

"I'm not that kind of girl either. Rosco liked to drink Baltika and read the paper out loud to me. That's Russian beer; I think it was comfort food for him. He loved it when the good guys failed."

A microphone squealed with feedback and I automatically covered my ears with both hands from years of being around bands that couldn't operate a sound system.

Mona laughed. "You look like the hear-no-evil monkey." She covered her eyes with both hands, then her ears and finally her luscious lips and laughed behind them. The motion made her gown dance.

I forced my eyes up to her face.

"Naughty," she said. "Take a deep breath, here he comes."

A tall guy in a black tux and a blue shirt strode the entire width of the stage to reach the podium stage right. Everyone applauded, so I followed along, thinking blue an odd choice before remembering colors had psychology. Blue supposedly inspired honesty and trust. It would also make him stand out from the crowd of white, be memorable.

He carried himself like a fighter pilot crossing the deck of an aircraft carrier after a successful mission. He stopped beside the podium, and waited for the applause to fade. I wondered if his computerized applause meter had recognized my face and was now rating me.

His jaw had the squareness successful actors seemed to share, and his dark hair hadn't started its trip to gray. Every not-gray hair was in place except for a slight curl that wanted to head south over his right eye. From this distance I voted for brown eyes.

He smiled, and I'd swear a stage light glinted off a gleaming white tooth.

"Friends. Thank you for your kind and generous support. As you know, these are difficult times for Chicago. But you are not alone, the entire great state of Illinois faces unprecedented challenges. Challenges that require bold leaders willing to take the necessary measures..."

I tuned him out and leaned toward Mona. "What do you think? Your kind of guy?"

She watched the stage. Squinted. Tilted her head.

"He's beautiful in a magazine cover sort of way."

I found my wine glass.

"His hands look strong." She pulled a lip in over her teeth. "I wonder if he knows how to use them?" She watched longer. "I'd say, fine for a few dates, but an underperformer in the long run."

"*Under*-performer?"

"Yeah. Too pretty. Life comes easily to him. He's probably a two-minute-hump chump."

I choked on my wine. The lady in red next to me turned and frowned.

I leaned toward the frown.

"Excuse me. Do you know if Mr. LaRuche was a fighter pilot?"

She straightened. "Of course not. A man like him wouldn't waste time in the military."

A man like him. My Barracuda-owning grandfather vacationed in Vietnam on Uncle Sam's dime. He hadn't cared for the sweltering jungle, but had never said it was a waste of time.

"Thank you," I said. "He seems so confident and powerful."

She relaxed a little. "That's because he is." She turned back to the stage.

I listened.

"We must stand by America in her time of need as she faces new threats from every quarter. Godless terrorists must be stopped by superior technology. Businesses must be free to innovate in an open market. Now is the time for our great state to take action. To be a leader, and reap the economic rewards of that leadership, will require your assistance in helping me to..."

His platitudes lacked content: no specific actions outlined, no concrete goals identified. His delivery, however, had everyone's attention, as if B.B. King were playing *Happy Birthday* on Lucille. I sat back and let his melodious voice flow over me. He wasn't singing the blues; he was singing the opposite — something filled with money and privilege, intent on expanding both. I wondered if Marvin could capture it in a song.

Oh I'm spending ten long a plate / but my woman is moanin' her meat's too rare.

My sad sad baby gonna make me pay twice / buy her another fancy gown to wear.

I chuckled. Mona leaned in close.

"What's funny?"

"I was imagining his pitch as a blues song."

Her eyes flicked to the stage and back. "No one writes blues about *having* money. Are you crazy?"

"Must be. I'm working for a stunning redhead in a paint-on gown and I haven't made a pass at her yet."

She shook her head. "How do you live with yourself?"

"I just remember a slow dance."

Her lips tossed me a kiss. "When the band plays."

I grew tired of Mr. Wonderful, and let my eyes meander over the crowd. Over forty, maybe even fifty. Not quite half were African-Americans. I eventually reached the last person at the last table far in back: a dark-haired woman facing away from me. I turned around and lifted Mona's chin with the tip of my finger; imagining her beside me driving across Indiana.

"What are you doing?"

"Admiring your exquisite bone structure. Your eye's a lot better."

She slapped my hand away, "Makeup. It doesn't *feel* better." She whispered, "Admire my tits, no one will notice that," then laughed and returned to drinking.

I watched the woman in back. She wasn't paying attention to LaRuche, she was discussing something with the man to her left whose face I couldn't see. I nudged Mona with my elbow.

"Do you know the woman at the last table? Black hair, talking up a storm."

She twisted around; her eyes took a moment to focus.

"Rumor has it she's LaRuche's money bitch."

Thirty-Four

THE LADY IN RED HEARD Mona say "bitch."

"Shh!"

Mona's tiny giggle ended in a hiccup.

"Sorry, ma'am," I whispered.

The conversation at the back table went on for a couple of minutes, then the two shook hands. She stood. Her gold gown revealed tan ankles and heels the color of the gown. She walked up the far side of the room. As she got closer I saw tinted lenses.

"Undergarments," Mona said.

LaRuche was explaining how important having the right governor would be to the future of Chicago. I glanced at the woman in red. She was entranced, as if a master magician were onstage preparing to make himself appear in the Governor's Mansion.

"What?" I said.

"That walk you're staring at. Curves. The allure. I'd move like that too if I wore anything under this gown." Her giggle sounded like the bubbles in champagne.

"You mean you're not…um…she's not shaped like that?"

"Not even close. Her hair is dyed, she hides her eyes, wears fake lashes. See the eyebrows? Waxed and drawn with a pencil. Boobs might be fake too, hard to tell with that much support. We girls have loads of secrets."

"I think she has purple eyes."

Mona finished her drink. "No one has purple eyes except that cool alien in the *Outer Limits*. Remember him? The *Hitman!*"

"You're way ahead of, er, behind me Mona."

"Not a fan?"

"Of a half-century old TV show?"

"The new one, from the nineties. I watched them with my dad when I was little. Now I play them over and over on the Internet." She wrapped her arms around her body. "Gives me shivers just thinking about it: *we are now controlling the transmission.*" She smiled at me. "I love that show."

I looked at a beautiful redhead that I swore had been in my car less than a week ago, and saw a ten-year-old frightened by a television.

"You're all right, Mona."

The dark-haired woman reached the side of the stage and stood beside the curtain, mostly out of sight, not more than ten feet from the podium. LaRuche realized she was there and made a slight motion with his right hand, never missing one word of his speech. She skipped up steps, handed him something, then disappeared again.

LaRuche glanced down at his hand but kept talking, segued into the value of donations and his appreciation for everyone's support, and that he had *just this very minute* received the endorsement of the Police and Firefighters Unions of Chicago—all thanks to donors like us. Then he promised to reduce crime in Chicago when he became governor of Illinois, though he didn't say how.

I leaned close to Mona's ear and whispered so the lady in red wouldn't shush us again.

"You said money bitch?"

"Handles everything about his campaign financing. Maybe even does his laundry. That's what Rosco told me."

This time she didn't get quiet at the mention of his name.

"Is he married?"

"Of course. Single men can't get elected. First table, fortyish blonde with the bare-backed pale green gown. Two kids, both girls. Lives at the gym. Needs contacts to find her car keys.

251

That's a real tan from a machine, none of that spray-on shit."
She paused. "Hairdressers talk."

"So he's not sleeping with the money bitch?"

Mona considered me from the corner of her eye. "N-a-i-v-e."

I shrugged. "Just asking."

I sipped sweet dessert wine, got bored listening to propaganda, and wondered how Tracy had come to be LaRuche's go-to money girl. It made sense that a rich guy would need a good banker. She had been on TV behind the mayor too, so she was traveling in circles well beyond my pay grade. I counted ten tables of ten people each down the left. Same for my side meant two hundred people at ten thousand per plate. My chest felt heavy.

Two million dollars. For one speech.

Applause brought my attention back to LaRuche alternating between bowing and holding up both arms victory style. Projected video on a huge screen behind him showed a crowd at a dinner like this one also applauding, apparently so we could all feel like one family.

I felt more like a cult member.

But I applauded so long my hands hurt because no one would stop. I sure hoped they weren't trying to get him to do an encore. Mona tugged the side of my jacket.

"It's like this every time."

"Is there a contest for applauding longer than the last dinner?"

She continued clapping. "Sort of. Didn't you hear him mention how long they applauded in Urbana? That was a hint."

"This sort of thing excites people?"

She shrugged. "It's a test of loyalty."

Finally the great Mr. LaRuche paraded off and we sat down. Workers skittered onto the stage. The podium disappeared, chairs and music stands arrived. A piano rolled into position. I timed them for fun: three and a half minutes and the guy in the blue suit was back introducing *Bridges Brass* and a trumpet player named Judy Bridges. The band took off into a swinging *Where or When*. Which made me think: *Who and How?*

Waiters took orders for cocktails. People started mingling. A tall thin guy dragged a woman in pale pale onto the dance floor and did a makeshift boogie-woogie. It took three more tunes before the band slowed it down. I turned to Mona. She was sucking on the swizzle stick from something on the rocks tinted pink. Rehab. Alcohol might react with her meds. I needed to slow her down.

She upended the glass and smiled through the bottom.

I stood and held out my hand. She took it, which was good, because it helped stabilize her when she rose. Heels put her eyes even with mine, just like at the Monkey. We reached the dance floor and she moved in close. I touched the gorgeous bare back that my hand couldn't forget.

She was easy to lead, her body seeming to flow wherever I moved.

"Been to Detroit lately?" I asked.

Her head rested easy on my shoulder. "That KISS concert." The liquor on her breath drifted my way. "And...hmm...not since the big fight."

I tried to think of a significant boxing match at Cobo Center, or something else she could be referring to. Came up empty.

"Fight?"

"Yeah. I haven't gone back. Not going to."

"Were you part of it?"

"Oh yes. Big part. Rosco was never satisfied."

We swayed. I tried to imagine why a guy wouldn't be satisfied with this beautiful gentle woman. An image of Betty popped up and said: *How about me?* Smart lady. Exploration. Good times. I couldn't get no satisfaction either.

Maybe it wasn't about the girl.

"What happened?" I said.

"I don't like to talk about it."

I danced and resisted the instinct to pull her closer because she felt good. If she wasn't going back, maybe there was something she wasn't going back to.

"Could it be related to our project?"

She shifted her chin on my shoulder. Her hand moved. "I don't think so."

I remembered the percentages of homicides between lovers in that news report.

"Did someone want to kill Hosco?"

"We both did. He lied, manipulated. Then..." Two choruses of a trumpet solo passed before she said, "I guess I wasn't a good girl."

She snuggled closer. Tiny points of light swirled around us; somewhere a mirror ball had started spinning.

"The naughty part of you cut a deal?"

I felt her cheek smile against the jacket of my rented tux.

"Funny. We didn't call it a deal. We agreed to dump him and his visions of sugarplums." A pause. "She said we should disappear."

"But..."

"Rosco found me. Made big promises. Delivered some too."

"And you slowly let him back in?"

She spoke as if recalling a dream. "I was lonely. Moved here. Got a club job. She tried to help, then disappeared. I searched. Maybe wanted a new deal, have her close again..."

I danced and waited. She was talking; maybe a part of her even wanted to.

"It wasn't slow. Once I unlatched the door, my legs opened shortly after."

"Poetic," I said.

I felt her smile again. "For awhile. Then it wandered. I made him promise to never go back to Detroit." She paused, swaying like a branch in time with the breeze of the music. "I wonder what other promises he broke."

"That hair the cops found in the tunnel?"

"You said it was mine."

"If it could hold on all the way to Detroit then be smart enough to fall off."

"That sounds silly."

"Has to be yours. The lab said so."

The band stopped playing. She looked up, pulled my face down gently, and kissed me. Saxophones played a fat sweet chord in my head. I expected to taste alcohol, but this was a vortex of swirling sensual warmth. We separated to applaud the band.

"No," she said. "It doesn't."

Thirty-Five

MONA AND I SAT SIDE BY SIDE in the back of the limo for the ride to the Pink Monkey. I watched the flare of streetlights as we rolled along: light, dark, light, then dark, mirroring my understanding of Mona's world.

"On the dance floor. What you said about—"

"No more talk. Rosco is gone."

I managed to keep quiet for two blocks. "Can I buy you a birthday present?"

The reflection of her face in the window was snowman still. "Not until December."

"A Christmas baby?"

"The fourth. You have to get me separate gifts." She laughed, but sounded sad. Another block passed. "I know you're trying to help, Tommy. This week has just...life sucks."

"May I ask a question?"

"Not about the past."

I slid across the leather seat until our hips touched.

"Is Mona your real name?"

"Yes. But I tell customers my last name is Manson. That starts a conversation about the musician or the serial killer. Either way, they remember me."

"Mona, guys don't need help remembering you. We need help forgetting you."

Her mouth twitched toward a smile. "Was that a compliment?"

I laughed, took her hand and squeezed. The limo stopped in front of the club.

"Thank you for a great dinner. I had no idea what ten thousand could buy these days."

"Oh stop it, you know how politics works. Besides, I'm only the messenger, it's not *my* money."

"Whose is it? Maybe she needs a date."

"Ha ha. I'll never tell."

"Seriously. What do you do next?"

Her bare shoulders shrugged. She stared out the window at the gray-canopied entrance to the Monkey. Her pile of red hair scraped the limo's roof liner. "Maybe nothing. Maybe I'm just a stripper."

"You've got a job, you can get by. Give it time."

"No warning," she said. She pointed a finger gun at the Monkey. "Bang. I feel so alone, like my soul is missing."

I waited, letting her stare at whatever she was staring at. Rehab meds in her blood, alcohol, one hell of a week. She had reasons to feel down.

"May I kiss you goodnight?"

She turned to me. Her green eyes were wet, but she nodded. I kissed her again, like on the dance floor. Backed an inch away. Hugged her. The floral scent of her hair enveloped me. I spoke softly, for her ears only. "You'll never be just a stripper."

She dashed into the club and I stood on the sidewalk watching the back of a shiny limo pull away. The license plate read: PNKMO9. I wondered if they really had nine limos. I turned and walked inside. Anna was leaning on the counter unwrapping a stick of gum from a lime-green box.

"Do you know where Mona is from?" I asked.

"An alien solar system where all the women are beautiful."

"Same place as you, huh?"

She smiled. "Detroit, I think. She talks about roads with numbers: five mile, six mile. And, you know what? She watches old science fiction shows. Don't know what that has to do with Detroit, but she said she's never ever going back."

"People say stuff like that when they're upset. You never know."

"I hear you. I told Mr. Hosco I'd never be a dancer. But this new guy seems nicer, and they sure make more money than I do. What do you think?" She spun in a circle. "Would I make a good dancer?"

"You have the assets," I said. "Depends on if you want to spend your time working the sale."

"The sale?"

"Sure. You spend all night trying to get money out of guys while they try to get you to hang around and take your clothes off while keeping their wallets in their pockets. It's a cat and mouse game. You have to give just enough so they'll put up money to get more."

She pursed her lips. "Could be fun."

I reached in my pocket and stuck a ten in her jar. "Your first tip."

She glanced to the jar, back at me; then lifted the front of her sweater to her shoulders, revealing she had forgotten her bra today. I counted to five before she pulled it back down.

"How did I do?"

"Fantastic. But you could have had the tip for nothing."

"I know, I was giving just enough."

I was laughing and shaking my head as I walked toward the Barracuda. Halfway there I lifted my pocket chain: midnight. That made me think of Lizz's watch, the gears inside, and where it was hiding.

And a safety-deposit box.

I drove to the W and parked along the side away from the water. Marvin was nowhere in sight. I got out, leaned on a fender and stared up at a moon that was halfway to something while thinking about two million dollars for dinner, a half-million of fake paper, and metal engraving plates. Mona's kisses intruded. My mind had drifted to Lizz peeling her shirt up over her head when Marvin called my name. I waved him over.

"Oh man, your wheels."

"Cops got it back for me."

"Maybe you should shoot it. Put it out of its misery."

"You're a veterinarian now?"

He gave me his smile. I wondered if I could ever be as happy as he looked.

"I bet you know just the guy to help me."

He nodded. "Marvin knows all. Chin of the Yi family is your man."

"A Chinese car mechanic?"

"More. Much more. Wait till you meet him." He put his head through the open driver's window and whistled. "You got grade-A damage. Those dudes wanted to find something."

"Or warn me to stay away."

Marvin pulled his head out and stood tall.

"Yeah. You get close to someone's woman?"

"Maybe." I paused. "And maybe I saw something. And maybe I know something. I'm not sure, because I don't really understand what's going on."

He whistled. "This all start with that hitchhiking fireball you told me about?"

"That's what I think. But the dots don't connect."

He pointed into the car. "Someone doesn't want them connected. You watch your back." He eyed me up and down. "Unusual threads. Do guitarists get paid more than bass players?"

"Had a dinner date. Her treat."

He whistled again. "You been taking lessons from Marvin. When we gonna play some more?"

"When you finish Anna's song so we can go back to the Monkey and play it for her."

"Hard to concentrate on music in that place," he said.

"We'll make Sorana stay downstairs."

He grinned. "Open mic at BLUES again?"

"Sure. How about you give me a song list so I can practice?"

His head shook emphatically. "Blues comes from the soul man. Why you gonna practice?"

"Because my fingers don't work as well as yours. It'll help if I send a telegram ahead of time."

He patted the back of the tux. "You're alright, Long Toe. Okay, I'll make a list tonight. Give you a head start."

"Anna's thinking about becoming a dancer."

I watched his eyes take a stroll up to the left. "Maybe that's my missing verse."

We shook hands.

I parked in my favorite spot in the public garage and walked the three blocks to Victoria's. I passed two cars but neither seemed to notice a guy in a tux. No one else was out walking the street. The darkness helped me relax.

Back in my room I pulled a small glass from my inside pocket and placed it on the nightstand. It had bright lipstick in three places. Mona hadn't been wearing gloves. I knew what Braden's team had concluded, but I wanted to check for myself.

I undressed and hung the tux carefully behind the door, then stretched out on the bed in my underwear. I reached for my journal and wrote: *Buckeye carousel, watchtower in the mountains, and pony express economics,* to remind me of what I had done with the three important keys. Then Mona's kiss on the dance floor floated through my head, inspiring me to create a kiss list.

Lizz's store. The longest on record.

In front of Penny's apartment.

Mona at The Drake.

Mona in the limo.

Mona visiting my room at Victoria's.

Mona, first night at the W.

After the list I wrote everything I could remember about each one. Lizz's ran to a page and a half.

I recorded Mona's "No, it doesn't" comment.

I scribbled an entry to remind me of our next B.L.U.E.S. gig.

I began logging the damage to my Barracuda, but started getting depressed, so I switched to a more practical matter: the insurance company would want pictures. I made a note to visit my fellow Buckeye to buy a digital camera.

Then I wrote December 4, rolled over, and turned out the light.

Thirty-Six

I STARED AT A CEILING slanted upward toward the headboard, wondering why it was so high; realized I was on the top floor of an antique house. Blurred shadows of a tree branch undulated on it. I'd bet the house was older than me, maybe older than any living human. Made me wish it could talk; advise me on what to do with my first Friday on the road.

A week since leaving Ohio, job, future in the suburbs…life with Betty. Ambitious Betty Cramer and what we half-jokingly called the Squeaky Hamster Wheel. First argue. Then talk. Adjust (you do this, I'll do that). Make up (the fun part). Rinse and repeat—as if we were recycling tension in a secret underground laboratory. Maybe those discussions boiled down to differing views of the future.

Or were just the going price of a relationship.

I didn't know in Ohio, and I didn't know now. But as I lay alone on Victoria's bed, I didn't hear squeaking.

The ceiling reminded me of a certain straight smooth quarter-mile of asphalt in the country. I missed the smell of burning rubber.

Maybe there was a place near Chicago, and I could convince Willy to come drag race before I got back on the road. Then I recalled an episode of *The Big Bang Theory* and the sexy blonde neighbor who worked as a waitress telling the super-brain physicist to cut clean his years-long relationship with string theory.

Cutting clean seemed like a good idea.

Then I considered the wisdom of taking life advice from a fictional character on a sitcom, and remembered what Mona had said about collecting cultural crap in my head: *brainwashing.*

I sighed. Only to Chicago, less than a day's drive from the house where I grew up.

Maybe it wasn't about the miles.

A dark ripple of depression began drifting in so I launched myself toward breakfast before it could land. Kim came by to pour coffee wearing sunset-orange lipstick. That made me think of the list of kisses in my notebook. Then I hit the road to search for Marvin's mechanic; got lost twice. I missed the talking directions from my cell phone, but not its incessant interruptions. Eventually I found a white building with red doors and trim that was hand-wax shiny. A small sign read: *Yi Chin Mechanic* in English, Spanish, and what I took for Chinese. A dozen cars were parked on the lot like pieces in a giant game of Tetris.

I introduced myself and mentioned Marvin's name. Chin bowed and made his way to my car. He walked around it three times clockwise, then three counterclockwise, eventually stopping directly behind the large rear window.

"Unusual condition," he said.

"It was stolen."

"Ah. Explain bad energy."

He walked away and back to the building whose structure shouted: *I was once a filling station.* When he didn't return I strolled inside. He was sitting behind a desk, also white, staring at two large flat monitors, and seemed to be playing a video game as angles changed and pictures popped up in rapid succession. Then I realized he was high-speed searching for Barracuda parts.

"This best," he said.

On the screen the seats of a car were spinning around the way they do in a TV commercial before the rest of the car is added by special effects. I stepped closer.

"Supple red leather," he said. "Perfect in good feng shui way."

"In a bronze car?"

"You wish I repaint car?"

"I like Turbo Bronze."

He nodded. "Yes, color suit you." He turned to the screen and watched the seats spin in a circle. "This be special, we should do."

I struggled to visualize my car with red seats. "How about repairing my old ones?"

He shook his head; pointed at the screen.

"Yes, let's do," I said.

For the first time he smiled, wrinkling his face.

"You need car?" he asked.

"If it's not too expensive."

He was out the door in a flash. I caught up with him standing beside a gray and black Smart Car about half the size of my Chrysler.

"Take this. Good in city. Favor to Marvin."

"Thank you, Chin." I bowed. He bowed in return and held out his hand. I gave him the keys to the Barracuda.

"I call when reach first step," he said, before spinning and gliding back into the garage.

I tried to see through the overhead doors of the two bays, but their dark windows reflected the sky. I slipped behind the wheel of the loaner to find the key in the ignition. It started and burbled like it was happy to be going someplace.

I maneuvered around the Tetris pieces and headed for the library. The car's dash spoke, "It's ten o'clock," just as I bumped the curb trying to parallel park. When I walked into the library Lizz was facing away from the counter writing in a notebook she was holding. A gold chain showed around the back of her neck. I leaned forward onto my elbows.

When she looked my way I whispered, "We have a problem."

She lifted one eyebrow. "Now it's we, huh?"

"I need to get into that box to check something."

"So *we* need a key?"

"Or we rob a bank."

"Okay," she said. "When?"

I didn't want to ask for too much, but I also couldn't wait for the Oberlin post office.

"Would after lunch be possible?"

"Easy," she said. "What else you got?"

I indicated the side room with my head. "Need to find something on your computer."

She led the way to the computer room that was starting to feel like a second home. Two people were already there: an older guy near the entrance who hadn't taken his coat off, and an Asian woman all the way to the back wearing a beige sweater. We got as far away from both of them as possible. I placed Lizz's copy of the *Idiot's Guide* next to the computer.

"What are we looking for?" she asked.

"Who," I said. "Birth certificate, places of residence, DNA science, things like that."

"Sounds fun." She pointed. "I'll be at the counter."

I started by searching for the history of women's lingerie. Then I opened the *Guide* to "skip tracing," and searched the recommended websites, including two I had to pay for with a credit card. It took an hour, but I learned a Mona Meyers had been born in Detroit General Hospital just shy of twenty-five years ago, which didn't quite agree with the *Tribune* article. My car was twice her age, which should have made me feel young, but didn't.

I tried to understand DNA profiling by reading Wikipedia pages. I was up to how it could be used to identify rapists with great accuracy when I tripped over a new technology. The details were beyond my college biology, but one comment stood out:

...will now be able to differentiate between monozygotic twins where current techniques fail.

I stared past the Asian woman's beige sweater, through the window, and into a gray sky. I tried to search for babies born on the same day as Mona, but the cheap access to the database I'd purchased would allow me to search for only one record at a time, not a whole list of them. So I searched for people named Meyers in Michigan, and compared the known addresses to the ones I had for Mona. It took twenty minutes, but a name showed up in a suburb of Detroit called Ferndale.

First name: Mala

My heart somersaulted in my chest.

I dug until I found Mala's birth information. Not the original certificate, but enough to show she had arrived in the world a few minutes after midnight, on December 5.

I whistled at the screen, then leaned back and stared at the pressed-tin tiles of the library's ceiling. I visualized Mona in her sapphire gown at the dinner, Mona with her thumb out, Mona the dancer, Mona the late night visitor, Mona in the hospital.

That foreign word in the hospital. Not prayer beads. Mona had been angry...about Hosco.

I searched for Hugh Hefner using a site called DuckDuckGo that promised not to track me. Hugh had assembled a long list of friendly girls over the years, but two surnames jumped out. Sandy and Amanda Bentley, known as the Bentley twins, had been Hugh's live-in lovers at the turn of the millennium. More recently, American glamour models Kristina and Karissa Shannon had lived at the mansion. I clicked through and was presented with nearly nude identical twins born in Michigan, both of whom had been Playboy Playmates—and Hefner's girlfriend—at the same time.

Hosco wanted to channel Hugh.

"That would turn out badly," I said to the Shannons.

"What?"

I spun around; Lizz was reading over my shoulder.

"Intriguing research. Do you like theirs better than mine?"

"Not even close," I said, without needing to lie. "Hugh sure gets around."

"He can afford the overhead. Did you find what you were looking for?"

"Found something I *wasn't* looking for." I tapped my finger on Mala's birth record on the screen. "My hitchhiker has a sister born a few minutes after her."

She was quiet as she read the document, then said: "Damn, that doubles the competition." She pointed across the screen. "What are those?"

"Me trying to understand women's undergarments."

She tilted her head and stared at me. "You got a secret thing for corsets and garters?"

I shook my head. "They never have my size."

She laughed and held up a small key between her thumb and index finger.

"Delivery."

The chain was gone from around her neck. I took the key, looked it over. It didn't seem different from when the bank gave it to me.

"Your guy does amazing work."

"He has good equipment and is very careful. I like that in a person," she said, moving closer until her leg touched my elbow.

"I've been practicing slow and careful with a wonderful librarian."

"Admirable objectives. Are you taking me to lunch? It's Friday; we can celebrate the end of the week."

I pulled out my watch. Eleven-fifteen. Held up the key. "Got to run an errand after I finish up here."

She gazed down at me with crystal eyes the color of clouds promising rain. I felt my heart accelerate.

"Yes, I'll take you to lunch. Could we make it one o'clock?"

She smiled her half-smile. "Perfect. Enjoy your nudie pictures." She turned and walked toward the front counter. I placed the key in the corner of my wallet, which suddenly felt very heavy, and turned back to the computer to learn more about someone named Mala Meyers.

Thirty minutes of work found a high school. The senior pictures made Mona and Mala twins to my eye. Just what Hosco was hunting for. The credit information from an apartment application showed an address in Chicago ten months old. After that, the databases couldn't find a whiff of her.

I thumbed to *obituary* in my *Idiot's Guide* for help.

No deceased Mala Meyers. I swallowed hard and tried Mona. Came up empty.

I scribbled the last known address in my journal.

I waved to Lizz as I passed the counter. She blew me a kiss with one finger as I pushed the door open.

A leaf chased a Hershey wrapper along the sidewalk under a bleak sky that seemed all wrong for nearly high noon.

Thirty-Seven

I DROVE CHIN'S LOANER to Penny's apartment enjoying the go-cart quick handling, and the miles of space around it on all sides that made the cramped city feel like a country road. When I pulled up at five after twelve she came running down the steps wearing a gold sweater and dark jeans that shimmered green carrying a black box. When she reached the car she held out her hands as if measuring it and started laughing. I pushed a button to roll down the passenger window.

"Small but mighty," I said.

She laughed harder. "All guys say that." She slipped into the seat six inches from my right leg and held the box on her lap.

"I used to have a tin box for fishing tackle," I said.

"Ever catch anything?"

"Walleye in Lake Erie. They're tasty."

She scooched sideways to face me. "You really went fishing?"

"Sometimes. Usually we used the boat to ski or find a beach."

"Yeah, I bet. A secluded beach where no cops would tap on your steamed-up window."

"Our boat didn't have windows. Is that it?"

She nodded.

"How long do you need?" I checked the rearview mirror and pulled out.

"Depends on the surface."

"Smooth hard metal. Almost like the cell phone."

"Metal is easy if the print isn't old. Didn't find much on the cell phone." She frowned in my direction. "Someone handled it an awful lot."

"Sorry. I wasn't thinking far enough ahead."

She tapped a dance rhythm on the box with two fingers. "What do you think about turning the phone on? Find out if there are more messages."

"Makes me nervous." I swerved left and snuck in behind a Chicago Transit Authority bus, whose exhaust, thankfully, came out its roof.

"It's a connection we're not using. Might tell us a lot."

"Might also get us found by people we don't want to meet."

"How? You said you took the chip out."

I shrugged. "I don't know. But if it's communicating, something is communicating back."

"Over Wi-Fi. Lots of people use that. I'll talk to Manford at school. He knows tech."

"How did you ever end up in a hi-tech crime school?"

She didn't answer for a big part of a minute. "It's complicated."

"Sorry. Not my business."

"That's okay. There's just so much hate in the world. I want to be part of the solution."

I entered a two-story parking structure around the corner from the bank and was amazed at how easily the little car slipped into a narrow spot on the roof marked *COMPACT*. The sky had grown so dark I thought the sun had set.

I stepped out of the car. "Does it rain here a lot?"

"Depends," she said. "On where you're from."

Penny carried the box under her arm like a purse as we walked to the bank. I stopped twice to study the street in both directions. A security guard in an olive-green uniform led us to a vault full of boxes where we inserted the key from Lizz, slid my box out, and took it to a tiny viewing room. The guard nodded at me, smiled at Penny, and pulled the door closed behind him as he departed.

"One more time before we pop the lid. I'm holding this for a person who left it with me in good faith."

"What do you have in there, a bomb?" she said.

"Please don't say that out loud." I flipped up the long top of the box to reveal two foam blocks. The tiny blue dots I had written on them still pointed to the back. This wasn't proof no one had accessed them, but it made me feel better.

Penny opened her case and removed a spray bottle, feathery brush, roll of tape, flashlight and flat things I didn't recognize. She also had a camera with a fat lens. I spread one foam clamshell, held it close to the counter and slid the metal block out without touching it. A balding Benjamin Franklin smiled up at us.

Her brown eyes shot from the plate, to me, to the plate, to me.

"Is that real?"

"If you mean, is it from the U.S. mint, I don't know."

She pulled out a magnifying glass the size of my palm and leaned within inches of the plate.

"This is spectacular. I've only ever seen pictures of intaglio for currency." She moved from one end to the other, hovering in spots. "Who would have the patience to engrave such a thing?"

"I've heard it's an art form."

She placed the glass aside and worked around the edges of the plate in silence. The metal was featureless until it finally revealed small smudges. She systematically took close-up pictures, pushed buttons on the camera, and waited.

"It'll take a minute, its computer isn't very fast."

"What's it doing?"

"Matching what I just lifted to the ones you gave me at the apartment. It's not as smart as the lab computer, but if we have something new, I want to know right now." She stared. "The entire plate is crystal clean, like it was polished, except for prints on the end. You think someone was in a hurry?" The camera beeped. She looked at the display on the back of the camera, then held it toward me.

I saw a pair of prints side by side.

"New one is on the left," she said. "The woman who was in your car handled these." She watched my eyes. "I think you knew that."

"They were wrapped in foam padding when I found them."

"So you didn't touch them?"

"No."

"Wait a second. You said they were left with you in 'good faith.' But you also said you 'found' them. You're not telling me something..."

"They were hidden inside what was left with me in good faith."

"Ah. So no one knows you found them." She stared at me. "Including the person who gave them to you."

I met her brown eyes. "Just you, Penny."

She bit her lower lip. "Let's do the back."

We flipped the plate over using little metal tools that reminded me of the dentist, then Penny dusted and scanned and photographed — but found nothing more.

"We're here; should we do the other one?" she asked.

I checked my watch, it was already five till one.

"What's your best guess?"

"It's just like this one," she said, "carefully cleaned. Your friend grabbed them, wrapped them and handed them off to you. No way these were being used on a regular basis, they had been stored. Or..."

"Your face says you're having a clever thought."

"Just a guess. They were cleaned, packed, and ready to go into the press. But before they got there — "

"You're thinking she stole them, aren't you?"

"You said the S-word. We've both read about the cop in Detroit. How many counterfeit operations do *you* know about?"

She started packing up her equipment, shook here head. "We're here; I only need a minute." While I moved the plate back into the foam, sealed it and positioned it with the tiny mark toward the back, she checked the second plate. Only one print, but it was slightly larger.

I repacked the second plate, closed and locked the box.

"How is he?" she asked.

I ran through our conversation in reverse. "The cop? Less than a year from retirement and now he's in limbo." I tried to imagine what it'd be like to be in the same job for decades. Beautiful and frightening both came to mind.

"You know what I read?" she said. "They brought his dog in. Placed his hand on its head. Even in a coma I bet he could sense its presence."

The guard led me to the vault where I reversed the long sliding action and locked the box in place. Halfway to the main entrance I stopped and grabbed Penny's arm.

"Back up quietly," I whispered.

We worked our way back and stood just outside the door where we had lifted the prints. I leaned against the wall and feigned looking for my wallet inside my jacket.

"See the dark-haired woman at the far desk? Bald guy sitting opposite her."

She scanned and found the right desk. "Yeah."

"She works for LaRuche, something to do with campaign financing. Can you tell what they're doing?"

She dropped to the floor and pulled her camera out of the tin box, then stood and hid behind me.

"I thought that was for close-ups?"

"In macro mode. I can use it as a telephoto too." I felt her arms press against my back.

"I've always longed to be a tripod."

"Shh, stand still, I'll get pics and video."

I stiffened my body and watched Tracy. She was wearing a blue business suit whose skirt reached below the knee. She had her legs crossed, showing a shoe with a low heel. Her black hair hung to her shoulders. She was wearing the gray glasses she always had on, and writing on a notepad on the edge of the man's desk.

"Can you read his name?" I asked softly.

"Vincent Cradel. Vice President of something."

"I wish I could hear them."

"Stay here," Penny said, and left her tin box open on the floor.

I watched her cross carpeted floor onto marble tile. Her boots clicked. She approached Cradel's corner desk, stopped, looked around the room on her tiptoes then took two steps to a white pillar and leaned against it with her shoulder. She was no more than ten feet from Tracy's back. Cradel hadn't even reacted to her approach. She pulled out her smartphone, placed it against the camera and began to text. She took small steps until she was on the opposite side of the pillar, and out of Cradel's view. She continued texting, one more customer engrossed in her phone.

I knelt and put the pieces back into Penny's box, then picked it up with the top open and studied the contents. If anyone asked, I was searching for my safety-deposit key.

Penny was still at the pillar when Tracy stood and shook hands with Cradel. I turned around so I faced into our viewing room. I found a mirror in Penny's tin box and watched as Tracy turned one-eighty and headed for the main entrance.

Penny followed her.

I followed Penny.

I stopped inside the main door and watched between the letters A and N of BANK as Tracy walked toward a black limousine with Penny following her. The driver opened Tracy's door and Penny kept walking without making eye contact. When the limo pulled away I tucked the box under my arm, put

Long Toe's sunglasses on, and walked directly to Cradel's desk. He was bending over scratching his ankle.

"Excuse me, Mr. Cradel. I'm Jake, Ms. Kane's driver. She thinks she might have left her pen on your desk."

He looked around and I placed my hand flat on the top of the desk.

"Maybe I took it, I do that sometimes," he said, and leaned to his right and pulled out a drawer. As his eyes turned down I peeled the top sheet off the notepad and moved my hand below the edge of the desk.

"I'm sorry, I don't see it. Tell Ms. Kane if it turns up, I'll hold it for her. It's the silver Mont Blanc that she likes to sign with, isn't it?"

"Yes, I believe so. She's a bit upset."

"The bank will get her a new one. She can even change the engraving instructions we have on file if she likes."

I thanked him and headed to the front door, the slip of paper tucked inside my palm. I found Penny on the sidewalk staring at her camera with an ear bud in her left ear. I stopped beside her and waited.

"She opened a new account with a fifty-thousand dollar deposit in the name of Tracy Kane. She had a check for the deposit; I saw it on his desk when I got there. I have it on video, but I don't know how much we'll be able to read. I need a larger monitor."

"I have to get to lunch, I'm late."

She pushed up the sleeve of her sweater to reveal a watch with a bright orange band.

"Shoot. Time flies when you're having fun. Can you drive me to class?"

"Sure."

We discussed our surprise at finding only one print. I had hoped it would be Hosco's. I gave Penny the small glass I lifted from LaRuche's dinner party. She dusted it while we drove.

Our testing was crude, but the print didn't match the one on the plate.

"Hey Penny, monozygotic twins have the same DNA, right?"

She was scrolling through pictures in her special camera. "That's a big word for a guy who eats at the Pig. But yeah, that's what the school books tell me."

"So they must have the same fingerprints?"

"Identical genetic material, sure." She waved her hand. "Wait a second, pull over. Reading in a moving car makes me sick."

I pulled up to an expired parking meter behind a gray Jeep thinking a whole lot of cars in this town were gray. Penny tapped on her phone. The sky was almost black.

A limo passed to my left. I tried to see into the back, but the windows were too dark. The license plate read PNKMO5. A Pink Monkey limo making a lunch run to the financial district — what a life some guys led.

"Check this," Penny said. "Fingerprints are dependent on conditions in the womb during pregnancy, so even identical twins have unique fingerprints." She looked up. "That's incredible."

I pulled back into traffic, growing ever more late for my lunch with Lizz, with one word throbbing in my head: Mala.

"I wonder how much Braden knows."

"Is that the cop who came to see you?"

I nodded. "He's working the Hosco shooting. He got my car back for me."

"Go see him. Share a little. Maybe he'll share back."

I pulled up in front of the DePaul University business building. She answered my question before I asked, which made me wonder if I was becoming old and predictable.

"They're making me take a course in business law so I can catch white-collar criminals."

"Have they taught you how a private investigator gets a license in Illinois?"

"Very slowly. There's a written test and stuff." She studied me, her brown eyes shifting like a crook with a question. "You planning to hang around Chicago?" She winked and hopped out of the car. "Can you keep the kit until later? I don't want to carry it around."

"Sure. I'll bring it by the Pig."

She waved and headed up the steps; her jeans twinkled green even under the stormy sky.

It took six and a half minutes to get to the library. I shoved the tin box behind the driver's seat and parked a little close to a fire hydrant, then ran to the building as fast as I could. Lizz wasn't behind the counter. I waited. No one showed up to help me. I checked the computer room. The man was gone, but the Asian woman was still working near the window, her sweater tossed over the chair beside her.

I went to the computer I had used that morning and found a short pencil in the drawer underneath it. I pressed the page from Cradel's desk flat and stroked the pencil across it like a kid with a crayon. Digits emerged from the gray strokes: 453-3217022. I tore a clean edge off the small page and wrote the number on it, put the original in my wallet and the other in my pocket, wondering how I could get a peek into that account.

I leaned right to catch a glimpse of the front counter.

Empty.

I'd been so busy I had forgotten about Brenda's chip. I dug it out of my wallet and pushed it into a slot on the computer. It contained a single movie file named IMG5749. A double-click started it playing on the screen.

The camera pointed out from a second story window at Brenda's stubby driveway, both sides of the road in front of her apartment, and a pool of light painted by a streetlamp. A tallish man stood against the side of a dark gray sedan staring toward where I estimated Brenda's garage door would be. Maybe it wasn't gray; in the low light everything appeared gray, could have been blue, or maybe even dark red. A mustang coasted backward into the street, across it and to a parking place on the far side. No lights, no sound. The driver's door swung open and the inside light popped on. I tried to see a face, but the driver dove out so fast the video was a blur. He turned to close the door carefully, his back toward me. The light went out. He seemed short beside the roofline of the Mustang. It could be a woman.

I backed the video up to see if the interior light would show me anything about the man beside the sedan. It didn't. I let it play. The short person walked toward Brenda's garage and disappeared. The other figure moved behind the sedan, remained still. I waited. Nothing moved. I leaned close to the computer's speaker; a rushing noise sounded like breathing.

No cars passed on the street below her window. I stopped the video. The file had been created at 3:03 AM, mere minutes after Long Toe left. No coincidence, someone had been watching.

That meant they had seen Long Toe Fowler leave the garage.

I blew air at the tip of my nose, and clicked play.

My Barracuda rolled down the driveway with the lights off and no one behind the wheel. It stopped at the crown of the road. I imagined the short man combing the inside of the garage, closing doors, locking up. So he should appear right about...

He walked down the driveway, a brimmed hat low over his eyes, and slid behind the wheel. The unmistakable idle of a V8 engine filled the night. I had the keys, so he must have prepared a hot-wire in the garage to be that fast. The car backed up and swung its rear to the left. The Cuda's taillights lit, showing me the side of a maroon Toyota Avalon.

The standing man glowed red. I paused the movie. I didn't recognize him in the tiny image, though something niggled at my mind, maybe because I *wanted* to recognize him.

The Cuda's headlights suddenly sprayed white cones on the asphalt. It drove away slowly until the taillights disappeared from the edge of the video frame. The red-faced man opened the passenger door of the Avalon, but the inside light didn't go on. Reflections of buildings in the side glass blocked my view into the car as it drove away in the opposite direction.

A woman's voice whispered, "Holy Moses."

The movie froze on the street, the pool of light alone now, revealing nothing: no men, no cars, not even a piece of loose trash.

Footsteps startled me. A woman in a gray skirt and jacket walking in spike-heeled boots that stopped at her ankle approached me. Black hair piled on her head added six inches to her height. She moved with a swaying grace that reminded me of Tracy. My watch said twenty after one. I'd need a really good excuse.

"Hi, Tommy," she said, stopping close to my chair. "Well?"

"Hello, Miss. I'm waiting for the librarian. Have you seen her?"

She popped me on the shoulder. "Stop it. Tell me what you think."

I watched an hourglass twirl. "Glamorous movie star from the forties, only sexier."

She smiled. "I caught you peeking the other day. Figured some things might look okay on me."

"Uh, way better than okay, Lizz."

Her smile grew. "Sorry I'm late, it took me a long time to find the boots I wanted."

"You mean stores stock that stuff?"

"Oh yeah, it's having a renaissance in some circles. Ever since *Mad Men* got people excited."

"Was that the forties?"

She shook her head and the mountain above shook with it. "No. This is more sixties than forties, but so long as you like it, pretend it's anything you want." She turned around, backed between me and the table and sat down on my lap with her arms around my neck. "Where are you taking me to lunch?"

"Somewhere to show you off. Any suggestions?"

"Let's go to Water Tower Place and walk around. I want to see how people react."

We drove to an eight-level shopping complex on Michigan Avenue, parked inside an attached garage, and strolled floors of shops chock-full of expensive clothing and trinkets, including a globe coated with gold. Two men broke their necks and one stumbled down the escalator.

"Are you enjoying this?" I asked.

"It's different. People usually scowl at my black eye makeup. Now they seem like they're admiring a painting in a museum. Plus, I feel tall."

"Between the heels and hair, you're almost average."

"Such a flatterer you are, Mr. Cuda."

We stopped on the second floor for lunch at a place called *American Girl Café,* which seemed appropriate given Lizz's outfit. We both ordered salads with a slab of salmon on top.

"What did you find?" she asked.

"The fingerprints match, but I was hoping for new ones that would lead somewhere. No luck." I reached across the table and placed the key beside her hand. "Thanks for getting this."

"Sure you're not going to need it again soon?"

"I'm not sure of anything. But I plan to stay far away from that box."

"Good idea; you can hang around me. Since I'm all dressed up, where are you taking me tonight?"

I frowned, thinking hard. "Did we have a date?"

"I'm sneaking into your schedule." She scooted toward the table and took a deep breath, lifting her breasts. "Unless you have one with someone else...or you don't like me." She smiled.

"Those are the only two options a smart artist can think of?"

"No, but they're in the top five."

"You're just fishing." I leaned closer and spoke softer. "I have new info to follow up on."

"You need help following up?"

I shook my head. "It'd be boring for you." Her right eye squinted. "Really. I couldn't pay attention to you like I would want because I have to keep watch."

"What are you watching?"

"An apartment."

"A peeping Tommy?" She laughed. "Can't you set up a video camera then pay attention to me?" She twirled her finger around a curl that had fallen over her right ear.

"I'll record video for sure. But binoculars will give me a closer look."

"At?"

"Whatever happens. That's why I have to be there, ready to take action."

"I see." She returned to her salad.

"Not to bore you by repeating myself," I said. "But you look fabulous."

"Inside or outside?"

"With and without."

She laughed. We made a game of estimating the total number of products in the multi-story mall (over fifty thousand), and guessing how many were required for happiness (fewer than a hundred, including chocolate). On the drive back she described everything she was wearing, and its purpose. I forced my eyes to stay on the road.

I stopped in front of the library, and waited for Lizz to reach the door. She turned and waved, a sight that almost made me cancel my silly surveillance plans. Especially because they were a long-shot hunch based on data nearly a year old that would probably add up to a lonely night watching trees grow along a Chicago sidewalk.

Thirty-Eight

I LEFT THE LIBRARY, drove five city blocks, and weaved Chin's little car to the curb where there was time on a meter. After rereading the section of the *Guide* on stationary surveillance I locked the car and headed for the pawn shop. The bell jangled as I entered. My friend was standing behind the counter paging through a black and white comic book. He didn't react. I stopped at the counter and tried to read his book, but it was too far away.

"Black and white comics?" I asked.

He nodded, still reading. "Original *Mutant Ninja Turtles.* This was good stuff before the big studios made everything green."

"In more ways than one."

His puff-of-air laugh sounded like, "Hah." He closed the book and dropped it on the counter. "Browsing or buying?"

"Good binoculars and a digital camera with a high-power optical zoom."

"Bird watching?"

I nodded. "Many interesting creatures along the lake."

"Hah." He moved to my left and pulled out a Nikon and a Canon. "Does it have to be small?"

"Any size is fine."

He brought out larger cameras: another Nikon, and an Olympus.

"Ten to one on the Nikon. Best I have."

I started with the best, checked that it would shoot HD movies, then pointed it out the window and ran the zoom back and forth. The tag hanging on it showed $150. When I turned back to the counter two pairs of binoculars had replaced the other cameras. One was black, the other green and tan camouflage.

"Night Owl?"

"Light amplifiers. You can watch birds at night."

They were also $150. Maybe everything was.

"What can I get both for?"

He pressed his lips together. "I'll throw in the binocular case." He brought a black case up and placed it on the counter.

"Any others I should consider?"

He frowned and shook his head, even though he had just put three cameras away.

"Two-fifty-three." He paused. "Plus tax."

I lifted the binoculars to the window. Gray clouds made a warning light flicker; it was too bright for Night Owl mode. I pointed the binoculars into a corner of the back room and pressed the NO button. The gray image showed detail of the side of a scratched metal desk. They would get me closer than the zoom.

"Deal with no tax."

I put my equipment in the trunk and headed to Victoria's. Halfway there I realized I'd be staring out a window at dinner time, so I swung by the Pig. I ordered a takeout sandwich from a young guy at the register named Jimmy that I hadn't seen before. The place was half full and three guys were coming up the steps when I felt a tap on my shoulder.

"Hi," Penny said. "I talked to Manford. You better watch out." She turned away with a tray full of food propped on one hand.

I paid Jimmy and tipped him with paper.

"Thanks," he said. "I'm saving for an amp."

His straight brown hair covered his ears, but didn't reach his shoulders.

I guessed. "Band?"

He nodded.

The three guys who had been on the steps stopped directly behind me to discuss the names of sandwiches and stare at their cell phones.

"What instrument?"

"Bass," Jimmy said.

"My friend plays bass. We were at BLUES for open mic."

The three guys behind me had stopped talking.

"I want to do that," Jimmy said. "But I need that amp."

One guy tapped my shoulder. "Can we order, man? We're in a hurry."

I thought of my cell phone beeping at me with a new message. I held up a finger to buy a few seconds.

"Not for open mic. They have one."

Jimmy wrinkled his nose.

The three guys ordered in rapid-fire succession.

Penny waved to me from the other side of the room. When I got there, she handed me a sheet of paper. It was covered with pencil doodles that brought crop circles to mind.

"Manford says Wi-Fi networks can be tracked. He tried to explain, but all I remember is companies like Google use the GPS location from cell phones and correlate, that's the word Manford used, *correlate* it to the Wi-Fi the phone is connected to. Then they create maps of the physical location of those Wi-Fi networks."

"Someone does this?"

"A bunch of companies. He told me all about a scandal at ShoutNot that was allegedly tracking the location of anonymous users."

"So if I turn the phone on and hook up to Wi-Fi, someone could find me using the name of the network?"

She nodded.

I flipped the paper over and tried to understand Manford's notes. The last sentence was perfectly clear: *If you do not want to be found, DO NOT connect to a network.*

"Thanks Penny, this is really helpful. No way we should turn that phone on."

"Unless..." She curved an eyebrow. "We drive somewhere to communicate, then get away quick."

I studied the crop circles. "Hit and run Wi-Fi?"

"Yeah, we'll have fun."

"Sounds dangerous."

She patted my arm, "Part of the fun." Then she ran off toward the kitchen.

I went back for my take out. Jimmy was counting the money from the tip jar. He slid the bag with my dinner across the counter without a word so I left him to dream about his new amp.

Back in my midget car I cogitated about the flick of an on switch stealing my privacy. Then I tried to guess how much Theo might know about such things. I was still speculating when I drifted to the curb a couple of blocks from Victoria's. The sky was darker. Fat drops started splatting against the windshield: one, two, twenty.

I ran to the hotel and was brushing water off my jacket when I reached my room. A sticky note from Kim read: *Call Chin. New discovery.* A number followed. I crossed my fingers for an option to the red seats. I went back downstairs and used my card to place the call. Chin answered.

"There is something you must see."

"Can you give me a hint?"

"Not on phone. Not sure what this mean. You must see."

I glanced down. Not yet four o'clock. I wasn't thrilled about a drive across town to the rhythm of slapping windshield wipers.

"Can it wait until tomorrow?"

The phone was quiet for a long time.

"Chin find something. You must see."

I figured that was enough "must see" to make this important.

"I'll head over right now. Get there as fast as I can."

"Good. Chin wait."

We hung up. I couldn't imagine anything about a trashed Barracuda that would explain Chin's persistence. I took the stairs two at a time and changed into black, scanned my footwear collection, and decided brothel creepers were close to gumshoe. Then I jogged back to my car and tried not to rush the drive.

The Tetris pieces had been shuffled.

I parked on the street. The rainstorm had morphed into a misty fog that penetrated my pants when I stepped out. No lights glowed inside or outside the garage. No Chin. Dark clouds reflected from the large corner windows. The door to the office where Chin had shown me the red leather seat pictures was closed.

I eased the car door shut, and walked away from the garage. At the corner I turned left, passed a rain-streaked window covered by pictures of Chinese food, and a magazine store with an entire wall of cigarettes. I snuck down a narrow walk between the buildings to the rear of the garage. Even the back wall had been polished. My Cuda sat in the far bay, the interior and doors missing. The bumpers stood vertically against a workbench. The place was glassy-pond-in-a-park quiet.

Maybe Chin had been called away. But something I couldn't quite put my finger on…I closed my eyes, exhaled slowly.

An image popped into focus.

The monitors on Chin's computer had been lit when I arrived. Why? Everything else had been shut down. I crept to the corner of the shiny building in short bursts, floating like a frat-boy ninja warrior sneaking up on the girls' dorm. I peeked over the roofs of the Tetris cars, dropped to my knees and felt dampness soak through my pants; then to one elbow to look under the cars for moving feet. In the furthest corner of the lot a long dark cylinder hid beneath a blue BMW crossover. I rose to one knee and surveyed the lot again. Empty. Still.

I stayed low and made my way between the cars until I was facing the front bumper of the blue crossover with my back to the fence separating the garage from the next lot. Tall plants along its length had covered the ground with white petals reflecting gray after-storm light. I lowered myself to check under the bumper, and saw the top of Chin's head.

He was on his back, his face turned toward the garage. He wasn't moving.

He didn't appear to be breathing.

I checked under the other cars, no feet. I moved to the side of the BMW. No moving shadows. I turned around to face Chin. His open eyes stared through me.

"Chin," I whispered. "Chin, it's Tommy."

He blinked rapidly. His chest lifted. "Are they gone?" he asked in a hushed voice.

"I don't see anyone on the lot or in your shop."

He scraped across the pavement on his back, his nose facing up at the chassis, until he was clear of the car. I put a hand under his arm to help him up and brushed stones and dirt off the back of his blue mechanics shirt.

"I was hiding. Found something you must see. When you called I see men." He held up his hands vertically a foot apart. "One tall, one short, walking street. Did not fit. These not the kind of men to walk."

"I didn't think you were breathing."

"Kung Fu method. Slow breath, keep quiet. Watch."

He led the way and pointed back at the BMW. "When they walk out of sight I turn off lights, activate security cameras, hide under car." He motioned with his hands. "Nice high car, easy."

"What did they want?"

Chin traced their steps while talking. "They enter main door, and go to garage to far side of car. They check right here." He indicated a section of the roof with two hands. "See?"

An eighth-inch hole had been drilled in the roof six inches from the side window. I'd never noticed it.

"I'm confused," I said.

"Come."

He led me to a black toolbox along an inside wall and motioned for me to push. We rolled it three feet to the left, exposing plain wall. He knelt and shifted a panel four feet wide and just as high. Behind it sat a safe built into the concrete floor.

"One moment," he said.

I walked over to my Barracuda and studied the inside. It had been stripped so thoroughly my chassis could have been coming down an assembly line. I hadn't even stripped it that far when restoring it.

"Here."

Chin stood beside me holding a black object the size of a pack of gum. It had a dull silver hook sticking out of one end. He placed it on my palm.

I stared at it. "Do you know what it is?"

He nodded. "GPS recorder." He drew a pattern in the air with his index finger. "Keep track of where you have gone."

I turned it over with a fingernail. "Does it transmit?"

"I think too small."

I pointed at the hook.

"Antenna to receive GPS signal. Usually these put under car, easy to find. This more clever."

I walked back to my car and found the hole. It was just the size of the antenna.

Chin wiggled a finger at me and crawled into the car through the passenger's opening. I poked my head in behind him. He pulled remnants of roof liner away where he had found the box.

"Slight lump here. I investigate. Find box. Call you."

"You're very thorough."

Chin smiled. "Liner mostly gone. Must install new."

I backed away from the car, my chest heavy. Someone tracking my Cuda? For how long?

"They may come to retrieve tracker. You take away."

I nodded, studied the smooth plastic. "Where would someone get one of these?"

Chin rubbed his chin with his left hand. "Police use them. Maybe they tell you where to buy."

Braden had found my car, called me to come get it. Or had someone wanted to know where the car went *after* I picked it up?

"Thanks, Chin. I'm glad you found this. Anything you need for the car?"

He walked a circle around my stripped Cuda; stopped by the left front fender; pressed his palms together, resting his chin on the fingertips. The headlight reminded me of Brenda's video.

"You have a security system?" I asked.

He brightened. "Ah."

I followed him to the front office where he brought up videos in the quadrants of his right monitor and started them all playing at once. The lower left showed his back as he exited through the main door. Everything else was still like a photo. We waited. He touched a button and the time indicators along the top ran fast.

"Searching for motion," he said.

In a few seconds, the numbers slowed and two men wearing brimmed hats walked through the front door and stopped at the counter. My shoulders tensed without me asking them to. The shorter guy looked around the room, but not up at the camera, so I didn't get to see a face. He pressed the service button three times. The taller one pointed to the garage and they went in. The upper quadrant camera tracked them to my car. The shorter guy crawled inside and examined the roof. The taller one turned his face back toward the office and I got a glimpse of a profile that convinced me it was a male without facial hair, but not much else. We watched them examine the roof from the outside and inside, beginning at the location of the hole and working outward. According to the timers, they were in the garage for just over three minutes.

"Both wearing gloves," I said. I reached in my pocket for Brenda's video. "Can you play this?"

Chin slipped it into the side of one of the machines. Moments later it was playing two feet wide. I watched the same sequence of cars moving and paid careful attention when the Barracuda's taillights came on.

"Same two men steal your car," Chin said.

"Seems that way."

"Why steal then give back?" he asked.

"They might be looking for something. They were tracking me to see if I would lead them to it."

"Is this something in your car?" Chin asked.

I shook my head. "I'm not sure what they want." Though I had a good guess. "Could I have a copy of the recording from your cameras?"

He fidgeted with his computer for a minute, then handed my chip back.

"Everything is there. I keep copy of car video." He paused. "Just in case."

"Thanks, Chin." I motioned toward the garage. "Let me know when you want help putting Humpty Dumpty back together."

With the videos in one pocket and Chin's find in the other I wandered back to the Smart Car. The dash read four twenty-eight. I headed straight for Braden's building. The car found a short parking space in front of the church. I jogged the stairs up to Braden's office. His door stood six inches ajar; I tapped on the glass.

"I'm out of here at five."

Braden's voice from behind the door.

My watch gave me eleven minutes. I eased the door open with one hand and stuck my head in. He was bent over an open folder with a red pencil vibrating between two fingers.

"Information to share, I can be quick," I said.

"What about?"

"Something possibly related to the Hosco case."

He waved me in with his left hand; his right moved the pencil as he continued reading.

"I'm off that case."

I stepped in, pushed the door closed, and stood in front of it. I knew nothing about how a police department worked.

"Did you find the shooter?"

He shook his head, still reading.

"Someone else take it over?"

The pencil stopped and he sat up. "Management shelved it. Not enough information to work with."

"So fast?"

His smile lacked conviction. "Doesn't take long to figure out you don't have anything. Especially when budgets are being cut...which is always."

"What if that hair found in Detroit belonged to Mona's twin sister?"

He stared at his pencil the way a smoker looks at a cigarette.

"No kidding. A twin. Have to be identical for the DNA to match."

"Minutes apart, different days. High school yearbook suggests identical."

"Where is she now?"

"Don't know. But the last address I found for her is here in Chicago."

He put his red pencil down, aligned it with the edge of the folder, leaned back.

"You think this mystery girl and your buddy Hosco were in Detroit? Then why is her sister in his Ferrari when someone puts three bullets into him?"

"Find her, maybe she'll tell us." I smiled.

"How old is this address you have?"

"Almost a year. I can't find anything since."

He rolled the pencil back and forth on the big blotter that covered the center of his desk.

"Long time." He looked up from the pencil. "She wasn't in the car. What do you think she can tell us?"

"Maybe a motive."

"Long shot, but if you give me the address, I'll add it to the file. It's a long file, though. Mr. Hoskova was a thug: arrests for narcotics possession, intent to sell, involved in prostitution, illegal possession of firearms. He owned a safe full of unregistered weapons. Maybe his lifestyle caught up with him."

"Hoskova?"

"Zhenya R. Hoskova. Came to the U.S. nearly ten years ago from Ukraine. According to his entrance papers, he was supposed to marry one Rebecca L. Staunch. He didn't. So he was supposed to go back. He obviously didn't do that either. The Rosco Hosco alias likely helped dodge Immigration."

Hosco had been a busy guy. I stepped to the desk. Braden handed me his red pencil. I wrote *452 Lockwood Drive*. He read it upside down.

"Apartments. Transients. It's been a year. Don't get your hopes up."

His face sagged as if the muscles had gone on strike. It must be hard being a cop, working with hints and guesses all day long. Probably all night too. I wondered how much sleep Braden had lost in all his years of service.

"Low odds Mona has a twin," I said.

"Even lower the sister had anything to do with a bum like Hoskova."

Hugh Hefner came to mind, but I didn't think Braden would take me seriously.

"Any convictions?"

"No. He always managed to slip through the court's fingers: technicalities, witnesses that didn't show up, that kind of thing."

I handed back his pencil, recalling the valet's comment about Hosco being connected. "Any theories?"

"Lots of them. Hoskova took the heat for leaking the location of that catacomb. Big operation, losing it could have pissed off someone important. Or the Detroit cop has friends that visited Hoskova as payback. Maybe Hoskova shouldn't have even been near Detroit, and the cop ID-ing him caused problems with his management."

"I didn't think Hosco shot the cop."

Braden shrugged. "Cop says no, but he didn't see who did. A confrontation like that, who knows what he saw, or remembers after being hit. You know the other two guys he sort of remembers might be the bodies in that grave. Cleaning fluid matches. Gangster stuff from the thirties: people who know too much can't be left dangling for the cops to find. Or maybe someone cut a deal, leaked information, got caught. No one has told me how they found an underground facility last used by bootleggers. Now you bring me a mysterious missing sister." Laughter grunted up from his chest.

His rapid-fire summary made me feel like a pulp-fiction character. "Did you find the weapon?"

He watched me, his lips rubbing together.

"Why so interested?"

"Trying to help Mona. She wants to know who killed her boy Hosco."

"Is she concerned?" He checked his watch.

I resisted the impulse to do the same. "About?"

"Being next on the list."

She had asked for drugs, not protection. This was far more complicated than Walmart.

"I don't get that vibe, but I haven't known her long."

He looked at his watch again. "You have four more minutes. Yes, we found a gun."

"That shot the cop?"

He shook his head. "No. But Hoskova had two on him when he died. One strapped to his ankle: a pocket Glock. Nine millimeter, just like the big ones."

"Man was worried."

"He obviously had reason to be." He made a V-sign with his left hand. "Two minutes."

I pulled the GPS unit out of my pocket and placed it on his desk.

"Have you ever seen anything like this?"

He pushed it around with the dull end of his pencil.

"Lots of 'em. We use them for tracking all the time. This is the mini with no radio. It's hard for the bad guys to detect because it only receives. Why?"

"It was hidden in the roof of my car."

"The one that was gutted?"

I nodded.

"Nice car. I remember the Barracuda. Before my time, but muscle cars have always appealed to me. This electric stuff we have nowadays..." He waved the hand holding the pencil.

"It's not yours?" I asked.

"Do you mean did the police plant it to track the whereabouts of a junked-out Chrysler owned by some kid from Ohio who managed to get it stolen from inside a garage?" He laughed briefly. "I read the paperwork you filled out to get it back."

I shrugged. "Sorry. Thought maybe it would help find the thieves."

"Looks like they found you. Do you know why?"

I could guess, and part of me wanted to talk about it, but an instinct to protect Mona (and myself) held me back.

"That car is worth something as a classic. But destroying it makes no sense."

"None at all. Sorry we don't have resources to pursue it." He stood and offered his hand. "Thanks for stopping by. The twin sister angle is amusing." He locked the folder he had been reading into his desk drawer and ushered me out the door. "Who knows, maybe she'll turn up and explain this crazy city."

Thirty-Nine

THE GRACE HAD ONLY EIGHT rooms, so it was a lot like Victoria's: comfy and smelling of decades of use. The room facing the street had been available, probably because each passing car sounded close enough to sideswipe the bed. It was perfect. I could see Mala's building, and the street in both directions.

The first thing I learned about doing surveillance work was it gave me too much time to consider alternative theories of my universe. Maybe my car had been stolen to put the tracker in, not to search for the hitchhiker's booty. Maybe it had been a warning. About what? Keeping my mouth shut regarding an encounter with a silver Ferrari would be a good guess.

I realized the red-haired girl had become "the hitchhiker" in my mind, and no longer simply Mona. I'd give two-to-one odds the hitchhiker was dear sister Mala.

But I had no one to bet against.

This left a fair chance the hitchhiker was Mona playing me for a naive college boy from Ohio; just because she was sweet and beautiful didn't mean she couldn't be evil. If I hadn't learned anything else from Raymond Chandler novels, I sure learned that. Then again, William of Occam said the simple explanation was the correct one: Mona the addict and Mona the angelic dancer didn't know much about each other's lives, and Mala had left town ten months ago.

I gazed through the tiny crack between the maroon curtains at the entrance to what had once been Mala's place. It was in a row of similar buildings, each with an upstairs and a downstairs apartment. I only had the main address, so couldn't be sure which floor Mala had occupied.

My Nikon camera with the zoom positioned to wide angle sat on the windowsill taking four pictures per second. At that rate, I could record for over twenty hours. It was backup. If something happened, I hoped to see it with my own eyes.

A long and low metallic blue Chevrolet went by.

I trained the binoculars on the entrance and tried to wish the door open. It didn't cooperate. No one had been in or out since I arrived around five-thirty. I pulled the table over to the window so I could see the display on the back of the camera, sat down, and unwrapped a Pilgrim's Progress from the Pig. I was halfway through the roasted turkey and avocado sandwich before growing anxious and returning to the binoculars. I tried Night Owl mode, but there was still too much light.

I wrapped the second half of the sandwich and put it in the tiny fridge thinking about the hitchhiker's phone. Like Penny, I wanted to communicate with Theo: find out who he was, why he had access to Hosco's phone, why he thought I could help him. But if Manford was right, Theo could find the phone the moment it connected.

By then, I'd have to be ready.

I lazed around and eventually ate the second half of the sandwich as traffic dropped to one car every couple of minutes. The street shifted from gray-filtered sunlight, to dusky gold, to the eerie emptiness of streetlights and, amazingly, a couple of stars despite the ambient city light. I was holding my Night Owl's to the curtain crack and pressing the NO button on and off when one of the side-by-side doors of the apartment opened from the inside. I held my breath and spun the little wheel to focus.

A woman in a shiny charcoal-gray coat backed through the doorway and locked the door with a key. Only the upstairs apartment showed lights. She spun and started down the walk, flashing a profile for a brief second. Then she turned away.

Only thing I knew for sure is she had dark hair, because it cascaded over the coat's collar.

I grabbed my car and room keys, ran down the steps to the front door; stopped, took a breath, and strolled out of The Grace with as much calm as I could muster. The woman was far to my right and making a left turn on the sidewalk. I started the Smart Car and realized it violated the *Idiot's Guide* recommendations for a chase vehicle because it was easy to remember—I'd have to hang back.

I drove fast for two blocks; swung left.

She wasn't on the street. The taillights of a car blocks away went out as it made a right turn. I slowed and looked for a person behind the wheel of a parked car. A white car passed going the other way. Then a pale green mini-van raced around me from behind. Both drivers were alone. I made a U-turn with surprising ease and cruised back. An elderly man came out of an apartment walking a poodle the size of a cat. No charcoal coat. I drove in a four-block square, and was about to go around again when I admitted I had lost her.

It was nine o'clock.

Shadowing would take practice.

I drove back to The Grace and sat around staring alternately at the front door of the apartment and the toes of my suede shoes. She was gone...which gave me an idea.

I grabbed the camera and went for a walk. When I reached the front of the apartment building, I turned up the path toward the door the woman had used, ducked to the right and circled the building with the camera taking four frames per second. Staying low, and with the creepers giving me silent footsteps, I held the camera up to each window, counted to five while rotating it slowly, and moved on to the next window. I avoided the front door because it was visible from the street, snuck onto a porch in back, and shot through a small window in the rear door.

I breathed easier when I reached the sidewalk, and easier still when I turned my key at The Grace. A quick replay showed a bedroom closet stuffed with a rainbow of clothing above a long row of shoes, a kitchen with no dishes in sight, and a living area sporting both a TV on the wall opposite a couch, and a desk in the corner with a flat computer nearly the size of the TV.

I restaged the camera at the curtain and sat for an hour wondering how I could have started that tail faster. Maybe a watched door was like a watched pot that never boiled. At times I felt electricity on my skin as if something were about to happen; then I grew bored and decided surveilling a month's old address was stupid. Eventually I went down to my car and pointed it toward B.L.U.E.S.

The band was playing a shuffle to a nearly full dance floor when I walked in. The atmosphere infused a bit of optimism despite my failed shadowing effort. A waitress stopped by my shoulder. I watched a tall thin guitarist make his instrument wail. I wondered why I was intent on helping the Mona who had tripped into my life. My amber beer arrived. Braden was right about Chicago being a crazy place — it seemed to be making decisions for me.

My thoughts turned to Lizz's kiss. Penny and her courageous approach to life. Marvin dropping out of college to pursue a dream. Kim saving to get into college to chase hers. I stared into the crowd moving to the music, wondering where Tommy Cuda fit.

I spotted her glasses first.

Same table as Monday.

Watching me.

I felt energy move up my spine. In all the confusion, I hadn't thought clearly about Tracy that night: what she felt, what she saw, why her last words were *go away*.

I made my way through the crowd.

"Was wondering when you were going to notice me," she said, her lips more smirk than smile.

"I was playing hard to get."

"You're a lousy actor. Care to join me?"

I sat down with my back to the band. "Thanks. I'm sorry."

"What for?"

"The other night. I should have made sure you were all right."

A smile touched her mouth then faded away. "That's okay. It happened fast. Sorry I freaked out." She lowered her eyes to her drink. "I was just so scared."

I worked on my beer. She turned toward the band. I tried to recall if she had sounded scared when she yelled that night. Or angry.

"It's not everyday you see fireworks like that."

"Right out in the open, " she said. "Your driving was impressive."

"I stomped on the gas without thinking. Survival instinct. Sitting in the street with bullets flying felt too…first time at a nudist colony."

She laughed. "It worked. You got us out of there."

The waitress who had brought my beer came close. I pointed at Tracy's empty glass. The girl nodded and walked away. Short black skirt and sneakers, lime-green laces.

"Is black your favorite color?" Tracy said, and laughed.

I smiled. "Depends who's wearing it."

The song ended and we listened to fifty people all saying nothing loudly. Then the guitarist strummed sweet chords and a girl singer began humming over it. Tracy looked at me and I noticed the purple eyes even through the gray glasses and remembered Mona talking about *The Outer Limits* and an alien hitman. I recalled eye color being based on reflection and thought the lights in the bar were contributing to the strange hue. Or maybe the silk blouse she wore under her jacket that matched her eyes. Then I remembered Lizz talking about contacts.

"Do you like my eyes?" she asked.

"Sorry for staring. The color...I haven't seen it before."

"I hope not. I had these custom tinted. Girls like to be unique."

"But —"

She interrupted before I could phrase a question.

"The contacts are corrective, I can't see things far away. I like violet. These —" she touched the dark frame of her glasses, "protect me from a certain light I'm sensitive to. You know Bono in U2? He has photophobia too. That's why we wear sunglasses all the time. I hate that I look like a librarian, but I hate headaches even more."

"You look great in glasses. Studious."

"Just the kind of girl you want to take home to mom."

A martini arrived in the hand of the waitress with the black skirt. I didn't watch her walk away. The singer moved into the chorus of the ballad, still only accompanied by the strumming guitar.

"The kind of girl I'd like to dance with."

Tracy smiled and stood. I followed her to the floor. This time I watched, tracing her skirt from its narrow waist below a short matching jacket, around the curve of lingerie-model hips, down to where it ended mid-calf. She turned and pulled me toward her.

My chin brushed her dark hair. Her scent lightened my head like the first feeling of alcohol. I concentrated to pick up the rhythm of the song in my feet, and recalled a random meeting in this very bar four days ago. A money girl for a big politician drinking alone on a Sunday. And again Tuesday. And now Friday. I wondered if she stopped at B.L.U.E.S. and drank most nights: a personal end-of-day ritual. Drinking hard liquor, but not tipsy. That took practice.

I rejected *what's a nice girl like you doing in a place like this,* and *do you come here often.*

"Do you like blues music?"

"It's my favorite. The stories and feelings are so real. I come here after hours to wash off the smut of the city."

"A frequent flyer?"

She pushed away enough to look up at me, her lips curves of orange under the colored lights.

"Not so much as to impair my work." She laughed. "I have one, two if a friend shows up." She watched me. "Then I head home because tomorrow is a big day."

"But tomorrow's Saturday."

"Even worse. I run fund raising events on weekends because voters are out relaxing. It's the best time to tap them for donations — when they're not expecting it."

The singer returned to humming.

"So you work seven days a week, and drink seven nights in a blues bar?" I squeezed her hand so she would know I wasn't totally serious.

"Depends on the next election. Sometimes there's only a tax issue on the ballot. Then I don't work so hard. Might even get a massage."

The music stopped. We drifted apart.

"And I thought you were here waiting for me." I laughed.

She tapped a finger to her lips. "I may have been keeping an eye out." She stepped closer. "Would you like to go someplace quiet where I can keep an eye on you easier?"

She instilled a desire to follow like the Pied Piper's apprentice. But a camera sitting on a windowsill beckoned.

"Sounds wonderful. But I have to go back to work."

"Now?"

"Soon."

"Are you playing tonight?"

I shook my head.

"What kind of work does a guy do late on a Friday night?" She paused. "If it's not too personal."

"I'm watching a house for someone."

She came closer still. "Then kiss me goodnight. I have a big day tomorrow." She turned her face up and closed those wild violet eyes.

I held her shoulders, kissed her gently. Hands on the back of my neck urged me forward. A lower part of my brain traversed the list of this week's kisses preparing to add a new one. Her tongue touched the tip of mine. A tiny memory bubble broke loose and rose up through a sea of neurons. She pulled away.

"Thank you for the drink," she said.

"But you haven't touched it."

She smiled. "I haven't left yet."

I followed her to the table as the band opened the next song with a guitar solo made from recycled power tools. She picked up the martini, slipped into the chair, and crossed her legs in one fluid motion. She drank half, held onto the glass, and smiled at me while tapping to the beat with her free hand. Her lipstick was slightly smudged, but she didn't seem to notice.

I finished my beer. As the song ended with another screaming solo she upended her glass and brought it down to the table.

"Thank you again, Tommy." She leaned forward. "Maybe I'll keep an eye out for you tomorrow night." She grabbed the collar of my jacket, pulled, kissed me with an audible smack, stood up fast, and headed for the front door.

I was staring at my empty beer when a short black skirt came up beside me.

"Another beer?" she asked, picking up my glass.

"Yes please, and the check."

"No need, the lady took care of it." The girl reached for Tracy's glass.

My left hand shot out and grabbed her wrist. "Wait. Could I buy that glass?"

A round face and lime-green eyeshadow that matched the shoelaces faced me. "We don't sell glasses here."

I held on. "Please." I reached in my pocket with my free hand, found a twenty, and pushed it into her hand. "Tonight was our first kiss."

She looked at her captive wrist, the glass, me. Her hand closed on the twenty and she smiled.

"You seem like a nice guy, take it." She winked. "I break them all the time." I released her; the bill disappeared into her pocket. "Be careful you don't finish last." She glanced over her shoulder, then leaned closer. "If you ever got lucky enough to kiss me you wouldn't need a souvenir glass to remember it." Her laugh accompanied the squeak of rubber heels as she walked away.

I could have thought about Hosco, or Mona, or the plates stashed in the bank; or Tracy's offer, or a red Fiat driven by an artist. But my mind formed the question: *Why lime green shoelaces?*

Forty

I WRAPPED THE GLASS in napkins and tucked it in the trunk where it couldn't roll before heading to raincoat-girl's apartment. The dash voice spoke, "Eleven o'clock," as I drove past the front. Both units were dark. The street was jammed with parked vehicles, so I drove a zigzag pattern until squeezing into a spot too small for my Cuda between a crosswalk and a pink Cadillac. I stared through splashing wipers at a name in the Caddy's rear window, and wondered how Mary Kay kissed.

I walked to The Grace in a steady drizzle, my creepers squishing puddles on the pavement. I shook my coat and draped it over a hardback chair near the heater vent, then knelt by the window. The camera was capturing pictures; my binoculars hadn't moved. A light came on at the rear of the first-floor apartment. I grabbed the glasses and peered along the length of the building. A yellow beam of light streamed from the back window onto the stone walk I had been on an hour before. I pressed the Night Owl button; the image turned gray, then sharpened. No movement. I considered possibilities.

A lamp was on a timer.

A motion sensor had been triggered. I checked the trees for a cat. Rain fell vertically. Not a breath of wind. No more stars.

The light could have been turned on over the Internet. My friend Charlie at college could do that with the furnace in his family's ski cabin up in Michigan. He called it the Internet of Things; I thought it felt like living in a video game, and missed starting a wood fire when we arrived to warm the place up.

I couldn't see around the far corner to know if someone was approaching the apartment from the back, so I watched the front and the lit window. I zoomed the camera and shifted it to see more of the rear where the light had come on. While I was making the adjustment a speck moved on the display.

I grabbed the binoculars.

The woman I had failed to tail was returning, long coat and all — hips swaying under a midnight blue umbrella. Her coat wasn't buttoned and her skirt reached below the knee. I focused the binoculars. She turned up the walk toward the apartment. I studied her back. As she unlocked the door the magnification of the field glasses showed me a clear profile.

Tracy?

My lips tingled. She pulled the door closed behind her. More rooms spilled light into Chicago. Steady rain made an electric sizzle outside the window. I stared through the glasses until there was no movement inside the apartment. I triple checked my camera, then stretched out on the bed.

And thought of her kiss.

I opened my journal and ran down the list: hitchhiker, waitress, librarian, dancer. I sorted kisses in my head like a little computer working on a spreadsheet: Saturday night, my room at Victoria's, barber chair, big band dance floor, limo.

"And BLUES," I said aloud.

I wouldn't swear on any kind of Bible. Tracy sure didn't look like the hitchhiker. The hitchhiker looked like Mona the dancer.

I stared at the ceiling for a long time. Then scribbled.

Dress like Hosco's girl. Confuse witnesses (me) and security cameras.

Could Tracy be Mala's roommate? Or someone who took over her apartment to run a sting for those hundred dollar plates?

Mala had disappeared.

Maybe Tracy…

I got up and studied the apartment with the field glasses. If Mona's twin had been printing money with Hoskova of the Hugh-Hefner fantasy when that cop and his dog showed up…then a hair from Detroit would match the hair in my car would match dancer Mona's hair in a DNA test.

And the fingerprints wouldn't.

I lowered the glasses; stared at the apartment building through a haze of falling water, breathing the freshness of rain.

Could Tracy be a transformed Mala?

I reached a hand to the wall; closed my eyes to concentrate. Red hair to black. Glamorous clothing inside and out. Glasses. Contacts. Lizz could create that makeover easily. And the DNA, a kiss, a silencer.

Hosco had to be the connection.

I sat down and watched Tracy's apartment for another forty-five minutes before the front light went out. Ten minutes later the back light went out. I resisted the temptation to break in and convince myself Tracy was really sleeping there. That wouldn't achieve much, and would be hard to explain to Braden.

I laughed. Tracy had extended an invitation, and I turned it down so I could go watch her place. Then I frowned; she had been at B.L.U.E.S. on purpose.

"Why?" I said, to an empty room.

I wondered if talking to myself was a sign of stress, changed the chip in the camera, and took the field glasses with me. I hung the DO NOT DISTURB sign on the outside doorknob in case housekeeping stopped by.

I jogged to the Smart Car, drove behind splashing wipers to Penny's apartment, parked across the street and watched for five minutes, concerned it was too late to visit. Then I noticed flickering light behind curtains on the left side of the front door.

At just past midnight, I rang her bell.

A slender girl with freckles on her nose and loose blonde hair hanging to her shoulders cracked the door open. She was wearing a long translucent robe that couldn't be keeping her very warm.

"Are you Tommy?" she asked.

"Uh, yes, but if..."

"Penny said you might stop by." She pulled the door open, waited for me to walk into the dark living room and closed it behind me. She turned and leaned her back against the door. "Would you like something to drink?"

"Beer if it's handy, but..." Her thin robe seemed to be her only clothing so I studied a painting above the couch that could have been sand dunes, except they were yellow. "Am I interrupting? I can come back — "

"A little." She smiled with toothpaste-commercial perfection. "But that's okay. Penny was hoping you would stop by; she's enjoying working on your little mystery." She walked past me to an open kitchen and pulled on the refrigerator handle. Light flowed from inside, silhouetting her slender body. "Stella?"

I nodded. She returned with an open bottle. I drank slowly, my brain still reacting to seeing Tracy enter Mala's ten-month-old address.

No coincidence was that big.

She sat on the couch and crossed her legs.

"Penny talks about you. She's having a bit of a," she tilted her head side to side as she spoke, "yes, no, buddies, platonic, bucket debate with herself."

"She mentioned a list the other day."

Her eyes scanned me, giving me an inkling of what a dancer like Mona must feel on a nightly basis.

"She's already thinking about dying. Drives me crazy sometimes."

I tapped my beer, watched the bubbles rise, wondered if the entire city of Chicago was filled with people I didn't understand.

"I'm just a clumsy car mechanic." I met her eyes. "I'm sorry, I didn't catch your name?"

"Amber." She hopped up, shook my hand. "Let me go chat with Penny." She waved goodbye as she strolled across the room and disappeared through the bedroom door.

I stared at my half-empty beer bottle, trying to think of Hosco instead of Amber. On a stool at the kitchen counter I journaled details of my meeting with Tracy, and visit to Chin's garage.

Who put that device on my Barracuda? Two guys that know their way around grand theft auto. Who did they work for?

The fridge kicked on and I jumped like a shot had been fired.

I moved the martini glass from my jacket to the counter, wishing I knew how to use Penny's fingerprint kit. What should be my next step? Talk to Mona. Get rid of everything. Figure out why she left cash and plates with a complete stranger.

Because they're very, very hot.

Then there was the unknown entity named Theo. How many messages had been sent that I hadn't read?

And Tracy.

"She's keeping an eye on you, Tommy," I whispered to her glass.

I turned to a fresh page in my journal:

Objectives:

Who killed Hosco?

Get rid of the plates.

Get rid of the money.

I stared at the list. Then added:

Stay out of jail.

Don't get anyone hurt.

I drew a timeline, made assumptions about who knew what when, and included the cop in the catacombs walking through a dark tunnel.

I wondered what the dog had done first.

The refrigerator rattled and stopped, leaving the room silent. The sky through the kitchen window appeared black. The rain had stopped.

I stared at the empty martini glass hoping Penny could find a good print. Then I calibrated my expectations: the print wouldn't match anyone. If I were very lucky, maybe Tracy could connect me to the prior occupant of that apartment.

I tried to translate objectives into actions. The plates needed to go back to the hitchhiker. Same with the cash. And the phone. I had to remember to get rid of that phone—and its SIM chip I was carrying around like a spare quarter.

As I grew more fatigued, other problems elbowed their way in. My car was a mess; I couldn't load my stuff and drive west even if I wanted to. Chin needed time. Mona needed an answer.

I peeked in the fridge hoping for another beer. While I was busy trying to guess where a woman's mind hid things the doorknob to the bedroom rotated. Amber emerged sans clothing, floating toward me like a ballerina.

I opened my mouth to defend myself, but couldn't form words.

"Boys are always hungry," she said.

"You forgot your robe."

She smiled. "Penny's tired. You're invited to come snuggle with us." She pointed at the fridge. "In the door, at the bottom. Help yourself, then come visit." She motioned toward the street. "Your side is by the window." She floated back to the doorway, turned, and tapped on the doorframe with two knuckles. "Don't knock, we might be asleep."

"But—" Too late.

I found half a club sandwich and another Stella in the door, sat at the counter, continued my staring contest with the martini glass, and thought about text messages and cell phones: the very things I was trying to escape.

Forty-One

MY ARMS STRETCHED ACROSS the back of a red convertible like the hitchhiker in *Fear and Loathing in Las Vegas:* wind in my hair, not a care, the whole world at my feet. Amber was at the wheel wearing her robe, Penny sat beside her pressing thumbprints onto a clear bottle half full of foaming beer.

"Tommy, Tommy."

Orange became pastel green as I inched my eyelids up. Bright light shone in my eyes. Nothing familiar came into focus. Why was I lying in underwear stretched tight...

I moaned, "Hallo."

An angel said, "He's awake."

"Tommy, it's Penny. Get up, you've got to see this."

A California earthquake shook my body. I remembered Penny...the Pig...someone floating through a room.

I sat up. Penny and Amber were standing fully dressed. I was in their bed, by the window.

"It's ten o'clock. I couldn't wait any longer," Penny said.

Amber giggled.

The lump beneath the light blanket was obvious.

"Amber finds them amusing," Penny said.

"What's going on?" I asked.

She poked my shoulder with a finger. "You're being lazy while I'm up working on our project."

I blinked my eyes clear and swung my feet to the floor.

"Is it like that every morning?" Amber asked.

"Many," I said.

"You poor boys. Such *hard*ship." She giggled herself toward hyperventilation.

"Fortunately," I said, "there are known treatments."

"Have *I* got a treatment," Penny chimed in, "but we don't have time. Take a cold shower and get dressed. We have to figure out what this means."

I started to ask what *what* means, but Penny pointed. I crouched and raced toward the attached bathroom.

Amber laughed.

"Such a waste," Penny said from behind me.

Full cold in a shower with giant yellow flowers on the curtain and the aroma of girls everywhere was invigorating. I tried not to drop any of the ten bottles along the side of the tub while searching for shampoo, of which there were four. Five minutes later I was sitting at the kitchen counter with Amber while Penny cracked eggs into a bowl beside a black electric stove.

"You're going to make me guess?" I asked.

Penny nodded.

"Are you going to be upset if I guess correctly?"

She looked at me over her shoulder. "Do you think you can?"

"Maybe. Something made me suspicious. That's why I brought the martini glass."

"What?" Amber asked, sitting directly across from me in an olive green T-shirt and blue jeans ventilated by a razor blade.

I looked at Amber, then at Penny, who was staring at me while the eggs sizzled.

"A kiss."

Penny frowned.

Amber smiled. "How romantic."

"Care to explain, Casanova?" Penny said.

"Good-night kisses a week apart mysteriously registered as similar."

"Are kisses like fingerprints?" Amber asked. "You know, no two alike?"

Penny caught my eye. "We need more research to answer that." She winked. "Time to guess." She turned to stir the eggs.

"There's a print on the martini glass. It matches the print found in my car that matched the print you and I, uh, discussed at the bank."

Penny smiled. "Nice work, Mr. Holmes. You found the hitchhiker."

"By accident."

"Accident?" Amber asked.

"It's a long story. I was trying to find Mona's sister when I found a woman who drinks martinis."

"Who's Mona?" Amber asked.

"A dancer at the Pink Monkey."

"Oh my God," Amber said. "I was in there once. Those girls are so beautiful."

"I'll ignore that," Penny said. "So, Tommy, do you have a plan?"

"I stayed up late last night sketching out an idea. Thanks for the sandwich, by the way. You two were sound asleep by the time I finished. I'm hoping you'll help me."

She slid scrambled eggs onto plates and brought them to the counter. "Do I get to kiss anyone?"

"Better. You get to operate that cell phone you're curious about."

Over breakfast I spelled out their part of the job as I had conceived it in the wee hours of the morning. Then Penny used a maps app to find every Starbucks within a twenty mile radius of Chicago.

"You have to move right after you turn the cell phone off. Please don't be tempted to stay just a little longer. The chance of the phone being tracked is too great." I gazed deep into Penny's soft brown eyes. "Promise?"

She and Amber both swore on Girl Scout's honor.

After breakfast I packed up the martini glass and headed for Braden's office. He listened graciously, but was dubious about drawing conclusions based on a college student playing with a dusting brush. I promised him more and he agreed to meet me, but that was all. He did, however, offer advice: be extremely cautious, Chicago was home to millions, only some weren't dangerous.

It was late Saturday morning when I left his office. I needed to find Marvin fast and had no idea where he lived. The sky was gray again, and whitecaps studded the lake as I drove north toward Brenda's place: as good a bet as any. I parked on the street near the spot the tall man had occupied. My hands tingled like a laser was reading my fingerprints. I pushed crazy thoughts of paranormal voodoo out of my head, chalked the feeling up to knowing too many songs from the Mississippi Delta, and headed toward Brenda's apartment.

Before I got to the door a young black woman in pink leather pants and a furry black jacket came running out, tossed her arms around me, and held on.

"Oh, Tommy, are you all right? I was so scared but I took the video anyway because I knew you would need it. I'm so glad they didn't find you. Marvin told me about your car."

"Hi, Brenda. It's nice to meet you."

She stepped back but held on to my hands. Her head tilted and she glanced over my shoulder. Her eyes became round white pebbles.

"Is that your new car?" She burst out laughing. "Sorry, it's just so...so..."

"Elegant? Economical? Smart?"

She pulled on my elbow. "Come on up, Marvin is having breakfast."

Brenda disappeared into an adjoining room while I talked to Marvin at a round table for four. In the center stood fresh-cut tulips in a glass vase with a tiny car that could have been a Mustang etched on the side.

"You brought her flowers?" I asked.

"What? No, she buys them from the guy on the corner. Likes to stick her nose in them."

"You always up before noon?"

"Didn't have a gig last night. Hey, since you're here, I got that list for you." He eased a sheet of Hotel W letterhead across the table. It had twelve titles and the key for each one.

"Thanks." I folded the paper into my pants pocket. "I've got a new problem."

"Yeah, Brenda whispered to me about your new car." He laughed a low husky roll.

"Much worse."

I outlined my plan for him, step by step, move by move. When I finished he reached for his coffee and gazed out the back window. I waited.

"What about cops?"

"I talked to a lieutenant. He'll meet us after, but won't help. Doesn't think there's enough, I quote, 'court-ready evidence.'"

"He won't interfere?"

"He was silent on that point."

"And you're sure?"

"The fingerprint, carefully analyzed by a college student, says so. The kiss, analyzed by yours truly, says so. The shared address is suspicious. That's all I have to go on." I shrugged. "There's a good chance we're wasting our time and nothing will even happen."

"And there's a small chance it will explode like a bomb test at Los Alamos."

I leaned onto the table with both elbows. "You have any suggestions?"

"That meet your list of objectives? Nope. You have a lot of plates spinning, my friend."

"Sorta playing by ear here."

He nodded. "Okay, I'm in. When and where?"

I laid out details for Marvin then headed for my last stop: the Pink Monkey. On the way I dug around in the glove box until I found the black-banded Apple Watch and iPhone placed there by Penny's tech-wizard friend Manford while I was at her place. As planned. It used encryption that even the NSA complained couldn't be snooped. When I reached the Monkey the valet appeared immediately.

"Hey, didn't you have a classic?"

"In the shop. This is a loaner."

"Good thing. You'll never get lucky with that. What's Smart about it anyway?"

"It's really good at finding parking places."

He handed me the claim ticket. "Well, that's something. We're not open yet; you'll have to wait outside."

At least it wasn't raining. "Any chance Mona is working this early?"

"I think so. Politicians are in town. They're set up inside for a crowd."

"Think you could get me in to talk to her before things get busy?" I reached in my pocket and came up with a ten.

"I'll give it a try. Have to park the car first; can't leave it in the street."

I waited under the gray awning and thought about how many things could go wrong over the next few hours while staring at a poster of Sorana advertising the club. I was betting big on an amateur fingerprinter and a hunch. Her smile seemed to be asking me if I really knew the score.

I answered, "That's why we call it improvisation."

My valet buddy didn't come back. It started to rain. Not a hard blowing rain, but a light mist of fog flowing downward like the mist that surrounds a waterfall.

I watched the street and checked the mini-computer strapped to my left wrist. Mickey held both gloves above his head. Manford was good. He had procured, on short notice, four Apple Watches because they had a walkie-talkie feature that apparently left no record: a neat trick in the surveillance-mad 21st century. I wondered how long Apple had worked to pull it off.

I walkie-talkied Penny. "Are you set?"

"Starbucks north of the city," she said. "It's really crowded, and half the people in here are texting."

"Good. I still have a lot to do at this end, but let's kick off. Reply to Theo with 'Twenty-five thousand delivery fee in U.S. Benjamins.' Let's see what he does with it. Abbreviate all you want college girl."

"Got it." I watched the rain. "OK, on its way," she said. "Moving right now."

"Thanks. Tell Amber I'll be happy to buy her a new robe. Her old one has worn awfully thin."

Penny was laughing as a smiley face came through on my watch. I drew a four-leaf clover back to her; we'd need it.

A tap on my shoulder startled me back to Hosco's punch. I turned to find Mona standing on the sidewalk in blue heels and white stockings. A lacy bra matched her shoes. Her furrowed brow prepared to fire a question.

"What are you doing here, Tommy?"

"Visiting my friend Mona if she has time and doesn't get pneumonia from standing on a damp street in her underwear."

She slapped my arm. "This isn't my underwear." The tip of her tongue swiped across her upper lip. "Thanks for going to that dinner with me. It helped."

"My pleasure. Can we talk?"

She glanced up and down the street. Light traffic crept through the foggy rain, wipers streaking damp glass.

I took off my jacket and wrapped it over her shoulders.

"No, you'll get soaked," she said.

"I'll change my shirt." I took her arm in mine and we strolled toward the parking garage I hadn't used this time. "You still want to know about Hosco?"

"Yes," she said, staring straight ahead. Her tall heels made sharp sounds on the concrete. She didn't elaborate.

"First, how are you?"

"Cold." We walked twenty yards before she continued. "Oh, that's not what you meant. It's getting easier, like you promised. Plus, they started giving me a cocktail." She laughed her gentle way. "That's what they call it, a cocktail of different drugs mixed together on that little piece of paper. I feel almost human."

"That's fantastic. Second, remember the money bitch from your fancy dinner?" I waited for her nod. "Could you look like her?"

Her spikes tapped for the better part of a blues chorus. "She's my height. Dye my hair, wear frumpier stuff, fake the walk a little. I could get real close. Why?"

"You need to fool someone into feeling confident."

She stroked her cheek with her free hand. "You mean someone who had something to do with Rosco?"

"It's still a theory. But yes, a lot to do with Rosco."

"Then yes, I'll try."

"He might kiss you."

She stopped walking, turned to me. "That's harder."

"I can help." I took her in my arms and kissed her. "Harder, with your mouth closed a bit." I kissed her again. "Better, more movement." I kissed her a third time, doing everything I could remember from Tracy's kiss at the club.

"Do I want to know how you know this stuff?"

"Money bitch was at BLUES last night. We had a conversation."

"Uh-huh. Later come have a conversation with me." She smiled. "We should practice more." She pulled me toward her and kissed me long and full. Dark lenses and purple eyes melded into my mind.

"You learn fast."

"Helps when you work in as few clothes as I do." She put her arm in mine again. We stood close in the rain gazing at gritty brick buildings enveloped in fog. "What's next?"

"Mona, there's something I have to tell you. But it's only a wild guess based on a tiny bit of circumstantial evidence."

"What kind of circumstances?"

"An apartment, fingerprints, timing."

She pulled my coat tighter around her shoulders with her free hand. "Go ahead."

"I think Tracy Kane, the girl you call the money bitch, is the hitchhiker I picked up."

Her eyelids fluttered like malfunctioning camera shutters.

"But you said the hitchhiker was a redhead who looked like me."

"No proof. Just a wild guess by a guy from Ohio." I waited, feeling unsure. Then said: "I think Tracy Kane is your sister."

The shutters froze open. She didn't speak; I didn't know what to say; we stood close together in the rain.

Her throat moved as she swallowed.

"What do you want me to do?"

I pulled a memory chip from my pocket. "There's a video of a closet on here. You need to be able to match whatever she happens to wear as close as you can. Sorry I can't be more specific."

She blinked three times and nodded.

I held up a small gold key; Lizz's friend had delivered again. "This opens what he's after."

She took the key, studied it. "This is all about money isn't it?"

I tried to smile but it didn't work. "In more ways than you think. Here's a key to my room at The Grace; we'll meet there. This phone and wristwatch are paired. That button will walkie-talkie to me so I can hear what's going on. Text if you need to. If I call, the watch taps your wrist. That means leave *right away*."

She hefted the equipment up and down. "I'll get a bigger purse."

I held her shoulders until she looked at me, then tried not to melt into her green eyes.

"Mona, we don't know who we're dealing with. He might get angry if he figures out what we've done."

"Good. That'll make two of us."

"Run if things get weird."

She reached up and stroked the stubble on my cheek; I hadn't shaved at Penny's.

"Things have been weird for a long time, Tommy. I'm happy you're here to straighten stuff out."

I grinned. "Trying to earn the money you're going to *eventually* pay me."

She opened my coat she was wearing, and hugged me hard to her blue dancing outfit.

Then practiced kissing me again.

Forty-Two

ON MY DRIVE BACK TO THE GRACE I felt a tap under my shiny new wristwatch. The row of traffic crawling to my right included a pickup truck with a bit of space in front of it. More tapping. I flicked my blinker on and pressed the walkie-talkie button.

"We've got a response from Theo," Penny said. "Want to hear it?"

"How long ago?"

"Just now. I called right away."

I glanced at Mickey. One-thirty. The pickup had slowed and there was a parking place ahead. I waved a thank you, slipped through the opening and stopped at the curb.

"Go ahead."

"'A reasonable offer. I accept.' That's it. Came in…fifty seconds ago."

"How long before you're at the next Wi-Fi location?"

"Five minutes."

"Tell him, 'Cash. Sealed envelope. Trade for key to treasure chest.' As soon as you send it, move on, okay?"

"We're playing it just the way we talked about this morning."

"I like that you're in a room with other people texting, makes you harder to pick out. Try to make sure no one IDs your car."

"Tommy, please stop worrying. You're not helping."

"Sorry, a little tense here. If you're forced to change the plan, please keep me posted, so I can stay with you."

"Amber says, 'Thanks for the robe, winter is coming.'" Penny was laughing again as she ended the call. This time two smiley faces appeared on my watch.

I had the same sense of not knowing where things were going that I sometimes felt when improvising with a band — told myself that the key was to *listen carefully.* I pulled into traffic, inched toward the hotel, and ended up parking five blocks away on a street lined with short trees growing through holes carved in the concrete sidewalk. I locked the car and walked fast.

I didn't hear any sound from inside my room, so I turned the knob and swung the door inward slowly.

The glowing light on my camera said it was dutifully taking time-lapse photos of Tracy's apartment. The rest of the room looked like a rummage sale after teenage girls on speedballs had rampaged through. Clothing was strewn on every horizontal surface: skirts, shirts, jackets, bras and garments whose names I didn't know. A row of boots and shoes formed a marching army surrounding the bed, and the dresser that had been empty when I left now looked like the cosmetics department at Nordstrom's.

I eased the door closed behind me and slid the deadbolt.

I called out: "Hello."

The rattle of something hard dropping on tile came from the bathroom. Light seeped from under the door onto the speckled-gray carpet.

The mouse showed five till two. I inhaled through gritted teeth. Maybe I was being too optimistic pushing this to happen fast, thinking it had a better chance of success if the opposition didn't have time to organize a response. I wanted him, them, her to get careless.

The door to the bathroom flung open.

"Hi, Tommy."

I choked. There stood Mona, her face relaxed, wearing...nothing. However, my brain didn't see Mona, it saw Tracy Kane. She had dyed her hair black, shortened it, added gray eyeshadow, tinted her face the shade of Tracy's tan; and perhaps most impactful, stared at me with stunning violet eyes.

She frowned. "Didn't I do a good job?"

I struggled to find my voice. "Mona, you're fabulous, amazing, the best. I'm speechless. Where did you get all this stuff? And those eyes?"

Her face broke into a wide smile, lips parting hauntingly like Tracy's. "I have two huge closets, and the girls at the club all chipped in after we watched your video. Everything we saw was from this past season, no old-fashion hard to find stuff. And..." She fluttered her eyelashes, "Optometrists like the Monkey too."

I took a breath. "Uh, would you like a robe? Don't want you to catch cold."

She padded toward me barefoot. "I'm not cold. I'm excited. I like performing."

I looked down at my toes so I wouldn't stare. "I'm not sure how long we'll have to wait."

"That's okay, I have to paint my toes." She pushed a blouse out of the way, sat on the edge of the bed, and reached for a bottle of polish on the dresser.

I went to the window and stared at Tracy's apartment. There was too much at risk to be distracted by a beautiful woman pretending to be another beautiful woman who might be her sister.

The watch tapped my wrist. I accepted walkie-talkie. Penny's voice came through.

"He came back with, 'When and where?'"

"OK, here we go. Tell him, 'Meet Tracy at three o'clock. No intermediaries. Location TBD.' You and Amber are on the move, right?"

"We left after receiving his last message. Longer drive this time. Sending now."

I crossed fingers on both hands. I could be very wrong about this.

"Everything okay?" Mona asked.

"We're right on schedule." I grabbed the field glasses, peeked in each window, found Tracy at the rear of the apartment flipping the flap open on a brown purse. She pulled a phone out, stuck it to her ear, and stared out the window over the kitchen sink.

"She's on the phone." I glanced over to check on Mona.

"I bet she's surprised," Mona said, holding a toe with one hand and painting it pale pink with the other.

"Could just be her laundry service calling."

She finished the pinky and brought her left foot up to blow on the toes.

I turned back to the window. Tracy lowered the phone and placed both hands on the edge of the counter, still staring out the window. Then she walked out of sight.

"She's moving." With the binoculars in one hand I found my new phone with the other and sent a Manford-approved, secure, encrypted text to Marvin: *Suzy Q is warming up.*

I tilted the camera to make sure it was seeing the front sidewalk. We waited. Mona finished her other foot and blew it dry.

"How long do you need once we know?" I asked.

She tilted her head and studied the room, a commander reviewing her troops. "Depends how special you want me to be. But I can do it in ten minutes if I have to."

I watched the apartment through binoculars. Mona straightened outfits on the bed, not bothering to get dressed. I checked and rechecked my wristwatch as Mickey's foot tapped out the seconds. Tracy stepped through the front door. Little hand on the two, big hand on the five.

"She's at the door."

I drew a Q and an arrow on my watch.

Mona's bare shoulder pressed against me. I held the glasses in place and stepped to one side. She stepped in, brought them down to her eye level. Tracy moved toward the street under a dark blue umbrella and turned away from The Grace, just like she had done the day I lost her.

"I have those boots. Darn, I wish she would turn around so I could see her top," Mona said.

"Patience."

Tracy walked half a block before a black limousine pulled up to the curb on her side of the street. She stopped and stared. Two black men who could have been linebackers for the Chicago Bears stepped out of either side and stood still. Tracy turned one-eighty and headed back towards her apartment.

"Perfect," Mona said, gently sucking her lower lip into her mouth and chewing it.

The limo pulled forward until it was two car lengths ahead of Tracy. Two more men got out. Tracy turned around. The first two men were close behind and engaged her in conversation. One took her umbrella, the other her purse and gestured toward the limo.

I received a text message on my wrist: *Suzy Q has been invited to the dance.*

Mona handed me the binoculars and I watched as she transmogrified via girdle, garter with lacy straps, black stockings, pale blue blouse, and a long skirt with matching jacket in gray with a faint pinstripe. She laced boots three inches above her slender ankles. Brushed her hair. Bent over, stood up fast. Slipped on glasses with dark lenses and brushed until she looked precisely like the girl in the binoculars.

SQ on her way to the dance came in on my watch.

"Well?" Mona said.

"You look magical. You are magical."

She smiled. "I have to put on lipstick." She fumbled through a dozen shiny tubes on the dresser and picked one. When she finished she put the tube in a small black purse.

"Key?" I asked.

She reached into the purse and brought out a small key, then put it back into a zipper pocket.

"Fantastic. One more time, OK? Or will that jinx us?"

She faced me and held her purse in both hands. "I arrive first, contact the safety-deposit person. Move the box to a viewing room. If a flunky shows up, you'll tap me with three quick taps. Then I walk out. If he tries to stop me, I tap...that's what you said right?" She lifted her wrist and smacked her big watch face with the index finger of her opposite hand. "Tap the watch over and over. How am I doing so far?"

"Perfect."

She grinned. "Get the envelope from him, put it down my blouse. Hand him the key. Wait until he opens the box and looks inside. When he's happy, give him," she dug into her purse, "this second envelope. Don't wait for him to open it, walk out and exit the bank through the main door."

"You have an incredible memory."

"It's just like a dance. First this step, then that step. Not so hard."

I stood back to admire the transformation of her being—the shading making her cheeks appear hollow, the black hair, the stockings—astonished at how an image could be manufactured.

I sure hoped it worked.

"Watch muted? Phone muted? We don't want anything making noise around you."

She double-checked her new gadgets.

"Mona." I waited until she looked at me and tried not to let the smoky glasses and violet irises freak me out. "Impersonating Tracy is dangerous. A lot can go wrong. I understand if you want to stop now." As I said it my own threat meter urged me to get in a car and drive away fast.

"I want to help catch the killer," she said. "Rosco was a lot of things, but he was mine...however little-girl stupid that sounds." She held my eyes for so long I wondered where her mind had gone. "Mala might be hiding inside Tracy. That's just another way of leaving."

That sounded so strange coming from the new "Tracy" I had to think it through twice. But she was right, Mala had abandoned her.

"OK, let's go."

"Wait no, I always pee before going on stage." She disappeared into the bathroom.

In minutes we were in the Smart Car.

"This is neat," she said.

"What?"

"This little car. I feel like a kid racing around a go-cart track. Rrrrrrrr!"

"I'm glad you're not tense."

"Oh, I'm all knots inside. But you can't let that out when you have to act."

"You'll be great, Mona. Break a leg."

She smiled, leaned over and kissed me gently on the cheek, then rubbed the lipstick off with the side of her fist.

I stopped the car across the street from the main entrance, and tried for an optimism I didn't feel.

"We'll get him, Mona."

She met my eyes. The violet of her irises messed with my head. She nodded, popped the latch, and stepped out of the car with her purse and a shopping bag.

I watched her glide down the sidewalk captivated by the way her movements were exactly right: a dancer doing a Tracy dance. Then I touched my watch to walkie-talkie Penny, and waited for her to confirm the connection.

"Send Theo the GPS coordinates."

I stared at the device on my wrist, connected by the magic of physics to another device on Penny's wrist. Five words to put a plan irrevocably in motion. The technology I wanted to escape.

Saving my butt.

Forty-Three

I STASHED THE CAR on the second floor of a six-story public garage and backtracked three blocks on foot. Before I reached the Ace Coffee Bar the watch tapped the back of my wrist. I accepted the walkie-talkie, and heard Mona ask for access to my safety-deposit box.

I stood in a long line to order a latte, scratching the back of my neck so the watch's speaker was near my ear. Two of the four customers in front of me talked on cell phones. The metallic scrape of the box sliding out reached me, followed by footsteps, and a soft thunk as it was placed on a table.

"Will there be anything else?" a male voice said.

"Colleagues may ask for me. Please show them in."

"Certainly, Ms. Kane. I will be happy to."

I carried a hot latte outside and sat at a table where I could see the door Mona had used. The trunk of a tree that had been growing on the street for decades partially blocked my view; I hoped it made me harder to see from inside the bank. I rotated the chair so my back was to Ace's wall, then sent a message to Penny.

Response to coordinates?

I plugged a wireless earbud into my left ear, and faked a conversation to blend with the casual chaos of the Ace crowd.

"Are you sure? I asked him to send a new estimate right away." Other caffeine consumers ignored me—one more hyped-up guy doing business on a cell phone on the weekend, living the American dream. Mona hummed a gentle song in my ear. I hoped it helped her relax, so one of us would be calm.

"No, I don't want to start work on the old estimate. It's too risky," I said.

None. Waited 5 min. In transit. ETA in 2.

Theo going silent seemed reasonable. There wasn't much to say now that he had the coordinates.

The latte was too hot to drink, so I blew across the foam, watched the bank entrance, and waited with focused attention, remembering Chin lying beneath an SUV. It was still too hot when a long silver ingot of a Lincoln MKZ pulled to the curb and dispensed two people from the right doors. Both moved immediately toward the bank. I saw shoulders telling me only that one suit was shorter than the other. They stopped halfway across the wide sidewalk. A third man glided out of the right rear and stood behind them. He was the tallest, and dangled a fat briefcase in the hand furthest from me. All wore business suits.

As if marching to the same drummer the three started forward. The silver car pulled away. My instinct was to warn Mona, but the plan called for silence. It was bad enough I was connected to the computer watch in her purse. I hoped they didn't search her.

The middle man held the door open. No one looked back. I prayed the bank's security system was recording faces.

I pulled out my phone, laid it flat on the table and texted Marvin. *The band has arrived.*

Mona switched to humming a Lovin' Spoonful tune; I couldn't place the title.

Thirty seconds later my Watch transmitted the sound of a door opening. I checked in with Mickey. Six minutes before three. Theo was early, maybe hoping Redhoof wouldn't be ready. I saw the first domino in a huge row silently topple forward.

"Hello, Tracy," a male voice said.

She probably nodded and smiled. Speak little, like we planned. I wondered if he kissed her hello. And if she passed.

Latches snapped. *Briefcase.* I tried to visualize the action in real time. *An envelope changes hands and disappears down Mona's blue blouse. The clang of metal says the top of the safety-deposit box has been removed and placed on the table.*

"What have we here?" The same male voice.

Mona points first to the engraved plates wrapped in padding, then to the half a million in counterfeit cash she carried into the bank in a Nordstrom bag. I gave him sixty seconds to examine everything. A gloved finger indicated three more minutes till three o'clock.

A text message arrived.

Two men in lobby. Main entrance. Cradel's desk. Curly-headed blonde making a deposit.

Penny was reporting from inside. A bunch of people, none of whom had ever seen each other, were now in a web.

"Good," the man said.

I crossed my fingers and texted Marvin: *Singer exiting stage.*

I went back to visualizing the unseen action. *Theo is satisfied with the plates. The cash is a surprise, extra credit. Maybe he smiles.* I hoped the bonus and Tracy's presence made him lower his guard; believe more fully in what was happening.

Amber pulled up to the main entrance in a pale-yellow Jeep and double-parked.

I was holding my breath, so I forced it out. *Mona hands over a sealed business envelope with a single sheet of paper inside. She turns and leaves.* I hoped Theo's curiosity would cause him to open it. The letter I printed at the library would inform the reader of the path the plates and cash had traveled to reach his hands.

Leaving out any reference to the driver of a dirt-brown Barracuda.

Mona came out the main entrance, walked across the sidewalk as Tracy Kane, hopped in the Jeep, and disappeared to the floor as Amber whipped into traffic. The taller sidekick exited the bank, checked the street in both directions, and walked back in. My subconscious poked at me but didn't generate anything useful.

I stared at a white glove. One more minute.

A black limousine turned the corner, drove past the main entrance so it couldn't be seen from inside, stopped, and dropped a passenger without pulling to the curb. It was gone before Tracy Kane reached the sidewalk and walked briskly to and through the main entrance, looking to the world as if Mona had forgotten something, turned around, and gone back in.

I sent the message to disengage: *Suzy Q is taking the stage.*

The mouse arms ticked to ninety degrees. Tracy was right on time.

A scribbled arrow above a smiley face appeared on my watch. Penny was on the move.

A dark sedan leaned as it came around the corner, stopping directly in front of the entrance. Braden stepped out the left rear door. He moved into the bank with two men beside him. If he did what we had discussed, three more of his men were entering the side entrance as Penny was leaving.

I stood, grabbed my phone, and speed-walked to my Smart Car. I reached the expressway in three turns and one red light. Then cruised north toward Wisconsin.

$ $ $

An hour later and many miles into the cheese state I turned off at a roadside rest stop and parked near an open concrete structure with a picnic table under it. I sat on the table and went back over the chain of events by scrolling through the messages on Manford's watch loan. I was up to *Singer exiting stage* when the clouds released a steady drizzle that sizzled on the roof above me.

I should have guessed who would arrive first.

A long black limo pulled up beside Chin's loaner, making the small car appear to shrink. Penny popped out of the passenger door hopping up and down.

"That was awesome!"

Marvin stood with the driver's door open showing his glistening smile that softened girls knees.

"Did she give you any trouble?" I asked.

He pointed. "You mean this one? No, she just won't shut up about how awesome today is. The other one swallowed the story that we had been hired by her boss to escort her to a secret meeting. She didn't say much after that, but she chewed off a fingernail."

"I wish I could have heard their conversation," I said.

"Me too," Penny chimed in, jumping from one foot to the other. "Damn, that was so cool. All those secrets unlocked." She splayed her fingers outward. "Pow!"

"We won't know how cool until Braden contacts me." I shrugged. "Who knows what will happen now."

A splash of yellow exited the highway and parked on the other side of my car making a Smart sandwich. Amber slipped out and ran over to hug Penny. Then she turned and handed me an envelope.

"Special delivery."

I slipped on the rubber gloves Manford had provided, insisting they were necessary for security reasons, and opened it carefully. Five packs. If each contained fifty hundreds, the man had delivered the twenty-five thousand as requested.

Marvin sat on the other end of the table, lifting it under me. "Think it's marked?"

I nodded. "And the serial numbers have been recorded and entered into a data base that watches for them to enter a bank."

"Not much good. Money you can't spend."

"It's fun to look at," Penny said. "All that cash is exciting." Amber put an arm around her and squeezed.

"I'll give it to Braden."

"Why did you bother with it?" Penny asked.

"Appearances. Theo would have been suspicious if I offered to give everything back out of good will." I turned to Amber. "Is Mona okay?"

Her face turned somber. "She was trembling when she hopped into the Jeep. I helped her into the club the back way, like you said. Sorana and Anna were there, they'll say she was dancing all afternoon for the convention. She seemed better once she took off the Tracy clothes, but she didn't talk much."

"Maybe a couple of drunk customers will claim she was there too. What did you do with those clothes?"

She moved her thumb. "The Jeep. I almost threw them away, but remembered they always find evidence in trash bins on TV."

"Let's move them to my car, I know a place to hide them."

When we finished moving Mona's clothes I gathered everyone into a circle. "Thank you for helping me. I realize this was a strange, dangerous endeavor. It couldn't have happened without all of you." They stared for a quiet moment, like me, probably thinking about men with guns who would use them.

Then they all laughed. So I laughed too. It helped melt the tension away.

"When will we know if we got him?" Marvin asked.

"I'll contact Braden secretly on Monday. But he might feed the story to the *Tribune*."

Marvin took me aside. "Speaking of Monday, got a call from BLUES. They want to know if we can do a full set Monday night." He shook my hand. "I told them yes. Congratulations on our move up from open mic, Toe."

We waved to the girls as they pulled away, the yellow Jeep seeming to bob with Penny's energy.

"Seems like such a waste," he said.

"You mean two girls in the whole world that Marvin can't have?"

He sighed. "No one can."

"They have each other."

"OK, Mr. Philosopher."

"Speaking of girls. How's Anna's song?"

He gave me that smile. "Polishing the lyric, man, polishing the lyric."

Forty-Four

I DROVE THE SPEED LIMIT south toward Chicago, the steady hiss of spinning tires on wet concrete helping me concentrate. The longer I thought, the more unanswered questions appeared. I hoped Braden would be given the budget to sort them out. When I reached Lake Shore Drive I turned west and headed straight for Get Over It. Just after five o'clock I parked on the street behind Lizz's Fiat and carried Mona's disguise into the shop. Lizz stepped out from behind the screen when the door opened, glanced at the bundle of clothes in my arms, and smiled when she recognized me.

"You brought a sexy outfit that you can't wait to see me model?"

"Great idea, but no. I'm hoping you can lose this stuff inside your collection so no one can ever find it."

She took the clothes and placed each piece on a hanger, examined it carefully, then hung it on a long chrome bar beside what was quickly becoming my favorite chair in the universe.

"Someone was sexy in an office sort of way," she said.

"A disguise so a woman would be mistaken."

"For someone else?"

I nodded.

"And now the evidence disappears?"

"What evidence?" I said, and almost succeeded in keeping a straight face.

"It's Saturday night," she said.

"Hmm...that means something special, doesn't it?"

"Only to guys who are dating a girl they hope to have sex with someday."

"I've got to wrap up the action from this afternoon." My jaw tightened with the thought. "There's a potential problem."

"Oh, are you dating someone?" She grinned the little curved line that touched my spine, like a photon exciting an atom into a higher energy state.

"I think I am. But I'm not sure she thinks so." I watched her eyes. They were soft and wet and inviting. At least in my imagination.

"That would depend."

"On?"

"On whether or not you've heeded her request."

I nodded. "Oh yes. I think about her all the time."

"That must be hard." She winked. "How do you get anything done?"

"I work while I sleep."

"Oh." She pouted. "So you don't dream about her then?"

"A man has to make a living sometime."

"Sad, but true." She wiggled a finger. "Come back here, I've got something for you."

I was anxious to leave for the Monkey to check on Mona, but I followed her through the narrow back door into what seemed to be a closet. She pushed the door closed behind me and the room went black.

"Hold out your hand, Tommy."

I lifted my right hand palm up. It didn't bump into anything. Her hand cradled the back of mine.

She whispered somewhere in the darkness. "This is the only copy."

Something small and hard pressed into my palm. I closed my hand around it.

"Copy of what?"

"Recordings."

I stared toward the voice but couldn't see a thing.

"What are you talking about?"

"Just review them as soon as you can. They'll be self-explanatory. Kenny helped."

"How did you get them?"

Her hand moved away; her body pressed against me. Hands grabbed my head and pulled. She kissed me.

I forgot about all my questions for Braden.

"Your car is easy to follow. If your problem isn't too big, come back and take me to a late dinner, okay?"

"I would like that a lot."

"Me too," she whispered. Then the door opened and light stunned my eyes into momentary blindness.

I left Lizz sorting through Mona's disguise and drove slow and easy toward the Monkey sweating about holding the sole copy of a memory chip. I made a careful legal U-turn at an intersection with two cameras guarding it. Minutes later I pulled the Smart Car into Chin's ongoing Tetris game, and went inside. I found him sitting cross-legged on the steel floor of my car, in a trance.

I poked my head through where the driver's window would be if there had been a driver's door to hold it. I waited.

"Hello, Tommy," he said, without moving his eyes. "Your car is saying many things to me."

"Is it pissed at me for getting it trashed?"

His face relaxed into a smile. "No, she is not angry."

I reached my hand through the window and held out the chip.

"I've got a problem, Chin. A friend handed this to me, says there are no copies. I've got to go help Mona."

He took the chip. It disappeared up the sleeve of his mechanics shirt.

"I will guard until you return."

"Please copy it if you can. I don't know what's on there, but I'd hate to have to tell my friend I lost it."

I ran back to the loaner and drove to the Monkey, squeezing the steering wheel tighter with each red light. At the last minute (realizing I had started to develop patterns that could be used to find me, just the way the *Idiot's Guide* said I should find other people) I skipped both valet and the parking garage and put the car on the street northwest of the club. I walked fast, feeling lighter for having entrusted the chip to Chin. When I got there Anna was leaning on her elbows reading, wearing a silky black top whose sleeves stopped in the middle of her forearms.

"Studying to become a doctor?"

She lifted the book so I could see the cover.

"There's a *Complete Idiot's Guide* to exotic dancing?"

"Step-by-step photos. I'm learning a lot."

"If you're going to read, why not go to college?"

"Students have loans. Dancing pays me."

"Maybe business school would be a good choice for you." I glanced into a club busy filling up on a Saturday night. "Is Mona here yet?"

Her face melted. "What did you do to her?"

"It was a strange afternoon."

"She's really upset. Go help her."

"I'll try, it's my fault she was there."

"Where's there?"

I hesitated. "Safer if you don't know."

She was still for a moment, her face placid like a child at prayer, then she looked at me and nodded.

I crossed through the club. Nearly every table was covered with stacks of chicken wings, oysters or cheese fries. Mona wasn't on the stage behind the bar. She wasn't on the back stage. I found Sorana, who said she hadn't seen Mona in half an hour, sorry she was too busy to talk, and ran off. I asked both first floor bartenders then headed up the elevator. The upper floor was also crowded with guys and tables of food.

The bartender was dealing with guys standing three deep trying to order drinks so I turned sideways and wedged my way toward the stage. Dancers were three and four to a table; Mona was nowhere. Then I remembered she no longer had red hair and focused on the brunettes in the room. My eyes landed on a guy on stage strumming an electric guitar. But the sound system was blasting a rhythm filled with synthesizers and computer bleeps, so I couldn't hear him.

He had his back to the audience and was wearing a long white fur coat Liberace would have liked. Dark hair hung over the collar, adding to the wild-creature-cum-rock-star vibe. I moved closer, but still couldn't hear the guitar. Finally saw that it wasn't plugged in. And the player wasn't a guy.

It was Mona.

She plucked a string with a fluorescent pink thumbnail she must have painted after ceasing to be Tracy, maybe in an effort to get her dancer persona back. She sat still as a rock until the string stopped vibrating, then slowly chose another, and plucked. Her left hand held the neck, but wasn't touching the strings.

I couldn't see what she was wearing under the coat.

The dance music ceased throbbing, revealing a jumble of voices in the room. The jumble was immediately buried by percussion that could punch a hole in concrete, and a muted trumpet crying through a sea of echo.

I made my way to the stage and crawled across the back behind the amplifiers and drum set on all fours. Mona was sitting on a chair so we were almost eye-to-eye when her head jerked up in wide-eyed terror for a split-moment before she recognized me.

"Tommy."

"Hi, Mona. I didn't know you played guitar."

She tried to smile, but her face only trembled. "I'm hiding."

"Did he frighten you? The man at the bank?"

Her forehead furrowed. "I saw him."

Her left hand squeezed the guitar neck with white knuckles.

"Do you want to tell me about it?" I asked.

Her hand relaxed. She plucked the high E string. Didn't speak.

I waited. The rhythmic songs changed again. Trumpet became flute.

"You saw him," I said, keeping my voice even, matter-of-fact casual. I worried what that new rehab cocktail was doing to her; worried she had taken too much; worried she was in a bar with easy access to loads of alcohol.

Her head bobbed as she plucked the D string.

"At the bank?" I asked.

Her head bobbed again.

I closed my eyes and put my mind in replay. Who did she see at the bank? The taller guy. His profile. My brain lit up with the shape of a jaw behind a bright explosion from a gun barrel.

"Mona...did you see the shooter?"

She stared toward the ceiling, glassy eyes back to green but hair jet black, familiar bangs drooping to shaped eyebrows; her motionless face alternately shadowed and colored by flickering stage lights.

"His eyes," she whispered. "That night. I thought he was going to shoot me." She turned to me, her fingers white on the guitar neck again. "You pushed us."

I could understand they might want Hosco for skimming. But why Mona? The catacombs. Cameras? Of course a facility printing money, even fake money, would have security. Shallow graves? Guys helping Hoskova. Someone saw a redhead...or maybe a professional gunman simply didn't leave loose ends.

That could only mean...

She reached out with her right hand and gripped my forearm the same way she was crushing the guitar. "Tommy, I'm going...going to...they want..." She focused on my face and tears started rolling down both cheeks.

How could I help? First, I figured she needed a rehab cocktail, her drug ration for the day was wearing off. Second, police custody? That tracker in my Cuda worried me. Run away to a land of redheads and blend in? Men with guns would find her. Remove the threat? Much easier said than done.

My fingertips started to tingle from lack of blood flow.

"Mona."

She turned toward me, but didn't relax her grip.

"No one knows you impersonated Tracy."

"It's my fault."

That stalled my thinking engine. I could see Mona as a victim in a web of crooks. But how could Hosco's death be her fault? I made sure she was looking at me, then said: "You didn't cause anything."

Her head rocked up and down. "I did. They were dating. Then he—"

I tried not to show confusion. "Rosco? Who was he dating?"

Her shiny green eyes stared at me. "Mala. We were dancers. Near the big airport. Men would hire us at the same time."

Mala and Rosco. Hugh and his twins. If Rosco wanted Mona…

"Rosco offered you drugs?"

"Just a little," she said softly. She plucked a string. "Then more." Another string. "She came home…caught us…on her favorite leather sofa."

Colored Lego blocks clicked together into a winding Great Wall of Logic in my head. I touched her arm to make sure she was paying attention, and said: "Mala got angry. You both agreed to dump him."

She nodded, staring as if she were watching events replay on my face.

"You were supposed to stay away, but he got you to come to Chicago." I could guess how, but I wanted to hear her say it. "More drugs?"

Her hands became still. "I like them too much. They feel so...fulfilling." She breathed in through flared nostrils. Out. In, out. "She tried to help." Mona turned to me. "I wouldn't listen. Finally..." She blinked repeatedly. "It's all my fault."

Blame wasn't going to get either of us anywhere. But she wasn't safe sitting here in her polar bear coat.

"Mona, will you go hide while I sort this out?"

Her fingers relaxed slightly on my arm. "How?"

I felt a tap on my shoulder. Anna was kneeling beside us.

"Tommy, Slim is on the phone. Says it's extremely urgent."

"Mona, I'll be right back. You play the guitar, okay?"

She nodded and released my arm to pluck a string.

I followed Anna to the elevator and shook feeling back into my hand while waiting for the doors to close.

"Is she okay?" Anna asked.

"Not yet. She thinks someone is out to get her."

"It's about Hosco, isn't it? I never liked the look in his eyes. I told her he was no good, even though he was strong and cute and rich—" She grinned. "She could do a lot better you know?"

"She could. And will." I gazed into a room packed with fifty men and a dozen lightly dressed dancers, and saw a flea-market crowd pushing and shoving to get what they wanted. I turned to Anna. "Are you sure you want to become a dancer?"

"Is this the fatherly warning?" She laughed. "You're not old enough."

"Brotherly. Get out of here and study real books."

The elevator doors closed, quieting the racket from the club.

"Did *you* study real books?" she asked.

"Sometimes. But I was drifting. Spent too long getting a degree I still haven't used. Find something you want to become; pursue it. Even if you're wrong, it will—" I stopped myself, a drifter should be careful about giving advice.

"I want to be a cop."

I started coughing and couldn't stop.

The elevator dinged its arrival, barely audible over the music from the club.

"You think that's funny?" she asked, blue eyes wide, slender body stiffening to defend itself inside the tight black blouse.

I held up a hand, knowing she had shared a secret. Knowing she was now open and sensitive and I could kill a dream just by spitting on it. I shook my head. "Not funny. Surprising, yes. But not funny."

"I could be a good cop." She glanced around the club as if searching for someone, or maybe making sure no one was near enough to overhear. "I hate what the guys around here get away with."

"Anna, you can be anything you want if you work for it. But it's not going to walk in the front door of the Pink Monkey."

She smiled.

The elevator doors opened.

I blinked, remembering. "What do you mean, *get away with?*"

"I don't know exactly." She put her finger on a button. The doors started to close. "I only know something is going on because a few guys have secret meetings after the club closes and talk about 'did you reach so and so?' or 'is the package ready for tomorrow?'"

"And you know this because..."

"Bartenders whisper secrets to dancers trying for favors." She grinned. "Of course, we girls never share anything."

"Maybe you should do detective work."

She released the button and the door popped open. She led me to the front entrance where a phone was lying on the counter. I hoped Kim hadn't hung up.

"Tommy here."

"I was just about to send sled dogs after you."

"St. Bernards. They use St. Bernards, with a flask of brandy around their neck."

"Not if they're going to bring your body back horizontal for making me wait."

"Sorry, Kim. Things are way out of hand."

"Tell me about it. Braden called. And called, and called. He wants you in his office, and I quote, 'Right now!'"

"On a Saturday night?"

"Yeah. He doesn't care how late it is, get over there."

"OK. I'm on my way. We have a new problem. Wait, don't tell him that."

Anna watched me sleepwalk the phone onto the cradle. Braden had the guy. He had the evidence. He even had my letter explaining step by step what had gone down. Needing to see me on short notice couldn't mean anything good.

I grabbed a ballpoint with the top chewed half off from the counter and wrote a note.

"Anna, will you make sure Mona gets to this address right away? Tell the owner, her name is Lizz, that Mona has to disappear."

Anna looked at the slip of yellow paper, then at me, then the paper, then me.

"I'll get someone to cover the door and drive her over myself."

I smiled despite Braden's call heavy on my mind. "An escort is a great idea. You'll make a good cop." I stepped closer and lowered my voice. "Please don't let Mona change her mind."

Forty-Five

WHEN I REACHED BRADEN'S office the door was closed, yellow light glowed behind its glass, and no voices seeped into the hallway. Smiling Mickey showed seven minutes before seven. I found the little rodent comforting, in no small part because the inside of that watch held a record of what had gone down, and when. I stared at *Lt. G. Braden* painted on the marbled glass and tried one last time to guess why he wanted to see me. I failed, let out a deep breath, and tapped with one knuckle.

"It's after hours on the weekend. Go away."

Braden's voice.

"Lieutenant, it's Thomas Kelsey. I received a mes —"

The door flung open.

His gray-flecked hair hung to one side, like he had been pushing it that direction with a broom. "Tommy, good to see you." His red eyes shot up and down the aisle. "Come in, quick."

I leapt through the door to prevent being crushed as he pushed it closed.

"Thanks for coming. We have a serious problem." He dashed around his desk, the wrinkled jacket of his brown suit following him like a kite tail.

His choice of personal pronoun blocked out other thoughts.

"Please, have a seat."

I sat in the green-backed chair I had used when retrieving my wrecked Cuda, which made me think of Chin, the chip, and why Lizz even had a chip.

"I'm glad you're here. First, I need your help."

My eyebrows levitated. If *he* needed *my* help, things were very far south.

"Second, the girl is asking to talk with you before she calls her lawyer."

I cleared my throat, but he continued before I got any words out.

"It's highly unusual, but this whole thing is highly unusual. So I'm going to let her see you." He dropped into his non-squeaky chair and stared down at a document as he continued. "If you agree, of course."

"Agree to talk to her?"

He nodded.

"I'm not a lawyer or anything. There's no confidentiality."

"We know. She knows. Says she doesn't care. Says we can record it all if we want."

"Are you going to?"

He shook his head. "No way. She might say something we don't want on record that we would have to disclose to the defense."

"Can't we get a lawyer in the room? Protect her?"

"We could, but she refuses. Says she doesn't know a single lawyer in Chicago she can trust."

I tried to think of a lawyer I could trust — came up empty.

"She thinks she can trust me?"

"She says yes."

"Even after today?"

"Especially after today. She likes the way you made things unfold." He looked up. His gaze made me feel like a fish in a small bowl. "And it almost worked."

I tried to swivel the chair out of habit, even though it had four normal legs, and banged my knee.

"The word 'almost' sticks out in that sentence."

He grinned. "It was a good plan." He felt around his desk until he found the red pencil. The point was flat. "But there are complications." He scribbled on a sheet of paper and handed it to me.

LaRuche — State Representative
Feron — Homicide
Stevens — Property Control

"I heard LaRuche speak at a fancy dinner a couple days ago. What's he have to do with this?"

Braden's eyes moved around my face as if searching for clues. "You really don't know?"

I reread the paper.

"Know what?"

He leaned forward on his elbows. "Who did you send into that vault?"

"You mean the girl?"

He shook his head. "No, the person meeting her."

"Someone called Theo who sent messages to a cell phone that doesn't belong to me. I think Tracy Kane is my hitchhiker. When I answered Theo, I expected her to get a call. She did."

Braden whistled long and low, like a buzz bomb falling on London in a World War II movie.

"Who did you think it was?"

I shrugged. "Based on not much, I guessed Tracy might be Mala version two-point-oh. She went to the catacombs disguised as her dancing twin. Theo maybe found out she had been with Hosco in Detroit, maybe even knew the whole plan, and was upset he didn't get his merchandise."

He chewed his upper lip with his lower teeth. The tooth on his right was chipped at the edge.

"It's worse than that."

When he didn't elaborate I read the list again. "One of these guys?"

"Your Theo didn't know the details of the operation. He was being ripped off by Mr. Hoskova, the guy you call Hosco. At least according to the Tracy Kane we picked up at the bank."

"Is there another one?"

He winked quick. Barely a twitch. "The one you sent in."

"Ah, now that's mixed up too."

"Not between us. You know you're dealing with criminals, so you use a safety-deposit box surrounded by bank security. Clever. The disguise keeps your delivery girl from being recognized. If recordings show up, they implicate Tracy Kane. I arrive with the cavalry to clean up. Only one thing."

I kept quiet. I counted more than one, but he was clearly ahead of me.

"Theo contacts a phone, receives your reply. Out of nowhere you want a meetup that includes someone named Tracy. He has to wonder who you are and what you know." He paused. Tapped his red pencil on the blotter. "Because Tracy Kane works for him."

The list of names stared up at me like a bad poker hand making me sorry I anted up. I visualized the back of the head and the breadth of the shoulders of the third man on the sidewalk, briefcase in hand, strolling confidently into the bank.

"LaRuche? But—" I found my breath. "If he received my reply, how did he get the phone number in the first place?"

"You ask good questions, Mr. Cuda. Tell me, when did you receive the first message from Theo?"

I thought back, remembered cleaning the Cuda in Brenda's garage. "After Hosco was shot."

"Correct."

"Wait, how do you know?" I asked.

"Because I now have in my possession what I believe to be the hitchhiker's phone courtesy of a conscientious citizen who turned it in to a bank teller. She claims to have found it on one of those glass tables with the shelves underneath that hold deposit and withdrawal slips." He paused, his eyes distant. "Easy enough to lay a phone down while filling out a form, be in a rush, forget to pick it up."

Good job, Penny.

"So LaRuche gets the number after Hosco is shot. How?"

"Speculation on my part," Braden said. He waited like a comic timing a punch line. "He has Hosco's phone."

I wondered if cell phones could be uninvented, save everyone a lot of trouble. "How? From what I saw on TV, the police were all over that crime scene."

"Yes, thanks to an anonymous call." He tapped his chest. "Hosco's phone was in his breast pocket. A bullet nicked the case, but the phone is still functional."

"So you cracked the phone to get his phone numbers and messages?"

"Didn't have to, Ms. Meyers knew the security code. Says she saw him enter 4-8-4-4 a hundred times."

I knew it didn't spell Mona. "But you're saying LaRuche got them too?"

"Within hours of when Hosco was shot."

I tapped the paper. "The other two names."

He rubbed his chin like he was checking to see if he needed a shave. "I'm afraid so."

"LaRuche is plugged into the department."

Braden was quiet for a moment, his jaw working slowly. "He votes for State monies to help this police department every year. Cops raise donations for his campaigns. In a you-scratch-my-back-I'll-scratch-yours way, he's part owner."

I tried to swivel in the fixed chair again. Crossed my legs instead. "So I stumbled into an ongoing investigation, and messed things up?"

"You stumbled all right."

Damn, the world was complicated. "Sorry."

"Not your fault. Hitchhiker dumps nasty problem on unsuspecting chump who gave her a ride. But you know what's odd? LaRuche said exactly what you just said: he was acting with Detective Feron in a counterfeiting investigation."

"Makes sense."

"It does." He scribbled with his red pencil, handed me the sheet of paper. "The first number is the time you sent your twenty-five thousand dollar offer. Good choice, by the way. It's easy to get that much cash from the department fast. Any more, bigger signatures would have been required."

"I got lucky from reading too many mystery novels. What's the second one?"

"The time the case number for LaRuche's investigation was entered into the system. It has since been amended...and backdated."

The chair was hard, so I stood and paced to the door to lean against the frame and study the numbers. "This case didn't exist when Hosco was shot. Or when someone accessed his phone numbers. Or when Theo sent an inquiry. But it comes alive after I make the exchange?"

"Many coincidences, it would seem."

"What does Tracy say?"

"Nothing. Says she'll only talk to you. But she had better start spilling soon."

"There's something else driving this?"

"We opened Hosco's safe. He was a gun collector. A little Glock 26 in a black ankle holster sitting on the shelf is especially interesting. Has a fingerprint on it."

"You're losing me, sorry."

"Don't be, I've been piecing the Hoskova case together since before you called me to raid the bank." He took a breath and blew it at his pencil. It rolled across the blotter and stopped at the stack of paper. "And ever since." He looked up, met my eyes. "Your hitchhiker, Tracy Kane. Her prints are in your car. And on the offset plates."

I got it. "And on that gun?"

He nodded.

"I'll take a stab. Ballistics analysis shows that little Glock shot the cop in Detroit."

He gave me a crooked smile. "Home run, Mr. Cuda."

"Tracy is freaking out. Why doesn't she want a lawyer?"

"Claims they all connect to the fine Mr. LaRuche."

I pondered the mechanisms. "LaRuche can get to them: bribes, political pressure, threats of losing huge public contracts."

Braden leaned back and stretched. "This is the Windy City after all. Political bluster has been our specialty since the eighteen hundreds. It's not just the weather." He stared down at his folder, but didn't open it.

"What would you like me to do?"

"Talk to Tracy. Give me everything you can. I'll attempt to prove it. But it's likely impossible with most of the department trying to defeat me."

"Why, Lieutenant?"

He opened the folder. "Why fight this, you mean? If you hadn't dropped it into my lap I'd be having a pleasant weekend fishing in a Wisconsin river. Now there are too many pieces that don't fit. But the real reason — " he opened the folder. "I think you've discovered the tip of a fat-cat iceberg." He met my eyes. "I want to destroy it."

"I'll be happy to talk to Tracy. Could I ask one more question?"

He nodded, his pencil poised over a stack of white documents.

"Did LaRuche say anything about a redhead?"

Forty-Six

MY JOB WAS TO EXTRACT details of the operation from Tracy. Braden would attempt to prove them. He showed me an FBI-style FD302 witness form just like the one described in my *Idiot's Guide.* Then reminded me that LaRuche's legal team would have access to her signed statement.

Our problem was one of trust. We couldn't trust anyone inside the building, telephones, conference rooms, and certainly not email. Taking Tracy Kane out of the building opened us to surveillance, which might add my face to LaRuche's list of people of interest. Braden insisted we avoid my being seen because it would limit my already limited usefulness.

All of which left us without a plan of action.

And me sitting on a hard chair staring down at a scuff mark shaped like a lipstick smear on Braden's tile floor while he doodled with a red pencil, having exhausted every trick we could conjure up.

My thoughts roamed from Tracy to Mona to the Monkey to Anna's elevator comment about what "the guys around here get away with." Little blue-eyed Anna, who wanted to be —

I sat up straight and said: "Make her a cop."

His pencil stopped drawing circles. "What?"

"Put her somewhere that no one will see her change into a uniform. Then let her walk out the front door."

"And?"

I pointed. "Can I use your phone?"

I lifted the handset of a black brick of a phone and punched in a number while Braden paced back and forth behind his desk. Chin answered on the second ring and recognized my voice.

"You must see," he said.

Knowing he would repeat it like Chinese water torture I agreed to drive to his place.

"Did I see a cab on your lot?" I asked.

"Yes, Prius. Need battery."

"Can I use it tonight for an hour?"

"Sure. Run on gas." A pause. "Maybe battery. Not sure."

I hung up and turned to Braden, who was still pacing.

"Figure out how we do it?" I asked.

"How long do you need her?"

"Hard to guess, because I don't know what she's going to say. Can you get me thirty minutes?"

He nodded. "I'll need prep time."

"Me too." I glanced at my wrist; thought hard about what I needed to do while watching a tapping yellow shoe. "Seven-thirty now. How about she walks out the front door at eight-seventeen sharp?"

"Then what happens?"

"A dark-skinned guy will pick her up in a Prius taxi. It's registered as *Out of Service* if anyone grabs the cab number. He'll drive around for thirty minutes while she talks, and drop her back at the front steps at eight forty-seven."

Braden was quiet for a moment. "I'll take her to a conference room personally and fake an interview in case they're listening. I can record her voice making few responses into a smart phone to play back intermittently. We just have to make sure nobody sees a female officer walk out of the room that didn't walk in."

"Think anyone is paying that close attention?" I asked.

"I'll be surprised if anyone pays attention to our Ms. Kane on a Saturday night; Chicago weekends are filled with fresh things to worry about. But the log will show I brought her out for interrogation, and which conference room we used. I'll make sure transcripts are available for prying eyes. She hasn't been talking much, so minimal fabrication will be required."

We shook hands. I jogged to my Smart Car and drove straight to Lizz's place. To the left of her front door a wrinkled, overweight woman slouched beside a grocery cart filled with overstuffed garbage bags. She was staring down at half of a paperback novel. I wondered if it was the first half or the second. Trying to miss the remnants of mozzarella, I dropped a ten in the open pizza box at her feet. She lifted a gloved hand off the novel to thank me, then used it to turn the page.

Lizz was sitting in her barber chair staring into space. The way it dwarfed her suggested a queen on her throne.

"Where's Mona?" I asked.

She blinked. "Hello to you too, Mr. Long Toe Fowler." She lifted an arm and rubbed her fingertips together. "I have sprinkled fairy dust on the lady whose name you have foolishly uttered and transported her to the land of enchantment. She is no longer visible from this dimension."

"Thank you, thank you. Can you help me become a foreign cab driver?"

"Not if you need a cab." She laughed and stood. "Please sit."

She plopped on a straight black wig with spray-painted gray tint. My eyebrows became thick and dark. She gave me a little black cap that I think was meant for a Greek sailor, a rumpled army-green shirt missing a button on the collar, blue jeans, and black Italian loafers she must have grabbed for a dollar at the Salvation Army. Then rubbed layers of cream into my face making me even darker than Tracy's tan.

Chin didn't recognize me when I walked into his garage. Until I said: "I must see."

That made him smile.

"I have twelve minutes," I said. "If you're sure the Prius will start."

He appeared thoughtful, nodded, and sat me down in front of his double monitors. "Watch."

I recognized the inside of the bank. A short curly-haired blonde woman ran up to a man and threw her arms around him. He pushed her gently away, saying something, though there was no soundtrack. She brought her hands up to glamour-girl makeup in a gesture of apology, then ran across the bank toward the door, bumping another guy on her way out. In a moment, she was gone.

"Audio files come separate. I re-sync."

"Are you a mechanic or a computer jockey?"

"Yes," Chin said.

I watched the men stand stone still, making no move to do banking. The round face of the bank clock on the wall showed three minutes before three. If it was correct, Mona was inside with the plates, the cash, and LaRuche.

"Listen," Chin said.

An audible click was followed by, "What a crazy chick."

"If she thought you were cute, bitch must be blind."

"Shut up, Stevens. You're just jealous."

"They're not being careful," I said.

Chin nodded. "Bored. Not ready to fight."

"Jealous? Over that midget?"

Laughter. I tried to connect faces to faint recollections of a profile in Chin's garage, and shadows on the street stealing my Barracuda, but couldn't be sure.

In the video the two men remained motionless. Penny drifted into view, collecting paper forms from cubbyholes in desk stands, being my eyes inside.

"When — " I began.

"Wait," Chin said.

I waited while Chin stared like he was seeing this movie for the first time. The first man sneezed, brushed a hand across his face.

"Did you see his watch?" Chin asked.

"Saw he was wearing one."

"Rolex Mariner. Very expensive."

"Maybe an award."

"Perhaps," Chin said, and returned to staring.

A woman in a gray skirt crossed the screen from left to right. She didn't make eye contact with anyone, but both men's eyes followed her. Mona dressed as Tracy leaving the bank.

"I told him not to bring her in. Dames can't be trusted." The first man's voice, barely a whisper. I suddenly remembered the names on Braden's list. His demeanor shouted detective. Feron.

He lifted a hand to motion to the second man, then followed Mona out of the video frame.

"Are they using radios?" I asked.

Chin nodded. "The blonde girl. I study her movements. Tiny bugs on floor behind men."

"Who's jealous now?" the second man said. Stevens. The guy from property management.

Feron had been gone only a few seconds and was returning to his earlier position. "She makes him think with the little head."

"Since when do politicians think?"

"We're never supposed to be seen together. His own damn rule, and look at this crappy setup."

"No warning," Stevens said.

The real Tracy came in headed toward the safety-deposit vault. They both tracked her movement carefully.

"Forgot her purse." Stevens voice.

"Something's not right," Feron said. "She's tense."

"Maybe the boss is mad. Her dragging us down here."

On the video, Feron's head shook. "The Man said, 'we've been invited.' Wouldn't say that if this was her gig."

Feron shifted on his feet, reached inside his coat.

I hadn't seen any of this from my perch outside at the Ace Coffee Shop. "What's he doing?"

"You want guess?" Chin said. "Adjusting pistol for quick access."

The video ran in silence for ten seconds. Penny moved causally up to a long narrow desk, then out of the frame.

"Who then?" Stevens asked, as if no time had elapsed.

"Someone connected to romeo hotel," Feron answered.

Stevens body grew taller; his eyes darted from bank customer to bank customer.

"You know this Romeo person?" Chin asked.

Forty-Seven

CHIN JUMPED UP AND RAN behind the counter. He tossed a black object into the air.

I caught it with my left hand.

"Electric." He thrust his hand outward. "Silent. Do not be fooled."

The yellow curve of the roofline of the aerodynamic car reminded me of a dinosaur egg I once saw at the Field Museum of Natural History right here in Chicago. I put the key in and dash lights came on. Nothing else happened.

I missed my Hemi's song as the car glided quietly out of the lot toward Braden's office, the consumption meter dropping every time I braked, and rising when I pulled away — a Pavlov-dog trick training me to save energy.

I stopped at the curb in front of the wide arch of the wooden doors of the church near Braden's office. Three minutes early. The car made no sound while I adjusted the brush-shaped mustache Lizz insisted I add before seeing Tracy. I double-checked the cab-available light to be sure it was off.

With thirty seconds to rendezvous I eased the car forward and stopped in front of the police station. I powered the passenger window down and listened to the sound of distant traffic. A bird squawked somewhere behind the car. I rested my eyes on the sidewalk in the distance where a tree root had lifted the concrete, and did my best imitation of a bored, disinterested cabbie awaiting a fare. Then footsteps: a rubber sole scuffing softly against the sidewalk. The right rear door was pulled open; the little car rocked as someone slid into the back seat.

I reached up and twisted the inside rearview mirror until I could see her face: violet eyes, no glasses, no makeup under a cop hat with a checkered band; hair tucked up out of sight, the puffed-up cap dwarfing her face — just like that inflated cap had done in the darkness of my room.

"Where to, ma'am?" I asked in a low voice.

"Wherever they told you to take me."

She stared out the window. I pulled away and headed north, drove three blocks and turned west. To my surprise, the car was still running silently on electric. I stopped at a light and powered the passenger window up.

"Why did you want to see me?"

She frowned, looked around for my cabbie's license, which wasn't there because I didn't have one, then back to my face. She bent far forward and studied my profile.

"Who the hell are you?" she said, then slid hard against the back of the seat.

"Let me tell you a story about a guy who picked up a hitchhiker. She lied about her name, and dumped enough hot property on the unlucky fellow to melt the gold in Fort Knox."

I drove steadily toward the lake, eyes forward, giving her time.

"Tommy?" she whispered.

"I researched your name. It means *the bad one.*"

"That's not true."

"You're not Mala?"

"No. I mean yes…I was. But I'm not like that. People don't understand."

I pulled into the drive-through lane at the smallest Starbucks I had ever seen. Six cars had gotten there before me.

"Braden gave us thirty minutes," I said. "We're not being recorded. Did you want to tell me something?"

"I didn't do it," she said, loud enough to count as a scream in the small car.

"You're ahead of me. Do what?" I inched the car forward.

"I didn't shoot the cop."

"Your print is on the trigger of the gun that matches the bullet. Circumstantial. But disturbing."

She stared out the window at the gray brick wall of the building next door. Black and blue graffiti at street level that might have been gang symbols decorated the bottom of a giant painting of a manga girl with huge gold eyes pointing a silver gun as big as her head directly at us.

"How about if you begin at the beginning and don't leave anything out? Try to save a few minutes at the end so we can plan a next step."

She took deep breaths, in-slow, out-slow like a yoga instructor, before turning toward the back of my head.

"LaRuche is an ass. I help him set up the laundry to move our paper through that confiscated property department the cops have. We substitute our bills before the seized cash is reallocated, usually to buy toys for boys like guns and gas masks. Millions of dollars flow through a government program called Equitable Sharing; so it's easy to hide a little here and a little there. "

She paused, did her yogi breathing again.

"I create other avenues too: stuff donation barrels, leak cash out through nightclubs, bribe people; all so he has more to spend than his opponents. Works like a voodoo charm—he has friends everywhere doing him favors. He makes big promises. Even bought me a sparkling engagement ring that I'm not allowed to wear—we have to stay secret because he's still married to the blonde. Tells me he has to keep up the image." She paused, staring into space with those unusual violet eyes. "Which became a huge problem when he suddenly decided his life won't be complete if he's not governor. But voters won't like Tracy LaRuche in the Governor's Mansion: too young, pretty, no wholesome American kids to show off on TV. The prick. I'm through waiting."

She gazed out the window at the brick wall and the silver gun. I crept forward.

"The prick," I mumbled.

"Hosco was LaRuche's printer, but you figured that out. It was Feron who introduced them. Anyway, Hosco finds out LaRuche is blowing Tracy off. Knows I'm pissed. Smells opportunity. He comes to me with a plan: make some money for ourselves. Literally make it — print a few extra runs. He has it all figured. We use the laundry network for our own benefit. I help him, he helps me."

Tracy Mala Kane Meyers finally wasn't lying, pretending or manipulating. She was scared.

"And you trust Hosco? After everything?"

"Just business. Trust has nothing to do with it."

"Does it work?"

"Starts to. Hosco gets a mill out over a couple of months. That's what we were doing in Detroit, making money."

The line inched forward. I heard the guy in front of me order fifty dollars' worth of hot water and sugar.

"The plates?" I said.

"Afterthought. We were almost finished with the run. Hosco knew where the security cameras were, had them disabled. I was in a little crawl hole where we hide things; the cover blends in with the dirt floor."

She stopped and stared out the window, her creamy cheeks taut beneath the puffy cop hat. I could just make out freckles along the ridge of her nose.

"You're alluring in uniform," I said, trying to keep her talking.

She turned, met my eyes in the mirror. "Tommy, this is serious."

"Why were you in the hole?"

"I was retrieving paper others had printed."

"Stealing it?"

362

"Sort of."

I pulled the electric car forward. Easy, like an amusement park ride. "How do you *sort of* steal money?"

"You change where it was supposed to go, pretend it went to the new place, and keep it for yourself."

"That makes sense?"

"If you understand our network. Once we stuff money in, it's hard to track...on purpose. Everything is fine so long as LaRuche the asshole gets his pervs. That's what we call them, pervs: perks and votes. LaRuche thinks it's funny."

"You reallocate it to your own pocket."

She was quiet for a few seconds. "That's one way to look at it."

Time was short, so I prodded. "You were in the hole retrieving money."

"A cop waltzes in with his dog, catches the guys cold. Not one of them did a thing. I'm shocked our security is so lax. Figure someone ratted."

I pulled forward, ordered two lattes.

"Extra foam," she said, from the back seat. I repeated her request to the barista.

"So you had to," I said.

"Either that, or we were all going to jail."

"So you shot a K9-patrol cop."

She wagged her head hard and fast. "No, no I didn't. I mean, yes, but no, I wasn't trying to."

I handed the clerk a twenty; didn't get much back.

I passed her drink between the seats and put mine in a plastic cupholder near my right knee. "Could you translate that?"

We pulled away in silence.

She blew into the little drinking hole in the top of her cup, her lips so like Mona's in the back of the limousine. When she stopped blowing she said: "I was in the hole."

"Out of sight."

"Exactly. I take action or we do time. Except LaRuche, he'd buy his way out. Might even help put us away if he figured out what we were doing to his wallet. You know, LaRuche always has his lawyer in the room so conversations are privileged and confidential — can't end up in court. He also makes sure he doesn't dirty his mind with details." She sipped her drink carefully. "His middle name is Plausible Deniability."

She stopped talking.

"We have eighteen minutes before I drop you back at the station."

She took a deep breath, stared out the window at window shoppers, sipped.

I couldn't tell if she was figuring how to tell her story, fabricating a lie, or scheming how to use me in the next phase of her plan.

"OK, you get the drift. Hosco and I are stealing fake money that we know how to launder. We want to get our piece of the action and drop out of sight. LaRuche can do whatever he wants; we're just not going to do it for him anymore."

"I thought Hosco already had a million."

"Men are *always* the problem. They think greed is macho. We were supposed to split the million. We got the million, but he spent his half." She paused. "You saw the car?"

"Subtle. At least it wasn't red."

"Right. So now he wants to go for *another* million. I try to talk him out of it; he threatens to tell LaRuche I've been robbing him, make himself out as Mr. Whistleblower. Who knows what LaRuche would do because the truth wasn't pretty. I wouldn't get far telling LaRuche, 'Oh no, I wasn't robbing you, we both were.'"

"So you can't take your half-million and bail?"

She shook her head while blowing on the cup.

I pulled into traffic. "So you go along?"

"I make him promise it's the last time. Promise not to wait for another press run. We just go in, take what's there, and print what we have paper for."

"And you believe him why?"

"I don't. I arrange for extra cameras to record Tracy's personal insurance."

"Extra?"

"LaRuche has tiny surveillance cameras hidden all over the place. But I take care of details for the fine Mr. LaRuche, who trusts me because he thinks I'm trapped by his charm. I added a couple that Hosco didn't know about."

"You handled anti-security."

"Right. When I told Hosco the room was clean, we went in."

"He trusted you?"

"Hosco wouldn't trust his mother. He figured if I recorded anything, I'd bury myself along with him."

I stopped behind a silver Prius at a red light. The silence in our car felt spooky, like the moment the world stops turning in a sci-fi movie.

"You say that like you're the invisible woman."

"Exactly."

I checked the mirror. She was drinking; her face serious.

I eased the pedal down and started rolling.

"We've only got a couple minutes. I'm not following you."

"Hosco never figured it out either. I had the tech contractor schedule tests on specific camera numbers at predefined times. Told him we were having blackouts."

"Hide and seek."

"You're quick, Tommy Cuda. Those tests encrypt video and store it for review. I'm the only one with the password to the test files."

"This is how you prevent techs from seeing things?"

"And other prying eyes."

"Did LaRuche know there were three guys and a redhead?"

She hesitated. "If the tech ran a test manually, instead of scheduling it like I told him, he might have seen something during setup."

"Yeah, a hot girl. Grabbed a pic for himself. Maybe talked about it."

She grinned. "Yeah, our tech might do that."

I made a right turn to carry us toward the station, wishing I had about three days to interrogate Ms. Tracy Kane.

"You want to know where the recordings are?" she asked.

"After you tell me what's on them."

"You won't believe me."

My mustache scratched my lip when I smiled. "I will when I see them."

"Cop has three guys at gunpoint. Dog is being very attentive. I slip in the hole, ease the hatch closed and stare at the clock on my phone. Yeah the one I gave you. I'm waiting for the scheduled camera test so it will see only three men. No one knows. Especially Hosco doesn't know."

"You're trapped."

"Right. I wait, the cops have us. I don't wait, the camera has us...including me."

"Tough choice."

"Not that tough. I don't have much faith in our judicial system, especially with LaRuche around. I crawl out of the hole and across the floor on my elbows. Even the dog doesn't notice me."

"So you're low. And you know about the ankle."

Her eyes flashed to the mirror. Then she slowly smiled and nodded. "Yeah, Hosco's carried that for a long time. He does a good job of not flinching while I pull it out. It's a Glock, so I don't have to mess with it to get ready to fire."

"And you shoot the cop."

She shook her head hard, dripping latte on the back seat of Chin's car.

366

"No way was I going to shoot a cop; that's a one way ticket to a long vacation. Much worse than printing a little money. I just wanted the hell out of there. I planned to shoot out the light, hope the dog went crazy, and we could deal with the cop hand-to-hand in the dark. I mean, there were four of us. The cop's backup hadn't arrived. It had been mere seconds since he found us."

I stopped in the parking place in front of the church I had occupied twenty-odd minutes earlier. The tower bells were ringing. She continued.

"There were two lights. I figured the one that would put us in darkness was the better choice."

"We're down to three minutes."

"I was flat on the floor. I lifted the barrel until the bulb glowed through the gunsight."

"The dog distracted you?"

"Hosco kicked me in the side; I fired as my body spasmed."

"And the bullet hit the cop."

She nodded.

"Let me guess the rest. Hosco grabs the gun. Knows your print is on it and it'll give him leverage. He runs, his buddies follow. Leaves you on the floor so the cop and dog have something to do."

She was staring again. "Yeah. He left the cop lying there."

"So you grabbed the backpack, and somehow remembered the plates."

"I needed them as a bargaining chip." She pressed her lips tight together. "I was scared the cameras had seen me with the gun."

"But you...never mind. How did you get out?"

"I figured Hosco would take the fast tunnel back to our SUV, so I opened number three. It's behind the steel barrel where we stash printing mistakes. I replaced the barrel and crawled out using my cell phone for a flashlight. That tunnel is small, so I couldn't go fast."

"Cops didn't find it?"

She shook her head.

"You stuck out your thumb. Got picked up by a trucker who saw a Mona lookalike."

"And found you buying a double-decker burger." She was staring out the window, her face expressionless.

The dash clock said we were a minute over time.

"Your sister misses you. And could sure use your help with her own monkey. You know she has problems, why frame her?"

"Frame? What are you—" She shook her head. "You have it wrong. I knew Mona would have the club as an alibi. And if LaRuche ever saw a video, he'd see Hosco with his drug-addicted stripper girlfriend, no matter what Hosco tried to tell him."

"Ah…which made Tracy invisible."

She didn't respond right away. Then said: "Even Hosco thought it was a good idea to keep Tracy in the background. So I could bail him out if things got messy with LaRuche."

The car was quiet until I said: "I don't understand why you needed a stranger named Tommy Cuda."

"I was in distress."

"And Tommy rode up on a brown turd of a white horse?"

Her lips, pink full and kissable even without shiny red gloss, managed a weary grin. "Too many eyes on me. LaRuche's guys watching Tracy. Hosco interrogating Tracy. I had to be able to look him in the eye and say I didn't know where the money was; I didn't have the plates. If I had hid them myself…" She shrugged.

"Did you have a plan for me?"

"Not you. Tracy was only planning to steal her belongings back." She paused. "At a safer time."

A sharp shadow slanting across the golden doors of the church made me think of sundials, and the passage of time, and my original objective.

"*Was* planning?"

"Unforeseen things happened," she said.

We sat in electric quiet.

The mirror showed me Tracy. I thought of Mala.

One of us had to say it. "Gunshots?"

Her lips rolled inward, as if she were suppressing tears. My mind's eye saw a gold smartphone on a familiar nightstand. On its screen a shiny bullet morphed into a copper-colored butterfly whose glistening wings flapped faster and faster, chasing me onto Chaos Road.

"So you lost control too?" I asked.

She burst into an alto laugh I hadn't heard before.

"No one has control, Tommy. That's the whole point."

I hoped she was wrong. And although the hole I was in might get deeper, I had to ask to help Braden. "So. Where are the files?"

"In Kinkos."

I thought of the Missing Mona flyers Penny and I had printed. "That copy company FedEx bought?"

"No silly, the computer system that runs security for the Detroit tunnels."

"Let's go to Detroit. Use the recordings to help clear you."

She shook her head. A strand of black hair escaped from the hat and flapped against her tanned cheek.

"No need. The computers are in LaRuche's house."

Forty-Eight

TRACY CROSSED THE SIDEWALK and jogged up stone steps to a waiting Braden. The street was empty in both directions, but I worried an observer would snap a picture of a cop using a cab to run out for a latte, and tweet it. I sure didn't want that kind of attention. As I pulled away I considered who should visit Braden with Tracy's information: cabbie, Long Toe or Tommy. I decided on Long Toe. The thieves had probably already seen him, and wouldn't be surprised he was talking to the cops about a missing car.

When I reached the garage, Chin had a copy of the movie ready for me, but I hesitated, fearing the distraction would interfere with my memory of Tracy's story. I didn't want to commit her words to paper—too permanent. And traceable. So I needed to see Braden right away.

Chin asked about the Prius.

"I was on electric the whole time. Mostly sitting in traffic."

"Engine never start?"

"Not once. Was it supposed to?"

"Yes. Maybe. I check."

I removed the mustache, and washed makeup into brown swirling water in the spotless little sink in Chin's restroom. Then I drove the Smart Car to Get Over It. The homeless woman was still reading on the sidewalk so I gave her another five. Inside, I traded the black wig for the Long Toe outfit including bronze pants and boots. A black beret replaced the Buddy Guy reverse hat I had tossed in a trash can. Lizz frowned; told me that had been shortsighted. She was, of course, correct.

The full loop took twenty-eight minutes.

Braden's door was closed. The same yellow light glowed through the glass. I was hungry, and a little buzzed from the caffeine on top of being far too close to cops and bullets.

I knocked.

Papers ruffled, the knob turned. Braden stared at me with the eyes of a guy who had tried to read the *Iliad* in one sitting.

"Tommy Cuda sent me," I whispered.

He faced me, unmoving for a moment.

"It's worse than I predicted," he said.

I put a hand on his upper arm and guided him into his office and to his chair. Then I closed the door and sat to face him.

"I've been verbally warned, and an official reprimand is coming, for having arrested Mr. LaRuche."

"But he was holding half a million dollars in fake bills, not to mention the plates required to print them."

"Apparently I was supposed to know that an operation was in place." He rubbed his eyes with curved index fingers.

"You checked. There was no operation."

"*Was* is exactly right. But there is now. Computer records currently show there was one then too."

"You mean the doctored documentation that matches LaRuche's fabricated story."

Braden managed a tired smile. "I wouldn't put it that way if anyone were listening. But yes."

I glanced around his small office. A couple of framed awards. A whistle in a glass cube. If they could bug a catacomb hundreds of miles away...

I said: "Your office is very clean."

He frowned at me for a moment, then recognition dawned. "I sweep once a week. But with so much dust in the air, it could get dirty the next day."

"There's a beautiful church next door."

He perked up. "Greek Orthodox I believe."

371

"I was admiring the architecture." I pointed at him, then the direction of the church, and held up ten fingers.

"A fine structure nearly a hundred years old. You rarely see that kind of craftsmanship nowadays."

"Do you need me to sign anything else for the car?"

He blinked a couple of times; figured it out.

"Oh, no, Mr. —"

"Fowler."

"Thank you. Your statement is fine. We shouldn't be needing you again."

I let myself out and strolled around two city blocks to approach the church from opposite the station. The main door was unlocked so I stepped inside and let it swing closed behind me with a thunderous clunk that echoed for seconds. Why a ceiling needed to be so far away wasn't precisely clear to me, but it created a majestic view that made me feel small and insignificant, yet mysteriously relaxed. I shuffled quietly to the back row taking in the bigger than life-size paintings along both walls, trying to think of a place where society built such tributes anymore. Six minutes later Braden came in a door on the right, and walked along the far wall. He sat down next to me and looked straight ahead at the altar.

"She claims LaRuche had Hosco printing fake bills and running them through dance clubs and political campaigns to fund his reelection. Uses them to bribe people. She also mentioned the cops: property management and an equitable fund. Isn't that real estate?"

"Not in this case," he said. "She's referring to material confiscated in the process of investigations: cash during raids, illegal weapons, drugs, artwork, vehicles."

"Somehow they're substituting fake bills and walking out with the real deal."

Braden sat very still. I waited, listening to the two of us breathe in perhaps the quietest place in all of Chicago.

"Clever," he finally said. "People would have to be paid off, but it could be done."

"That's what we're up against." I scanned the open expanse of the church out of habit. Or fear. Of course we were still alone; churches weren't that popular on Saturday night. "It gets stranger. Tracy, aka Mala, claims there were cameras hidden in the Detroit catacombs that only she knows about."

"Convenient."

"She was buying insurance. Says LaRuche gave her an engagement ring, she developed the laundering operation, he gets cold feet."

"A politician reneging on a deal?" He laughed from his stomach, the sound reverberating like rolling surf in the cavernous church. He shook his head. "Hard to prove."

"We can find the ring and receipt," I said, then pressed on, wanting to get everything out of my head before I forgot it. "Hosco was seven-figure skimming. That's why they were in Detroit. Two things. The cameras were set to record at specific times. She wanted to be invisible, but have blackmail material over Hosco."

His head bobbed in agreement. "Smart lady. Sexy and smart. That combination seems to lead to trouble."

"Sexy leads to trouble all by itself," I said, smiling.

"What's the second thing?"

"Remember, she was dodging cameras. She's hiding when the cop shows up because she knows a recording is being made, but has to deal with the situation. So she crawls along the floor and pulls Hosco's ankle gun, planning to shoot out a light. He kicks her; she fires, hits the cop."

"Probably Hoskova's intent. Seems like the kind of guy that'd shoot a cop instead of going for the light."

"We can't ask the three guys that were with her; they're all dead. But if she wasn't aiming at him, isn't it a whole different crime?"

Braden leaned forward and clasped his hands. He looked like he was thinking, but he might have been praying.

"You're about to tell me where these recordings are, aren't you?"

"I can only relay what she told me."

He took a deep breath and blew it toward the floor.

"I've been with the force for over twenty-six years; never seen anything like this. A cop on the take here and there, sure. But a mass buyout woven into the political system?" He turned to face me, his hands still clasped. "And it's going to get me."

"Unless you get it first."

He smiled like a professor trying to get a lesson across for the umpteenth time. "You kids, all optimists." He gazed toward the large arched ceiling above the gilded altar at the front of the church. "Do you like Tom Cruise?"

"Yeah, he's okay. Brings a certain intensity to his work."

"Remember the film *Minority Report?* Those three people lying in fluid predicting where crimes were going to be committed? I feel like one of them. I can see what's going on. Only in my case, I don't have any resources to try to fix it."

"Where's Tom when you need him?"

"Probably making another hundred million on a blockbuster built on a Philip K. Dick story."

Braden looked tired. The kind of tired even a vacation in the Bahamas with umbrella drinks delivered to the beach wouldn't fix.

"You watch a lot of movies?"

"Yeah," Braden said. "I watch the ones I couldn't predict over and over, try to see what I missed the first time. And why I missed it. People see what they're looking for, you know."

"You mean the guy in the gorilla suit experiment where no one sees him because they're counting basketballs?"

"Yeah, Simons and that blasted invisible monkey. Destroyed me. I missed a six-foot tall gorilla...counting damn bouncing balls. And I'm supposed to be observant."

"You were following directions," I said. "And I bet you got the ball count right."

He nodded. "Still missed the gorilla." His jaw worked up and down. "OK Tommy Optimistic, hit me. Where are these recordings we have to get?"

"A computer at LaRuche's house."

His head snapped left to face me, eyes wide awake. "His house? Not a bank, or military base, or the bowels of a submarine. Just a house?"

"Tracy says he monitors the cameras in Detroit from a computer system at his house he calls Kinkos. No copies exist anywhere."

Braden stood up so fast I felt a breeze. "I know just the guy."

Forty-Nine

I SPENT SUNDAY WITH BRADEN and another man in Braden's basement around a fold-up card table working through minute tactical details under a 60-watt lightbulb swinging from a brown wire. Braden asked me six times if I wanted to go through with it. I told him each time, yes. I wanted to help stop LaRuche; I wanted Mona to have closure on the bum Hosco; I wanted to know if Mala was lying about the cop; and I especially wanted to get back on the road and see Chicago growing smaller in my rearview mirror.

At five o'clock Braden read an oath as part of deputizing us for the duration of the current emergency situation. The other man said his name was Sony, like the Japanese company. He refused to explain why, but insisted his mother chose it. Braden thought that being deputies might save us from the hottest water if we got caught.

"We're not going to get caught," Sony said. "Think that clearly. The more you think, the better off we are."

"You believe that *Secret* book about attracting things by thinking about them?"

He shot me a twisted frown. Not over five-foot-five, he wore a long black coat almost to his ankles and thin black leather gloves that made him look like a surgeon from the dark side.

"Are you crazy? I believe in the power of confidence and focus. We have a complex series of actions to undertake. All we have to do is think about them and nothing else." He wagged a finger at me. "Every time you think about failure you lose a little bit of your edge. Think about it enough —" he let his hand fall sideways.

I imagined a sentry falling asleep, and being court-martialed.

Braden said, "You both have maps?" We nodded. He put a folded piece of paper in each of our hands. "These are copies of a search warrant. What we're about to do is a little..." he rolled his lips over each other, making his cheeks puff out, "unconventional. It will help if you leave one behind, preferably in LaRuche's hand." He turned to Sony. "I couldn't go to the DA, don't know if he's connected. I got Judge Hayward, who issued the warrant, to write this for you." He handed an envelope to Sony, who shoved it into his coat without bothering to open it.

"How about the judge?" I asked.

"Hayward is solid. He wrote up the papers and promised to delay entry into the computer system until close of business tomorrow. It will all be over by then, one way or the other."

"Think positive," Sony said. He reached into his left pocket and unfolded a diagram. "Last time. Are we sure the girl knows the layout of the house?"

"Says she's been there on multiple occasions," Braden said. "Last visit was three weeks ago with Hosco."

Sony used two outstretched fingers like calipers to measure distance on the diagram. He nodded. "I hope you run fast, Tommy."

"Four-forty in high school," I said.

"Which machine?" Sony asked.

I held out a hand. "Tower on left, third machine down."

"Kane better be right," Braden said.

"Very messy," Sony added, but he had a wild smile across his face. "Time check."

I pulled on my chain. We verified our watches: 8:11 pm.

"Can we depend on the girl?" Braden asked.

Sony said: "Her cute ass is on the line, she'll be right on time." And he had never even met her.

I followed Sony's black coat up steps that hadn't ever been painted. We refrained from wishing each other luck, exited through the back door, jogged across Braden's grass, and pushed through the hedge to climb his fence. The old wood shook, but held firm. We speed-walked a block to Sony's black pickup truck with a black cap over the bed.

Sony pulled away and drove for nine minutes before he spoke.

"Timing is everything. This guy has multiple perimeters: electric fence, dogs, motion sensors. Margin for error is minuscule."

I grinned. "You're going to tell me that's the easy part."

He nodded.

Sony drove to the Bourgeois Pig where we met Penny and had his meal of choice before a job: chicken Caesar salad and water. We ate slowly and chatted about everything except what we were about to do. Sony even informed me that I would get wet one out of every eight days in a Chicago summer. He insisted I skip Penny's cookies: we needed to be thinking and acting fast, not nosediving from a sugar crash at exactly the wrong moment.

We left at ten sharp.

At ten-fifteen houses along the road grew larger and further apart.

At ten forty-five we parked at the curb behind a metallic olive Mercedes, the houses now occupying grounds as large as a city park.

Sony opened the back. Everything inside was black. There was no light.

"You work at night a lot?" I asked.

"Always and only. Harder for me to see, but harder for everyone else too. I know what I'm looking for; they just see shadows and shapes and confuse the cops with conflicting eyewitness accounts."

He handed me a backpack. "Put it on, take it off, put it on. Make sure nothing hangs up. Be sure you can do it fast."

I practiced while he transformed. First a rifle and scope over his left shoulder, then a backpack, and finally a pack that clipped to the backpack's straps, but rested on his chest, making him more video-game hero than human.

He lowered the hatch silently, nodded. We returned to the front seat of the truck.

He glanced at my pack. "Sorry you have to handle the Play-Doh, but one of us needs to shoot."

"Your instructions were clear. I'll do it exactly as we practiced."

"Can you see the porch?"

I found the binoculars in the glove compartment and pointed them far down the street. A cherrywood door held a silver knocker the size of a cantaloupe. Flickering lanterns on either side looked to be real gaslights.

"No one yet."

"Three minutes," Sony said.

I felt my heart accelerate. I focused on the first action. The fence. Remembered Mona saying: *It's just like a dance. First this step, then that step. Not so hard.*

We waited.

I stared through the binoculars.

A low white car stopped in front of the gaslit porch. A redheaded girl stepped out.

"She's going up the walk."

Sony started the truck: a whispering purr in the night's stillness. I wondered if his mufflers were black.

"Knocking," I said.

He put it into gear but held the brake.

"Door opened. Opened wider. Hand on her wrist. Pulling her inside."

"Mark time," he said.

The truck rolled forward. We passed the low white car, turned right, skirted along the side of the property. Stopped.

"Fifty-eight seconds," I said.

We put on goggles, and breathers that would filter the air.

Sony took three long deep breaths, then put the truck in reverse, held the brake.

I counted down from five.

"...two...one...zero."

Sony jammed the accelerator down. The truck backed up the street, over the curb, and directly at the rear fence to the house with the gas lights; tearing up golf-course grass along the way. He stopped twenty yards short of the fence, jumped out, zipped open the pouch on his chest, tossed two grenades at the base of the fence, then jumped back in and yanked the door shut.

Before the debris stopped falling we were both out of the truck and running through a car-sized hole ripped in an expensive iron fence. Dogs barked all along the street, making it hard for me to locate the ones I needed to worry about.

Then I remembered my dance steps. *Run! Do not think about dogs.* Sony's sage advice.

I sprinted to the near corner of the house, heard myself wheeze through the breather then paced off fourteen steps across the back of the building, exactly as I had done in Braden's basement a dozen times.

Snarling growling barking stood the hair up on my neck, down my arms, and immobilized my hands. I shook my wrists to loosen them, unclipped, and swung the backpack to the ground. Yanked two zippers, grabbed a gray block in each hand, replayed Sony's voice *(hard, so they stick)* and slammed them against the stone wall close to the ground. Reached back into the pack, put two above those. Five times and I had a semi-circle of fireworks glued to the back of the house.

I reached for the pack.

A Doberman coming my way flickered in my peripheral vision. I froze. It wobbled, stumbled and slid snout first into my backpack. I threw the pack on my back, flicked ten tiny switches on the ten blocks (left to right), grabbed the hind legs of the dog, and was ducking around the corner of the house when a blaze of fire erupted, tripping me to the ground face-to-tail with the dog.

"Sleep well," I said.

I stood up fast. Felt woozy for a second. Ran fourteen paces through a wall of dust, dropped to my belly, and scrambled across pulverized Sheetrock on my elbows.

As promised I was in a dark closet, glowing LED eyes blinking everywhere. Two towers. I wanted to know the time and see how far we were into the operation. Sony yelled in my head: *Do your job.*

One. Two. There was no computer three down in the left tower. There were only two machines.

I squeezed around the rack and into the small room. Tracy would have seen the towers from the doorway, not from a fresh hole blown in the wall.

The other rack, three down. I grabbed the power screwdriver from a backpack sleeve and spun out the screws holding the third computer, pulled it from the rack, yanking out the power plug and network connector. I stuffed the thin machine into my pack where the explosives had been, closed the zipper, and unrolled a long tie-wrap. Around the rack's vertical bar, around and around the doorknob, zip closed. Braden's idea to slow them down.

Footsteps and voices in the next room.

I dropped and crawled as fast as I could move.

The dog was struggling to stand, head wobbling. It saw me with glassy eyes, but didn't bark.

I blinked behind the goggles, and found the tailgate of the black truck.

Then I ran like the starting gun had just fired.

I reached the passenger door and dove in wearing my pack. The truck started rolling. The door swung at me. I stopped it with the sole of my boot, yanked it closed.

Sony was behind the wheel half his earlier size: no packs, no tranquilizer gun. As we accelerated his right hand reached out, found a covered switch taped to the dash. His thumb moved the cover, he glanced in the mirror, and flicked it up.

The black sky behind us glowed red and a crater opened where our truck had been parked. Braden had suggested obliterating as many foot and tire prints as possible, this was Sony's solution.

Sony swerved as he reached pavement and shot through the neighborhood at double the posted limit. He drove one mile, turned at Bankhurst and stopped in a dark cul-de-sac.

"Be ready," Sony said.

I took off my pack and shifted it to my lap, still breathing like a sprinter at the finish line.

A blue and white police cruiser came around the corner with its headlights off and stopped behind the truck. Braden stepped to the pavement.

We jumped out.

Without conversation Braden drove the pickup away.

I threw my pack into the trunk of the cop car. We ripped open Velcro seams and stripped off one-piece black jumpsuits, and tossed them in too.

Now we were cops in blue uniforms wearing goggles with air filters. We had even been deputized.

Sony drove back to the main street in the dark, then hit the lights and siren and headed for LaRuche's house. He parked the car across the driveway and we ran to the front door. Sony knocked loud twice before we shouldered the door down.

Dust floated in the dancing light from a fireplace to my left.

"Police," Sony shouted, the sound muffled through his mask. "Answering a domestic disturbance call."

We moved through the house. Sunken rooms. Indoor lap pool. Billiard table. Kitchen large enough for handball.

No one.

Sony met my eyes through the glass of the goggles.

I said: "He'll protect his data."

We dropped down half a flight of stairs two at a time, hustled toward the back, and found people bunched around the door to the computer closet I had recently vacated. LaRuche stood to the left of two muscular guys with buzz cuts in black polo shirts (who clearly weren't Feron and Stevens) struggling to open that door against my tie-wrap. To their right a girl wearing neon pink tennis shoes and a thin green sweater covered with pale pink stars huddled against the wall. One guy saw us coming and grabbed her around the biceps with a fat paw of a left hand.

"It's okay, officers," LaRuche said. "We've had an explosion, but everything's fine."

We moved forward.

Sony shouted through his mask: "Neighbors reported a domestic disturbance."

LaRuche smiled at the girl. "Not here, was it, honey?"

Green eyes found mine. Her upper lip trembled.

Sony spun a boot upward and caught the guy holding her behind the knee. The guy let her go as he went down.

I grabbed an arm and pulled her toward me.

Smoke rolled through the crack of the door they had been struggling to open.

"What the hell are you doing?" LaRuche shouted. "Do you know who I am? I'll have your badge." He turned to the guy still standing. "Stop him!"

The guy turned toward Sony, who touched him on the side of the neck with something I never saw. He dropped to the floor. Sony faced LaRuche.

LaRuche took two steps back.

Sony reached out with the search warrant in his hand.

The girl and I ran together out the front door and across manicured lawn. I stuffed her into the back of the patrol car. By the time I jumped into the front seat, Sony was racing around the front. He flicked on the gumball lights and burned rubber.

My heart pounded.

Sony turned to me, his eyes even with the top of the steering wheel. I knew he was grinning behind the goggles.

I said: "Are your jobs always this subtle?"

Fifty

SONY DROVE FAST with lights flashing. Emergency vehicles flew by in the opposite direction to reach the explosions at the LaRuche estate that had likely been reported by a dozen frantic neighbors. He cruised for two minutes, then made a turn onto Lake Shore, flicked the lights off and slowed. I watched the rearview mirror on my side, and had to grin at the way traffic moved away from a cop car.

Mona's quiets sobs chased away my moment of levity, and dragged me back to the danger that remained.

"Will they come after this car by number?" I asked.

Sony shook his head. "It's checked out to Braden. By the time anyone figures that for a problem, it'll be tucked in the garage where it belongs. With luck, it'll go out later tonight or tomorrow morning."

"You mean to destroy evidence we might be leaving here?"

"Are you a cop?"

I shook my head. "No, I read novels." Sony laughed a high-pitched squeal that had me visualizing hyenas feasting over a gazelle.

"Where are we going?" Mona asked from the back seat.

"On our way to a friend's place," I said. "Just a few more minutes."

"Am I going to jail?" she said in a voice so thin it threatened to tear.

I twisted around in my seat as far as I could under the seat belt and found her eyes through the metal mesh between the rows.

"No Mona, you're not going to jail. Sony and I might, but all you did was go in and have a conversation."

"But I told him Rosco was stealing from him."

"That wasn't news," I said.

"He wanted to know how I knew if I wasn't there."

"And you told him Tracy Kane revealed it to the police."

"Yeah," she said.

"And he wanted to know how you found out." I watched her nod slightly. "And you said, 'She's my sister.' Is that about right?"

"Yes," she said quietly. "He said he didn't know that Tracy had a sister, but he could see the resemblance."

"All of which kept him distracted and at the front of the house so Sony and I could do the demolition dance."

"It was so loud," she said. And while I watched, her lips became the hint of a smile.

"Yeah, it was," Sony said. "Man, we were totally professional." He slapped the wheel with both hands. "Boom boom boom, first strike to exit in seventy-three seconds."

We left the highway and Sony pulled the car onto Chin's lot and up to the left hand door. A tan car cover in the back of the lot was shaped like my Barracuda. The garage door went up and Sony inched the police cruiser in. The right-hand stall where my Cuda had been was occupied by two young Asian men unbolting the front fenders of a black pickup truck.

Sony switched off the cop engine.

"What color did you pick?" I asked.

"Silver. If I can't be invisible with black, I might as well confuse 'em with the most popular color in the USA."

"Always thinking," I said.

"I like silver," Mona said.

Sony pointed a thumb to the back seat. "See."

Chin came out of the office carrying a laptop in one hand, a black metal box in the other, and loops of wire draped over both arms. Braden was right behind him. Sony opened the driver's window and stuck his head out.

"Truck looks great."

Braden smiled. "You'll love the new color. Chin says it's metallic silver with a hint of black flake."

Sony laughed his squeal again.

Chin jumped into the back seat of the cop car beside Mona. I hopped out, Sony popped the trunk release. I grabbed the pack with the computer we had just lifted from LaRuche's place.

Braden poked his head in through Sony's window.

"Ms. Meyers, do you want to stay here or ride with these thieves?"

She turned to Braden, then me.

"Wherever you feel safe," I said. "But this box I'm holding is contraband. You might want to be far away from it."

"I'll call out for Chinese," Braden said.

Mona smiled. "I love Chinese."

"Smart girl," Chin said. "You stay here, enjoy garage. Watch men work. They like to show off for pretty American girl."

Mona laughed. It was a pure genuine sound that made me glad we had hit LaRuche's place. I let her out of the rear door of the cruiser.

She blew me kiss. "Thanks, Tommy."

I gave a little salute and a smile because I had seen an actor do it in a movie. Then I hopped into the shotgun seat.

Sony backed the car out carefully and the three of us headed for Central Illinois—not because there was anything of particular interest in Central Illinois, but because we needed time to work where we wouldn't be found.

Chin passed cables to me through the mesh divider. One went to power from the car, another from his black-box AC converter into the back of the stolen rack-mount computer server. A network cable back through the mesh connected to his laptop. In minutes he was operational.

"Trying the admin passwords Ms. Kane provided. If her intel is good, this will be easy."

I listened to Chin type and hoped Tracy had the right info.

"In with second password. You want to hear it? Sure you do. LovekanesbOObs...with capital O's. Did she bribe this man?"

I watched the lights on the flat computer in my lap flicker, thinking about how little I knew about, essentially, everything.

"Data structure is simple. Folders by camera number. Reverse-chrono order for each day."

Sony changed lanes and pulled up to pass a tractor-trailer hauling two giant rolls of steel.

"Those will crush you if they come off," he said, pointing.

"Is that why we're cruising along beside them?" I asked.

He laughed. "Afraid all your luck is used up?"

"Camera one-five has seventeen test files. Opening now."

Lights flickered.

"Scanning test file one."

I rode in silence, waiting, crossing my fingers Chin would find something that made the past hour seem like a smart move.

"File thirteen won't open. Just lucky." He laughed. "It has additional encryption."

"That numeric code she gave me. Tracy said we would need a key."

More clicking. Sony started humming something that sounded like *The Star-Spangled Banner* on a vintage 78 RPM shellac recording that had been used for a Frisbee.

"I'm in," Chin said. "View from behind a person in uniform. Three guys with hands on their heads."

I twisted around. He lifted the laptop so we could both see the screen. Nothing changed until a bright flash low to the floor near Hosco, and to the side of the press, strobed the interior of the cave.

"Not definitive," Chin declared.

He went through the files for that camera and two others, using the extra passcode each time. File nineteen on camera three-nine contained pay dirt. It showed a redhead who looked like Mona crawl across the dirt floor, lift a gun from Hosco's ankle, and aim it up to her right. As we watched, a boot shot across the frame and landed on her ribcage. She contorted, a flare erupted from the barrel, and something blurred past the camera.

"What was he trying to achieve?" I asked. "A kick has no accuracy."

"Speculation," Sony said, who hadn't even seen the video as he drove. "He kicks her, she screams, gun goes off. Cop is distracted by the shot, and the woman's voice. You do know the female voice is the most recognizable sound to a human male, right? The cop can't help himself; he reacts to the broad screaming. Gives our buddy time to pull a weapon."

"However," Chin said. "The kicker is lucky. She shoots cop by accident. This shows man then ran as a yellow-belly from the jaws of the tiger."

"So Tracy speaks the truth," I said.

"There is more," Chin said.

Sony glanced my way. I shrugged, waited for Chin's play-by-play.

"The three men are gone, the policeman lies on the ground, dog sniffs near him, wondering what is wrong with his master."

"What about the girl?"

"She has disappeared."

Sony turned to me. "You got enough?"

"I'm not a lawyer. But Tracy seems to be telling it straight."

"Here," Chin said. "Girl is wearing large backpack."

"Is it black with pockets down both sides? Silver reflectors?" I said.

"You have eyes in back of head," Chin said.

"That's the one Mala aka Tracy gave me when she told me her name was Mona."

"This has printing plates in it?" Chin said.

"By the time I got it, they were hidden in the sides."

"She's helping the cop," Chin said.

Sony twisted his head around. "What?"

"She dropped the pack and is...yes, she is pushing handfuls of money under shirt where he was shot. The dog is running in circles, doesn't know if it should stop her."

"She's trying to stop the bleeding with cash?" I said. "She didn't tell me that."

"Probably thought you wouldn't believe her," Sony said.

"She is gone. I will search for another camera now that I know the correct time stamp."

"What's the dog doing?" Sony asked.

"Sniffing the money," Chin replied.

"Think we got enough?" Sony asked.

"It's hard to know what Braden needs," I said. "But we found new evidence. Let's head back."

Sony pulled off at the next exit and stopped at a diner called the Endless Cup across from a gas station: he was hungry and wanted to celebrate. He and I went inside to get burgers while the police car idled with the windows down. Chin insisted on surfing through more files.

Sony faced me in a booth with red vinyl seats where I could peer out the window beneath the word Endless. Across the street an orange shield-shaped sign at the top of a fat white pole said Phillips 66. I turned to Sony. Up close the wrinkles around his eyes said he was about forty, and amazingly relaxed.

"I'm new to this, Sony. How did we do?"

He popped three fries into his mouth at once.

"We did great. Fast in and out. That was the plan. That's what we did. You managed to grab the right computer and find your little movies." He upended a giant diet Pepsi. "A good day's work."

"I know why I did it, but why did you?"

"The judge cut me a deal. Reduces my sentence to probation only from a, uh, previous experiment."

Chin opened the door to the restaurant, looking back over his shoulder at our car repeatedly.

"You must see."

Sony looked at me. I nodded as I stood. "Yes, we must see."

I stuffed a handful of fries in my mouth and followed Chin. When we reached the cruiser we all got in the back and left the doors open.

Chin started a movie on his laptop.

"I go back in time for Tracy tests. Find much."

The dates spinning in the corner showed the movie to be six weeks old. The angle was up high, looking down to where the cop had been lying. The printing press sat near the middle of the frame. A strip of paper came out of it—covered with hundred dollar bills.

Sony whistled. "What a way to earn a living."

"They must have a cutting room," Chin said.

"Interesting to watch an old press," I said. "But I don't see how—"

Two figures entered the frame from the left. The one in back was LaRuche: tall, handsome and wearing a suit like always. The other was clearly Zhenya Hoskova minus the mustache.

"Why would he have cameras running?" Sony asked. "It's stupid to create evidence."

"Tracy Kane's insurance," I said. "That invisible trick she tried to play on Hosco when the cops came. She turns the camera on at a known time and captures everyone but herself. I bet that wasn't the first time she did it."

"And no one knows," Chin said. "Because they do not think to look for movies that are not supposed to be there."

"She must be working with at least one tech," I said. "These show up as test files, something innocuous that everyone else ignores."

"Until she needs them," Sony said. "Sneaky bitch. I bet I'd like her."

"I wonder if it's enough for Braden?"

Sony faced me. "Can't hurt. A district attorney is going to have a hard time ignoring surveillance films of an underground facility where a cop was shot. Ought to end LaRuche's political career if it doesn't put him in prison."

"My friends," Chin said. "I am very nervous." He waved his hand at the parking lot. "We are out here alone. These files have no backup."

"Can you make copies now?" I asked.

He nodded.

Sony and I moved to the front seat for the drive back to Chicago. We reached Chin's garage just after midnight and deposited the first set of backup chips in his vault. Sony hid a second set in the toolbox under the bed of his truck. Chin put another into a priority mail envelope that made me think of my key on its round trip to Ohio, and where Lizz had hidden hers. I buttoned a chip into the pocket of my black shirt after changing out of the uniform.

And we made two sets for Braden.

"Almost done," Sony said. "To the post office."

We dropped the envelope, addressed to a friend of Chin's who lived in Chinatown in San Francisco, into the blue box in front of the post office.

Sony looked at me.

"One more stop," I said.

He pointed the car toward the police station. Halfway there we pulled into the parking lot of Dunkin' Donuts. Three cars in the lot; four people on stools inside the small diner. Pedestrians on the corner stared at the cruiser, then drifted down the street in the opposite direction.

I held the little SIM chip between two fingers; saw Made in Malaysia printed across the bottom. I tucked the chip above the driver's side sun visor so it was completely out of sight.

We got out and locked the car.

Sony went into the shop first. I followed thirty seconds later. Braden was alone in a corner booth sipping dark coffee, a half-eaten powdered donut on a plate in front of him.

I sat at the end of the counter with Sony to my left, the car keys between us.

I ordered coffee and anything with apples in it from a gray-haired waitress I had never seen before. Sony ordered three different kinds of donuts and orange juice. While we waited to be served, Braden came to the counter and reached between us to pay his bill.

We remained silent. No eye contact.

When my apple surprise arrived along with a stack of donuts for Sony, the cruiser keys had been replaced with a rental car ring from Avis: the folks who try harder.

Fifty-One

I FELL ASLEEP AT VICTORIA'S dreaming of a sunny Monday, looking forward to putting the steamroller of events set in motion by Mona's *find-me-Tommy* note behind me. Braden could deal with it. He was a professional, and not on vacation.

When I woke, rain pattered against the window like the dancing feet of fairies scattering magic dust. I thought of the ballerina on Mona's music box. The only feeling I could identify was anxiety: did Braden have enough evidence, could Mona get her life back, what would happen to Mala, were Sony and I going to be busted for burglary?

I checked the outside of my door. No sticky messages.

I tuned my blue guitar and sat on the edge of the bed in my underwear playing through Marvin's song list. It was ten o'clock before I went down for breakfast. Slim wasn't around so I retrieved my own coffee from a silver tank with a hand pump. Victoria was in the kitchen doing dishes, saw me, and offered fried eggs, even though I was officially late.

While eating slowly, I scanned the newspaper and found a tiny article about a residential fire in the suburbs. No injuries. The reporter speculated it may have been caused by a gas line explosion like the one that killed eight people in Northern California in 2010.

After eating I went up to my room and tried to play through the tunes again. I managed two, then couldn't summon the energy to move my fingers. I wondered if Sony also felt despondent the day after he blew things up. In the excitement, I had blocked out the reality of clay that could kill me instantly, even managed to slap it against LaRuche's house. But now, in the aftermath, every time I thought of that gooey brick smacking against masonry an image of my hand being blown off rattled my brain.

I put the guitar away. It was 10:33. The rain had stopped.

I took a hot shower and dressed in a dark blue T-shirt and jeans, wanting to look like other people today. I pulled open the drawer where I had stashed the hitchhiker's half-million and stared at the envelope LaRuche had given Mona at the bank.

Twenty-five thousand dollars.

I figured it was U.S. legal tender because I couldn't imagine LaRuche being careless enough to pass fake cash with his own hands. It was surely marked, or the serial numbers recorded, so it would leave breadcrumbs to find me: a person I hoped he didn't even know about.

Crumbs.

Did the envelope contain a GPS tracker? Stuff like that was easy for wizards like Chin, and LuRuche certainly had tech people. I grabbed my jacket and picked up the pack with a napkin from the Monkey in a crude attempt to avoid leaving fingerprints. On my way out I borrowed the second section of the *Chicago Tribune* from a table and jogged to the Braden-supplied rental car.

I circled Lincoln Park counterclockwise, running north on Cannon toward Stockton and back to Fullerton, until I was confident I wasn't being followed. Then I parked in the marina to the northeast and walked back toward the North Pond restaurant with the folded newspaper under my arm, thinking of dinner with Lizz, a key, and the fun we could have had in a warming hut for ice skaters.

I followed the pond trail to a place called the Laughter Gazebo. It was empty. My pocket watch showed 11:21. I sat facing the water, my back to the footpath, wondering about the name until my eyes landed on a faded plaque with the inscription: *Laugh for no reason* above an invitation to laughter-yoga classes. I smiled, thinking that must be a great way to keep the mind flexible.

I placed the folded newspaper on my lap and read the article that happened to be facing up. A World War II Wildcat fighter plane had been pulled out of Waukegan Harbor after seventy years, having been used to train Navy pilots to land on aircraft carriers on Lake Michigan. I was happy to see that the pilot had been rescued, and lived to be eighty-five. I tried to imagine landing on a little dot floating on the water and marveled at the skill, and bravery, of human beings.

A man came into the gazebo and sat to my right. He wore a wide-brimmed brown hat and a long trench coat. He gazed out over the pond, the hat low over his eyes.

"I enjoyed the movie," he said.

"How did you like the ending?"

"Quite a surprise." He tugged his hat brim. "The District Attorney is running for reelection. Harry, that's Harold Carter our mayor, has been building a platform on crime rate reduction. They're teaming up. This case will be key."

"You're getting help?"

He nodded. "Now there's budget for everything I ask for. Even forensics on those graves in Michigan."

We watched wind-ripples dance across the pond like brushstrokes on a giant painting. I wanted to ask a question, but didn't want to hear the answer.

I finally said, "How's Tracy?"

"They'll reduce the charge. But she had the gun in her hand."

"Mona?"

"Who's Mona?" he replied.

I smiled, happy he was keeping the dancer out of it. I moved the folded newspaper from my lap to the bench.

He said: "Feron held on to the gun, didn't think it'd ever see a ballistics lab." He paused for several seconds. A couple of ducks quacked to our left. "After he shot Hoskova."

On the water's surface I saw the reflection of a dark Chicago street; saw orange flare from the barrel of a silencer; watched Feron trip over the front bumper of a low silver car; felt my foot press the gas. I took a long slow breath.

"Overconfidence?" I asked.

The hat nodded. "In his boss." He reached inside the long coat, came out with a folded copy of the *Tribune*, placed it on top of mine. "You want to know why?"

"Unless knowing the answer is dangerous. I've had enough danger."

He grunted. "Always money and women. You'd think some creative genius would invent a new reason for a crime." He scratched his temple, stared out over the water. "He was jealous of Hoskova. Especially when Tracy suddenly started spending time with him. And Feron? Did she spend time with him? Lead him on? Manipulate him to gain access to those security cameras? I don't know if she did. But I also don't know that she didn't. I do know she went to the trouble to legally change her name to Tracy Kane, so anyone hunting Mala Meyers would hit a dead end."

I recalled finding that dead end while sitting in the library. I thought about a hotel room at the W, and how much of what transpired Tracy might have planned while riding through Indiana in my Barracuda.

He continued. "Feron saw Hoskova spending money like LaRuche was rewarding him for some kind of right-hand-man work. Right-hand man was Feron's job, and he wasn't going to let a thug muscle in on his gravy train. Feron saw you meet with Hosco and Kane, figured you were working with them; thus, the little search of your car. He convinced LaRuche Hosco was ripping him off. It was true, of course, but according to LaRuche, Feron was supposed to have a talk with Hosco, not shoot him."

"The talk got out of hand."

"That's what he told LaRuche."

I watched skyscrapers twist and turn on the pond's surface. "Do you believe any of these people?"

A pair of brown ducks paddled close to the shore.

"I believe Tracy," he said. "But she needs to choose her friends more carefully." He shook his head. "She sure confused things by posing as her twin sister."

"A lot went wrong," I said.

He pushed his newspaper aside and picked up mine, slipped it inside his coat.

"Does Feron know Tracy has a twin?" I asked.

He smiled. "That might have solved everything." He stood and walked toward the ducks until he was on the other side of the gazebo.

I glanced at the paper on the bench, then back out at the pond.

"From a raid," he said. "Hasn't been recorded." He tapped his jacket. "We will log Mr. LaRuche's gift."

I wanted to stand and shake his hand. Wish him luck. Tell him how much I respected the risks he was taking with his career.

But Braden turned and left without looking at me.

Fifty-Two

I TUCKED BRADEN'S NEWSPAPER under my arm and walked the long way around the pond to the marina. The path was still wet and a sheet of gray clouds hung over the black waters of Lake Michigan. I thought of Sony laughing behind the wheel of his new silver truck. That made me smile. I hopped into the rental car, placed the paper on the passenger seat and drove toward a parking garage near the library, watching for a tail at every turn. I pulled into the garage and wound my way to the top floor.

I left the engine running.

All alone.

I flipped the paper open twice. It contained a thick white envelope. I opened it and counted twenty-five thousand dollars in hundreds and fifties. Braden was an interesting cat. I divided the money into five equal stacks, had second thoughts, peeled five hundred from each stack and made a short stack. Then I wrapped each one in a sheet of newsprint and folded the edges in to make six clean packages. In the glovebox I found a plastic ballpoint pen with no cap, and wrote a name on each package:

Mona, Penny (and Amber), Marvin, Chin, Lizz

On the short stack I wrote *Eve.* I figured Braden would take care of Sony, and the reduced sentence for Tracy was payment enough. I laughed at myself. She probably had more money stashed away than all of us put together. That reminded me of the account number I had lifted from the pad of paper at the bank. I'd get it to Braden; maybe he could trace activity to assist his case against LaRuche. Or help Tracy.

I spent the next hour delivering packages. Mona cried on the second floor of the Pink Monkey. I invited her and Anna to come see us play at B.L.U.E.S.

I found Penny working the Pig lunch hour. She barely had time to say hello, so I stuffed the package into the little black apron that she wore to hold her order book, and invited her to see us play at B.L.U.E.S.

Marvin wasn't in. I considered taking a chance and leaving the package with the cashier, figuring a W employee wouldn't be the kind of person to steal other people's money; that way, Marvin could dig the surprise when he got to work. Long Toe Fowler reminded me that shit happens in the world. I decided to give it to Marvin tonight at the club, personally.

Victoria was standing behind the registration desk tapping coins into paper rolls. I gave her the short stack, confident she could convince Kim to accept it. She reminded me that the B&B offered a monthly rate. And to call my mother.

I found Chin eating from a bowl with chopsticks while the two young guys who had been there Sunday night stripping the truck sprayed a bumper luminous silver.

"They need practice," he said. "Start on bumpers."

I placed the package next to his noodle bowl.

"This is for helping a friend. I'll pay for the Cuda separately when it's ready."

He moved noodles to his mouth without taking his eyes off the newspaper.

"Not necessary."

I nodded. "I must do."

His dark eyes met mine and held. Then he nodded and smiled.

I parked a block from the library and wondered if Lizz worked on Mondays. My hand reached for a cell phone that wasn't there. I gazed at my fingers, and thought about tradeoffs. Put my hand in my pocket. Then I realized I couldn't even remember what day I had met her. In Chicago for only ten days and I had been so busy living I was forgetting important stuff.

I walked to the library with my heart pounding behind her package in my jacket pocket.

She wasn't at the counter.

She wasn't in the computer room.

She wasn't in the storage room where they kept piles of books that needed to be re-stacked.

She wasn't making drip coffee in their tiny kitchen.

I found her descending stairs from the second floor. I hadn't even realized the library had a second floor, though I should have guessed from the height of the building outside.

She stopped ten steps from the bottom and smiled.

"Are you taking me to lunch?"

"If you like. I'm wide open until our gig at BLUES tonight. Are you coming?"

Her smile deepened. "If you want me to."

I nodded slowly, watching her face. Then I noticed her clothes.

"You're wearing that sixties stuff again, aren't you?"

She held out her hand. "I was hoping you would come by."

She pulled me up the steps. The second floor couldn't decide if it was library shelves or offices. She chose an office and closed the door behind us. I sat behind a wide gray desk in a swivel chair that squeaked. She sat on the desk and pulled her skirt up above her knee, revealing the silky strap of a blue garter belt.

I pulled the package out and placed it on the desk so she could read her name.

"Only gift wrap they had," I said. "Before you open it, could I ask you something?"

A flutter of eyelashes said *sure.*

"How did your friend make that key so fast from all those tiny parts?"

"Three-D printers are really quick." She paused. Ran a finger along the strap of the garter. "But he didn't." Her crystal-gray eyes studied my face. "Is it over?"

"Yeah. I just saw Braden. The DA is going after LaRuche. Plans to make it a high-profile case to fuel his own reelection, and help with the mayor's too."

"So we won't have to hide the key again?"

"Not that key at least."

She pulled a watch from deep between her breasts and leaned over with the chain still around her neck. She flicked the cover open.

It looked like a perfectly normal watch to me, just like it had the entire time.

"You lied to me," I said.

"To protect you. I knew you'd think so long as the parts were in the watch, no one else would figure it out."

I leaned back in my swivel chair and nodded. "That's exactly what I figured."

"Well...so long as you believed that, why bother cutting the key up? I just put it in the little tin box under the counter we use to store stubby pencils, and locked it up with the other supplies."

"Stubby pencils?"

She smiled, her lips deep red, and shiny like fresh hot rod paint. "My favorite kind."

I shook my head, then sat up straighter. "Hey, where did you hide Mona?"

Lizz dug into a hidden pocket in her skirt and handed me fifteen dollars.

"Mona said you already did too much for her."

I stared at the two bills. "That was Mona in front of your shop?"

Lizz smiled without parting her lips. She gazed at me for what felt like a Sunday afternoon double feature. I didn't look away because it felt so good.

"What now, Tommy?"

"Tonight we rock. We're going to play Marvin's new song, the one he wrote for Anna."

"The coat girl at the Monkey?"

"Yeah, but she thinks she wants to be a dancer."

"Maybe she will; maybe she won't. Her heart will tell her what to do next." She paused. "I meant a little longer term than tonight."

"Well, since we blew the back off of LaRuche's house —"

"*You what?*"

"Sorry, shouldn't have told you that. After we stole the encrypted movies that finger the bad guys —"

"You're teasing me now." She lifted her chin and looked down her nose at me.

I waved my hands. "Forget all that. Last night I was sitting in the Endless Cup diner staring at a gas station."

"Is that porn for you car guys, staring at a gas station?"

I laughed. "Sort of. I was gazing at a big shield with the number sixty-six on it, the Phillips Petroleum logo."

"Mmm, get your kicks on route —" she traced a pair of sixes on her chest with her index finger.

"Exactly. I want to drive from Chicago to LA, like the song says."

"Alone I bet." She said it without showing emotion that I could read.

I nodded. "I'm trying to discover something."

She stood and walked to the window.

"Have you been doing your homework?"

I frowned thinking *what homework?* "Oh, I'm doing really well at not doing. Been busy wearing out my gumshoes."

She touched two strings and the clatter of blinds flipped the room into darkness.

"I like men with self-control. Without that, they're useless."

She unbuttoned her blouse and let it fall. A midnight-blue bustier encased her slender body. She unbuttoned and unzipped her skirt. It floated to the floor. Her garter belt didn't have matching panties.

"Lizz?"

She walked toward me with slow strides in tall heels, her curves creating heat inside my body, like working on a warm Hemi in an Ohio summer. For a fleeting moment I recalled the warning to a Greek god about flying too close to the sun.

She stood beside me, reached out both hands, and turned them palms up. Each held a square foil wrapper. One black. The other could have been painted Turbo Bronze by the Chrysler engineering department in 1967.

"Our favorite colors," she said.

She dropped the packages on the desk and stepped close. One hand pulled my face up to her mouth, the other touched the inside of my left thigh.

After she stopped the kiss, which might have been two or three days, I said, "Lizz."

"I like it when you say my name."

"Lizz, I'm leaving."

"All the more reason."

"As soon as Chin has my Cuda ready."

Her hand reached higher up my leg.

"Then we had better hurry, Tommy. Shame we can't wait for the back seat."

ACKNOWLEDGMENTS

Thanks first to you, for your interest in and support of my novels. Readers like yourself enable me to continue to write. Thanks also to those readers who have posted reviews of my books, each one is greatly appreciated, as it helps me reach new readers in this vast new world of eBooks.

Thanks to colleagues who reviewed early manuscripts and provided thoughtful insight and suggestions including: Amy Brekeller, Michele Bighouse, and Catherine Kuchers. I also greatly appreciate the meticulous review by my friend Jim Elliott, who has been reading my work from the beginning, and the copyediting assistance of Pierce Sheats.

A Barracuda tankful of appreciation goes out to my intrepid editor Robyn Russell who again provided her keen insight into the internal workings of narrative fiction. Finally, a giant thank you to R, who continues as first reader and number one supporter of my undertakings.

ABOUT THE AUTHOR

Joe Klingler has been a programmer, research scientist, software executive, and entrepreneur. He is the author of the award-winning thrillers *RATS* and *Mash Up,* and is fascinated with the interplay of people and the technology they absorb into their lives. His thrillers intertwine digital technology and his passions for music and motion. Joe currently resides in California with a Mac, a couple of motorbikes, and a guitar. *Missing Mona* is his third novel.

Please don't let impersonal corporate-driven social networks come between us...

Join *Joe's Readers* directly at:

www.joeklingler.com

to occasionally receive news on book releases, previews, discount promotions and more.

Made in the USA
Lexington, KY
15 December 2016